LAST SONG SUNG

OTHER CULLEN AND COBB MYSTERIES

Serpents Rising
Dead Air

LAST SONG SUNG

A CULLEN AND COBB MYSTERY

SUNG

DAVID A. POULSEN

DUNDURN
TORONTO

Cover image: City: istock.com/ ImagineGolf; Blood: istock.com/redhumv
Printer: Webcom

Library and Archives Canada Cataloguing in Publication

Poulsen, David A., 1946-, author
    Last song sung / David A. Poulsen.

(A Cullen and Cobb mystery)
Issued in print and electronic formats.
ISBN 978-1-4597-3986-4 (softcover).--ISBN 978-1-4597-3987-1 (PDF).--
ISBN 978-1-4597-3988-8 (EPUB)

    I. Title. II. Series: Poulsen, David A., 1946- . Cullen and Cobb mystery.

PS8581.O848L38 2018   C813'.54   C2017-905724-3
                                             C2017-905725-1

1 2 3 4 5   22 21 20 19 18

Conseil des Arts du Canada   Canada Council for the Arts   Canada   ONTARIO ARTS COUNCIL CONSEIL DES ARTS DE L'ONTARIO
an Ontario government agency un organisme du gouvernement de l'Ontario

We acknowledge the support of the **Canada Council for the Arts**, which last year invested $153 million to bring the arts to Canadians throughout the country, and the **Ontario Arts Council** for our publishing program. We also acknowledge the financial support of the **Government of Ontario**, through the **Ontario Book Publishing Tax Credit** and the **Ontario Media Development Corporation**, and the **Government of Canada**.

Nous remercions le **Conseil des arts du Canada** de son soutien. L'an dernier, le Conseil a investi 153 millions de dollars pour mettre de l'art dans la vie des Canadiennes et des Canadiens de tout le pays.

Care has been taken to trace the ownership of copyright material used in this book. The author and the publisher welcome any information enabling them to rectify any references or credits in subsequent editions.

— *J. Kirk Howard, President*

The publisher is not responsible for websites or their content unless they are owned by the publisher.

Printed and bound in Canada.

VISIT US AT

 dundurn.com | 🐦 @dundurnpress | f dundurnpress | 📷 dundurnpress

Dundurn
3 Church Street, Suite 500
Toronto, Ontario, Canada
M5E 1M2

In memory of my dad,
Lawrence Allen (Larry) Poulsen,
who shared with me the joy of reading

In memory of Wayne Lucas,
who shared with me the joy of friendship

And always ... for Barb

PROLOGUE

February 28, 1965

The cigarette smoke stung her eyes. She threw the cigarette down, regretted it right away — hated to do that to a Lucky Strike, damn good smokes — and looked around.

Looking for Joni. Joni Anderson, who said she'd be there for the last set before taking the stage herself. But Joni wasn't there. Not yet. Or at least not here in the alley, smoking, laughing, tuning her guitar in one of those crazy, brilliant, completely open-string, Joni-esque ways that few could follow, let alone play.

She rubbed her eyes, trying to drive the sting away, and squinted at the back of the building. Not old, not new, just one more building in a row of structures that offered no more or less than this one.

The Depression. She'd always felt it was a weird name for a folk club. First of all, people often mistakenly thought the name referred to the mood, not the social and economic shock that had devastated so many of the world's economies in the 1930s. *This* Depression was *that* Depression; it had nothing to do with the state of mind. The old newspaper clippings that dotted the walls, virtually the only decorations to be found in the place, provided the proof as to which Depression was being referred to.

Instead of Joni, the only other people in the alley were her two band guys: Jerry Farkash, who'd been with her from the beginning twenty-one months ago, and Duke whatever-the-fuck his name was, surely to God the worst bass player to ever stride on stage with an Airline electric around his neck.

She glanced at her watch. 10:50. She'd begin her last set at 11:00. Joni would take the stage just after 11:30, play for an hour and a half with barely a break, and everyone would love her. Like they did every night.

She *really* wanted Joni to catch her last set. Especially the new song, the one she'd co-written with the shitty bass player. The guy *could* write lyrics. That was the only reason she'd kept him around this long. But even with his ability as a lyricist, she knew he'd have to go. He was killing them on stage.

And the guy was weird. What kind of name was Duke? And his last name was just as crazy. *Prego*, that was it. Prego. *You're welcome* in Italian, for Christ's sake. Not his real name, obviously. *Who calls himself Duke You're Welcome?* The guy had to go, and before her Vancouver date at The Bunkhouse. She'd pay him something for the lyrics and then send him on his way. She'd rather play The Bunkhouse without a bass player than have Duke fucking Prego on that stage.

She looked at her watch again. Just time for one more Lucky Strike. She turned away from the biting wind to light it and didn't see the car come up the alley. She heard it, though, and once her cigarette was lit, she turned to see if it was Joni. Maybe she'd caught a ride with some guy, or —

As she turned, she heard the screeching of brakes. The car doors were flung open. Then *pop, pop, pop* — not loud like you'd expect gunshots to be, but they *were* gunshots. She realized that when first Jerry, then Duke went down clutching his chest, groaning, then gasping like he was trying to get air. Then two men — one of them holding a gun — were racing toward her.

She tried to run, but it all happened so fast. There was one fleeting moment of recognition. A scream … a curse. Then the first man, not breaking stride, hit her with his fist, and it was all over.

ONE

There was something Holmesian about it.

Cobb and I were sitting in his office, drinking Keurig Starbucks, me looking out the window at 1st Street West below us and watching a beautiful twenty-something blonde cross the street and head toward Cobb's building.

My memory told me that was how several Holmes stories began — except, of course, it was Holmes's apartment on Baker Street that he and Watson were in and Holmes was either playing the violin or reading the newspaper. Cobb had spent the last hour invoicing clients and telling me in general terms the nature of their cases. To my knowledge, Cobb did not play the violin.

There was, however, a bit of a similarity between Watson and me. Although Holmes's companion was a doctor and I had spent most of my adult life as a crime writer, first for the *Calgary Herald* and then as a freelancer for the last several years, the fact was that, like Watson, I was something of a chronicler of the cases Cobb and I had worked on together. I was, at that time, working on a couple of articles I hoped to shop to magazines — articles that recounted the details of our recent investigation into the violent deaths of a number of right-wing media luminaries. That was the reason my computer sat at the ready on a small table in one corner of Cobb's second-floor space on the corner of 12th Avenue and 1st Street West in the Beltline, an elder statesman among Calgary neighbourhoods.

"You're about to have company," I said, not looking away from the street or the young woman, who had clearly favoured denim when she had made the day's fashion decisions. I was confident of the correctness of my assertion because at the moment, Cobb was the lone tenant of the building, all the others having been temporarily evacuated while renovations were taking place. I'd asked him how it was that a private detective was not inconvenienced with having to vacate his office when other firms with more office space and several actual employees had been. Cobb had smiled as he told me that, as soon as the building manager had mentioned Cobb would have to leave the building for a couple of weeks, Cobb made as if to begin the packing process, pulled several firearms from his closet, and set them on his desk. The manager, apparently not certain whether the weapons were part of the move or had been taken from the closet for some other purpose, decided that Cobb's office looked "okay as it is" and backed out the door with considerable dispatch.

"Male or female?" Cobb asked, without looking up from his own computer.

"Decidedly female," I told him.

"And you know she's coming here because …?"

"Because (a) there's bugger all else on this side of the street, (b) she keeps looking up here as she gets closer, and (c) she's now entering the front door of the building."

"Ah … that last one's a dead giveaway."

He closed up his computer in an apparent attempt to look more detective-like for the new arrival and had just completed that task when the knock came at the door. I turned from the window, crossed the office, my slippery city shoes (as Ian Tyson called them) drumming on the aged hardwood, and opened the door. My closer look at the young woman confirmed what I had been fairly certain of from my window view of her. Though the September wind had done her mid-back-length blond hair no favours, she was striking. Young — twenty-ish, I guessed — and ... striking.

"Is this the office of Michael Cobb, private detective?" she said in a voice that was breathy but firm. My first impression of her was that she was no-nonsense.

"It is," I said, and stepped back to allow her to move into the office.

She stepped inside, and Cobb stood up to greet her. There was a momentary look of confusion on the young woman's face as she looked from me to Cobb and back at me.

I gestured in Cobb's direction to allay further confusion.

"I'm Mike Cobb," he said, "and this is my associate, Adam Cullen. Please have a seat." Cobb indicated a brown leather chair that, until I'd stretched my legs by moving to the window, had been my spot. I took a new position on a hard-backed, hard-seated, cloth-covered thing that offered a comfort level equal to that of a church pew.

When she was settled into her chair, Cobb looked at the young woman. "What is it you think I can help you with, Ms. ...?"

"Brill. Monica Brill."

"Would you care for a cup of coffee, Ms. Brill?"

She shook her head, sat forward in the chair, and

looked at Cobb with eyes that confirmed my earlier assessment. She was all business.

"I'm interested in hiring a private detective, but I need someone who does more than spy on wayward spouses in divorce cases." She wasn't smiling.

Cobb was. "I won't lie, Ms. Brill, I did a few of those back in the day, but haven't for a long time. I'm an ex-cop, worked robbery for a few years, homicide for a few more."

She nodded, then looked over at me, eyebrows lifted. "That's what my research indicated. Your partner does the divorce work now?"

"Neither of us does, actually," Cobb said, as she turned back to him. "Mr. Cullen is, as I mentioned, my associate. We occasionally work together. Mr. Cullen is particularly good at conducting research. I tend to be more at ease … in the field."

"Will you be working together on this case?"

"That depends on the nature of the investigation you want me to carry out. Maybe you should tell me how I can help you."

She nodded, pursed her lips, and said, "Maybe I'll take that coffee, after all."

"On it," I said, heading for the Keurig machine. *Adam Cullen, researcher and gofer.* "How do you take your coffee?"

She smiled. "One sugar, please. No milk." She turned again back to Cobb. "I'd like you to find my grandmother."

"Your grandmother is missing?"

"She is. That is, she has been for some time."

"How long has your grandmother been gone?" Cobb asked.

"Fifty-one years."

"Make that two coffees," Cobb said to me.

There was silence in the room for a few minutes, but for the gurgling of the coffee machine. I glanced over my shoulder at the two of them. Cobb was studying the young woman, a quizzical, slightly surprised, but not thunderstruck look on his face. I had never seen Mike Cobb look thunderstruck.

Finally, he spoke. "And are you certain your grandmother is still alive?"

"I'm not certain of that." Monica Brill shook her head. "That would be part of your assignment. I want you to find out if she's still alive after all this time … and if she's not, I want to know what happened to her."

"Maybe you should start at the beginning, Ms. Brill."

I started toward her with the coffee, but before I could make the delivery she stood up and walked to the window, standing in almost the same place I had left moments before to answer the door. "You might want to take a look," she said.

Cobb and I looked at each other, then followed her to the window, Cobb moving up alongside her, me standing just behind her, looking over her shoulder.

She pointed. "See the Italian restaurant there?"

She was pointing at Parm, a place Cobb and I had been to a few times. Decent food, better-than-decent pizza, and extremely handy — directly across the street and maybe fifty steps from the front door of Cobb's building.

"Parm," I said, to confirm that we were all looking at the same place.

She nodded. "Do you know what it used to be?"

"You mean pre-Parm, or fifty-one years ago?" Cobb's eyes were still focused on the restaurant.

"In the sixties there was a coffee house located in the basement of that building. It was called The Depression."

I nodded. "I'd forgotten that," I said. "I've read about the place. It was Calgary's first coffee house. Did fairly well for a time, I think. A few big-name performers appeared there early in their careers. Neil Young, the Irish Rovers, Gordon Lightfoot, Joni Mitchell —"

"Except her name wasn't Mitchell. Not then."

She turned away from the window. Cobb and I followed suit. Monica Brill settled back in her chair; I set her coffee on the desk in front of her, passed Cobb his coffee, and returned to my spot on the concrete slab disguised as a chair.

"Anderson," I said. "She was Joni Anderson back then."

"Very good, Mr. Cullen." Monica Brill nodded and glanced approvingly at me, making me feel like I had just passed some test.

She sipped coffee, set the cup back down, and took a breath. "On February 28, 1965, my grandmother was playing The Depression. She was on the same bill as Joni Anderson. My grandmother stepped out into the alley behind the building between sets to have a cigarette. She was never seen again."

"Right," I said, "I remember reading about it. A couple of guys were shot, and a third person — your grandmother, I take it — disappeared. The police were never able to solve either the shootings or the disappearance."

"That's right. No one has solved the case … up to now."

"I assume you have a reason you'd like this looked into after all this time," Cobb said.

"Our family has lived without knowing what happened to my grandmother that night. I don't want to live like that anymore. Even if the news is really bad, as it very well could be … I want to know."

Cobb rubbed one hand over the other, then changed hands and repeated the gesture. He was thinking.

"Ms. Brill, you want to engage my services to conduct a search for your grandmother, who disappeared a half century ago. I'm not in the habit of taking people's money under false pretenses. And that's what I'd be doing if I were to accept this case. Almost all of the people your grandmother knew back then, and those who knew her, will be either dead or in a home, some with limited ability to be of help. If we can even find them. I have quite a high regard for my ability to do my job. But this case offers so little likelihood of being solvable that, I say again, I feel like I'd just be taking your money."

Monica Brill didn't answer. She reached down into the satchel she had set at her feet and pulled out a file folder. It was fairly thick.

"This is what I've been able to do on my own," she said, setting the folder on Cobb's desk. "In this folder are press clippings, a photocopy of the police report from the original investigation, photographs of my grandmother performing, and a map of the street as it was back then. I put that together myself. I might have one or two of the businesses wrong, but I think for the most part it's quite accurate. The two detectives who first worked the case were Lex Carrington and Norris Wardlow. Mr. Wardlow died in 2003, but Mr. Carrington is still alive and is a resident of Cottonwood Village Retirement Centre in Claresholm, which is about an hour south of Calgary. I tried to get in to see him, but the people in charge wouldn't allow it, so I don't know if he remembers the case or is even mentally competent. That's as far as I went with my own investigation. I decided it was time for a professional to take over."

I could see Cobb was impressed. He opened the folder, flipped through some of the material in it, read a couple of the clippings, and finally looked up at the young woman sitting opposite him, who showed no sign of impatience.

"I'll tell you what I'll do," Cobb told her. "We'll work this for a week — make some calls, see if there's any chance that there might actually be some leads out there, something we can take hold of and follow up on. If after that time I feel there's any point to continuing the investigation, we'll talk again. If, however, I think I'd be wasting my time and your money continuing, then I'm out."

Monica Brill nodded. "That's fair."

"Now, is there anything you're not telling me?"

"What do you mean?"

Cobb leaned forward on the desk.

"Often with cases that have been unsolved for this long, when someone wants the investigation restarted, it's because something has suddenly turned up — a long-lost note, a letter from the missing person, a mysterious phone call, something like that. Is there anything along those lines that might be the reason, or at least part of the reason, you've come to see me?"

Monica Brill hesitated. It was her turn to think. "I guess … I guess there *is* something that's kind of, well, puzzling."

Cobb looked at her but didn't say anything.

"Five weeks ago, I received a CD."

"A CD."

Monica nodded. "I wasn't going to say anything, because I was afraid you'd think I was a crackpot and not take the case."

"How did it come to you?"

"It was left in my car."

"In your car," Cobb repeated.

"My car had been locked. I'm sure of that because I remember locking it with my remote, and an older couple who were nearby glared at me when it beeped."

"So, someone broke into your locked car and left a CD."

"Yes."

"And where was this?"

"At the grocery store. A Safeway just a few blocks from where I live. I didn't notice it right away. I loaded my groceries in the trunk, and when I went to get in the driver's seat, the CD was lying there. I almost didn't see it."

"Was it in a case?"

"Yes."

"And what was the CD of?"

"It's a song."

"One song," Cobb repeated.

A slow nod. "Yes, one song ... and ..." Her voice trailed off, and she looked down at her hands.

"And what, Ms. Brill?"

"I'm sure it's my grandmother singing."

"Did you recognize the song?"

She shook her head. "I've heard my grandmother's voice before. On some old reel-to-reel tapes. She'd signed a record deal but hadn't recorded anything before she disappeared, at least nothing commercial — just those tapes. But I've listened to them, and I'm quite certain it's her voice on this CD, even though the recording is poor quality."

"Poor quality as in *old*?"

She shrugged. "Maybe. It's quite scratchy, and there are a couple of places in the song where her voice fades out almost completely."

"And the song she's singing on the CD wasn't on any of the tapes you'd heard previously."

"No. I went back and listened to them all again, and this song isn't on the tapes."

"Anything identifying the CD?"

"What do you mean?"

"You know — an image, a graphic, like an album cover?" She shook her head again.

"Any writing on the case or on the CD itself?"

"No, nothing. The case was dirty, but there wasn't anything about what was inside."

"Is this the only thing you've ever received that might connect to your grandmother?"

"I … I think so."

"And no phone calls, letters, nothing else that you or anyone else in your family might have found out of the ordinary?"

"Nothing. And I'm sure if anything like that had come to someone else in the family, I'd have been told about it."

Cobb looked down at the folder again. "Is the CD in here?"

"I made a copy. The copy is in there."

"The copy." Cobb repeated.

"As I told you, I was afraid you'd think I was a nutcase and refuse to take this on, so I didn't bring the original … if the one I received *was* the original."

I was having trouble with her thinking that the first CD would make her seem like a nutcase but a copy wouldn't. I wondered if Cobb would let that go. He did.

"I'll need you to bring the original CD with its case and the tapes of your grandmother performing earlier," he told her. "I'll see if a voice analyst can match up the voices."

He looked over at me, eyebrows raised, offering me the chance to ask some questions.

"What about your mother, Ms. Brill?" I asked. "Is she with you on this investigation into finding *her* mother? Is she aware of it?"

"My mother passed away four years ago. Breast cancer. She was only forty-seven years old."

"I'm sorry."

Monica Brill's expression didn't change. "Her name was Alice; she changed it to Alicia as a young woman. She moved to Calgary when she was twenty, married my dad, and they divorced after ten years. We talked about my grandmother several times before my mother died. She never knew the woman who was her birth mother and never heard a word from her or about her after that night." She pointed in the direction of what was once The Depression. "My mother was raised by an aunt — one of my grandmother's sisters. Who, by the way, also knew nothing about what happened to her sister."

When I didn't have any more questions, Cobb looked back at Monica. "What was your grandmother's stage name?"

"She didn't have one. She went by her real name."

"And that was?"

I answered the question. "Ellie Foster."

Monica Brill turned to me. "Wow, good memory!"

I shook my head. "I wasn't around during The Depression days, but like I said, I've read about the place and what happened in that alley that night."

"If your grandmother had made any commercial recordings, Mr. Cullen would probably have them in his collection," Cobb said, with a nod in my direction. "He has an accumulation of Canadian music that is likely unmatched."

"Accumulation?" I said.

"It means you have a lot." Cobb smiled.

"Thanks for clearing that up for me."

Monica continued to look at me. "Sounds like you could be the perfect guy to have on the case."

I shook my head. "Uh-uh." I pointed at Cobb. "He's the investigator. I help out once in a while with research. Maybe I can contribute in that area."

She looked at Cobb.

"One week," he said after a long pause. "Then we meet again to determine if there's any point in continuing."

"And that week will cost me …?" Cobb quoted the figure, and she nodded her agreement. "Do you require a deposit?"

While they sorted out payment, I picked up the file folder from Cobb's desk and glanced through it. It was thick and heavy — further testament to the work Monica Brill had done on her own.

I picked up one piece of paper, the eyewitness account of someone named Guy Kramer, who had stepped into the alley just as the car had come racing down it. He had dived behind some garbage cans as the first shots were fired, so he didn't see much, although he indicated in his statement that he had peeked over the bins at one point and had seen two men dragging Ellie Foster to the car and pushing her inside. He'd identified the car as a 1962 or '63 Ford, dark in colour. Kramer didn't get a licence number. Other than noting that there were two men and that one was tall, he wasn't able to offer a description of either man. He thought, though he couldn't say for sure, that both men were carrying guns. Someone had written at the bottom of the page, "This witness passed away in September 2003."

. I set the page back in the folder and looked up as Ms. Brill stood up and reached across the table to shake Cobb's hand. I also stood and returned the smile she offered as she shook my hand.

"I'll see you in a week," she said.

I nodded, afraid to say something that would offer encouragement in what looked to me like the biggest long shot since the 1962 Mets.

When she'd gone, I offered the folder to Cobb. He shook his head. "Why don't you take the first run at it? Lindsay and I are doing dinner tonight at her brother's, and it's a command performance. Get it back to me tomorrow; I'll read through it then and we can compare notes."

"Does that mean this is another Cullen and Cobb extravaganza?"

"Maybe. Like the lady said, who better to have on this case than an expert on Canadian music? There is one thing, though."

"What's that?"

"I'd rather refer to them as 'Cobb and Cullen' extravaganzas."

"I'm a writer. I know what sounds better. 'Cullen and Cobb' rolls off the tongue. *And* the pen," I said.

"This may require further discussion." He smiled, then nodded toward the folder. "Impressive."

"Yes, quite an accumulation," I said, grinning.

"Happy reading."

TWO

The reading was a long way from happy.

Cobb had wanted to get home to have time to get ready for the evening's social function, so I gathered Monica Brill's file and pulled on my peacoat — a bit of overkill, as fall had been easy on southern Albertans so far. My destination was the Purple Perk seven or eight blocks away; one of my favourite coffee haunts in that part of the city.

Monica Brill's file wasn't comprehensive, but there was enough there to answer some of the questions I had and to prompt some I hadn't thought of. It contained at least part of the homicide file. Having already read the statement of the lone eyewitness about what had happened in the alley behind The Depression fifty-one years before, I decided to go to the police report next.

It looked to my untrained eye like the work of the two police investigators, Norris Wardlow and Lex Carrington, had been both thorough and well documented. They had interviewed club management and staff, as well as several, though not all, of the patrons who had been there that night. The officers acknowledged and were frustrated by the fact that some of the audience had fled as word of what was going on in the back alley had spread inside the club. The two cops even talked to a couple of cleaners who had been working in a nearby building. The cleaners had heard the commotion but seen nothing. Because the area was commercial, there had not been the usual canvas of nearby residents.

During the first days of the investigation, Wardlow and Carrington had focused on two things: learning all they could about Ellie Foster and the two shooting victims, and trying to find the car that had been used by the two gunmen. They had checked out several cars that answered the minimal description given by Guy Kramer. They were unable to find the one used in the commission of the crime. As for Monica's grandmother, while the two officers were able to put together a fairly detailed account of Ellie Foster's early years, they'd been less successful at discovering much about her life as a professional performer or anything that might have provided a motive for her kidnapping.

Ballistics identified the murder weapon as a Colt Python and determined that both victims had been killed with the same gun. Six rounds in all were fired — three struck one of the victims, two hit the other, and one round missed both men and ended up embedded in the back wall of the building that housed The Depression.

The investigators surmised (admitting it was only a theory) that one man had driven the car and that the second man, the passenger, was likely the shooter. Though the witness, Guy Kramer, had been very sure both men had gotten out of the car, he wasn't able to say for certain which one was the shooter. And though he thought both had been carrying guns, he hadn't been willing to state that fact with certainty. The investigators had guessed that the reason for his uncertainty was that he had ducked for cover behind the garbage cans as the shooting had started and may have had only a couple of glimpses of what actually happened — afraid to take a longer look for fear of being seen and ending up as the next victim. Understandable.

Carrington and Wardlow had also interviewed Ellie's family members: a sister, June, who was three years older and lived in Moose Jaw, Saskatchewan (it was she and her husband who had raised Monica Brill's mother); Ellie's mother, who lived in London, Ontario (Ellie's father was deceased); and a cousin, who lived in Walkerton, Ontario, a couple of hours from London. I read the transcripts of the interviews, and beyond shock and sorrow, none of the family members were able to shed any light on what had happened in the back alley, or why.

Only one comment of even mild interest came of those interviews. In response to the question, "Had your daughter seemed worried or anxious in the days or weeks before she was kidnapped?" Ellie's mother had replied, "No, not worried or anything like that, but she seemed different. Sort of cold and unhappy, and that wasn't my daughter." Though Carrington and Wardlow had asked follow-up questions, Mrs. Foster had no explanation for her daughter's altered personality other than, "Maybe she wasn't handling becoming successful very well."

The detectives also spoke to the caregiver who had looked after Ellie's baby girl, Monica's mother, in London, Ontario, where Ellie had lived for the previous two years when she wasn't on the road performing. Again, nothing. The investigators were not successful in finding the baby's father. It was one of the questions they'd asked in every one of their interviews, but apparently Ellie Foster had not divulged that information to anyone — at least not to any of the people the cops questioned. Either that, or the people who did know the father's identity had been sworn to secrecy and weren't willing to betray a confidence, not even after the death of the person who had asked for that confidence.

I read a while longer. What I found in those pages confirmed my belief that the two officers had worked hard. Wardlow had flown to Ottawa and talked to several people at Le Hibou, the club Ellie had performed at before her Depression gig. The two detectives also contacted a club called The Bunkhouse in Vancouver, where she was scheduled to appear the following week. The trail quickly became cold, and as I read and re-read the police report I could sense the growing exasperation of the two men. There were virtually no leads, nothing that would even remotely explain what had happened that night. They dug into the backgrounds of the two band members who were shot, thinking that maybe Ellie Foster wasn't the main target of the attack. Again, nothing.

Eventually I sat back in my chair, drank espresso, and thought about what I'd read. I concluded that, a half century after the fact, the chance of our solving this case — one that two apparently competent and dedicated cops with the advantage of working it right after the crime had taken place had struck out on — was next to nil.

After pondering that sad reality for several minutes, I pulled the CD copy out of its paper-bag wrapper and, with earbuds in place, spent the next half hour listening to the lone song over and over, trying to find some hidden clue or message buried in the lyrics. I struck out. With authority.

I figured Cobb would repeat my effort the next day, after which he'd decide there was no investigation to be conducted, admit defeat, and move on to something — anything — more promising.

My cellphone rang. This week the ringtone was Robbie Robertson and the boys: The Band. A few bars into "The Weight," I clicked answer and was listening to my favourite voice in the stratosphere, that of Jill Sawley, the woman I had been seeing for almost a year and with whom I was very much in love.

"Hey, what's up, Mister? There are two women over here who are hoping you're having a lovely day and that you're up for what folks in these here parts refer to as a strawberry shortcake fest. Kyla knows it's one of your favourites, and apparently thinks we should spoil you. I tried to talk her out of it, but without success."

"Hnh," I said.

"Excuse me, but that sounds just a little south of enthusiastic."

"That's because, as I am outnumbered two to one, said fest is likely to be followed by my being subjected to a chick flick, a film genre that ranks just slightly above horror on my 'most hated' list."

"Colour me guilty." She laughed. "Sorry, but the testosterone extravaganzas offered by the likes of Stallone and Schwarzenegger are seldom on the bill at the house of Sawley."

"'Seldom' as in …?"

"Never."

"Exactly. However, the promise of strawberry short-cake will offset the pain of having to watch *Love Actually* one more time."

"Thought that might happen." Jill laughed again.

I turned serious. "Is strawberry shortcake okay for Kyla?"

Jill's nine-year-old daughter, who had stolen my heart within minutes of our first meeting, had been diagnosed with Crohn's disease a few months before, and I was constantly wary that this or that food item might cause her discomfort, or worse.

"It's not something she should be having often, but in moderation I think we're okay."

"Then count me in. Want me to pick up a movie on my way over?" While most of the video stores had disappeared over the last couple of years, there was still one that I frequented and it seemed to stay busy, perhaps because the selection rivalled, and likely surpassed, that of any online carrier.

"Already handled."

"I was afraid of that."

I had a couple of hours and spent much of that time writing out and studying the lyrics from the Ellie Foster song, hoping I had missed something in my listening. Scratched out on paper, the words offered no more meaning than they had through the earbuds. I stared long and hard at them.

Summer sun. Summer fun. Some were done
They walked the gentle path
At first asking only that the wind and rain wash
their shaking hands
Stopping peace to fame
That person's name

Man at the mike … so, so bad
But good at play
And always the sadness, the love over and over
The long man points and tells
An owl sits and stares, sound around and through
his feathered force
So much like the other place. And so different …
Midnight. Not yesterday, not tomorrow. A time
with no day of its own
The last of sun. The last of fun. The last time won
They circle the windswept block
At first telling the youngest ones it's only a dream
See the balloons, hear them popping
Are they balloons?
No more the sadness, the hate over and over
The long man points and tells
An owl sits and stares, sound around and through
his feathered force
Midnight. Not yesterday, not tomorrow. A time
with no day of its own

Eventually my eyes ached and my frustration level had
me shaking my head and tapping the page hard enough
to break one pencil and threaten the welfare of another.
And still I saw nothing. The inaccessible ranting of a phar-
maceutically modified mind? Or a message? Or something
else? Or nothing?

I was having trouble believing that a CD containing
one song would suddenly appear fifty years after the disappearance of the person singing the song without there
being anything significant about it. It made as much
sense to me as the lyrics themselves. I hoped that Jill or

Cobb would have more luck deciphering the thing and closed my notebook.

I decided to try something else. I'd been in situations before when having a story appear in the *Herald* and other national newspapers had been helpful. This was one time when I thought we really had nothing to lose. If reading and remembering the story jarred even one mind to recall a detail that had previously been unknown, then the story would be worth the effort.

And writing it would force me to review again what we did know — mostly from newspaper accounts and the file folder Monica Brill had given us during her visit to Cobb's office.

I tapped at my keyboard for the next seventy-five minutes, constructing a piece I knew the *Herald* would use. I forced myself to stay away from conjecture and used only the information that was known: the details about what had happened in the alley behind The Depression that night and the few meaningful facts the police had managed to piece together as to what had happened after that.

As I read it over, I realized the story was pathetically incomplete. But it was all we had for the moment. I added a plea for anyone knowing anything at all to please get in touch with either Cobb or me, and I texted Cobb to let him know what I'd done and that I'd like him to see the piece before it ran. I wanted to be there when he read it to gauge his reaction and answer any questions he might have. I added that I'd read through Monica Brill's file folder and would bring it along. He got back to me in less than a half hour to say he liked the idea and to suggest we grab coffee or breakfast in the morning.

I texted him back saying I was just heading out the door en route to Jill's house and that I'd bring Monica's file folder and a copy of the song lyrics the next morning. Then in capital letters I typed "BREAKFAST." I was already running late for the strawberry shortcake festival, so I didn't wait for the answering text.

Before picking up my car from the parking lot behind Cobb's building, I stopped off at the two-storey brick structure that had once housed The Depression. Parm promised terrific pizza and great wine; neither was an unworthy goal, in my opinion.

Though Cobb and I had been in the place a couple of times, I'd paid little attention to the layout or decor. Once inside, I ordered a beer from the pleasant server I'd seen there before. She told me, in answer to my question, that she had been working there for a little over a year.

While I waited for the beer to arrive, I looked around. Parm was pleasant, clean, and friendly. And offered nothing in terms of instant clues to the world that had existed there fifty years before.

When the server delivered the beer, I asked her if she was aware that the basement of the building had once housed Calgary's first folk club and coffee house. She shook her head and regarded me suspiciously. I introduced myself and told her I was writing a story about the club and other similar establishments from yesteryear for the *Herald* — sort of a "Where Are They Now?" piece.

I was skirting, or at least stretching the truth, but didn't want to scare her off by relating that the place had been the site of one of Calgary's most infamous unsolved crimes. Later when she came by to ask if I wanted food or another beer, I asked if I could have a look at the basement.

"It's just storage now," she said.

"I understand," I told her. "Just a quick look — it would really help me with the story I'm writing."

She looked around and apparently decided the young girl who was serving a couple three tables away from me could handle things for a few minutes while she showed me the downstairs area. She led the way to the stairs that wound their way to the basement level, turned on a light near the bottom of the stairs, and stepped aside at the bottom to allow me to see.

"Like I said, we use it for storage." She sounded apologetic.

"No problem," I said, and stepped past her to get a better look around.

The ceiling was low. One wall was decorated with a carousel that was a symbol of a later club that had occupied the space, and most of the rest of the place was, as she had stated, storage. Metal shelving units, beat-up chairs, some dishes, a few pots and pans, and one worn but decent-looking chesterfield were the highlights.

I stepped further into the room and tried to imagine where the stage might have stood, pulled out my phone, and snapped a couple of pictures of the space.

The truth was, there was nothing there to indicate that the place where I was standing had once been a happening folk club where Mitchell, Lightfoot, Cockburn, and others had performed in the earliest moments of their careers. I'm not sure what I'd expected. Spirits of long-passed singers? Discarded programs from 1965? A dust-covered microphone?

None of those things, of course, existed. And try as I might, I was unable to get any kind of feel for what had been there fifty years before.

It was a storage area.

I turned to the server and nodded. "Hard to imagine it as a club, huh?"

She glanced around, shrugged. "I guess."

I thanked her, and we returned to the main floor. I finished my beer, paid my tab, and left what I hoped was a generous tip. Outside, I stood on the sidewalk and stared at the front of the building for a long while, again unable to conjure up ghostly images of yesteryear. I looked up and down the street, trying to determine what buildings still remained of those Monica Brill had noted on her map of the street as it was in 1965.

I walked down the block until I found an opening that led to the alley and circled around to the part of the lane that was directly behind the restaurant. I was standing in the vicinity, at least, of where two people had lost their lives in a hail of gunfire and a young woman had been abducted and never seen or heard from again.

Until now.

If the CD that had been left for Monica Brill was, as she and I suspected, her grandmother singing. I kicked a few rocks around, snapped a few more pictures, and made my way back to the street. I crossed it and then walked to the parking lot at the rear of Cobb's building. I climbed into my Honda Accord and headed off for strawberry shortcake and a painful movie experience.

I hadn't gone more than three blocks when I got a call — my first opportunity to try out the hands-free device I'd installed a few days before.

"Hello." I hoped I sounded like a veteran hands-free guy as I spoke.

"Marlon Kennedy," the voice on the other end of the line said.

I hesitated. "Kendall Mark," I said.

"Yeah."

"You got something?"

"I want to talk to you guys."

"Sure," I said. "Got a time and place in mind?"

"Belmont Diner. Thirty-Third Avenue Southwest. Nine o'clock tomorrow morning."

"Yeah, I think …" I started to respond, then realized I was talking to a dial tone. Kendall Mark, now known as Marlon Kennedy, had hung up. That call had removed any indecision as to where Cobb and I would be meeting in the morning. Except that now there would be three of us.

I fog-walked through the rest of the evening, even the strawberry shortcake that was, I seem to recall, pretty damned wonderful. And the movie, when I was able to concentrate at all, was okay too. *Mean Girls* … Lindsay Lohan. I laughed a couple of times and nodded dutifully whenever Jill and Kyla gave me their *told you this would be amazing* look.

After Kyla headed off to bed, a copy of Kathy Kacer's *The Night Spies* in hand, Jill poured us each a glass of a Tuscan red and sat next to me on the couch.

We didn't talk much. Often we didn't, content to be close to one another, allowing the music — she had selected R.E.M.'s *Automatic for the People* — to move through and between us. During the second glass of wine I told her of Monica Brill's visit to Cobb's office and the search for Ellie Foster that would be our focus, at least for a while.

I showed her the lyrics of the song; she read them, shrugged, and said, "That's going to take more concentration than I'm capable of right now."

"Roger that." I nodded.

"Although there is one thing I might be able to manage to concentrate on." She placed a hand on my thigh.

"Wicked woman." I smiled at her.

"The Eagles were singing about me."

"That was '*Witchy* Woman,'" I pointed out.

She took my hand and began leading me down the hallway. "Like I said, they were singing about me."

THREE

The Belmont Diner is located in Marda Loop, another of the older neighbourhoods in Calgary, and one of the coolest. A movie theatre called the Marda, long since gone, gave the area its name. Cobb and I were in a booth near the back of the Belmont by 8:30 the next morning, both wondering what Kendall Mark wanted to talk about.

Cobb knew Mark much better than I did, having worked with him back when both men were detectives in the Calgary Police Service.

Kendall Mark had been one of the investigators assigned to the 1991 murder of a nine-year-old girl, Faith Unruh, in a neighbourhood not far from where Jill and Kyla now lived. I'd learned of the little girl's murder a few months before, when one of Kyla's friends dropped it on us at dinner one evening.

I had become fascinated, perhaps even obsessed, with the case of the young girl, who had been walking home from school with a girlfriend. When the two parted at the friend's house about a block from the Unruh house, Faith had continued on toward home. She never arrived, and her body was found the next morning in a nearby backyard. It was determined that she had been murdered shortly after leaving her friend, meaning the killing had taken place in broad daylight in a populated residential part of the city.

Cobb had filled in some of the details of what had happened with the investigation. Police initially thought it would be relatively easy to find and apprehend the killer, given the circumstances of the murder. But that was not the case. Though officers worked hard and long for weeks, and then months, and eventually years, they had come up empty in the search for the killer. Cobb told me that the two lead investigators were never the same, the result of an emotionally charged investigation that failed.

Cobb had also told me of a third policeman, Kendall Mark, who, while not directly assigned to the case, had developed an obsession with finding Faith Unruh's killer. He had left the force and disappeared, the belief being that the stress of the case had gotten to him and he had simply "lost it" and gone away.

My own fixation had taken me to the neighbourhood many times. I'd driven the street and alley where Faith had lived and died; I'd walked and stood near the yard her body had been found in — not in some ghoulish fascination, but simply, as I had hoped for with my visit to the site of The Depression, to get a feeling for the area and a sense of the place where the horror of Faith Unruh's death had unfolded.

Which was how I met Kendall Mark face to face. Well, not exactly face to face. I had been jumped and taken down in the alley behind my apartment one night. The man I initially thought was a mugger turned out to be a dramatically altered Kendall Mark, who had spent the years since the murder watching the former Unruh home and the spot where her body had been found. He had set up an elaborate surveillance system with cameras and monitors, all in the hope of one day seeing the killer if and when he returned to the scene of the crime.

It was crazy, of course, the sad compulsion, the mania of a man who could not — would not — let go of the idea that he would one day confront the murderer of Faith Unruh.

The cameras were located in the house Mark had purchased not long after the murder. It sat across and just down the street from the murder location. The cameras had filmed my presence at the scene. Kendall, who had changed his name and his appearance, came close to exacting his long-awaited revenge on the person he thought had to be the killer when he mistook me for that person. I had been fortunate to survive that night.

Now Marlon Kennedy, a black man — formerly Kendall Mark, Caucasian — wanted to meet Cobb and me to talk about … something. Cobb and I had spoken with him a couple of times since the night in the alley when he'd been close to dispensing justice on the wrong person. In part, our conversations with him were designed to gain his assurance that the kind of vigilante action that had nearly ended my life wouldn't happen again. I was fairly certain our entreaties had fallen on deaf ears. Kennedy had grudgingly agreed that he'd at least let us know before he did anything drastic, an assurance I wasn't convinced would hold up if he once again felt that he had the killer in his grasp.

Neither Cobb nor I said much at first. We drank coffee but decided to wait on ordering breakfast until Kennedy arrived.

"Any ideas?" I said after a few minutes.

"About?"

"What he wants to talk to us about."

Cobb shook his head. "No clue. Maybe there's something he wants us to check out that he can't since he's gone underground, or maybe he just wants to throw out some ideas, although I doubt that…. Mark isn't a real team guy. I'm not sure he ever was. Or maybe he just wants to buy us breakfast because he likes our company. So, to repeat: I have not the faintest idea why he called us."

I nodded, drank some coffee.

Cobb said, "You?"

I shook my head. "I mean I guess it's possible he's got something and your little pep talk about the evils of vigilantism has him wanting to play by the rules and involve us in the apprehension of the killer."

"Yeah, not likely."

"I know I've asked you before, but do you think he's … I don't know …"

"Unhinged?"

I set my coffee cup down. "Well … yeah."

"I don't know." Cobb spoke slowly. "I'm not a psychiatrist or a psychologist, so I can't answer that. I'd say he's damaged. This case did that to him, or at least it was the one that put him over the edge. But is being that consumed with finding a killer any stranger than being obsessed with making money and never thinking about anything else … or a guy wanting to reach some magic total on an Xbox game and spending twenty hours a day locked in a room playing the damn thing … or someone spending twelve or fourteen hours a day bodybuilding? Hell, if obsession equals crazy, then there's a lot of wingnuts out there."

"Actually there *are* a lot of wingnuts out there."

Cobb held up his hands. "Fair enough. I'm just saying a lot of us have obsessive behaviours. I'm not sure that necessarily means we're nuts."

"So what's your obsession?" I asked.

"Right now it's breakfast. I hope he gets here pretty damn quick."

"One more thing," I said. "What the hell do we call him?"

"Tell you what, why don't we ask him?"

On cue, Kendall Mark, a.k.a. Marlon Kennedy, walked into the restaurant. Without, it seemed to me, ever actually looking at us, he made his way slowly in our direction, his eyes taking in the room like there was actually a chance that Faith Unruh's killer might be in here.

Habit, I guessed.

He sat down next to Cobb, which I found a bit strange. The two bigger men were sharing a space that clearly hadn't been designed with people that size in mind. I guessed that, as with a lot of cops, current and former, journalists were not his favourite people, and he preferred a little discomfort to having to share space with a member of the fourth estate.

The waitress returned to our table with a coffee pot. Mark nodded at her, and she poured him a cup and topped up Cobb's and mine.

"Ready to order, gentlemen?" she said.

"Yeah, I think so," Cobb answered. "I'll have the breakfast special, please — eggs over medium with rye toast."

She looked at me.

"Pancakes, please," I said. "With sausages, and I'll have a small orange juice."

She turned her attention to Mark.

"I'll have what he said," he aimed a thumb in Cobb's direction, "but with whole wheat toast."

The waitress moved off; no one spoke as we doctored our coffee.

Cobb broke the ice. "I'm guessing you'd prefer that we call you by your new name."

"Yeah, I'd prefer that."

I made the mental adjustment and nodded that I was onside. A minute or more passed before Marlon Kennedy spoke again. "Nine thousand days."

I didn't have an answer for that, and Cobb lifted an eyebrow as his response.

"In a month or so it'll be nine thousand days that I've been watching Faith's house and the place where they found her body. Nine thousand days that I've either been watching or checking tapes with the cameras working. Not one day off. Some milestone, huh? I'm thinkin' that a lot of people — people like *you* — would think that's some crazy shit."

I thought it best not to mention that we'd just been having that very conversation. Kennedy took a swallow of coffee, and when neither of us answered, he went on: "A white guy takes oral medication and bombards his body with ultraviolet rays to change his skin to black, changes his name and stakes out a place for twenty-four years — what the hell's crazy about that?"

It was a funny line, but there was no humour in either Marlon Kennedy's voice or his face.

"Why'd you call this meeting?" Cobb said.

"Couple of reasons. First one is I need to be away for a few days."

"And?"

"I need somebody to be there."

"You've got your cameras and tape machines."

Kennedy shook his head. "They need to be checked — make sure they're working right. And I need somebody to look at the tapes, see what's been happening at the two locations. And to be there … a pair of eyes when mine can't be."

The waitress arrived with the food, so the next couple of minutes were given over to distributing, passing, salting, and peppering. All three of us took a couple of bites before Kennedy set his fork down and looked first at Cobb, then at me.

"My ex-wife's dying," he said. "We split about a year and a half after Faith was killed. She just couldn't take me anymore. She said I'd changed, and she was right. But it was never a hate thing between us. I never blamed her for leaving. In fact, she's the only person, other than you two guys, who knows about … what I do."

The eyes that were normally as intense as any I'd ever seen were softer as he spoke of his ex-wife.

"She moved to Nanaimo maybe ten years ago. Her sister called a couple of days ago. Meg hasn't got long," he said. "She kept it from me until now. But they told her it's only days now until …" The voice trailed off, and the eyes looked down.

"I'm sorry, Marlon, I really am," I said. "I know what you must be feeling."

He raised his head, and the look he gave me was cold enough to force me to look away. "What the fuck do you know about —" A couple of heads turned our way.

That was as far as he got. Cobb leaned his elbow on Kennedy's arm and pressed down. Kennedy tried to pull it free, but Cobb pressed harder and spoke in a low voice:

"I don't want you making a scene in here, Marlon, do you understand? And just for the record, Adam knows exactly what it's like. Except that they were still together when he lost his wife."

I could see Kennedy's face beginning to contort from the pain in his arm, and I thought he might try to hit Cobb with his free hand. But he didn't. Instead, he held up that hand.

"I didn't know," he said, looking at me. "That was way out of line. Sorry."

I nodded, and Cobb moved off his arm. Kennedy flexed it a couple of times and smiled. "I forgot how tough cops are — even former cops."

"When are you leaving?" I asked him.

"As soon as I can get packed and gone. Later tonight. There's a twelve-thirty flight."

I looked at Cobb. "I know you want to stay on the Foster case. I can do some work on the research side from Marlon's place while I'm tending video cameras and checking film."

"I don't know how long I'll be gone," Kennedy said. "Might be a week; might be longer. I'll check in with you once I'm out there and I know more."

I nodded.

"I know I'm asking a lot here and —"

I held up my hand. "We'll make it work."

"I appreciate it."

For a few minutes we turned our attention back to our breakfast. After a few minutes, Kennedy laid down his fork and looked again at me.

"I hope you don't mind my asking, but your wife … what —"

"She died in a fire," I said. "The fire was deliberately set."

He looked at me for a time, then nodded slowly. "You're *that* guy. I remember now. You finally got the bitch who did it. I read about it."

"Yeah." I looked down at the breakfast I was losing interest in. "Yeah, I'm that guy."

"Jesus, man. I'm sorry I was such an asshole before." He held out his hand across the table.

I shook it. "No apology needed."

"Yeah, there is." He turned to Cobb. "To you, too."

Cobb nodded as the waitress came by and topped up coffee cups one more time.

We ate in silence for a while. Kennedy looked up again and spoke in an even more hushed tone than before. "Something I want to say ... or maybe *ask* is a better way of putting it."

Cobb finished spreading jam on a slice of toast, set it down and turned to face Kennedy. "Yeah?"

"Does this thing seem, I don't know ... off to you? I've read the homicide file probably a hundred times. We should have nailed this bastard in no time. It should never have been this hard. Don't you think that's weird?"

"I don't know if *weird* is the word I'd use," Cobb said. "*Frustrating*, for damn sure."

"Yeah, well, here's the thing I've been wondering — and maybe it's that frustration you mentioned, or maybe it's the obsession I have with this case that cost me my family — but lately I've been thinking, what if it was a cop? I mean, I get that it's out of left field, but sometimes I think, why didn't this piece of evidence happen? Or, why didn't that turn out to be a match? Stuff like that. An investigation that should have been a twenty-four-hour slam dunk is a twenty-four-year-old cold case. And I've been asking myself if it was maybe possible that somebody was on the inside making things a lot more difficult than they should have been."

"You think it could have been Hansel or Gretel?"

Cobb had told me earlier that one of the lead investigators was a guy named Hansel, which meant that his partners tended to get saddled with *Gretel*. This Gretel was actually Tony Gaspari.

Kennedy shook his head. "Not them. At least, I don't think so…. I knew those guys. So did you. Looked to me like they busted their asses on this. Look, I know this sounds like I'm even crazier than you already think I am, but Christ, just think about it, Mike."

Cobb waited a long moment before answering. "All right, I'll think about it. I doubt like hell that there's anything there, but I'll take a look. And I want you to write down anything you think might be a little off with the investigation."

"Fair enough. I've already jotted down a few notes. When I get back from the island, I'll put some thoughts together and send them along."

"Sure. I'll look at them, but it might not be for a while. We're working on something right now that's going to keep us busy."

"I'm okay with that. It's not like this thing is going to get any colder if we don't get right at it. But listen, if you guys are tied up with something, maybe you don't have time to take over the surveillance at my place right now. I'll totally understand if —"

I held up a hand to stop him. "The things I'm doing on this other case I can work around helping you out. It's fine."

He looked at Cobb, then back at me. "If you're sure."

"I'm sure. When do I start?"

"When *can* you start?"

I shrugged. "Right away, I guess."

"Why don't you come by around ten tonight? I can show you the setup before I have to leave to catch my flight."

"I'll be there."

He stood up as if to leave, then put his hands on the table and bent down.

"I'm not expecting you to do this for nothing."

I held up a hand and shook my head. "Why don't we talk about that later? For now, let's just get it done."

He straightened, looked like he wanted to argue, then changed his mind.

"See you later tonight," I said.

"I got breakfast," Kennedy said.

"Not necessary," Cobb said.

"Actually, it is." Kennedy turned and headed for the counter.

Our server came by and collected plates and cutlery from our table, giving Cobb and me time to think a little about the points Kennedy had raised during breakfast.

When she'd gone, I sipped coffee and said, "Well?"

"Interesting," Cobb said.

"The thing that I come away with from that meeting is that the guy is not a crazy person."

Cobb took some time before answering. "I think you're right. He was pretty lucid today. But let's not forget this is the same guy who's been living in a house staring out at a crime scene for twenty-four years, and when he's not staring at it he's videoing the area. And this is also the same guy who took you down, and we don't know how close he was to taking you out."

"Yeah, you're right. So do you think I was stupid to offer to watch over things while he's away?"

"No, I can't say that. But one thing I want to make really clear: You see something or you spot something on a tape that seems a little off, you don't go jumping in your car and racing off after somebody. You call me."

"I'm totally onside with that. The life of the swashbuckling crime fighter is not for me."

"Swashbuckling?"

"Think Errol Flynn."

"Right."

"What did you think about his idea that we should be looking at the cops for this?"

"Like I told him, I have to think about that."

"Interesting premise, though. Might explain why the investigation went sideways."

"That would be one possible explanation." Cobb nodded slowly. "I'm not sure it's the most logical one. Anyway, let's talk about things more current — the Ellie Foster case." Cobb tapped the Brill file folder.

"Right." I reached into my pocket and pulled out the story I'd written, handed it across the table.

He unfolded the paper and read for a few minutes while I checked my phone. I remembered how much I hated seeing people do that in restaurants and put the phone away, signalled the waitress for more coffee. She came over and topped up my cup. Cobb looked up just long enough to shake his head.

"Your friend is a generous tipper," said the waitress, whose name tag indicated her name was Betty.

Cobb looked up again. "Really?"

"That surprise you?" Betty asked.

"No, I guess not," Cobb said.

I shrugged to show I didn't have an opinion, and Betty headed off in the direction of a table of elderly women who, judging from their loud and never-ending laughter, were having a quite wonderful time.

Cobb read for another minute or two, folded the paper, and handed it back to me. "I like it. I'm not sure it will net us any results, but I can't see a downside."

"Okay, I'll talk to a couple of editors I know, see what we can get going on it."

"You adding a tip line?"

"What?"

"A number people can call. You going to put contact information in there?"

"Oh, right. Yeah, I thought I'd put in our cell numbers."

Cobb shook his head. "Correction. *Your* cell number. This stuff usually nets a couple hundred crackpot calls for every legitimate tip. I'd get yourself a disposable phone just for this. That way, you can throw the damn thing away if you're overwhelmed with idiots."

"Disposable phone it is."

"And I think we should maybe divide up the chase a little bit," Cobb said. "You're the music guy. How about you tackle that side? Former agents, club owners, other musicians, anybody you think might be useful — realizing, of course, that a lot of those people may have passed on or could be damn hard to find."

"That's stuff I can do while I'm tending Kennedy's surveillance stuff. I mean, he has a job, so obviously he isn't sitting at the monitors twenty-four seven. I'm sure if I need to leave to talk to people face to face, I can do that and then check the tapes later to make sure I didn't miss anything."

Cobb nodded. "He works in a couple of parks or something, isn't that what he told us?"

"Grounds maintenance. Works a few hours a day to bring in some money."

Cobb nodded, then rubbed his chin with the back of his hand. "Okay, you concentrate on the music; I'll work the other side — family, friends, cops who might have been part of the investigation — anyone I can find. Let's talk again in a couple of days."

"Here's something else." I pulled out a second piece of paper, this one with the lyrics of the song Monica Brill had received in the mail, and passed them to Cobb. "In your spare time maybe you can take a look, see if there's anything there that might point us in the right direction … or any direction at all."

"Thanks." He glanced down at the lyrics, and then looked back up at me. "You see anything in them?"

I shook my head. "I read them so many times, I've pretty well got the thing memorized. But I'm not seeing anything that jumps off the page and says 'Yeah, better check this out.'"

"I'll look them over tonight. Maybe have the family take a peek too. They're probably smarter than me on this kind of stuff."

"Not a bad idea." I nodded. "I'm having Jill and Kyla do the same thing."

"When will the story hit the paper?"

I shrugged. "Newsrooms have been gutted in recent years. A lot of my former contacts are gone. But there are still a few people around that I can talk to. I should be able to get something happening in the next few days."

Cobb started making moves like he was leaving, then stopped and looked at me. "You sure you're okay with going to Kennedy's place tonight?"

"You think I shouldn't be?"

"Hard to say. Like I said, he seemed pretty with it this morning, but I keep reminding myself that this is a guy who jumped you in a back alley and threatened to kill you."

"I think if he wanted me dead, I'd already be dead."

"Probably right. I think the story about his wife is legit. But once he leaves the house for the airport tonight, you call me." He stood up.

"Will do. And thanks for the concern."

I expected a joking reply but got a slight nod as I stood and joined him in the walk to the door of the restaurant. On the street, Cobb said again, "I'll be waiting for your call tonight."

"Got it," I said, watching as he headed off in the direction of his Jeep Cherokee.

Before I climbed into the Accord, I pulled out my phone and keyed in Jill's number.

"Hey, handsome," came her throaty voice seconds later.

"How's the woman I love?"

"Better now. How's your day?"

"Interesting. What have you guys got on later? I'd kind of like to get together, fill you in on some stuff."

"Well, my daughter attends school, as do a lot of nine-year-olds, and I'm hunched over books and calculators like Ebenezer Scrooge in the counting house."

"I doubt Scrooge had a calculator."

"Good point. So much for my literary allusions. Anyway, why don't you come for dinner? Or do we need to talk sooner?"

"Dinner's great. How about I pick up Chinese?"

"Sounds good. Just make sure it's not all deep fried."

"Check. How *is* Kyla?"

"Pretty good. Scale of one to ten, I'd say seven."

"I'd prefer a nine."

"Me too, but compared to what we went through in the summer, we're doing pretty well."

There had been a few weeks that summer that had been damned stressful until the doctors determined what was causing the intense intestinal issues that had knocked a tough kid flat on her back. We were eventually informed about Kyla's Crohn's disease and that lifestyle changes would be necessary to help her cope with the illness. Kyla was the strongest of the three of us and had made it clear that she would tolerate no feeling-sorry-for-Kyla behaviours from anyone. And with that as our mission statement, we were all doing okay.

"Okay, lots of veggies it is. See you around six. Love you, babe."

"I love you too. I've got wine, so we're good on that score."

"Perfect. See you then."

I rang off and decided to grab my computer out of the car and get a little work done. I needed some kind of a gateway into the life and times of Ellie Foster. Cobb had mentioned agents, club owners, musicians. That was a good starting place.

I spent the next few hours drinking coffee in the Phil & Sebastian Coffee Roasters on 4th Street and googling everything I could think of that might open a door to the coffee house music scene of the sixties. And finally, at around 3:30, I had my first positive result.

There was a book about Le Hibou, the folk club in Ottawa Ellie Foster had played a few weeks before her Depression gig. I found excerpts of the book online and they were interesting, but the part I thought might be helpful was the list of people — performers, owners, staff, and volunteers — who were part of the history of the club at that time. I googled several of the names and found what appeared to be something fairly current relating to a guy who'd been the assistant manager at the time of Ellie's disappearance, a guy named Armand Beauclaire.

I googled the name and tracked a phone number for an Armand Beauclaire who lived just across the river from Ottawa, in what was Hull and is now Gatineau. I punched in the number and was greeted three rings later by a cough, a clearing of a throat, and a rumbled "Hello."

"Mr. Beauclaire?"

"Yes."

"My name's Adam Cullen. I'm a freelance journalist, and I'm researching a piece I hope to write on the life of Ellie Foster. She was a folksinger in the sixties who disappeared while performing out here in Calgary. That's where I'm calling fr—"

"The Depression."

I paused before replying. "Yes, that's where she was performing at the time of her abduction. I was wondering if you knew her at all."

"Of course I knew her. In fact, I booked her. She'd performed twice at Le Hibou, and she was scheduled to come back a few months after her last appearance. But then she …

she … " There was a hint of a French-Canadian accent, but the guy was clearly bilingual. I wouldn't need Cobb and his fluency in French — at least not yet.

"Mr. Beauclaire, I —"

"Armand, just make it Armand."

"Okay, Armand. Listen, I'm sure you've probably thought about it a lot, especially at the time of her disappearance, but do you have any ideas at all as to what might have happened, who might have had a reason to want to kidnap Ellie Foster?"

There was silence on the other end of the line for a time. "You're damn right I've thought about it. We all did. Denis Faulkner was the co-owner and ran the place. It hit him really hard. Ellie was a sweetheart. I can't say I knew her that well, but audiences loved her. Everybody loved her. There was absolutely no reason in the world for that to happen. Unless the kidnappers got the wrong person — one of those mistaken identity things, you know?"

"When you hired Ellie for Le Hibou, did you deal directly with her or did she have an agent?"

Another pause. "There was a guy. Not a booking agent, nothing like that. He called himself her business manager, I remember that much. It was him I talked to."

"You remember his name?"

"Hmm, let me think about that. The guy was a loser, so he wasn't somebody I *wanted* to remember all that bad. Last name was Bush — that's all I got. And I remember that only because we all made jokes about him being 'bush-league.' The guy wasn't well-liked, if you catch my drift."

"Any reason for that?"

"I don't know. Maybe, maybe not. People form opinions about other people. Smoke a little weed, have a coupla beers, and make a determination about someone. I did that a lot. All of us did. Maybe the guy was an asshole; maybe he wasn't. Half a century later … I can't honestly say."

"Did you see him after Ellie disappeared? He come around at all?"

"No, never."

"So he didn't represent any other artists?"

"None that we hired."

"So you can't tell me if the guy's still alive, or where he might live if he is alive?"

"Sorry, can't help you there."

"Anyone else who was around Ellie — roadies, band members, boyfriends — anybody you think I should maybe talk to?"

"Jesus, it was fifty years ago."

"Yeah, I know, Armand. I know it was fifty years ago. Just thought I'd ask."

He cleared his throat. "No, no, you're right. And I do remember Ellie like she was standing across the room, her guitar around her neck, singing some sad song I didn't totally understand but would have listened to all damn night, you know?"

"I've heard that about her."

"I'll tell you something." Armand Beauclaire's voice was quieter now. "Ellie Foster was going to be big, and I'm talking about as big as Joni. That's the gospel truth right there. And whoever pulled her into that car in a goddamned back alley in Calgary, they took that away from us."

"Look, Armand, I understand that the prevailing sentiment is that she was loved by all. I've heard that from everybody I've talked to. And I hope this doesn't sound callous, but somebody didn't love her. Somebody abducted her, shot two people, and drove off. Can you think of anything or anyone I should be asking about … looking into? However remote … anyone at all?"

Long pause. "Jesus, it's tough, you know? And like I said before, I loved her to death, everybody did, even that last time."

I waited a few seconds for more. None came.

"What did you mean by 'even that last time'?"

Beauclaire cleared his throat. "Like I said, she'd played Le Hibou two previous times. This time, she wasn't the same. It wasn't big, like she was a raving, weird-ass bitch or anything, but she was just different. Quieter, maybe. Introspective. Almost like there was something on her mind, something she wanted to talk about, but never did. But hell, maybe it was a lover or something. I mean, that shit happened all the time. But it was like after she played the other place, she was a little different."

"The other place?"

"Yeah. There was another club. Up in Little Italy. Wasn't around long. Maybe a year, two at the most. Ellie was one of the first acts they hired. I think they wanted to kick our asses. Didn't happen. Ellie said she'd never play there again. And she didn't. Nobody did. At least nobody who mattered. And then it was gone."

"Remember the name?"

"Sure. The Tumbling Mustard. Cool name. But that was the only cool thing about it."

"You ever go there?"

"Once. Cold coffee. Bad talent. I didn't go back."

"You know the club operator?"

"Nope, not really, except there were two of them, I remember that. Blew into town from the States somewhere,

Arizona maybe, or California. Gone in a year or so. Maybe back to the States. I didn't pay a lot of attention once I figured out they weren't real competition."

"Remember either of their names?"

Another pause. "Christ, I can't remember where I left my glasses, but I've got one guy's name. Fayed. Middle Eastern dude. Ahmad or Abdul or something. Anyway, I think he was the main guy. I can't remember the other guy's name. Listen, what kind of story you writing about Ellie? You're asking some questions that seem a little strange to me."

I thought about it.

"I am writing a story about Ellie, but that isn't the whole truth." I told him about Monica Brill and our investigation, figuring he'd be pissed off about my lying to him. He wasn't.

"Do me a favour," he said. "You find out what happened to Ellie, I'd like to know. I don't think you will after all this time. But like I said, I'd appreciate hearing what you find out."

"You're officially on the list. We find anything, I'll call. That's a promise."

"I appreciate that. And I wish you luck."

"Thanks, Armand. And thanks for your time. If you think of anything else, I'd appreciate a call. Does your phone have call display?"

"Yeah, and I even have a computer. I may be old, but I'm not prehistoric." He chuckled, but I wasn't sure if he was laughing at me or at himself. "I can see your number. I'll write it down, and I'll call you if I come up with anything."

I ended the call and banged together a summary of the conversation. I attached it to an email to Cobb and received a reply within ten minutes. It said only, "Good job. Let's talk later."

The Chinese food was good, and the hot topic of conversation was volleyball, Kyla's latest passion.

"So you've made the team, then?" I said, after she gave a detailed account of the first few practices of the season.

She shrugged. "I don't know yet. We have a game tomorrow night. After that, Mr. Napier's going to tell us who's on the team."

"And what do you think your chances are?"

"Pretty good, but it's not like when your mom's the manager of the baseball team. Then you'd really have to suck to not make the team. This isn't like that."

"I'll remember that during next season's tryouts." Jill laughed. Then she turned to me. "Now, there was something you wanted to talk about. Is this an adults-only topic, or can all of us be part of the discussion?"

"Actually, this is something I'd like to share with both of you."

It was Kyla and one of her school and baseball buddies who had first sprung the shocking news about Faith Unruh's murder on us a few months before. Josie, it turned out, lived on the same street Faith Unruh had lived on — and died on — many years before. And Josie had heard snippets of conversation about the murder. She'd shared those snippets with Kyla; then, the two of them filled Jill and me in on what they knew over dinner one night.

I figured Kyla deserved to know that Cobb and I were aware of the case, and while we weren't exactly conducting a full-blown investigation, we did have our antennae up and at the ready should any new information present itself.

I told them about the meeting Cobb and I had had with Marlon Kennedy. I didn't mention my earlier meeting with Kennedy in the laneway. Jill already knew about it; Kyla did not, and my desire to keep no secrets from her did not extend to sharing stuff that might scare her.

"And so tonight you're going to his house for an orientation into the surveillance he's been conducting on his own all these years," Jill stated.

"Yeah, and then I'll be sort of looking after the stuff and filling in for him during the time he's gone to be with his ex-wife."

"That is so totally sad," Kyla said softly. "He sits there every day watching those two houses and videoing everyone who comes around?"

"Yeah," I said.

"It is sad, honey," Jill agreed. "It's really sad."

We sat silently for a while, watching the evening shadows forming on the street outside.

"I hope whoever did that to Faith — I hope he comes by there one day and Mr. Kennedy gets him."

I put my hand over hers. "I hope so too, sweetheart, but one thing that's really important — Mr. Kennedy has to do things in a lawful way. He has to report what he finds out to the police and let them handle it. It wouldn't be right for him to take the law into his own hands and try to get some kind of revenge on the person — even if he was 100 percent sure he actually had the killer. You can see that, right?"

She thought about it for a minute, then stood up and said, "Yes, I can see it, but it's still really sad. I'm going to bed to read for a while. Is that okay, Mom?"

"Of course that's okay."

Kyla kissed me on the cheek, gave her mom a long hug, and headed off to her bedroom. After a minute or so, I turned to Jill. "Was I too preachy?"

Jill smiled. "I don't think so. It was a useful message to share with her. Kyla likes to think about things before she makes decisions. She'll think about this, and in a day or two she'll come back to it."

"Are you okay with me doing this?" A couple of times the projects I'd worked on with Mike Cobb had turned ugly. Ugly as in *dangerous*. I didn't see any danger in what I was about to do, but there were no guarantees.

"Actually, this is fine," Jill said. "I've been feeling really guilty that I haven't been volunteering at the Inn lately, and I've wanted to get back to it. This is the perfect opportunity."

The *Let the Sunshine Inn* homeless shelter and food bank was where I had first met Jill during a search Mike and I had conducted for a young runaway addict.

"Damn boyfriends get in the way of the good stuff," I said.

Jill smiled and shook her head. "Uh-uh, this boyfriend *is* the good stuff. No, a lot of it has been due to Kyla's being sick. And even though she's a lot better, I've been reluctant to get very far away from her. But I think I'm ready to let things return to normal now."

Normal. Ordinary. Surprising how words like that felt really good after a difficult summer filled with worry over the health of someone we cared so much about.

I looked in the direction of Kyla's bedroom, then back at Jill.

"God, I love you two people."

"Us two people are pretty darn crazy about you, too. Or is that *we* two people?"

"Doesn't matter … as long as the two people's names are Jill and Kyla."

"Turns out you're in luck."

FOUR

I rang the front doorbell of Marlon Kennedy's house a couple of minutes before ten o'clock. I'd been standing on the front step for a long minute looking around, taking in a yard and house that were remarkably unremarkable. An ordinary house in an ordinary neighbourhood, where, years before, a little girl had died a violent, terrible death.

Kennedy opened the door and stood looking at me for so long that I began to wonder if he'd forgotten I was coming. And I thought back to the night he'd attacked me — the action of a man pushed over the edge. Not a madman, I didn't think. *But mad people surely didn't act like they were mad all the time. Did they?*

Finally he stepped back to let me enter. I'd thought about what the place might look like during my drive from Jill's to here. Not a long drive — that was one of the things about Faith Unruh's death that had hit home, the close proximity of Jill and Kyla's home to the death scene that had played out in 1991.

Now as I moved inside the house that had been the home and workplace of Marlon Kennedy for so long, I made no secret of my curiosity. I stepped to the middle of a large front hallway and looked around. To the left was what looked like the dining room — at least in Kennedy's configuration of the house. A vintage dining room suite that was a little the worse for wear but still held charm despite its age occupied most of the space in the room.

Like the neighbourhood that surrounded it, the house, or at least this part of the house, was mundane, almost dull. Nothing to indicate that this was surveillance central for a decades-old murder. Or that the occupant of the home was living an obsession.

Only one picture in the room, on the southernmost wall. Not a painting — a large two-by-three-foot photograph of a little girl. I recognized the photo. I'd seen it before. It was the one several media outlets had used. Faith Unruh when she was eight or nine, a quizzical smile playing over full lips, soft friendly eyes. Trusting eyes … perhaps too trusting.

I surveyed the rest of the room. The wall opposite the one with the photo contained a doorway leading, I guessed, to the kitchen.

I let my gaze wander in a semicircle to the right. A larger room spread out before me. It looked to have once been a living room. While I was scanning my mind for words to describe what I was looking at, Kennedy led the way into the room.

"The business part of the place is right here in the living room on this floor and the back bedroom upstairs." Kennedy pointed to the far end of the room.

As I stepped into that space, I noticed right away that the *living* part of the living room was absent. It was something like a combined study and A/V centre. Two video cameras, tape playback machines, a table with a computer at one end, notebooks and pens at the other. Latest technology and old school sharing the same surface. And it *was* the latest technology. I stepped to the window. One camera was on a tripod and stood maybe chest high. A stool was in place so that the watcher could sit and have the camera roughly at eye level.

"Tapes?" I asked him. "All this and you're still using tapes."

He shrugged. "That's what I started with. I know there's newer technology, but this is what I know, what I'm comfortable with. And it does the job."

I looked through the camera and knew that I was looking at the front yard and the front of the house that Faith Unruh had lived in at the time of her death. Three doors away and on the same side of the street. Kennedy's house was slightly more forward on the lot it occupied, thus offering a clear and unimpeded view of what had been the Unruh home. I also noted I was looking through the branches and leaves of a couple of trees that stood outside the window.

I looked at Kennedy. "Camouflage?"

"Yeah." He managed a tiny nod. "The neighbours might get nervous if they thought it was them I was watching. I planted those trees the first year I was here. Now I have to keep pruning them back to allow me a clear view of the house."

He spent a few minutes telling me how he wanted the comings and goings of people from the house and the area in front of it recorded in one of the notebooks on the table.

"I'm not going to tell you about the people who live there. I don't want you getting lazy on me. You watch, you write down everything and everyone you see, and you'll figure it out for yourself."

I thought that attitude a bit childish but didn't bother to tell him that.

"You got this part?"

"What about this second camera?" I asked.

It sat on a smaller tripod, or at least one with the legs not extended. It was in the corner near the window, but not facing the window, as the other was.

"Backup. Everything here has a backup. If there's a breakdown with one piece of equipment, I can be back up and running in seconds, minutes at the most."

"Makes sense," I said, though I wasn't sure it did. I wasn't sure that any of this made sense.

"You okay with this part?" he repeated.

"Yeah, I think so."

"The rest is upstairs. Follow me." He began the climb up to the second floor, and I followed. There were three bedrooms and a bathroom on that level. He led the way into one of the bedrooms.

"I cleaned this up a little for you, got a bunch of my shit out of the closet. There's a couple of extra blankets in there, if you need them. I don't use the upstairs bathroom, so you can treat it like it's yours. I hope it's all okay."

Along two of the bedroom's walls were bookshelves. I'm not sure why, but I hadn't expected Kennedy to be a reader. I noted that a lot of the books were hardcovers, but I didn't look at any in detail. There'd be time for that later, or at least I hoped there would be.

"It's fine," I assured him. Actually, it looked more than fine. Like the rest of the house, it was neat and clean. Not that Marlon Kennedy was a neat freak; the place wasn't perfect, but it was pretty damn good.

He led me down the narrow hall to the last bedroom on the east side of the house, and I followed him into a space that looked to be about the same size as the room he'd designated as mine for the next while. Again, there was no furniture but for one table sitting just off-centre from the middle of the room and covered with more notebooks — several piled high, the record of almost nine thousand days of surveillance. Kyla had been right. The word to describe what I was seeing was *sad*.

The rest of the room was a maze of recorders, computers, and video cameras. I turned to see that in one corner of the room, a high-powered rifle leaned against the wall. Kennedy noted my reaction to seeing the rifle.

"Emergency only," he said.

"Good," I said.

"The part you need to know about is over here." Another high-backed stool sat in front of the window and next to another video camera on a tripod. "I've got everything set up, so it should pretty much run itself, but I'll take you through any problems that could pop up."

For the next twenty minutes I was given an intensive albeit brief seminar in video communications. He was remarkably thorough. There were two recorders so that when he was checking the tape from, for example, a time when he'd been away, another recorder was capturing the scene in real time. I got the idea that it was from this view that Kennedy thought there was a better chance of one day seeing the killer. And I had to agree. If the person who took Faith Unruh's life was to return to the scene, my guess, like Kennedy's, was that he would do it at the actual murder scene as opposed to the place the little girl had lived. I made a few notes, especially relating to the tapes I'd be checking when I couldn't actually be watching the two houses. I had to admit Kennedy not only knew the equipment backwards and forwards, but he was also able to communicate what I needed to know very well. I'm not sure why, but I hadn't expected communication to be one of Kennedy's strengths. Maybe because that hadn't been the case the night he'd jumped me in the laneway behind my apartment.

The last thing he went over was the scene outside the window. Across the street and five doors down was the house and yard where Faith's body had been found. I knew the place, but this was a different view — from the side and slightly above. Kennedy had chosen his home well. The exposure to the scene was perfect: a clear view of the garage in the backyard and the alley behind it. It was there, next to that garage, where Faith's body had been found the morning after her disappearance, naked and lying under a four-by-eight sheet of plywood.

Kennedy had been lucky to find a place that offered an unobstructed look at the two places he needed to see.

"Any questions?"

"Not about the technology," I answered him. "I think I've got that figured out."

"Yeah?"

"One thing, though. Besides me, how many times in all these years have you seen someone who maybe looked a little suspicious?"

"Count 'em on one hand."

"I don't know whether to admire you or feel sorry for you for doing this."

"Well, let me put your mind at ease. I don't give a rat's ass which one you choose. Or what you think of me. This is what I'm going to do until I get that bastard."

"And you really think you'll get him?"

His shoulders slumped a little, and his voice dropped to a near whisper. "Some days I'm convinced that I'll never see him, that he's dead or he's too smart or, like I said, he had cop help to get away with it and I'll never get any closer than I am right now." While he speaking he bent down to look through the video camera. "But there are other times when I know … I can feel it, that he's still out there and one day he'll walk into my camera shot and I can spring the trap. By the way, something I forgot — binoculars on that shelf over there."

He pointed, and I looked at the shelf he was indicating, saw the binoculars.

I glanced at my watch. "You better get going."

He nodded. "You good?"

"I'm good."

"My bag's down in the hall. I'll grab it on the way out. House keys are on the table right by the front door. There's some stuff in the fridge if you get hungry. I'll text when I know more."

"Listen, Marlon. I got this. Why don't you just think about what you need to do in Nanaimo? And I want you to know I'm sorry about your wife."

"Yeah." He left the bedroom, and I heard him descending the stairs.

"One more thing!" he yelled from the main level of the house. "That rifle's loaded … just so you know."

I looked over at the rifle, a .30-06, and was still looking at it when I heard the front door close.

I walked back and forth between the two workspaces Kennedy had set up in the house. After twenty minutes of that I called Cobb, left a voice mail to say Kennedy had gone to catch his flight and all was quiet. Then I called Jill.

Though I was fairly sure I'd woken her, her voice gave no sign. I heard, "Hey, cowboy," after she picked up. "How's the spying going?"

"Okay," I said. "Kennedy's left for the airport. I've been checking the place out. The crazy part is that I can picture myself actually being sort of busy between watching, recording what I see, and checking the tapes to look at what I missed."

"No, sweetheart," Jill countered, "that's not the crazy part. The crazy part is that you're in a virtual stranger's house looking for a clue into something that happened twenty-four years ago."

"I guess," I said.

She paused. "I'm sorry. It's not right that I'm making light of it. I honestly feel terrible for that poor man who has given up his life for this. And I'm glad you called. I was kind of worried about you. Everything's okay over there?"

"Everything's fine," I assured her. "I mean, this feels weird to me too, but I wanted to do this for the guy so he can be with his wife. And what's weirdest of all, it feels like fishing. You sit there, you haven't had a bite for hours, but you keep looking at your line in the water like at any second some fish is going to grab the hook, and bingo, you got 'im."

"And you think you might see someone who could be the guy?"

"I don't know," I said. "I mean no, I don't really believe that. But I also find it impossible to say I'm *not* going to see someone. That's the fishing part. I guess that's how it must be for Kennedy. Anyway, I miss you and I need to hear the voice of the young lady who lives with you … if she's up."

"She's lying here right beside me. Wouldn't go off to her own bed until we'd heard from you. I think she has a crush on you."

I heard a "Mom!" in the background and could picture the pained expression on Kyla's face.

She came on the line. "I don't know why you even go out with her." I could hear the urge to laugh in her voice.

"I do it only to get her out of the house and give you a break."

The laugh surfaced then. We didn't talk long, but she did tell me she'd thought about it and decided that Mr. Kennedy should not take matters into his own hands. Jill had been right about her daughter's need to analyze.

"You're a terrific kid, you know that? It must be about time we hit Chuck E. Cheese for a night of my beating the tar out of you in every game in the place."

"You wish!" She laughed again.

"You know what I really wish? I wish I could give you a hug right now."

"What you have to do is give me a think hug."

"And I do that how?"

"You think about the hug, and I think about the hug at the same time. It's not as good as the real thing, but it's better than no hug at all. Wanna try?"

I wondered if Kyla and her dad used the "think hug" method — then decided it didn't matter.

"I sure do," I told her, and I actually closed my eyes and imagined holding her.

"Did it work?" she said after a few seconds.

"You're a genius," I said. "I'm not going to be around much for the next little while, so we're going to have to rely on think hugs, lots of them."

"Okay."

"Have a good sleep, okay?"

"You too, Adam."

I promised her I would, but as we ended the call I knew it would be a while before I slept.

For the next three hours, maybe a little longer, I alternated between the upstairs and downstairs locations. I spent more time on the upper level — on the stool and looking some of the time through the camera and some of the time through the binoculars at the garage and the alley behind it — two of the places Kennedy had spent something like half his life watching.

The stools were the tall kind you see in some bars and coffee places — comfortable for maybe an hour, nasty after that. The best part was the walk between the two surveillance locations when I was able to stretch and rub the numbness out of most of the lower back half of my body. I finally retrieved two of the blankets Kennedy had told me about and manufactured a couple of almost cushions, which helped. I took breaks every couple of hours to do bending and stretching exercises, a new appreciation for Kennedy's dedication already firmly formed in my mind.

During the time I was watching from the upstairs perch, I saw one car go down the alley, just before midnight. Nothing and no one else. Sometime around 1:30 in the morning, I checked the cameras to make sure that they were working and properly aimed, that I hadn't accidentally knocked one off target. Then I went out to the Accord, grabbed my gym bag out of the trunk, and went back inside.

I checked the kitchen, more out of curiosity than hunger. Kennedy had stocked the place pretty well before he left. I wasn't surprised by that, except that he would have had to do the shopping between our chat that morning and my arrival that night. Another example of the man's attention to detail.

I took a shower and, after one last look out of the main floor window at what had been the Unruh house, I headed off to my own bedroom. I glanced quickly at Kennedy's book collection — almost all non-fiction, with a strong bent toward biography. Again, I was surprised. Being a fiction guy myself, I went to bed with the copy of Miriam Toews's *A Complicated Kindness* that I'd brought with me. I fell asleep with the light on and the book still propped on my chest, woke up a while later, and for a minute had to remind myself where I was. I shut off the light and thought for a while, mostly about the fact that I had just completed night number one of my surveillance. Just 8,999 short of Kennedy's record.

FIVE

The next morning I made a pot of strong coffee and was back at my upstairs bedroom post just after 7:00. I watched the departure of the man who lived in the house where Faith's body had been found. At 7:34 he came out the back door of the house, walked to the garage, and disappeared inside. A minute or so later, a brown Chrysler 300 backed into the alley, turned left, and headed west, disappearing from view in a few seconds. I noted that the man was thirty-something, wore a good-looking, lightweight suit, and carried a briefcase. I recorded his departure in the notebook Kennedy used to diarize all "sightings" on either property.

Seventeen minutes later, a woman came out of the house. She had a little girl in tow, and they, too, entered the garage, then after a couple of minutes drove away, this time in a Nissan Murano. Nice vehicles — this family didn't appear to have been affected by the downturn in the Alberta economy.

They were too young to have been living there when the murder had taken place, unless one of them had grown up in the house. I wondered if either of the adults — I assumed they were either husband and wife or live-in partners — was aware that they parked their vehicles just metres from where a little girl just a few years older than their own daughter had lain as the life drained out of her. I wondered, too, whether real estate agents were obligated to tell prospective buyers about horrific events that had taken place in or around properties they were trying to sell.

I drank coffee and watched for a while longer, then went downstairs. At 8:22, a red Equinox pulled up in front of the house where Faith Unruh had lived. An eleven- or twelve-year-old boy, backpack over his shoulder, dashed from the front door and down the sidewalk and then climbed into the back seat of the Equinox. The boy was dark-skinned, perhaps East Indian or Pakistani. He rapped knuckles with another boy, similar in age and Caucasian, already in the back seat. The driver — I guessed he was the second boy's dad — pulled away from the curb, and I could see someone else in the passenger-side front seat, an older sister, maybe. All of them were likely heading for the kids' school.

I recorded that departure too. I took a break between 9:00 and 10:00 to take in yogourt and a bran muffin and thought about the fact that I hadn't, during my time in the surveillance rooms, listened to any of my music. Music was part of virtually every one of my days. It had been the therapy I relied on after Donna's death. Yet it had felt somehow wrong to have even that small pleasure while I looked out these windows hoping to spot a killer. I wondered if Marlon Kennedy looked at his time on the surveillance stools the same way.

Cobb texted just after eleven o'clock:

Read again your report on the conversation with the former assistant manager of Le Hibou. Good work. Want to hear your thoughts. Interesting the attitude change in Ellie after she'd played the other club. Might be a good idea to do some checking on the place when you get time. I've got a lot on my plate today — some domestic, some case-related. I'll call when I get some time.

And that was my morning. For lunch I went down to the kitchen and made myself two baloney and lettuce sandwiches and took them and a Diet Coke back upstairs. But this time I decided to take my laptop with me. I pushed aside cords and power bars and made space on the table that occupied much of the centre of the room. I set up to do a little work on the Ellie Foster disappearance while I kept an eye on the scene outside.

The afternoon went by surprisingly quickly. I divided my time about equally between surveillance and research, looking, as Cobb had directed, for connections to Ellie Foster's music career. And I spent a fruitless hour and a half trying to find out something about the coffee house known as The Tumbling Mustard. Found one mention — actually, a poor-quality photo of a poster from the club dated October 17, 1964. It was promoting a singer who called herself Angie. That was it — just the one name. Nothing on anyone named Fayed. I wasn't sure I'd learn anything even if I was able to track down Mr. Fayed, but I was intrigued by the notion that Ellie had undergone some kind of personality or attitudinal change during or around the time of her Tumbling Mustard gig. Maybe Fayed could shed some light on that.

On a whim I checked out performers named Angie and actually surprised myself when I discovered a Wikipedia mention of a "Fredericton-born folksinger who enjoyed a brief career in the early and midsixties and retired to a sheep farm in the Shuswap area of B.C." I tried to find more about the elusive Angie, who may or may not still have been raising sheep in British Columbia, thinking she might be able to direct me toward Fayed, but I turned up nothing. Then I came across a brief notation that offered "prayers and thoughts to the family and friends of Angie Kettinger, the wonderful New Brunswick–born singer who passed away last night in the Salmon Arm hospital at just sixty-six years of age." The piece, dated April 29, 2011, included details of a memorial service to celebrate Angie's life and music.

I was hoping that the passing of Angie Kettinger wasn't a harbinger of things to come as Cobb and I tried to track people with some knowledge of Ellie Foster's life and disappearance.

When I broke for dinner — a pizza warmed up in the oven — I had an almost blank page where I'd hoped several lines of meaningful text would be. After I'd cleaned up the dinner dishes — one plate, one glass, my kind of cleanup — I once again returned to the surveillance locations. As I sat on the upstairs stool looking at the quiet scene that was the house across the street, I realized how little I had accomplished that day. At eight o'clock I broke for a run, weaving my way around the pleasant neighbourhood and passing in front of both of the houses I had been watching on cameras. Back in Kennedy's house I spent twenty minutes sitting in the dark of the dining room, trying without success to pull together even one thought that would move the Ellie Foster investigation forward.

After a quick check of the two cameras I was back at my computer feeling, more than anything, useless and depressed. For the next while I again immersed myself in the musical career of Ellie Foster. It wasn't a long career. She had sung professionally for just over two years, but even in that time — as I read reviews, promo pieces, and comments about her from those who had seen her perform at Le Hibou in Ottawa, the Louis Riel coffee house in Saskatoon, a couple of Toronto and Vancouver clubs, or even Caffè Lena in Saratoga Springs, New York — it was clear that a great many people thought she was a special talent.

There were countless glowing commentaries and predictions of a major musical career that would rival those of Baez and Mitchell. I put in another hour of Google searches and phone calls and finally came up with something. Nothing major, but something. I tracked the number of a former *Herald* writer who used to write a music column. I'd met Bert Nichol a couple of times, but he'd retired by the time I started at the paper, so I didn't know him well, and I doubted he'd remember me at all.

I had no idea how old he was, but I figured *old* was the operative word. Nevertheless, I hoped he could tell me a little about The Depression … if he was still lucid. And willing to chat. I called the number. It was coming up on ten o'clock, and I knew I was pushing my luck, but maybe the guy was still up and about.

A woman's voice came on the line.

"Hello. Is this Mrs. Nichol?"

"Who's calling, please?"

Ah, careful. Good girl.

"This is Adam Cullen. I used to work at the *Herald* and met Bert a few times, although I didn't really have the opportunity to get to know him. Right now I'm working with a detective on the Ellie Foster disappearance from 1965. We've been contracted by a family member. I was hoping I could speak to Bert if he's still up."

There was a long pause.

Finally she said, "He's still up, the damn fool. He watches reruns of those game shows — says it's research for when he's a contestant. I think he's kidding, but with Bert you never know. I'll take the phone to him."

"Thank you," I said.

I'll take the phone to him. Bedridden? Wheelchair bound?

A couple of minutes later, a voice that would have fit perfectly on an old 78 rpm record came on the line.

"This is Bert."

I went through the self-introduction again, hoping I wouldn't have to repeat it a third time. No danger there. Bert was 100 percent sharp. And business-like. Or maybe I was keeping him from one of his shows and he just wanted to get rid of me.

"What can I do for you?

"I wondered if you covered The Depression when you were writing music for the *Herald* and if you could tell me a little about the place?"

"I didn't get the music beat until ten years or so after The Depression was gone from the scene."

"Oh," I said, knowing my disappointment was likely evident in my voice.

"But hell, I guess I knew the place as well as anybody. Went there lots — even took Rose a time or two — that was Rose, my wife, you were talking to before. I saw Ellie Foster perform maybe three or four times. In those days I was just dipping a toe in the music world, and I remember I wrote two or three pieces about her for a couple of smaller music publications — the ones that paid in free copies and once in a while an album in the mail. In fact, me and a couple of friends of mine, we were supposed to be there the night she was kidnapped or whatever the hell happened to her. But one of the *Herald* sports guys asked me to cover for him. The Saskatoon Quakers were in town to play the Calgary Spurs. Senior hockey. He was supposed to do a piece on Fred Sasakamoose, who was travelling with the Quakers at the time. You heard of Fred Sasakamoose?"

"I have, yes." I'd caught a CBC documentary some years before on Canada's first-ever First Nations player in the NHL. "Cree elder. Former NHLer."

"Exactly right." Bert sounded like he was happy I was up on my hockey history. Which I wasn't. But I did know of Fred Sasakamoose.

"He'd retired as a player a few years before," Bert Nichol went on, "but he was coming to Calgary with the Saskatoon team, so I got to interview him. Good guy, as I recall. But it meant I missed that night at The Depression, all the shooting and shit … ah, sorry, Rose … all that stuff that went down that night."

He dropped his voice a decibel or two. "Heard about Ellie when I got home later that night. A goddamn … uh … bloody shame." He dropped his voice even lower, to a whisper. "My wife doesn't approve of bad language."

"I understand," I said. "Listen, Bert, do you still have any of those stories you wrote about Ellie Foster?"

A pause, then normal volume. "Naw. That was a long time before computers. I'd write 'em and send 'em off — lots of times, the editors didn't even get back to me, especially if they didn't use the stuff. Probably just chucked 'em. End of story." He chuckled. "Literally."

"Yeah. Listen, Bert, any chance we could maybe have coffee and talk about The Depression a little?"

"After all this time?"

"It's a long shot, I know, but her granddaughter is hoping to bring about some kind of closure to it, and —"

"Granddaughter?"

"Yes."

Another pause, longer this time. I was beginning to think I'd lost him when he finally said, "Listen, I know if it was my grandkids, I'd want people to help any way they could. Why don't you come over here tomorrow afternoon? I don't get out much, so meeting you somewhere might be a little difficult."

"That would be great. Can I bring anything?"

A pause. "How about a Peters' Drive-In milkshake? I could do with one of those."

"Done. What flavour?"

"Chocolate and orange mixed."

"Got it."

"I don't know if I'll be much help, but what the … the … what the heck, right? Always worth a chat."

He gave me the address, and we ended the call.

I had just put my computer to sleep and was about to head back downstairs to the ground floor camera when my phone offered the first few bars of Loverboy's "Turn Me Loose." I picked up, expecting to hear Jill telling me something she'd forgotten to say the night before. I was wrong.

"Just checking in," Cobb's baritone voice informed me. "Making sure you're not lying in a ditch somewhere."

"No ditch. Everything's fine here, or at least as fine as terminal boredom can be."

"I can imagine," Cobb said. "Actually, I had a couple of reasons for calling. Wanted to keep you up to speed on our other case."

"Ellie Foster."

"Yeah. I called in some favours. I got the actual homicide file from the shootings and Ellie's disappearance. What Monica Brill gave us was bits and pieces, a summary."

The homicide file, I knew, was a comprehensive collection of witness statements, the reports of the investigating detectives, crime scene photos, forensics reports — in short, every piece of documentation pertaining to the homicide being investigated. I knew as well that some jurisdictions, particularly those in the States, called that collection the *murder book*. But the Calgary Police Service used the term *homicide file*, sometimes abbreviated to *the file*.

"Anything there?"

"I've given it only a cursory glance. I want to spend some time on it tonight. How about I stop by in the morning and we take a look at what we've got?"

"Human contact. What a concept. I'll have the coffee on." I didn't bother telling him about my conversation with Bert Nichol — figured that could wait until morning.

Cobb laughed. "See you then."

I stood up and took a quick look out the upstairs window. Nothing to see but a house and backyard at peace. I ran tapes for an hour, took one last look at the Unruh home from downstairs, then did the same thing upstairs with the murder house (the name I'd decided to give it to keep them straight in my mind).

A quick glance, then I was turning away to call it a night when something brought me back to the camera — a movement, or maybe just a shadow. I grabbed the binoculars and brought them to my eyes, and while most of my being was telling me it was nothing, I couldn't control the racing of my heart.

"Come on," I said out loud. "Kennedy's been watching for years, but you're going to stumble across the killer in a few hours? Give your head a shake."

But I stayed in place for another half hour, watching ... and seeing nothing. I ran the tape back and watched it three times. Something had moved in the alley behind the garage. I was sure of it. I was almost equally sure that what I'd seen was a dog or cat, or maybe a waving tree branch caught by a gust of wind.

Almost sure.

My eyes were aching and tired from the strain of trying to see something in the blackness of the alley. I wanted to go to bed, to sleep and dream about something pleasant.

But there was a part of me that wouldn't let it go ... couldn't let it go. What if I'd had the chance to spot the killer, but ignored it, and he went on to kill again? And again. How would I live with that?

I decided to walk across the street and have a look around. Total darkness had long since settled on the street, and I took one last long look before I left the house. Earlier I'd noticed a flashlight on the windowsill next to the rifle, and now grabbed it. I hesitated and actually considered taking the .30-06. I shook my head at that insanity — just what the neighbourhood needed, a stranger wandering the back alley with a weapon. Yeah, that would hardly draw any attention at all to the house where the street's recluse lived.

Instead I pulled on my jacket, tucked the flashlight into a pocket, and descended the stairs. I stopped in the kitchen long enough to take a nearly empty bottle of bread and butter pickles out of the fridge. A glass jar, surely a dying breed. I dropped the last couple of pickles onto a side plate, rinsed the long, skinny jar, and stuffed it under my jacket. Not as effective as a .30-06, but possibly useful in hand-to-hand combat. *So did you take a knife, a hammer, brass knuckles? No, I opted for an empty pickle jar.*

As prepared as I thought I could make myself, I slipped quietly out the front door. It was just after eleven, and the street was in the process of settling for the night. Several houses were already in darkness, including the one I was headed for.

I took a minute to look at the houses where it appeared that at least one person was still up. I looked at the windows, most with curtains pulled and muffled light behind them as residents read, watched TV, tapped away at computers, or got ready for bed. No one at any of the windows was looking out on the street as a stranger crept carefully along, flashlight now in hand.

I went the opposite way down the street, turned left at the corner, then left again at the alley. The house was seven in from the corner — I'd counted while I walked down the street. I hadn't used the flashlight at first; there was sufficient light from the street lamps to allow me to navigate. But once in the alley, by the fourth house in, darkness had pretty well encircled me, and I flicked it on.

I slowed my pace as well, listening to my breathing and the crunch of the gravel beneath my runners as I walked — convinced that anyone within a two-block radius would be able to hear both. At house number six I stopped and pointed the flashlight first one way, then the other. Saw nothing, detected no movement. Heard nothing but the distant hum of an occasional vehicle.

I tried to determine where the movement I'd seen had been. Everything looked different once I was actually in the alley. I kept my hand over the flashlight, removing it periodically and letting the beam illuminate the alley for a few seconds at a time before covering the light again. My eyes had adjusted to the darkness, and I moved again now, slowly and carefully inching forward until I was behind the garage on which the camera was trained. I looked across the way, and between houses I could see Kennedy's house, knowing that I would now be on the tape. I bent down close to the ground and could no longer see the window of the Kennedy house. The back fence of the property blocked my view of the house from this angle. Which meant that the camera could not now see me. And *that* meant that something — or *someone* — creeping along close to the ground would likewise not be visible from Kennedy's roost.

The significance of my discovery, it seemed to me, was minimal. A dog or cat could move through the alley undetected. So could someone crawling along the ground. But it seemed to me people seldom slithered, snake-like, along gravelly — or any other — surfaces. Unless, of course, that someone was somehow aware that there was a camera trained on the area and that he or she could be seen if walking upright. Rather hypothetical. Rather ridiculous.

What was more likely, of course, was that it had been a small animal that I'd seen, or that animal's shadow, thus rendering my evening's excursion utterly unproductive.

Nevertheless, I wanted to be thorough. I again cast the beam of the flashlight around the area behind the garage. Saw nothing. Then I went over the ground in smaller pieces, moving the light and my vision back and forth across the alley ... again, seeing only gravel, dirt, and a couple of garbage cans against the fence. They, too, would be invisible from Kennedy's vantage point, and I stepped closer to them, thinking, though not with great certainty, that whatever I had seen had to have been in this general area.

The garbage cans, their grey metal shining when I splashed the light on them, were on a small wooden stand maybe a foot off the ground. I scanned the area again and saw nothing ... except for a single piece of paper, clearly something that had escaped the confines of the trash bins. I picked it up and stuffed it in my pocket, if for no more reason than to avoid returning from my wild goose chase completely empty-handed.

One last look around, splaying the light first here, then there. Nothing. Not even a second scrap of paper. I made my way back up the alley to the street and retraced my steps to Kennedy's house. Once inside, I returned the flashlight to the upstairs windowsill and out of curiosity rewound the tape to see what I had looked like prowling the lane behind the murder scene. I first saw flashes of light created by my placing my hand over the flashlight, then removing it. Then I was on the screen, moving slowly, clearly visible despite the darkness and shadows of the alley. I rewound the tape, watched it again, and was surprised to note that as dark as the alley had been, and even though I was never in the flashlight's beam, I was recognizable — a testimony, I supposed, to the quality of Kennedy's equipment. Watching the tape, I realized my expedition had, in fact, borne some fruit. Going down there had been useful in terms of providing a frame of reference for what I was seeing when I looked through the viewer of the camera.

And having provided at least a little justification for my nocturnal prowl, I reset the tape and headed off to bed. I was asleep in seconds, but it wasn't a peaceful night. I woke several times, tossed and rolled around the bed, and dreamed of shadows.

Unpleasant shadows.

SIX

Cobb arrived just after nine and came, as he always did, bearing gifts: Starbucks coffee and bakery items that had definitely not come from Starbucks.

Before we sat down to coffee, I showed him around the place, augmenting the tour with commentary explaining Kennedy's way of conducting the surveillance and recording of what he observed. Cobb was silent during the tour of the two rooms, nodding occasionally but offering no comment until we were sitting at the kitchen table, coffee poured and butterhorns warmed and buttered.

"He hasn't spared any expense," Cobb commented after a sip of the Pike Place.

I nodded. "State-of-the-art equipment, and up to date, meaning he must upgrade fairly regularly."

Neither of us spoke for a couple of minutes, but I noticed Cobb shaking his head.

"What?"

"Damned sad," he said in a soft voice. "You spend virtually every hour of your life staring at two places; you spend all your money making that possible, and the first break you take from it in over twenty years is to be with your ex-wife while she's dying. I'd say that's pretty damned sad."

Kyla had expressed much the same sentiment.

"Can't argue that." I broke off a piece of the butter-horn, chewed, and swallowed. I looked at Cobb. "You ever tell anybody about …" I looked around the room. "About this? About finding Kennedy? Any of the guys you both worked with?"

Cobb shook his head. "Didn't think that would be a good idea."

I nodded, and that was the end of conversation until we'd finished eating. I topped up the coffee with some I'd brewed before Cobb had arrived. He snapped open an old-school briefcase and pulled out a long manila file folder thick with pages.

I looked at the folder as he removed a long elastic band from around it. He extracted an envelope, reached inside, and pulled out several photographs. He didn't say anything until he had them spread out on the table between us.

I scooched my chair around a bit to get a better look at them. Cobb pointed. "There are more, but this is a pretty good representation. This one," he said, laying a hand on one of the photos, "is Jerry Farkash. He played guitar and occasionally keyboards. And that's Duke Prego, who played bass; he had joined the group only a couple of months before they came west."

I studied the two pictures — the first, of Farkash. He was face down in the alley, head turned away from the camera, much of the back of his skull blown away.

"Shot from behind," I said.

Cobb nodded. "Might have been trying to run from the shooter. Hard to know for sure, but that seems likely."

The second photo showed a man sitting with his back up against a tall, wooden fence that bordered one side of the property. He looked like he was resting after a hard workout and would be getting to his feet when he caught his breath.

Except for his eyes. Even in the floodlit back lot and alley, even in the slightly grainy black-and-white photo, it was clear that the life was gone from Duke Prego's eyes … and wouldn't be coming back. There would be no catching of breath ever again. I looked at the victim photos for a couple of minutes — trying to take in every detail of the bodies and of the ground around them, knowing that Cobb had already done that. I saw nothing that offered up anything that might be useful.

There was also a photo of the garbage cans; I assumed they were the ones Guy Kramer had taken shelter behind. There were four, they all looked to be metal, and one was on its side. I thought back to my nocturnal prowl of the night before, the garbage cans behind the house where Faith Unruh's body had been found.

The last two pictures were of the alley, one labelled "looking south," the other "looking north." I remembered from my other reading that the car had come from the south — that had been in Kramer's statement.

I stared at the south-facing photo for a long moment, then looked up at Cobb.

"They had to know."

"What?"

"The killers had to know Ellie and the band guys were out there. Either they went for a smoke break at exactly the same time every night, and the shooters knew when that was, or one or both of them had been in the club that night. When Ellie and the guys went outside, they left, got in their car, and drove down that alley."

Cobb said, "I've thought about that too. I think it's the latter. I just don't think you could count on the break taking place at exactly the same time every night."

"So that means one of the shooters ... or both ... was in The Depression that night while Ellie was performing."

"Or a third person was in the club and communicated with the killers that Ellie and the others had gone outside. Either way, it's clear, or at least likely, that someone in the club that night was part of this. And I'm fairly sure Carrington and Wardlow had the same thought. Carrington wrote that he was frustrated that they couldn't talk to more of the people who were in the club that night, that quite a few had left during the chaotic moments that greeted the news of what had happened outside. They tried to get names, got a few, but Carrington admits they missed some, including maybe some who left while the band was taking its break and before the shooting started."

I looked at the photos for a moment more, saw nothing that told me anything significant.

I drank some coffee and looked at Cobb. "Any chance that either Farkash or Prego was the target? And that Ellie was just there and they grabbed her because she was a witness ... or maybe thinking they'd have a little fun with her before killing her?"

"Another theory of the original investigators," Cobb said, "but they got nowhere with it. Doesn't mean we shouldn't keep it on the back burner as a possibility."

"Anything else that might be useful in there?" I tapped the folder.

He shrugged. "Hard to say. A couple of names, maybe. And one or two things we might want to check on."

"For example?"

"For example, Guy Kramer, the fourth person in the alley that night."

"The guy who hid behind the garbage cans."

"Yeah. He died in 2003."

"I remember reading that."

"What you may not have read is that Guy Kramer's wife still lives in Calgary."

"And that's significant because …?"

"I'm not sure it is. But this is what I've learned. The police report Monica Brill had in her file folder was one of the early reports, maybe even the first. Typically as the investigation goes on, the detectives investigating the crime update their notes, add stuff — new evidence, transcripts, or at least notes of conversations and so forth. Monica's material didn't have that."

"You found something Kramer said later?"

Cobb shook his head. "I didn't, or at least nothing helpful. But what was significant is that Wardlow and Carrington talked to him several times over the course of six or seven weeks after the shooting and kidnapping. They logged times and dates of those conversations."

I didn't get it, and my face must have shown it.

"He was the only eyewitness," Cobb said. "It makes sense that they'd question him at least a couple of times. But several times? That suggests maybe they thought there was something there — that Kramer was either having trouble remembering or wasn't being truthful. The note after one of their visits to his house said, 'Nothing. Again.' That sounds like frustration."

"Or maybe the realization that he really had nothing more to offer."

Cobb nodded. "That's a possibility. But I'd still like to have a chat with Kramer's widow."

I pointed my coffee cup at the file folder. "Anything else?"

"I think our best course of action is to concentrate on Ellie herself. There were some areas that may have been overlooked. Or if they were looked at, they didn't make it into the report."

"It looked to me like the investigators were pretty damn diligent, at least in that early report I saw."

"And I'm not suggesting otherwise. But we can't assume they didn't miss something. Even good cops working hard can make a mistake. Or overlook something significant."

"I imagine it's like writing. I can look at something a half dozen times and miss a word I left out every time. It's why they have something called *editors*."

"And it's why unsolveds get pulled out of the vaults for years after the first investigation so that more pairs of eyes can look at them. Just in case."

We sat in silence for a couple of minutes, both of us staring at the file folder.

It was Cobb who finally spoke.

"Okay, let's talk Ottawa."

I brought him up to date on my unsuccessful efforts to learn anything about The Tumbling Mustard, Fayed, or the other partner. I told him about Angie Kettinger, the Maritimes singer who had passed away in 2011.

He nodded sympathetically — at least that's what I thought the nod signified. Or maybe like me he was resigned to knowing that so many of the figures we would have liked to talk to were dead.

"Still, there might be some significance to the place, especially if whatever was going on with Ellie Foster's mental or psychological state came about during her time there as a performer," he said.

"And we're relying on Armand Beauclair's recollection on that."

"True enough, but let's not throw that strand onto the scrap heap just yet."

"Duly noted," I said.

"So like I said, there are a few things I'd like to know. Where did Ellie stay while she was here performing? How did she get to and from The Depression? Who did she hang with, and what did she do when she wasn't actually performing? And I'd like to apply those same questions to her previous gig, in Ottawa at Le Hibou. And maybe further back than that."

I thought about that. "Clearly, there were some things I missed in my chat with Armand Beauclair."

Cobb laughed. "If I had a loonie for every time I had to go back to a witness because of something I'd forgotten or not thought of asking, I could buy a yacht and live on the French Riviera. So don't beat yourself up over that."

"Thanks, Coach. By the way, I'm meeting with a guy, Bert Nichol, who used to be a music writer for the *Herald*. Frequented The Depression. Even wrote some stuff about Ellie, though not for the *Herald*. I'll throw a couple of those things at him."

"He still have copies of the stuff he wrote about her?"
I shook my head. "Doesn't sound like it."
"Damn."
"Yeah."
"Still, he sounds like a guy worth talking to."

"Guess I'll find out."

"I'm meeting Monica to get the originals of the old Ellie Foster tapes and the CD. I have an appointment to have some voice analyses done."

"I'm betting the voice on the CD Monica received is Ellie Foster."

Cobb stood up. "My bet, too. I'd better hit the road."

"Thanks for the breakfast," I said.

He nodded and headed for the door.

When he'd gone I made my bed, cleaned up in the kitchen (Kennedy was apparently an inspiration), then put in a couple of hours on surveillance detail.

Saw not a damn thing.

Bert and Rose Nichol lived just off 4th Street Northwest, a couple of blocks from James Fowler High School. I was met at the door by Bert's wife, Rose. She smiled as she ushered me inside the sixties bungalow that was one of the last of the original houses on a block that was almost all infill.

Rose Nichol's coiffed grey hair suggested she had recently been to a beauty salon, and her attire — blue pants and patterned top — like the house and yard, bespoke a woman for whom neatness and order were important.

She shook my hand as we exchanged greetings, then led me into a living room that looked like it hadn't changed since it was originally furnished. Maroon sofa and easy chair, both old and well worn, but still service-able and comfortable looking. Both pieces of furniture came with doilies and reminded me most of all of the home of my former mother-in-law. Donna's mother, Joan, would have liked this room and these people, and for a second there was a grab at my chest, as there always was when I thought of Donna. A glance around the room told me the Nichols loved all things porcelain; figurines of girls in swings, bears with cubs, and horses, a lot of horses, were among the ones that caught my eye.

I was right. *Old* was the first word that came to mind in describing Bert Nichol. Old, but not decrepit. Tall and thin, bordering on gaunt, he was wearing pressed dress pants, an orange sweater, and recently shined loafers. I would soon learn he had a sharp mind and eye, and an even sharper tongue.

He was standing and offered his hand as he said, "You've met Rose."

"Adam Cullen," I said, as I shook his hand. I held out the milkshake I'd brought, and he accepted it with a smile.

"Mother's milk," he said with a grin.

"Tea, Mr. Cullen?" Rose smiled at me.

"I'd love some, but only if you'll call me Adam."

The smile got bigger. "I think I can manage that."

I was having trouble putting an age to Rose. She was clearly younger than her husband, but I couldn't have said by how much.

"If you do a bunch of damn swearing in here, as I've been known to do from time to time, Rose just might poison your tea." Bert spoke in a volume generally reserved for people with a hearing impairment.

"I'll do my best on that score," I assured them both, as Bert laughed and Rose shook her head at what I guessed was a long-standing joke — probably more humorous to Bert than to his patient wife.

"After that, you might wish to change your mind about the tea, Adam," Rose said, "but I'd still be happy to bring you some."

"And I'm still happy to accept your offer," I said as she withdrew.

Bert pointed at the couch, which sat opposite a blue recliner, also old, that I suspected was *his* chair. We both sat and studied one another.

"I remember you now," he said. "And I've read some of your stuff.... You're pretty good."

"I appreciate that, Bert, especially coming from someone like you."

"The new generation of journalists," he said, after a swallow of milkshake, "I'm not much impressed with." Before I could answer, he held up both hands. "I'm sure there are some good ones, some like you, but I'm pretty underwhelmed with the group as a whole."

I nodded. "Newsrooms have changed, Bert, and so have the people in them."

"What people? There's nobody in newsrooms anymore, for Christ's sake. Rival papers share the same newsroom, the same writers. What kind of BS is that?"

"Can't argue that. Journalism's different from what it was."

"Journalism's disappearing, that's what journalism's doing."

I was hoping we'd move on from this topic soon. Bert was right, and normally I'd have loved to discuss the plight of the newspaper industry, but I really wanted to get to Ellie Foster.

Maybe he sensed my thinking. He started to nod his head but opted for a shake instead. "Let's talk about something else. You didn't come here to talk about the good old days. Besides, maybe they weren't all that goddamned good." He glanced in the direction of the kitchen. I guessed he was hoping his epithet hadn't been heard by the matron of the house. I wasn't sure why this one worried him more than the others.

"I'd like to hear your thoughts about Ellie Foster."

He looked at me, then closed his eyes, and I got the feeling he was hearing her, remembering a song she'd performed so long ago.

He opened his eyes but didn't look at me. His gaze cast downwards at the floor. Finally he said, "What a dreadful thing."

"Can you tell me about her?"

"What do you want to know?"

"What was she like? I mean, I know about the talent, but I'd like to know … *her*."

"Yeah, well, first of all you *don't* know about the talent. If you never heard her, never sat close to that tiny stage at The Depression and listened to her sing the world better, then you don't know squat about her talent."

"Fair enough, Bert. You're right."

He waved his hand. "I didn't mean to sound harsh. I just meant we — all of us — lost so much when she disappeared. Think if there'd never been a Joni Mitchell or a Baez or a Cohen — think how different, how much emptier our world would be without their music. And she would have been right there in the same conversation with them, with Neil Young, with Dylan, with … all of them."

I didn't answer, because clearly I couldn't contribute to a conversation about a singer Bert Nichol had quite rightly stated I knew nothing about.

"She was a bit of a heller, you know." The corners of his mouth turned slightly upward.

"In what way?"

"She didn't mind disturbing a little sh—" He glanced again at the kitchen. "Disturbing things a little," he amended.

"What kinds of things?"

Before he could answer, Rose returned to the room with a tray. Two teacups and saucers, chocolate-covered cookies on a plate, some napkins, and fixings for the tea. She came to me first.

"Adam?"

I took a cup, added a little milk, and took a cookie. "Thank you, Rose. See, Adam is so much nicer than Mr. Cullen."

She smiled and moved off to serve Bert, who accepted a couple of cookies, then she settled on the couch that sat to my left, Bert's right. She and I sipped tea while Bert worked the straw in his milkshake for a minute or two. (You don't *sip* a Peters' shake.)

I didn't want to rush things or spoil the tranquility of the moment, but I did want to keep moving forward with the interview. "You were saying Ellie Foster was something of a rebel."

Bert swallowed a bite of cookie while he dabbed at his mouth with a napkin and nodded.

"I don't mean to overstate that," he answered me. "I guess they were all rebels to be doing what they were doing. She sang songs about war and sex and standing up to the government, taking back the land, you know the stuff."

"Protest songs."

"Except for the ones about sex. I'm not sure you could classify those as protest songs."

I smiled. "Probably not."

"Thing is, when you looked at her, what you saw was this innocent-looking, childlike little thing; she *was* tiny, and yet here were these words coming out of her that, I don't know, didn't fit the person she was, you know?"

"The *physical* person she was," I said.

He looked at me for a while before nodding. "You're right. Like with a lot of people, the real Ellie was the person inside, and there was nothing tiny about that — the spirit, the talent you talked about, the things she wanted to say."

"How did audiences react to her?"

"Loved her. I mean *loved* her." He paused, drank some more shake. "And not just audiences. She was someone everybody wanted to be around. Staff, other performers, people like me … she had a quality about her that others wanted to be a part of."

"Even though she was a heller," I said.

"Yeah. Even though."

"Did she have any close friends … anybody she hung out with out here?"

Bert picked up the milkshake but didn't take a drink, just stared at the container while he thought. Finally, he looked up at me and shook his head.

"I don't think so. I mean, the reality is I can't remember. That's a long time ago. Sorry."

"No need to apologize, Bert. I appreciate your trying, and I get that it's close to impossible to recall some things from that far back."

He didn't respond to that. At least not right away. Sucked on the straw again. "Mighty good shake … thank you."

"You're welcome."

"Chocolate and orange together. You ever try it?"

I shook my head.

"Should," he said, as he set the container down on the carpet next to his chair. "There was a young guy worked in the place, odd jobs kind of guy, sometimes served coffee to the customers. I remember he took quite a shine to Ellie. Don't know if that's helpful, though. I remember talking to him at The Depression a few weeks after Ellie disappeared. He still seemed pretty upset about what happened to her."

"Upset how, Bert? Angry? Sad? Stunned?"

"Well, yeah, stunned, for sure. We were all stunned. Two people get shot, another is kidnapped. But I'd say he was also pretty broken up about it. Heartbroken, I guess."

"You remember his name?"

A pause.

"Just the last name. And that's because I knew his dad. The old man worked for Calgary Power back when it was *called* Calgary Power. We both played on the Calgary company fastball team. O'Callaghan. Don't remember the first name … of the kid, I mean. The dad's name was Gary. But yeah, the young guy worked at The Depression, and I'm pretty sure he wanted to get something going with Ellie. Maybe he did. I wouldn't know about that."

"You ever talk to him about what happened that night?"

"Sure. But he couldn't tell me anything. Didn't see anything. I remember he said it was really busy … good crowd, a lot of people coming and going."

"He mention anyone unusual, anybody who caught his attention?"

"No, he didn't. I'd remember that, and I'm sure he didn't mention anyone."

"What was it like in the club at the time right around the shooting … he say anything about that?"

"Just that he didn't hear anything from outside. It was too noisy — they played recorded music between performers. So that was happening when Ellie was outside. Then the other guy who was out there when it happened, the guy who was hiding —"

"Guy Kramer?"

"Yeah, him." Bert Nichol bobbed his head up and down. "He came running in, and he was yelling. O'Callaghan said he was pretty hysterical, and it was a few minutes before anybody figured out what he was hollering about. People went out into the alley to check it out. The O'Callaghan kid said that's when things got kind of crazy, a little panicky. People running back inside yelling to call the cops and an ambulance. Some customers just left. The kid also said that at first, everybody thought it was just a shooting. Until finally Kramer was able to spit out that there were two guys and that they took Ellie and drove off."

Rose Nichol stood and poured me more tea. I held up my hand at half a cup, then nodded thanks. She sat back down and the three of us sat for a while, saying nothing. I finished the tea and set the cup on an end table next to me.

Bert cleared his throat. "You know she had a kid, right?"

I nodded. "I do know that, yes."

He paused, then nodded and smiled. "Of course you do — you told me about the granddaughter. It's her that has you looking at it again. Trying to find her grandmother."

"She's hired Mike Cobb and me. She thinks her grandmother might still be alive."

Bert digested that for a minute.

"Damn. A grandkid." Then he shrugged. "Makes sense, though. Ellie has a kid. That kid has a kid, and now she's trying to find out what happened to her grandmother. Yeah, that makes total sense. Kind of makes me wish I was still in the game. Be a hell of a story."

I noticed he seemed to forget the no-profanity rule of the house as he became more animated. I waited a minute to let his excitement settle.

"You happen to know where Ellie stayed while she was performing here?"

Bert thought about that. "I don't know, but I'd be willing to bet she stayed with some local performers. I remember there were three or four of them that would take in touring acts. Charge a little bit and get some mentoring."

"You mean like music lessons?"

"I guess you could call it that. I mean, think about it: You're just starting out and first of all, you've got some big-name performer staying in the room down the hall. And then you get to sit down with that person and absorb some of what they know … jam a little bit, learn some stuff. I'd call that a win-win."

"Remember anybody who did that — who took in touring performers?"

I could see Bert was tiring. I needed to wrap this up. A glance at Rose told me she was thinking the same thing.

"There was a guy back then, played house parties, did the Will Millar thing too ... you know who Will Millar is, right?"

I nodded. "Irish Rovers. Started out playing at a pancake house here in Calgary, I think. The Rovers played The Depression too, as I recall."

Bert smiled. "By God, you do know a few things. Good, I hate talking to somebody who has no idea what I'm talking about. Anyway, this guy, he played in local eateries, probably played for burgers and fries. He did everything he could to break in to the business, including, if I'm not mistaken, providing accommodation for a few people. Don't know if Ellie was one of them, but I guess you could ask."

"You have a name?"

Bert's smile became a grin. "Two names this time. First and last. Roosevelt Park. Black guy. Back at a time when the only black people in Calgary either played for the Stampeders or were entertainers. I'm exaggerating, but you know what I mean. Anyway, Roosevelt still lives here, or at least he did. I saw him a couple of years ago. I think he was working at the university, in shipping and receiving or something. He might be retired by now, but maybe you can track him down."

"He didn't make it in the music business, then?"

"There wasn't anybody who tried harder. But there also wasn't anybody who sang worse. Played an okay guitar and some harmonica, but his voice? Fingernails on a chalkboard."

Bert chuckled at his word choice, and I smiled. Glanced again at Rose, then back at Bert.

"I know you've probably thought about it, Bert, maybe thought about it a lot. You have any ideas as to who the two people were who shot those guys and took Ellie Foster?"

He didn't answer right away. Finally, he shook his head slowly. "You're right. I've thought about it and thought about it. Not as much in recent years, but after it happened — for a long time that was *all* I thought about. And I've got no more idea today than I did the day after that night in that alley. Who they were, why they did what they did ... where they took Ellie. Nothing. I've got exactly nothing."

I started to stand up. Hesitated, then sat back down. "One last thing."

"Sure," Bert said, but I could tell he was close to spent. I didn't want to cause the man to have a heart attack or stroke. "Don't feel you need to answer this right now ... we can chat again another time, but I was wondering if you noticed anything different about her in the days before she was taken. Like, maybe she was worried about something. Like something or someone was bothering her."

A pause, then a slow head shake. "Thing is, I didn't know her well enough to be able to say if she was behaving any differently than any other time. I'd interviewed her a few times, but I can't say that I knew her. Not like that, you know?"

This time I got all the way to my feet. "I don't want to take any more of your time. I appreciate the conversation," I turned to Rose, "and the hospitality."

She stood up. "I'll walk you to the door, Mr. Cullen."

I turned back to Bert and nodded my appreciation again. He held out a hand, and I stepped forward and shook it.

"Thanks, Bert. It was great to meet you."

He nodded. "Likewise."

Rose and I started for the front door.

"One thing I do know," Bert's voice boomed a little louder. One last burst of energy.

I turned back to him. "What's that, Bert?"

"The grandkid's right. You're going to find her."

I took a step back toward him. "How do you know that?"

He shrugged. "I don't have any proof, and I don't know where she is. But she's out there. I can feel it. I don't know if somebody has kept her captive all this time, or just what, but it's like that TV show from a few years ago. The truth is out there. You will find her."

He pronounced those final words like a judge reading a sentence.

I managed a half smile. "We're going to try."

Forty minutes later, I was back in Kennedy's house alternating between upstairs and down, checking tapes and looking through camera lenses and binoculars. And thinking about what Bert Nichol had told me. And how confident he was that we'd find Ellie Foster. Probably a lot more confident than I was.

It had been a long day, slow-moving, with tenuous progress at best. I made a set of notes based on my conversation with Bert, emailed them to Cobb, and kept a set in the folder I'd labelled "Ellie Foster."

I looked at my watch. It read 9:30. I called Jill and felt bad that I'd just missed Kyla. Last night had been an exception. I'd have to call earlier.

"Just wanted you to know that I love you to Alaska and back," I said.

"Alaska?"

"Hey, I'm a writer. I can't use the same words as everybody else."

"But Alaska?"

I laughed. "Okay, I'll work on it for next time. How are things at the food bank?"

"Food bank, good; shelter, not so much."

I'd always thought Let the Sunshine Inn was a hokey name for a shelter, but hadn't told Jill in case she was the one who had named it.

"What's the problem?"

"It looks like we're going to lose a lot of our funding," she said. "A letter from Social Services came to the shelter a couple of months ago. I just found out about it yesterday. Our fiscal year-end is the end of October. We've got just over a month to find alternate funding for at least 70 percent of next year's budget."

"Social Services give a reason?"

"Lots of reasons, but none of them alter the fact that we can't operate after a 70 percent funding cut. Celia told me she thought this might be coming. She'd kept it from me and the other volunteers so that we wouldn't worry."

I'd met Celia previously. Crusty but dedicated. I could see her wanting to bear the burden of impending bad news by herself — not wanting to stress out the Inn's volunteers.

"Any chance of finding some magic alternate sources?"

"In a month? In this economy? I don't like our chances. Celia's been working on it but hasn't had any luck so far."

I'd known the answer before I asked the question. "Well, we've got a little time. As soon as I'm wrapped up here, we'll sit down and do some brainstorming."

"That's not all we're going to do when you've wrapped up there."

I knew she was trying to convey that all was normal, all was fine. I also knew it wasn't, but I played along. "I like the way you think."

We ended the call with both of us missing the hell out of each other.

I looked at my watch again and decided it wasn't too late to make one more call. It turned into seven calls — there were several *R. Parks* in the directory, but on call seven I got the voice mail of Roosevelt Park. The message said he was out of town. I identified myself and said I was looking into the disappearance of Ellie Foster from fifty years before. I fell back on the writing-a-story-for-the-*Herald* explanation, which was becoming less and less far-fetched as I went along. The idea of actually freelancing a piece to the *Herald* — something more than the Crime Stoppers update I'd already written — was becoming more appealing by the day. I left my number and expressed the hope that he'd be willing to chat with me.

I hadn't yet contacted any of my friends from the editorial brotherhood, mostly because every time I looked at the piece I'd written on Ellie's disappearance, I saw something — or several somethings — I wanted to change. The curse of the writer: the reluctance to let the damned thing go.

Uneventful days slogged by. Next to no progress on Ellie Foster, and no more shadows in the laneway across the street. I spent some time editing proofs for my new book, the follow-up to my kids' book, *The Spoofaloof Rally*. I'd been surprised a few months earlier when my publisher (I do love those two words) called to say that sales of *Spoofaloof* had suddenly taken off after a year and a half of it being on the top-ten list of non-sellers. And they wanted a follow-up book, if I was interested. Now that second book was nearing completion, and I was still coming to grips with the fact that I was an actual writer.

And I finally had the Ellie Foster update piece completed to my satisfaction. I'd fired it off to four people I knew and a couple I didn't. I heard back from three right away — the *Calgary Herald*, *Edmonton Journal*, and *Ottawa Citizen* would all run it the following week. The *Saskatoon StarPhoenix* replied to say they would take it to their next editorial meeting. I hadn't heard back from either the *Vancouver Sun* or the *Globe and Mail*, but was confident I'd receive a favourable response from the *Globe*. A guy I'd worked with and liked a lot was on the city desk there, and I liked my chances. I wasn't as sure about the *Sun*, only because I had no personal contact there and would have to rely on someone having an interest in a case that hadn't had the same impact on that city that it had on Calgary, even though Ellie Foster had been scheduled to play Vancouver's Bunkhouse not long after her Depression gig.

Kennedy called on Friday morning just after seven. I had just poured a cup of coffee and started up the stairs; I had to turn back to pick up the landline phone.

We exchanged hellos, then he said in a voice soft and full of pain, "She passed last night."

"I'm sorry," I said, and meant it.

"The funeral's on Monday. I'll be home Tuesday. You okay there till then?"

"Take as much time as you need. I've got things under control here."

"Okay," he said. Several seconds passed before he added, "Thanks," then hung up.

Twenty minutes later, Cobb called.

"I finally got to your email. Looks like we've got a few more people to talk to. Any luck coming up with a first name for O'Callaghan?"

"Not yet. Still working on it," I told him. "I had better luck with Roosevelt Park. I have an address and a phone number. I called, but his message said he'd be away until the end of the week. Thought I'd call him again today, see if he's back."

"Good," Cobb said. "That's good. And no surprise — the voice on the CD Monica Brill found in her car is almost certainly that of Ellie Foster."

"You're right," I said. "No surprise."

"I've got a meeting this afternoon with Guy Kramer's widow. Wondered if you wanted to be there. She lives in Bowness. I can pick you up if you feel like coming along."

"Yeah, I'd definitely like to tag along. What time?"

"I'll come by at one thirty."

After ending the call with Cobb, I tried Roosevelt Park's number again. Same message.

Over the next few hours, I alternated between watching tapes, checking the two houses, and cleaning up the place. I hadn't been comfortable with eating all of Kennedy's food, so I'd taken to either picking up food or having it delivered, with a clear preference for pizza and Chinese, which meant that a fair amount of cardboard and Styrofoam needed to be sorted and packaged up for the recycling and garbage bins.

I was having no luck tracking the O'Callaghan Bert Nichol had mentioned. I'd googled, called information, checked the phone book, and tried the Henderson's Directories at the closest library branch — all to no avail. Hadn't found a Gary O'Callaghan at all, and no leads on his son's first name.

Back at my computer I googled O'Callaghan again, with the same non-result. Finally I gave up and made myself two sandwiches and poured a glass of milk for accompaniment. Which was stupid, since I hate milk except in coffee or on cereal. But I felt as uneasy about drinking Kennedy's beer as I did about raiding his refrigerator and had forgotten to pick up a case, not once but three times.

The sandwiches were okay, the milk less so, but I reminded myself that I was taking in calcium, surely a good thing. The opening guitar riff from "Taking Care of Business" — I'd changed my ringtone that morning — announced that I had a call, and I swallowed the last of the second sandwich as I reached for my cellphone.

Bert Nichol's voice crackled a garbled greeting.

"Hello, Bert, how are you today?"

"Something I thought of after you left." A hacking cough followed.

"What's that, Bert?"

"There was a woman. She did little things around The Depression — printed up the programs, made posters. Like a lot of them, she was dedicated to the music, willing to do whatever just to be there. Anyway, she tried to write a book a few years ago, maybe ten or twelve, even."

"A book on The Depression?"

"Yeah, but she discovered the same thing a lot of people do who think they're going to write a book. It isn't nearly as easy as they think. So no book. But I had a drink with her back when she was working on it, and she showed me some of her notes."

"Her research."

"Yeah. She'd done a pretty good job, had a lot of stuff I didn't even know. And I'm pretty sure she planned to devote a chapter or maybe more to the shooting and Ellie being kidnapped. I can't remember her notes for that part, but I'm guessing she'd done at least some background work on it. Might be worth a call."

"Great, Bert, I appreciate this. You recall her name?"

"Lois. Lois Beeston. She owns a fabric store or something like that, gives classes in knitting and some of the other stuff people do with fabrics. Store's on 17th — Fabric Magic or something like that, I'm not sure on the name. I had coffee with her in there once. Does a pretty nice little business … or at least she did back then. Haven't seen her for maybe three years, so I can't say for sure what's going on with her, but I thought, hey, maybe she's got something you could use."

"This is great, Bert. Thanks."

"Listen, do me a favour. You find Ellie, or you find out what happened to her, I'd like to know."

"I'll make sure that happens, Bert," I said.

I decided to waste no time in calling Lois Beeston. I got the number for Fabrics Sew Magic (seriously, that was the name) and placed the call. A woman's voice answered.

"I wonder if I could speak to Lois Beeston," I said.

"She's just away for lunch, but she should be back any … whoa, nice timing, she just walked in."

I could hear muffled voices as the woman on the phone and presumably Lois Beeston conversed. And a few seconds later, a new voice was on the line.

"This is Lois Beeston. How can I help you?"

"Ms. Beeston, my name's Adam Cullen. A mutual acquaintance suggested I should call you. Bert Nichol."

"Oh, Bert — my God, I love that man to death. Haven't seen him in way too long. How is he?" The voice I was listening to was two-thirds Georgia plantation owner and one-third junior high school teacher. Both parts exuded a warmth that made me like her, despite our being less than fifty words into knowing each other.

"Bert's doing pretty well, I think," I told her. "He mentioned your name in connection with the disappearance of Ellie Foster back in '65."

"The Depression," she said slowly.

"Bert indicated that you had worked on a book for a time and may have some information that could help my partner and me to find Ellie."

"Find Ellie." She repeated the words the way people repeat things that don't make sense to them.

"Sounds crazy, I know, but her granddaughter approached us to see what we could do about locating her, or at least finding out what happened to her after that night. My partner's Mike Cobb — he's a private detective and former cop. I was a crime writer with the *Herald* for a number of years, and now I work with Cobb on some of his cases."

"And you want to see how much I can remember, and if I have any clues to help you with this investigation."

"Pretty well sums it up," I admitted.

"Well, I'm certainly willing to do whatever I can to help find Ellie, but do you seriously think you'll be able to do much after all this time? So many people will have died or won't remember what they had for breakfast, let alone something that took place fifty years ago...."

"You're right, of course," I replied. "But we're going to do what we can. I guess we'll see where that takes us."

"Well, I admire that sentiment, I suppose. And yes, I'm happy to share what I did for the book, although I'm not sure there's anything there that will help."

"Understood," I said. "I'm wondering what your time is like later today. Cobb and I have an appointment at one thirty, and maybe we could meet you after that, if it's convenient."

"I suppose I could make that work. The good part is I have all my research notes in my office here at the store."

"I'd be happy to take you for a late lunch, if that works for you."

"There's a Chopped Leaf in the Deerfoot Meadows Mall. It's not that far from the store. You okay with healthy?"

"More than okay," I told her. "How about three o'clock?"

"I'll see you then. I'll bring my notes."

Cobb arrived a couple of minutes ahead of 1:30. Once we'd settled into his Grand Cherokee, I told him about the upcoming meeting with Lois Beeston.

"Good work, but I'll have to drop you back here so that you can go on your own," Cobb replied. "I'm getting together with our client."

"Monica?"

"You'll remember I agreed to take the case for a week only and then let her know at that time whether we would stay with it."

"I remember, but I'd lost track of time. You have to let her know today?"

"I'd like to," he said, nodding. "What do you think?"

I thought for a while before answering. "Tough call. I feel like we've made some progress, but my God, Mike, this thing took place before either of us was born. So much of what evidence there was is gone, just like so many of the people who might actually provide that evidence. Still, there's a part of me that wants to keep trying. I hate to lose, and I hate giving up even more."

I could see Cobb's hands gripping the steering wheel a little tighter than they had previously.

"I feel the same way." His voice was tight. "But I also don't like the thought of taking that girl's money and not being able to deliver. And the truth is, I don't know if we can do this."

We drove in silence for a while. As we pulled up in front of a small, older bungalow just off Bowness Road, I turned to him.

"Just so you know, I'm okay with whatever you decide. But can you hold off on a definite answer until after I've talked to Lois Beeston and Roosevelt Park? And maybe this O'Callaghan guy, if I can find him? If none of them gives us something we can use, we're running out of people to talk to."

He nodded. "The week isn't up until tomorrow. I just wanted to give her an update so she doesn't think we're stringing her along."

We stepped out of the car, and as he came around to join me on the sidewalk leading to Mrs. Kramer's front door, I clapped a hand on his shoulder.

"I doubt if Monica Brill or anybody else will ever accuse you of stringing them along."

Before he could press the doorbell, the front door opened and a short, stoutish woman with hair the colour of weathered brick stood looking at us, a near-smile playing at her lips.

"Mrs. Kramer?"

"Yes."

"We spoke on the phone. I'm Mike Cobb, and this is my associate, Adam Cullen."

She nodded and stepped back to allow us in. Cobb held out his hand as he went by, and she shook it.

We stepped into the room, and Mrs. Kramer closed the door behind us. She gestured toward a brown leather chesterfield.

"Can I offer you something to drink? I have beer, juice, and water. Not a terrific selection."

"I think we're fine, Mrs Kramer." Cobb smiled at her. "But thank you. We don't want to take a lot of your time."

All of us sat, Cobb and me on the chesterfield, Mrs. Kramer on a rocker. "Well, this feels a little like *Dragnet*, doesn't it?" The smile grew larger on a face that looked like it smiled a lot.

"Dum de-dum dum," I sang.

Cobb looked at me, then back at Mrs. Kramer, electing apparently to let the *Dragnet* conversation end. "We appreciate your taking the time to talk to us."

She nodded, the smile still in place. "I'm happy to help … if I can."

"Your husband, Mrs. Kramer …"

"Guy," she said.

"Yes." Cobb nodded. "Guy. Did he go to The Depression often?"

"No more so than the other clubs he went to."

"Was he with anyone that night?"

"He told me he went there with a customer, but the customer only stayed for one cup of coffee. Other than that, if he wasn't with someone, it wasn't for lack of trying."

"Are you saying your husband went to The Depression and other places to meet people?"

"Only certain people, Mr. Cobb."

"He liked to try to pick up women. That's what you're telling us."

Mrs. Kramer nodded. "That's exactly what I'm saying, Mr. Cobb. Except that *trying* might be a bit inaccurate. Most of the time, he succeeded. Guy was a good-looking man. And charming. Women liked him. And he liked that they liked him."

"And that night?"

She shook her head. "That night, he came home. I guess maybe people getting shot and kidnapped put him off his game."

"Did you talk about what happened that night in the alley? What he saw?"

"Not at first. I brought it up a few times, but he was reluctant to talk about it. What he saw scared him. And changed him. He stayed home a lot more after that. I was pregnant with our first, and the baby was born a couple of months after that terrible night. He actually became a pretty good dad and a better husband than he had been."

"But eventually you talked about that night at The Depression."

"Guy talked. I listened."

"I know it was a long time ago, but if you can remember what he said, it could be very helpful. And I know you've probably repeated it dozens of times, but if you've got one more telling in you, we'd really appreciate it."

"He told me he got there sometime after nine. Guy was a salesman with a company called Kleen Limited — they sold janitorial supplies. He'd met with a customer after work, then they'd gone to The Depression. To answer your earlier question, he hadn't been there more than a couple of times. For one thing, the place was a coffee house, didn't sell booze. I think the whole picking-up thing probably works a little better if there's liquor involved."

"I'm guessing you're right, Mrs. Kramer. Did he say why he went into the alley? A cigarette?"

She paused for the first time. "He said it was for air. He wasn't a smoker."

"And did you believe him?"

"I suspect the club was smoky, so maybe he was telling the truth. Or …"

"Or?"

"There was only one person in that alley who would have been of interest to him."

"You're saying he was hoping to talk to Ellie Foster?"

"He never admitted that, but I'm saying it's possible."

"And do you know if he did talk to her … before the car showed up?"

"I don't know that. He never ever said one way or the other. Like I said, he never admitted that that was his reason for being out there."

"What did Guy see that night?"

She paused again; this time it looked like she was gathering her thoughts. Remembering long-ago conversations.

"He said the other three people, Ellie and the two guys in the band, had been out there for a few minutes. He told me he went up some stairs to the main level, opened the back door of The Depression, stepped out, and saw the three of them. Ellie was off to one side a bit. The two guys were smoking. And the three of them were talking. He'd been out there for only a minute or two when the car came roaring up the alley and stopped. Two men jumped out of the car and shot the band guys. Then they grabbed Ellie and dragged her into the car, and drove off. He said it happened really fast."

"Did he say what Ellie and the two men were talking about in the moments before the car arrived?"

"He didn't hear much, but he did say it sounded like they were talking about some other club they'd played recently. He didn't get much more than that; at least, that's what he told me."

"Okay, so the car pulls up and the two guys jump out. What did he say about that?"

"He said he knew right away that something bad was happening. He saw that one of the men was carrying a gun. He didn't know if the other one had a gun. He thought so, but he wasn't sure."

"Which one was he sure had a gun?"

"The one who got out of the passenger side. He said he couldn't see the driver at first because he was blocked by the car. The driver was on the far side. By the time he got around the car, the first man had started shooting. Guy remembered seeing one of the guys in the band fall to the ground. There was more shooting after that, but by then he'd taken cover behind the garbage cans and he didn't see anything more."

"Could he tell anything about the gun?"

"Only that it was a handgun … a pistol or revolver of some kind. My husband knew nothing about guns, so he wouldn't have been much help there."

"Did he describe the men at all, what they looked like? What they were wearing?"

"He said the passenger was the taller of the two. He couldn't say what they were wearing or how old they were … nothing. Either he didn't see much at all or he was in shock or something and never remembered."

"Okay, what about what he heard?"

"He said the men in the car didn't say anything until after the shooting stopped. Then he heard them say, 'Get in the car,' and he heard Ellie Foster scream and yell 'No!' — stuff like that. Then all he heard was car doors slamming and the car racing off."

Cobb paused for a minute, looked at me.

I said, "Did your husband say if he looked out from where he was hiding? Did he peek out while the kidnapping was happening? See how the men got Ellie into the car?"

She took some time before answering. "Something you have to understand: My husband felt very guilty about his role in what happened that night. He thought of himself as a coward and was convinced that other people saw him that way too. He didn't look out until well after the car was gone. He didn't do anything to help that girl or to try to stop what was happening. He was convinced that if the two men had known he was there, he'd have been killed. I think he was right."

"I think he was right too, Mrs. Kramer," Cobb said. "And we don't think your husband was a coward. He did what most of us would have done, and if he'd done otherwise we would not likely be having this conversation. And we're sorry to cause you the pain of going through this again. These are things we have to ask."

"I understand."

"What did he do then?"

"He finally came out from behind the garbage cans and looked at the two men who were shot, in case he should do something. But he said he was sure they were both dead, so he ran inside the club. He said it was crazy at first. He just grabbed anybody he saw and said, 'Call the cops, there's been some shooting outside behind the building.' At first he said people laughed or pushed him away, thinking he was drunk or on something. But finally he found the manager, or at least the person who was in charge that night, and that guy went out into the alley. Guy was never sure what happened after that, who actually called the police. He said he just sat down and drank some coffee and waited for the police to come, because he knew they'd want to talk to him."

"And while he was waiting for the police to arrive, did he see anything unusual, anybody behaving in a manner that seemed … I don't know … suspicious?"

"He said quite a few people left even though the manager was telling everyone to stay and wait for the police. But he couldn't make people stay, and Guy said several people just got the hell out of there. I guess not wanting to be involved. Or maybe they were scared."

"Did Guy say anything else, no matter how insignificant he may have thought it at the time, anything at all?"

"The only other thing he said was that he thought he had heard Ellie yell something like 'You bastard!' and just the way she said it, he wondered if she actually might have known the men in the car. He wasn't at all sure, and didn't ever say that to the police because he was afraid it might send them off on the wrong track. But he said it to me. A few times."

I looked at Cobb and could tell he wanted to yell something like, *He should have told the investigators and let them decide how to deal with the information!* He stayed composed, however, and leaned forward on the couch.

"Your husband heard Ellie say 'You bastard' — not *bastards*, plural?"

"No, it was *bastard*. I remember thinking about that at the time. Wouldn't you have called them both bastards?"

Cobb nodded but didn't comment. After a few seconds, he asked, "And Guy was fairly certain that Ellie had said '*You* bastard,' not just 'Bastard'?

She paused before answering. "I wouldn't swear on a stack of bibles or anything, but I'm pretty sure that's what he said — 'You bastard.'"

Cobb appeared to consider that before continuing. "Is there anything else you can recall him saying?"

"I've been over this so many times … I haven't left anything out."

"One last thing — you mentioned your husband had gone there that night with a customer. He say who the customer was?"

She shook her head. "I don't think so, but if he did, I don't remember who it was."

Cobb stood up. "We're grateful to you for taking the time and for being so forthcoming with us. Very grateful."

Mrs. Kramer got to her feet, and I followed suit.

"I can't imagine that you're going to be successful after all this time, but I wish you well."

"Thank you, Mrs. Kramer." Cobb pulled a business card from his pocket and handed it to her. "If you've seen any crime shows on TV, you know this is the moment when the investigator says, 'If you think of anything else, please give us a call.'"

Mrs. Kramer managed a half smile and nodded. "I've seen those shows." Her voice had settled to the monotone that is often a sign of stress or exhaustion. She looked like she was struggling with both at that moment. Remembering had been difficult.

Cobb opened the door and stepped out onto the front step. As I passed Mrs. Kramer, I touched her shoulder and said, "Thank you. You were terrific."

She managed a second small smile and closed the door behind us.

Neither Cobb nor I spoke, even after we were back in the Cherokee. Finally, at a red light, Cobb slammed the steering wheel. "Jesus, there's a possibility that Ellie Foster knew her abductors, or at least one of them, and Kramer didn't think he should tell the cops."

"In fairness, there's also a possibility she *didn't* know her abductors. But you're right — the only eyewitness, and not only does he not see much, but he also holds back something that could have helped."

We were both quiet the rest of the way back to Kennedy's house, both of us seeing, or at least *trying* to see, the scene that had unfolded in the alley behind The Depression that night. As we pulled up in front of the house, Cobb glanced at his watch.

"That took longer than I thought it would. You'll have to move fairly quickly to make your next meeting."

"Our talk with Mrs. Kramer impact how you're going to approach your chat with Monica?"

"Not sure. I'm thinking about that. What do you think?"

I shook my head. "Can't see why it should. She didn't give us anything earth-shaking, even with the 'you bastard' thing."

"Maybe, maybe not. Like I said, I'll think abut it."

"Fair enough. And maybe Ms. Beeston will be the breakthrough."

"Yeah, maybe." He didn't sound convinced. "Anyway, you better get moving."

"Right. Later." I jumped out of the Jeep and ran for the house.

A decent break in traffic and an Escalade pulling out of a parking spot right in front of the Chopped Leaf reduced how late I was for my appointment with Lois Beeston. When I stepped inside at five minutes after three, I spotted her right away, in a back booth along the right-hand wall, which wasn't so much wall as windows.

Pages of notes were spread over most of the table in the booth. She had a coffee in front of her, and she was tapping her teeth with the eraser end of a pencil while staring intently at one of the pages.

I stopped at the side of the booth and cleared my throat. When she looked up at me, I was looking into an ever more pleasant face than I had anticipated. Lois Beeston's face expressed curiosity, friendliness, and warmth.

She was wearing a baggy brown sweater and some kind of headband thing that might have earned her the title "old hippie" with some.

"I'm Adam, Ms. Beeston," I said.

"And I'm Lois, Adam."

I nodded, and we shook hands as I slid into the booth opposite her. In seconds she had pushed, gathered, and piled paper until there were clear areas in front of us. She passed me a menu.

"I got two when the server came by," she told me. "And for the record, you don't have to buy me lunch."

I smiled at her. "For the record, I *want* to buy you lunch."

She returned the smile, and for the next few minutes we talked about Bert and she explained the menu to me, ending with a recommendation for something called Whole Bowl No. 1.

I took her advice, and later, when the food arrived, I was glad I did. Until then we talked in general terms about The Depression. She talked about her time there, mentioning several of the performers; she was a big fan of Gordon Lightfoot, adored Joni Mitchell, and didn't particularly like Ellie Foster.

"Why was that?"

"She was … different," she said slowly. "Today I guess we'd use the word *entitled* — back then she just seemed a little too sure of herself. At least to me. I know most people thought she was wonderful. But for me it was like she knew she was going to be a big deal and the rest of us had better start getting used to the idea. At least that was the way she was around the people who worked there. Never with the audience; when she stepped up to the microphone, it was magic."

Our lunch came, and for the next several minutes we devoted ourselves to the food, which was easy — Whole Bowl No. 1 was a nice mix of black bean corn salsa, avocado, cheddar, cilantro, pita chips, and sour cream, all served on a bowl of warm brown basmati rice. As Lois Beeston had said on the phone, healthy.

When I thought it was appropriate, I set my fork down, took a drink of Five Alive, and looked across the table at her. "You were right, Lois, this place is excellent. Thanks for suggesting it."

She smiled and picked up her napkin.

I said, "A few minutes ago you used the word *magic* to describe Ellie's performance. What made it magic?"

"I'm not sure I can find words that would properly describe what she could do. There was her voice, of course. I would say Joni was the best there was, but Ellie wasn't far behind her. But it was more than her voice; it was the way she looked at every person in that audience like they were the most important people in the world to her. And I think that was sincere. It was like she and everyone out there were making love. And I don't mean that in a suggestive or even sensual way. It was just … you see, I told you I couldn't describe it properly."

I was fairly sure I detected a bit of colour in Lois Beeston's cheeks. She looked down at the table.

"I think you're describing it perfectly. Please go on."

She took a forkful of food, chewed, swallowed, and finally said, softly, "She rarely talked between songs, just 'Thank you,' you know? But when she finished a set, you had the feeling that people loved her … and I mean that in the truest sense of the word, not 'Oh, I just *love* your casserole, Aunt Polly.' It was, as I said earlier, magic."

When Lois Beeston was finished, I realized she had made me want to believe that Ellie Foster was alive and that Cobb and I could find her.

I pointed to her bowl. "Why don't I let you finish up, and we can talk more after we're done."

She nodded, and we ate in semi-silence, pausing occasionally to exchange thoughts about the food, the place, and the weather. Small, small talk.

When we'd finished and the table was cleared, she once again manoeuvred paper, having, it seemed, a plan for how she wanted me to see the various pieces.

She did. She pushed one piece of paper toward me.

"Here are my chapter titles; you'll see that chapter eight was devoted to Ellie Foster and the night she disappeared."

I looked down and noted that the title she'd assigned chapter eight was, "Singin' the Blues: The Disappearance of a Future Star."

"And this is the outline for that chapter." She pushed another piece of paper my way — a half page of typed text with a few notes pencil-scribbled in the margins. I read it and learned nothing I didn't already know. Not surprising: it was, after all, only an outline.

"Do you have more detailed notes about that night, your research notes?"

"Just rough stuff," she replied. "I'd abandoned the book before I got to the real work on that chapter."

"Why?"

"Why what?"

"Why did you give it up?"

She shrugged, a frown pulling at the corners of her mouth.

"You're a writer," she said. "I'm not. If I were to give you one of my early chapters to read, you'd see that. I didn't at first.... I believed I was creative, artistic — how hard can it be, right?" She shrugged again, and the frown became a wry smile.

It was a story I'd heard before. The person with that story in their head, and all it needed was to be on paper and the big royalty cheques would start rolling in. *No, that's not fair.* Often with wannabe writers, money was not the prime motivation; more often it was about getting the story told, a story that had meant a great deal to that person for a long time, offering it to a world in which some might even read it. The problem, as Bert Nichol had noted, was that writing was so much damn harder than many people thought.

"Can I look at your notes for chapter eight?"

She sifted through more pages, taking some from one pile, a couple from another, then another, and after a couple of minutes, passed me the lot.

"I think those should be roughly in order. Why don't you look at them while I get us some coffee?"

I nodded agreement and fell to reading, looking up only briefly to acknowledge her return with the coffee. There was too much to read without keeping her there all afternoon, so I skimmed and speed-read what I could in fifteen minutes or so. By the end, I was nodding and tapping pages that contained what looked like useful information.

Finally I looked up and said, "You've done some really good work here, Lois."

"Do you think so?"

"I do. Research is a big part of what I've done most

of my working life, and this …" I tapped the pages again, "this is going to be helpful. If you have time, can we walk through a couple of parts I have questions about?"

"Of course."

"You've included a list of people who worked at The Depression."

"Yes."

"Any way of knowing who was actually working that night?"

She pointed. "The names are in blue and green. Blue for there that night, green for not."

I laughed.

"Is there something funny about that?"

"No." I shook my head. "I was actually laughing at myself. I thought the two-colour thing was just to dress it up — make it look a little prettier. I should have known better."

She smiled, then turned serious again, watching me as I looked through her notes a second time.

"How many of the people who were there that evening did you talk to afterward?"

"All of them. By that, I mean all of the staff and volunteers."

"And you have notes of those conversations included here?"

"Yes, as well as conversations I had with several of the customers who were there that night."

"That part, I don't understand. You did these interviews several years after the shooting and kidnapping. Likely The Depression was closed by the time you did all this work?"

"That's correct, yes."

"How was it that after so much time had elapsed, you still remembered who was working that night, and even which customers were there?"

"I didn't."

I raised my eyebrows. "Sorry?"

"I've wanted to be a writer since high school. And I knew that life experience was important for any writer. So I started a diary in … I think it was maybe grade eleven or so. A very detailed diary, and I was pretty disciplined, wrote every day, wrote a lot. When I was working at The Depression, I thought there might be some grist for the mill. Obviously I wasn't thinking about something like what happened in February of 1965, but these were entertainers — there was some interesting stuff going on around the place pretty much all the time. My diary entries were quite extensive — names of people, what they did, how often they were at the club, anything I thought might find its way into my imagined book."

"And you were able to contact all of the people you'd written about in your diary?"

"Not all, no. But most. Some took some work to find, but I was fairly successful. There were people who raced out of the place as soon as they learned that something bad was happening, and some of those I was unable to connect with. So, to be accurate, I interviewed most but not all who were there that night."

"Tenacious."

She smiled. "I prefer *determined*. Tenacious makes me think pit bull."

"Would you be okay with my borrowing these?" I indicated the papers on the table. "We'll be careful, I promise you. But I'd like to spend some time with what you've done, and I know Cobb will want to as well."

"No, I don't mind. I just can't believe any of this will be of help."

I smiled at her. "It may not lead us directly to the two men who took Ellie Foster that night. But every piece of information we can gather, especially with something that happened that long ago, will be helpful."

She thought about that before nodding. "I understand. And I want to help any way I can, believe me."

"I absolutely believe you, Lois. And I wasn't kidding before. You've done some amazing work here."

She seemed genuinely pleased. "Do you just want the notes for that night?"

"Actually, I'd like all of it, if that's okay. Again, I'm fairly certain there's useful background information that I'd like to look over."

"That's fine. I just have to organize things a little better." She fell to shuffling and stacking papers once again.

I watched her for a moment. "You knew everybody who worked there," I said. "You remember someone named O'Callaghan?"

"Darby O'Callaghan?"

"I don't have a first name. Bert mentioned a guy who worked there some, and had a crush on Ellie. Said this O'Callaghan was heartbroken at what happened that night."

"That's Darby." Lois spoke slowly again, thinking as she formed the words. "He was smitten, all right, no doubt about that. I don't think Ellie thought nearly as much of him as he did of her. And I do remember he was terribly upset after."

I looked down again at the collection of paper. "If we wanted to follow up with any of the people you talked to, do you have up-to-date addresses or ideas as to where we might find them?"

"Not many." She shook her head. "The truth is, quite a number are dead; others moved away to God knows where. There are a few, I suppose, that I have a fairly good idea of where they might be. But not many."

"Understandable," I said. "What about Darby O'Callaghan? Any idea where he might be these days?"

"I ran into Darby a couple of years ago at the farmers' market on Blackfoot Trail." She nodded. "He lives outside of Calgary. I can't remember which town, but I think I have a note somewhere. I could check."

"I'd appreciate that. And any contact information on any of the other people you interviewed at the time, as well."

She had the pages organized to her satisfaction and pushed them in my direction. It was a large stack, and I knew I'd be at it for a while. I had fortuitously brought along my briefcase, so I shoved the lot inside.

"One last thing," I said. "You mentioned that there were things about Ellie that you didn't find altogether likable. But someone has commented that she seemed somehow different in the weeks just prior to her disappearance. I'm assuming you had met and talked to Ellie prior to that last gig?"

Lois Beeston nodded. "She played The Depression once before, a few months earlier. I met her then; we chatted a few times." She paused. "That's interesting and something I haven't thought about a lot. There was something in the days before her disappearance — I don't know how I would describe it. Distracted, maybe. Like she wasn't totally focused on the conversation, not just with me, but with others. To be honest, I chalked it up to guy problems. Ellie was … um … active in that regard. But thinking back on it, maybe there was something else going on. I mean, it wasn't a big thing, which I suppose is why I haven't given it more thought. But maybe there was something there."

"Thanks for all this, Lois, including the introduction to the Chopped Leaf. I'll be in touch. Can I drop you somewhere?"

"I think I'll stay here for a while, have another coffee." She reached down and pulled a pen and the thickest diary I'd ever seen from her bag. The diary was full of bits of paper of various kinds — I could see that some were newspaper and magazine clippings, while others looked like coupons, though I couldn't be sure in the moment I took to look at it, figuring it would be rude to stare at the thing. She opened it to a blank page, smiled at me, and began to write. I hoped I'd get a favourable review.

I wanted to tuck into Lois Beeston's research notes as quickly as possible, but when I got back to Kennedy's, I opted for a run and a shower first. I followed that with an hour at the cameras and tape playback machines, then decided I could wait no longer and settled down at the kitchen table with a Rolling Rock and the stack of pages Lois had given me.

I started with the notes on chapter 8, the "Singin' the Blues" chapter. I reread what I'd skimmed at the restaurant, this time in detail. Sadly, Lois was right. While the work she'd done was extensive, even exemplary, there just wasn't much there beyond the names of the players that might be helpful to our investigation.

I was disappointed, pushed the stack of paper away, swore out loud, and took out my frustration on the beer, throwing it back with little attention to taste, thirst, or enjoyment. I sat for several minutes, willing myself to read more, procrastinating, dreading the thought of darkness where I had hoped for at least a little light, and finally turning on a clock radio that sat on the kitchen counter, opting for oldies rock.

I thought about food (the Whole Bowl No. 1 was wearing off), I thought about another beer, I thought about the lyrics to "Ahead by a Century." And I thought about Lois Beeston madly scribbling in her diary during her time at The Depression. All interesting thoughts — none of them productive.

I decided I would begin at the beginning of her notes and read until I found something … *anything* that would provide a clue, an insight, a shred of knowledge that might be useful, however remotely. It was a childish notion and I knew that, but I needed some incentive to plunge back into something that would take hours and may not offer much reward.

Happily, I was wrong. It didn't take long. I changed my tack after the first-chapter notes and decided to read them out of order, to choose bits that sounded at least interesting. And relevant. An hour or so into my reading, I came to an untitled chapter: the lyrics to songs written and presumably performed by various performers.

Half a dozen pages into the section, I came to the heading, "The Songs of Ellie Foster." I doubted that what followed was all of her songs, maybe not even most of them, but they were worth a read. Hell, they might even offer some insights into the kind or person she was, this woman we were hoping to find … and find alive.

Ellie Foster's songs, or at least some of them. Eight or nine songs in, I found it. The lyrics I'd seen before.

Summer sun. Summer fun. Some were done
They walked the gentle path
At first asking only that the wind and rain wash
their shaking hands
Stopping peace to fame
That pearson's name
Man at the mike … so, so bad
But good at play
And always the sadness, the love over and over
The long man points and tells
An owl sits and stares, sound around and through
his feathered force
So much like the other place. And so different …
Midnight. Not yesterday, not tomorrow. A time
with no day of its own
The last of sun. The last of fun. The last time won
They circle the windswept block
At first telling the youngest ones it's only a dream
See the balloons, hear them popping
Are they balloons?
No more the sadness, the hate over and over
The long man points and tells
An owl sits and stares, sound around and through
his feathered force
Midnight. Not yesterday, not tomorrow. A time
with no day of its own

The words to the song on the CD that had been left in Monica Brill's car, the CD that had brought her to Cobb and me.

I read and reread the words, just as I'd done before, noting the typo in line six, wondering if the mistake was Ellie Foster's or Lois Beeston's, realizing it didn't matter. In fact, maybe the lyrics didn't matter except that they confirmed the song on the tape was actually written by Ellie Foster and, one would surmise, performed by her as well.

This time the song had a title, "Dream of a Dying." It was as impenetrable as I'd found the lyrics of the song to be.

Still, I'd fulfilled my self-imposed mandate of finding some kernel to ponder. My second bottle of Rolling Rock was, while not exactly celebratory, at least enjoyable. I headed back to the main floor camera with a spring in my step, and even joined Ann and Nancy Wilson as they reprised "Magic Man." Timing is everything.

I sent an email to Jill. It read:

Have either you or Kyla had any luck trying to unearth meaning from the lyrics of the Ellie Foster song? BTW, found song title: "Dream of a Dying." If you guys come up with anything that might have any significance at all, I will take both of you to the restaurant of your choice, and I'll even watch an entire chick flick without a single complaint.

Love you both,
Adam

I hit "send" and went back to Lois Beeston's research notes, then found a chapter that she had actually written called, "In the Beginning." It was a history of the coffee houses and the folk music that had "claimed its place alongside rock and roll — led in Canada by people named Joni, Ian, Sylvia, Gordon, and Bruce ... before the British invasion headed by The Beatles and the musical rebellion they ushered in."

As I read her words I realized she wasn't wrong in her doubting assessment of her own literary abilities. I felt bad about that but pushed the thought out of my head and concentrated on the story she was telling, not how well or badly she was telling it.

And it *was* intriguing. She took her dreamed-of readers across the country and into clubs in Toronto, Ottawa, Winnipeg, Regina, Saskatoon, and, finally, Calgary. She stopped there, I guessed, because her focus was on The Depression, but I thought it odd that she didn't conclude the journey in Vancouver, with its rich tradition of live music, including folk in the fifties and sixties.

I was interested in her discussion of Le Hibou. Lois noted that Ellie Foster had played it not long before her fateful gig at The Depression. Of course I already knew that, but she added something I didn't know. Not only had Ellie performed more than once at Le Hibou, but also, her most recent performance there — the one that immediately preceded her fateful gig at The Depression — was one of special significance. It was, in fact, the final show at the Bank Street location of Le Hibou, on February 7, 1965. Ellie had been joined that night by Carol Robinson and Amos Garrett, and four days later the same threesome opened the new location of the club at 521 Sussex Drive.

All of that only a couple of weeks before her life changed so dramatically — and horribly — in a back alley in Calgary.

Then came a second find. A separate piece of paper that had been incorporated into a chapter listed Ellie Foster's performance schedule dating back several months before her disappearance. If what had happened to Ellie had its genesis prior to her Calgary gig at The Depression, the schedule could prove useful.

August 19–24	Louis Riel coffee house — Saskatoon
August 26–31	4th Dimension coffee house — Regina
September 3–15	The Tumbling Mustard — Ottawa
September 18–23	The Mousehole — Toronto
November 12–17	The Inquisition Coffee House — Vancouver
December 5–6	Caffè Lena, Saratoga Springs, New York
February 7, 11–12	Le Hibou — Ottawa
February 24–March 3	The Depression — Calgary

Lois Beeston had been a diligent and thorough researcher, and reading her notes and even first drafts of some chapters gave me an insight into the Canadian music scene at that time, something I was very much lacking.

I set her work aside and concentrated on mine, alternating between running tapes and peering through cameras and binoculars until my eyes were blurry and my head ached. Satisfied I had missed nothing while I'd been out and that nothing was brewing in either location tonight, I ran myself a bath, took two Tylenol, and promptly fell asleep in the tub, narrowly avoiding dropping Ian Rankin and Inspector Rebus into the water.

I awoke just after seven with an idea, towelled off, and though a quiet evening with a book and early bedtime beckoned, I dressed again in street clothes and headed off into Calgary's falling darkness to set the idea in motion.

Bryan Adams and the first few bars of "Summer of '69," another new ringtone, roused me at 8:12 the next morning. I did my best been-awake-for-hours impression, but Cobb saw through it in seconds. Hard to fool a seasoned detective.

"It's damn near afternoon," he told me in a voice that was way too jovial.

"First of all, no, it's not," I said, "and secondly, it's Saturday. In civilized countries, people get to sleep in on Saturdays."

"Okay." I heard him chuckling, doubtless enjoying ruining my morning. "But I thought you'd want to know that I met with Monica yesterday, and we've got another week."

"That's good. I found a couple of things in Lois Beeston's research notes that might be useful, and I'm still working on Roosevelt Park and Darby O'Callaghan."

"Darby."

"Yeah, I got the first name from Lois Beeston."

"Good. Any luck with the lyrics?"

"I worked on that, too, and so far, nada. But I've got better minds than mine working on them now."

"My strategy exactly. You up for coffee?" he asked me.

"As opposed to more sleep?"

"Life is all about making choices."

"And if I choose sleep?"

"I phone back every ten minutes."

"I figured something like that. The Starbucks on 1st Avenue. Thirty minutes."

"There are Starbucks closer to Kennedy's house. You missing your 'hood?" he asked.

"Actually, I am," I said, as we ended the call.

I was sitting in an armchair when Cobb arrived, a few of what I thought were the more relevant pages from Lois Beeston's work sitting on the table beside me.

"I don't see a coffee anywhere."

"I thought you might want to buy. Life is all about making choices."

"You're a bitter man." He chuckled and headed for the counter.

When he returned a couple of minutes later with two grande Pikes with milk, I held up the piece of paper detailing Ellie Foster's schedule. And I'd found a second list, this time noting the places she was scheduled to go after her Calgary gig. Vancouver's Bunkhouse for a week, another week in Victoria, back to Ontario for a two-week gig in Toronto, then a return date at Le Hibou in Ottawa, where she clearly had been a popular figure.

Cobb and I sipped coffee and traded pages back and forth for a few minutes before he finally said, "This has me thinking."

I looked at him. "About?"

"If the song has some significance — and I'm guessing it does, or why was it left in Monica's car? — and the song was presumably written before Ellie played The Depression, then there could have been something going on in her life before she got to Calgary that led to what happened that night."

I studied my coffee mug for a while before I answered. "Then why did the kidnappers wait until Calgary to do something?"

"Yeah, that's the one I've been wrestling with."

"Given how hard it's been to find useful information from fifty years ago right here, I hate to think how much tougher it's going to be trying to find leads in Toronto or Ottawa or Halifax."

"Yeah, I thought of that too." Cobb nodded.

"Something *I've* been thinking about."

Cobb raised his eyebrows, looked at me over his coffee mug.

"I wonder who put the CD in her car."

"That would be nice to know, but if it were that easy, there'd be no need for people like us to investigate things."

I thought about that. "I guess, but I mean, it hardly makes sense that the kidnappers have had a change of heart after half a century and decided to offer the granddaughter some previously well-concealed clue to her grandmother's whereabouts."

"Yeah, I'd say that's not what's happening here."

"So that leaves two possibilities, it seems to me," I said.

"Let's see if your two possibilities are the same as mine."

"Okay." I took a sip of coffee and then leaned forward. "One is that the tape has no significance beyond someone providing a nice souvenir memory of a long-lost relative."

"In which case, why break into her car — why not just hand it to her?"

"Exactly," I agreed. "Which means there *is* some significance to the tape, and the person leaving it had a reason to want to be anonymous."

"I had this conversation again yesterday with Monica, and that's pretty much the conclusion we came to as well."

"So what's next?"

"You keep tracking the two guys from The Depression —"

"O'Callaghan and Park."

Cobb nodded. "I'm going to work the phones." He held up the two pieces of paper with Ellie Foster's performing schedule before and after Calgary. "This will help. I'm sure Carrington and Wardlow did some checking. But maybe they didn't work that angle as hard, or maybe they missed something. Even though Wardlow actually went to Ottawa, I didn't see anything in their reports that indicated they looked hard at some out-of-town angle. Looks like they ruled it out after his trip out there."

I nodded. "That's what it looked like to me."

"I'll see if I can find any other cops who were around from that time — maybe there was something going on that will give us something to look at."

"Doesn't sound easy."

Cobb smiled. "You know what they say … if it was easy —"

"Yeah," I said, cutting him off. "I know what they say."

I'd stopped by my apartment to pick up a few more clothes, a box of CDs, and a combination CD player and turntable to help me get through the remainder of my tenure at Kennedy's place.

I was back at Kennedy's and looking at the upstairs tape from the morning when Bryan Adams and the guys informed me of an incoming call.

"Hello."

"Roosevelt Park. Hello back at you."

I pulled back from the tape machine and sat at the working table, where I had a notebook and pen at the ready.

"Mr. Park," I said. "Thanks for getting back to me."

"In your message you said you wanted to talk about Ellie Foster."

"That's right. Her granddaughter has hired a private detective named Mike Cobb to see if he can find out what happened to Ellie and to find her if she's still alive. I'm working with him. We thought you might recall something that could be helpful in our efforts."

"Shit, what's it been, forty, fifty years?" Park was laughing as he said it. "You boys got zero chance of finding Ellie Foster."

"I understand your skepticism, sir." I worked at keeping my voice even. "But we believe our chances are a little north of zero. I'd like to sit down with you, kick around a few things about The Depression. I know some of the performers stayed with you when they were appearing there. Was Ellie one of those people?"

"Yeah, Ellie stayed at my place. At least some of the time. When she wasn't camped out with the dude she'd hooked up with."

"You know the dude's name?"

"Uh-uh. She never told me, and I never asked. Wasn't any of my business."

"I'd be happy to buy you a coffee, Mr. Park. If you have time."

"Hey, I got time up the yingyang. But I don't drink coffee. What I do is eat lunch." He laughed again.

"In that case, I'd be pleased to buy you lunch. Have you eaten yet today?"

"Hell, no. Well, that's not exactly true. I have eaten, but not so much that I can't manage a little more. Especially when it's free."

Park sounded like a piece of work. Lunch could be interesting.

When I stepped into the Swiss Chalet on Macleod Trail, it quickly became clear that Roosevelt Park was a *large* piece of work. It appeared that he'd "managed a little more" fairly regularly over the years. I'm not good at guessing weights, but I was fairly sure that the first number on the scale would have been a three.

He was sitting at a window booth about halfway

down, and apparently he figured out who I was as soon as he saw me, because he waved me over. He didn't get up, but stretched a monster hand across the table and we shook. At least *he* shook. My hand just went along for the ride.

There are two kinds of people who weigh three-hundred-plus pounds. There are big people, and there are fat people. Roosevelt Park was not a guy with a belly that looked at you over the top of the table. He was big all over.

He grinned at me. "I ordered us a beer. Hope that's okay." He pointed at the can of Bud Light that sat at my place.

"Beer is always okay," I said as I slid into my spot.

"You ever been to a Swiss Chalet?"

"I'm a newbie to the experience." As I glanced at the menu, I got the feeling that it might differ slightly from the Chopped Leaf in terms of its attention to healthy eating.

"I recommend the chicken," Park said.

"I bet when you go to A&W you order a burger."

"Damn straight." He nodded. "They got a few other things here, but you wanna go with the chicken."

We ordered chicken, and when the woman who took our order had moved away from our table I pulled my notebook and pen out of my jacket pocket.

"Oh my," Park said. "Official."

"More like bad memory." I tapped my head. "How long have you lived in Calgary, Mr. Park?"

"We gonna get along, you need to stop calling me Mr. Park. I answer to Rosie."

I smiled at that. "I answer to Adam. How long, Rosie?"

"Came here in '62. Stampeders signed me. I played a total of four games — two pre-season, two regular season.

Tore my Achilles, and that was that. No more football. But I liked the place. Never left."

"Where'd you play college ball?"

"Oklahoma. I'm a Sooner, baby." He grinned again, which I was figuring out was Park's default facial expression. Hard guy not to like.

"I might not be able to buy you lunch, after all," I said. "I'm an Oklahoma State grad. Cowboys, baby."

"Shit, we kicked your asses all over the field." He laughed.

"And we kicked yours all over the diamond."

He laughed even harder at that. It became clear that Rosie Park was a regular at this establishment, and that was even more evident when "the usual" that he had ordered arrived at our booth. The usual for Roosevelt Park consisted of what I guessed to be at least two complete chickens — maybe more. Bordering on a flock.

I'd settled for a quarter-chicken dinner. Cobb and I had skipped breakfast that morning, and I was pretty hungry myself. We fell to eating and finished at about the same time. Rosie didn't take many conversation breaks. The lunch — all of it — consumed, Rosie worked his way out of the booth with surprising dexterity and made a trip to the washroom. On his return, with coffee in front of us, we at last resumed conversation. I kicked it off.

"You talk to the cops after Ellie Foster disappeared?"

"Sure. A couple of times."

"You mention the boyfriend?"

"Well, I'm sure I did. But, of course, I didn't know who the guy was, so I couldn't tell them much. And, on top of that, *boyfriend* might have been the wrong word altogether. I don't even know that there was only one guy. I just know there were some nights that Ellie didn't use her bed at my house."

"You sure her companion was male?"

"Oh yeah, that I am sure of. Ellie was hetero. She liked men … maybe a little too much."

"So how do you know she wasn't camped out at a friend's place?"

"Stuff she said. How she looked when she showed up to change clothes. I knew."

I thought of something. "The two guys in the band — where did they stay?'

"Don't know. Not at my place. She wouldn't have wanted that anyway."

"Really? Why is that?"

"She couldn't stand one of them. Only kept him around because he was a hell of a songwriter. And even then, she was planning to run his ass after the Calgary gig."

"Which guy was that?"

"The bass player, Duke Prego. Came from the Maritimes or something. Guy was an ass."

"What was it about him that made him an ass?"

"Hey, we're going back in time here. But I remember for a guy who was as bad as he was on bass, he thought he was amazing. That drove Ellie nuts."

"How did Ellie get back and forth to The Depression from your … wherever she'd spent the night?"

"Caught rides. Didn't need to rent a car; everybody wanted to give that lady a ride."

"Okay, let's go back to the night she disappeared. Were you there that night?"

"At The Depression?"

"Yes."

He shook his head. "No, I had a job. The Stampeders helped me out — got me a job as a shipper-receiver. I was working late that night. Went home and crashed. Didn't hear about it till the next morning on the news."

"What did you think when you heard it?"

"What do you mean?"

"Did you have any thoughts at all about who might have done it?"

"Well, shit, of course I had thoughts. Everybody had thoughts." He stopped long enough to drink some coffee. "But I didn't have any idea, not really. I mean the damn thing made no sense." Another pause, more coffee. "I honestly thought she'd show up again. That whoever took her would release her, or the cops would find her. For the first while I was sure that somehow, some way, she'd come back to us."

He lowered his head, looking down, remembering something he wasn't likely to tell me about. After a minute or so, he raised his head and looked at me.

"But she never did."

"No," I said, "she never did."

"You find her, I'd like to know about it."

I nodded. "I'll make sure of that."

I'd just climbed into the Accord when my phone chirped an announcement that I had a text. It was Lois Beeston letting me know that Darby O'Callaghan lived in Cochrane, just northwest of the city. She also gave me a number to reach him at. I called, got his machine, gave my regular spiel, and asked him to call me.

* * *

Back at Kennedy's place, I went through the report from Carrington and Wardlow's initial investigation. I'd studied it, been through it a few times, couldn't remember any mention of Ellie Foster seeing someone — or more than one someone — during her time in Calgary. I found the notes that followed their initial conversation with Roosevelt Park. There was a description of Park, even a photo of his house, a big old two-storey, and a notation that Ellie stayed there while she played The Depression. But no mention of a possible lover, boyfriend … nothing. Either the investigating detectives had thought it was insignificant and hadn't pursued it or they *had* checked it out but didn't record what they had learned because, again, it wasn't germane to the case, or because they hadn't found the guy or guys.

I texted Cobb a summary of my conversation with Rosie Park — I left out the details of the meal — and turned my attention to my surveillance duties. I was in the upstairs bedroom staring through the camera lens at the house across the street when Cobb called back.

"Ready for a road trip?"

"Sure. But only if it's to Hawaii, Mexico, or maybe Greece — I'd like to see the Acropolis," I replied.

"How about Claresholm?"

"Claresholm, Alberta?"

"You've heard of it."

"Heard of it, driven through it, and I'm sure it's nice, but it doesn't really bump Hawaii, Mexico, or Greece out of my top three."

Cobb chuckled. "Sometimes I don't get you at all. I think it's time we had a chat with Mr. Carrington."

"Is he able to chat?"

"I called the seniors home he's in. Cottonwood Village. Talked to a nice lady who said he's lucid, has some issues with short-term memory, but some days he's pretty good. She said as long as we don't cause him a lot of stress or tire him out too much, we can talk to him."

"Okay, Claresholm it is. But next time I want Honolulu."

"I'll pick you up at nine tomorrow morning."

SEVEN

Claresholm is a little more than an hour south of Calgary. Cobb was uncharacteristically late getting to my place, so we rolled into Claresholm a little before eleven and stopped at Roy's Place, a restaurant situated on the highway going through town at the one intersection that sported a traffic light. I quickly learned two things: neither member of the couple that ran the place was named Roy, and the food was terrific.

We took our time over a couple of omelettes, then made a valiant attempt to get through a cinnamon bun chaser that was the size of a small aircraft. Only a person with the body shape and bulk of Roosevelt Park could get through one of those things in a single sitting. A rancher sitting at the next table recommended Bloat-Aid, a product apparently given to cattle that have overeaten. I thanked him for the advice and made up my mind to purchase several bottles prior to my next visit to Roy's.

Our first half hour at the Cottonwood was spent wheeling Lex Carrington around the grounds. It felt a little strange, wandering here and there with a man neither of us knew, and with all three of us saying nothing until the walk part of the visit was completed.

Finally we took up a spot at a vacant picnic table. Carrington rolled expertly up to one end, politely refusing my offer of help. He clearly didn't need it. Cobb fetched coffee for the three of us, and once the delivery and distribution was completed, Lex Carrington stared at us over the top of his Styrofoam cup.

"You want to talk about Ellie Foster," he said finally.

Cobb nodded and explained our interest in the case.

"Julia told me you were wanting to talk about that, so I've been thinkin', you know? Rememberin'. Bitch of a thing." Carrington shook his head sadly. "We worked it hard, thought we had a couple of suspects, but the leads dried up faster than dog piss in the desert."

He spoke slowly, and there was a gentle but persistent tremor to both his head and hands.

"Who made your suspects list, Lex?"

"Big black guy, forget his name, different name —"

"Roosevelt Park," I said.

"Yeah, him. She was staying at his place. Wardlow, my partner, thought for sure Park was shaggin' her and liked him for one of the killers, but the one wit we had said it was two white guys in the alley that night, and besides, the guy had a solid alibi. Even so, Wardlow kept on him. Figured maybe he hired the guys who grabbed her that night. When I asked him what he figured the guy's motive was, he had this cockeyed theory about Park killing the band guys because one of them was also shaggin' her, then kidnapping her for his love slave. Even wanted to get a warrant to search the basement of Park's house — figured we'd find her chained up down there. Wardlow was a good cop except for one thing: He was the most racist bastard I ever knew. Hated pretty well everybody who wasn't white. And he hated blacks most of all. Couldn't stand 'em."

Cobb was digesting all of that.

"Park told us she didn't sleep there every night. He figured she had a boyfriend she was spending time with. You do anything with that?"

Carrington stared at the cloudless sky for a while. "Yeah, I remember him saying something about that, and I seem to remember we checked it out. Decided she was a woman who liked the occasional one-nighter, you know? No boyfriend, just sex partners."

"You check them out?"

"Tried to. Didn't get far. We didn't have any names, and after she disappeared none of them apparently felt like coming forward."

I wondered if Wardlow's leaning toward Roosevelt Park as a possible suspect might have been the reason Ellie's male companions weren't pursued with a little more diligence. And I wondered, too, if Carrington had kept mentions of Park's name to a minimum to protect a racist partner.

I could see Cobb was working at not being critical of the earlier investigation — probably a good idea. I figured Carrington would dry up fast, maybe even faster than dog piss in the desert, if it looked like we were finding fault with the detectives' work.

I leaned forward. "One thing, Lex — we're hearing two conflicting stories about the kind of person she was. You or Wardlow have any kind of take on that?"

He looked at me for a while before answering. "Yeah, that was one of the things I had trouble with. People talked about how she was great with the audience, but not nearly so great with everybody else. I remember talking to the owner of The Depression about that. He said it hadn't always been like that. She'd played the place before, and she was a sweetheart. But not that last time. It was like she was pissed off. Political and pissed off."

"Political?"

"Yeah, like strident: 'This is what I believe, and if you don't think like me you're an asshole.'"

"Can you remember who characterized her that way?"

A pause, then a head shake. "No, I can't, but I'm thinking it was more than one person said the same thing."

"And she hadn't been like that on her previous time in Calgary?"

"Apparently not."

"Anybody suggest what it was that precipitated the change in attitude?"

"Well, you ask people something like that, they're going to speculate … but nobody gave us anything more than *maybe*s and *possibly*s. We checked out every damn one of their suggestions. Or at least the ones that weren't totally nutso. End of the day, it was like every other lead we chased: nothing."

I was amazed at how much Carrington was able to remember and how well he could articulate those memories. Especially if, as had been suggested to Cobb, he was suffering from a little dementia, or at least short-term memory loss. There was damn sure not a lot wrong with his long-term memory.

One of the caregivers from the centre came by carrying a blanket. She was both pretty and friendly.

"Are you warm enough, Mr. Carrington?"

He grinned up at her. "I'm cold as hell, C, but nothing a couple of hugs wouldn't cure."

"C" shook her head and laughed. "Blanket's the best I can do, Mr. Carrington."

"Damn," he said, chuckling. "I'm fine, C, but thanks."

The pretty caregiver moved off and, once out of Carrington's sightline, signalled to us that we had ten minutes. Cobb looked at me, eyebrows raised, inviting me to join the discussion if I had something more. I did.

"Lex, you ever hear of a place called The Tumbling Mustard?"

Carrington looked blankly at me for a few seconds, then shook his head. "What the hell is it?"

"Just a name that came up — a folk club from back then. Ottawa."

Carrington shook his head again. "We checked out Ottawa. Wardlow went down there — budgets said only one of us goes. But I never heard him say anything about that place. Either it never came up, or he checked it out and didn't think there was anything there. Anyway, when he got back here we went over every conversation he'd had out there, everything he'd learned. And I guarantee you he never mentioned anything called The Tumbling ... what was it?"

"Mustard," I said. "The Tumbling Mustard."

"But he checked out Le Hibou?" Cobb asked.

"The place she played right before she came here?" Carrington nodded. "That was the main reason he went down there. Like I said, Norris was a good detective, other than the racial thing. I think he got all there was down there. If he didn't mention that other place, then it didn't need mentioning."

I was starting to re-evaluate the work the two men had done on the case. Even if Cobb and I were wrong and The Tumbling Mustard was meaningless, it damn sure warranted at least a mention in their reports. I wondered whether Carrington didn't have an overinflated appreciation of his partner's talents. I admired the loyalty, but wasn't sure I could agree with his faith in Norris Wardlow, at least based on what I'd seen so far.

I looked over at Cobb and nodded, giving the ball back to him. Cobb turned back to the former police investigator.

"I imagine you've thought about it in the years since that night," Cobb said. "Ever come up with any other thoughts, something you think we should maybe follow up on?"

Again, Carrington took his time answering.

"I look back at it and I ask myself whether we tried hard enough. And I honestly don't know what more we could have done. I know there was something we missed; somebody shot those guys and took Ellie Foster. We didn't find out who, and we didn't make an arrest. That was our job, and we failed, plain and simple. Even now, I wish there was something I could give you that would help you find the truth." He shook his head slowly from side to side, lips pursed, shoulders slumped. "But I can't."

On the way back to Calgary, Cobb was moody. Or at least pensive. I figured it was because he felt pulled in two directions by the earlier investigation. As a former cop himself, he wanted to give Carrington and Wardlow the benefit of the doubt. More than that, he wanted to believe they had done a thorough and effective job, but after our chat with Lex Carrington, he may have been having some trouble maintaining that belief.

Finally, he inhaled, let the air out slowly, then spoke: "I think we need to make some follow-up calls, see if we can find out more about what might have precipitated the mood change. We've heard about that from a few sources now. We need to chase that down, if we can."

"Might be tough. Hell, she could have found out she was pregnant, or had a fight with one of those boyfriends Park talked about. It's just as likely something like that as some weird thing to do with the other coffee house." I realized in saying that I probably sounded exactly like Norris Wardlow had sounded.

"Maybe. Maybe not," Cobb said. "But we have to try. Any luck finding anybody connected to that place?"

I shook my head, inwardly glad that Cobb had assumed I'd already tried.

"Might be worth another shot," he said.

"Fair enough. I'll get back on that right away."

It's easy to say, *I'll get back on that right away*. It's a little harder to get back on that. Especially when you've already exhausted what you'd thought was pretty much every possible lead out there.

Cobb dropped me off at Kennedy's place just before 6:00. I spent a couple of hours on the surveillance vigil, but it would be a lie to say I gave it my undivided attention. There was something else occupying my mind, and for the second night in a row, I set out to do something I was dreading but felt I had to do.

Again, my plan ended in frustration — a waste of an evening. Maybe it was a sign that I should abandon a plan as foolish and precarious as this one, but I knew I'd be back out there trying again.

Soon.

I'd promised Cobb, so the next morning, after the obligatory check of tapes and the two scenes under surveillance, I set about trying to find out more about The Tumbling Mustard. I did have one idea. I was, after all, first and foremost a newspaper guy. I figured that there had to be a print source, whether in an ad or the occasional promo piece for upcoming gigs — something in the *Ottawa Citizen* that mentioned The Tumbling Mustard (surely a sixties name if ever there was one).

I packed up keys, reading glasses, wallet, and cellphone and headed for the downtown central branch of the public library. I spent a couple of mind-numbing hours poring over the *Citizen*'s archives, during which time I learned that the hottest day of 1965 was June 28, when the thermometer reached thirty-two degrees Celsius, that the CFL's outstanding player that year was Ottawa's Russ Jackson, and that a 1965 Ford Fairlane 500 two-door sedan could have been purchased for $2,312.

And finally, on page 27 of the October 19, 1964, edition of the paper was a small ad for The Tumbling Mustard, noting that Sonny Terry and Brownie McGhee would be performing at the club from October 25 through 29, and that the Saskatoon Princess, Paula Pendergast, would be there the following week. I stayed at it another hour, but that was it. Not even an ad in the days leading up to Ellie Foster's performing there.

That left me with one shot. I knew that both Sonny

Terry and Brownie McGhee had long since passed away, which meant that the Saskatoon Princess was my lone hope. All I needed was for Paula Pendergast to be (a) alive, (b) findable, (c) in possession of her mental faculties, and (d) willing to talk to me.

Piece of cake.

Back home. *Jesus, I've begun to think of Kennedy's place as home.* Google time. With Heart (*Dreamboat Annie*) and The Hip (*Yer Favourites*) providing the soundtrack (the oldies radio station had clearly inspired me), I went to work. There was a three-line Wikipedia item on Paula Pendergast saying she had been a teenage sensation who had played blues and folk clubs in the sixties and early seventies. She had left the business in 1974 to start a family. She had one recording, an album called *Rhythm of the Ramble*. I called Hot Wax Records on 10th Street in Kensington. The place was amazing. Probably 20 percent of the albums in the collection that covered much of my living room floor had come from there. I'd never called and come up empty.

That record remained intact. One copy of *Rhythm of the Ramble* was put away for me — twenty-eight bucks.

I had planned to go get the record the next day, but after another fruitless Google search for the Saskatoon Princess and twenty minutes of looking at the two houses through Kennedy's cameras, I decided instead to pick up the record right away, congratulating myself on my earlier decision to bring my CD player/turntable unit back with me.

The trip to Kensington was quick except for the last couple of blocks, when inner-city traffic slowed to sloth speed. I visited with the guys at Hot Wax, collected the album, and was back at the house in just under an hour.

I was more interested in the liner notes than the music, but was surprised at the quality of both the songwriting and the performance of those songs by the Saskatoon Princess. The liner notes, on the other hand, were a disappointment, telling me virtually nothing about Paula Pendergast, offering instead a few paragraphs of what I guessed was sixties social philosophy that left me scratching my head.

Nevertheless, I figured I was on a roll, so my next plan was to start calling telephone information services and to hope like hell that Ms. Pendergast had kept her maiden name or gotten divorced and gone back to her original name.

I decided on a Montreal theme to backdrop my calls and put Arcade Fire, then The Dears on the CD player, noting, as I had many times before, the difference fifty years made in the popular music of the day. Yet I was also aware that there was an interrelationship, however thin. It was, after all, music; there was kinship and connections, however tenuous.

I was mildly optimistic. If the Saskatoon Princess had begun raising a family in the midseventies, I reasoned she would have been maybe twenty-five to thirty-five at that time. Add forty-ish years, and there was a reasonable chance she was still alive.

I started with Saskatoon, then hit other Saskatchewan cities. When I had struck out in the Wheat Province, I moved over to Alberta. I started in the south with Lethbridge and Calgary and then worked my way north, again with zero results.

Until Grande Prairie. There, I learned that there was a *P. Pendergast* living in a small community just outside the city, a place called Wanham. I got the number and made the call, convinced I would soon be talking to Peter or Patricia Pendergast. I was wrong.

The female voice that said hello was soft but firm. And I guessed it belonged to an older person.

"Hello," I said, willing my voice not to sound like someone who was sick of talking on the phone. "I was hoping I might be speaking to Paula Pendergast, the former folksinger who was known as the Saskatoon Princess."

"Yes."

I didn't know if she was saying, *Yes, I understand the reason for your call,* or *Yes, I am the Saskatoon Princess.*

"Are you that person?"

"Who's calling, please?"

"My name is Adam Cullen. I'm a journalist in Calgary, and I'm working on a story on Ellie Foster, a contemporary of Paula's. I'm trying to get information on The Tumbling Mustard, a club both women played in the sixties. So I guess that brings us back to my earlier question — are you Paula?"

The answer was a throaty chuckle, then, "Isn't that the dumbest name ever?"

"The Tumbling Mustard?"

"Well, that too." The chuckle again. "But actually I was thinking of the Saskatoon Princess. Oh, and yes, I am *that* Paula Pendergast."

"Wow," I said, meaning that I was stunned at my luck in having found her as quickly as I had.

She may have taken the *wow* for something quite different.

"Oh, I wasn't really that big a deal," she said.

I thought about telling her how much I loved *Rhythm of the Ramble,* but I thought that might be laying it on a bit thick. Instead, I said, "Is now an okay time for you to chat?"

"Ellie Foster," she said, drawing out the name. "I never thought I'd hear those two words again."

"Did you know her, Ms. Pendergast?"

"Not well.… In fact, I barely knew her at all. I met her and heard her a few times, of course. She was … enchanting on stage. I admired that so much because I wasn't like that at all. I was never really able to captivate, to beguile an audience like she could. In fact, performing wasn't really the part of the music business I particularly liked. For me it was the writing and recording — I preferred the studio to the stage."

"*Rhythm of the Ramble*," I said.

"Mr. Cullen. You have just stolen an old lady's heart. I realize that you probably just googled it or whatever it is you do, but I am flattered that there is anyone at all who knows of that record."

"The album cover is sitting here on my desk, and I just finished listening to the album a few minutes ago."

"My goodness," she said, with another chuckle. "I finally have a groupie."

I laughed with her. "Yes, you do, Ms. Pendergast. I'm wondering if this is an okay time to chat a little more about the club," I repeated.

"I think so," she said. "I suppose that will depend on what you want to ask me. And I'll answer only if you promise never to call me Ms. Pendergast again."

"Deal," I said. "Paula, what can you tell me about The Tumbling Mustard?"

She thought for a while, and when she answered, she began slowly, as if wanting to choose her words carefully.

"It wasn't like Le Hibou," she said. "That was where the big names played. The Tumbling Mustard was like the — what do they call them? The minor leagues."

"That's what they call them. And yet I noticed that Sonny Terry and Brownie McGhee played there just before you did in 1965. They were big league even then."

"Actually, that's not true, Mr. Cullen."

"Oh?"

"They were scheduled to be there, but they cancelled a couple of days before they were supposed to perform."

"You happen to know the reason for that?"

"There were rumours at the time, but, of course, I never found out the real reason."

"What were the rumours saying?"

"Money. One of the stories I heard was that the owners didn't forward the advance money they were supposed to. Told the guys to just come on up to Ottawa and they'd get looked after when they got there. I imagine Sonny and Brownie had heard that one before."

"Was that a common occurrence at The Tumbling Mustard?"

"Cancellations, you mean?"

"That, and performers not getting paid."

Long pause. I was about to ask if she'd heard me when she spoke again. "How much do you know about The Tumbling Mustard, Mr. Cullen?"

"Next to nothing," I confessed. "But I'd like to learn more."

"It was owned by two guys, one of them was Middle Eastern. I remember his name, I'm not sure why — but it was Abdel Fayed. I don't know what country he came from or how long he'd been in Canada. I do remember that he was extremely intelligent and spoke almost perfect English with very little accent. The other guy was creepy. He was really smart, too, but creepy smart. I remember he said he hadn't lived in Ottawa for very long, but if he said where he came from I didn't hear it, or at least I don't remember it."

"You remember his name?'

"Uh-huh. Laird. Cameron Laird. Always Cameron. Never Cam."

"And he was creepy smart."

"Yes. I know that sounds almost silly, but the thing was, The Tumbling Mustard wasn't like other coffee houses. In those places, it was always about the music. The TM wasn't … like that."

"The TM?"

Another chuckle. "People got sick of saying 'Tumbling Mustard' all the time."

"I can't imagine why," I said, with a chuckle of my own. "If it wasn't about the music, what was it about?"

"That's the part I'm not too sure I can tell you. It felt like every time you looked over at the coffee bar, you'd see either Abdel or Cameron, or both of them, huddled with somebody in this deep conversation. They hardly ever paid attention to what was happening onstage, and I don't think they paid an awful lot of attention to the customers either. Maybe that's why the place didn't stick around long."

"How long was the … uh … TM part of the Ottawa folk scene?"

"About a year and a half. Started up in the late summer or early fall of '64, and it was gone by the spring of '66."

"How did Fayed and Laird treat you?"

"I had no complaints. I got paid on time. Of course, I wasn't a big-ticket item like Sonny and Brownie would have been. But they treated me all right. Except that Laird kept asking me out. Well, not *out* exactly. He wanted me to come over to his place. I never did."

"Any particular reason you didn't want to do that?"

"A few, actually. I had a boyfriend, for starters. And Cameron, I don't know, he sort of scared me."

"Scared you how? Was he physically imposing?"

"No, that was Abdel. He was a big man. Not fat … big. Lots of muscles. People said he spent a lot of time at the gym, which would make sense, given his build. But Cameron Laird was skinny. Tall but very slight. Not a lot to the guy. So that wasn't what scared me about him. It was just that he was really intense. Always looked forbidding. And then with all their little hush-hush discussions going on all the time … no, you couldn't have paid me enough money to go out with that guy."

"These secretive discussions — did it seem like the people they were talking to were the same ones all the time?"

She thought for a minute before answering. "Often it was the same ones in the same place, leaning on the counter, their heads all together and whispering away at each other. It probably wasn't really whispering, but you know what I mean."

"Surreptitious," I said.

"The perfect word for it. But there were other people who were part of their little conversations. Some of them I saw only once or twice."

"Always men?"

"Mostly men, but not all the time. I seem to remember at least one or two women getting in on the tête-à-têtes."

"Would you say that it looked like they were talking about illegal things? Maybe making drug deals ... anything like that?"

"I can't say that, because I just don't know. Mostly it was just this big secret thing. Almost like they were plotting. Or maybe just gossiping, I really don't know. All I can say for sure is that it wasn't a nice place to perform."

I'd been scribbling notes, but I looked up now and stared out Kennedy's living room window while I thought about what Paula was telling me.

"You ever see Fayed or Laird after the club closed down?"

"I never did. I was in and out of Ottawa a few times, but I never played the TM again. I went there a couple of times to see other people perform. But after it closed down ... no, I never saw either of them again. Of course, I didn't try to."

"Ever hear anything about them? Where they got to, anything like that?"

"Uh-uh.... No, wait, that's not true. I seem to remember a few years later somebody said one of them, I don't know which one, ended up in California. Maybe L.A., although I can't say for certain."

"One last thing, Paula, and I really appreciate your taking the time to talk with me — Ellie Foster played the TM. Did you ever see her perform there?"

"I did. She was there early on and for quite a long gig — maybe a couple of weeks. I was in Ottawa rehearsing with some new band guys. I saw her a couple of times, actually, and she was just as amazing as ever. In fact, when Ellie was performing, those were the only times I ever saw the little huddle break up and the people at the counter — *all* the people — actually pay attention."

"Listen, I —"

"Oh my God," Paula said, interrupting. "I just thought of something. I hope I'm not making this up, some memory that didn't really happen at all, you know? But I'm sure that she not only got the little discussion group to disperse when she was performing, but also, at least once, when she wasn't on stage, I saw her right there with them. I can't remember if it was during a break or after she was finished for the night, but I'm almost 100 percent sure I saw her in one of those damn huddles … head down and looking just as … surreptitious as the rest of them."

"Did you ever think about what happened to her? Wonder where she got to? Who took her?"

"I guess everybody thought about those things." Paula was speaking more slowly now, as if she was thinking about them again. "I mean, if it could happen to Ellie, maybe the same thing could have happened to me. I guess that sounds a little self-important — I was a long way from being Ellie Foster. But I can still remember getting goosebumps thinking about her, wondering where she was, if she was still alive. But after a while, as horrible as it is, you stop thinking about it as much. You move on, as the expression goes."

"I understand," I said. "Paula, can you remember when Ellie's two-week gig at the TM was? Even roughly?"

She took some time with that. "I know it was before me, because I remember thinking there was no way the audience would love me like that when I stepped on that stage. I was there the first part of November; I remember that because my gig ended on Remembrance Day. I played a couple of songs that I had hoped were appropriate for it. So I guess that would put her there in September or

October.… No. I'm pretty sure it was September. Which would be about right, because I think she was one of the first acts they had there."

Paula's recollection corresponded perfectly with the schedule I'd found in Lois Beeston's notes. I scrawled a notation of my own. "Paula, I want you to know that you've been amazing. And I want you to know something else. I'm an avid collector of Canadian music. And I'm very glad *Rhythm of the Ramble* is part of my collection."

"That's very nice of you to say, Adam. I really hope you find her even after all this time. And I hope that maybe there's a miracle waiting for you and that she's okay … somehow."

"Me too, Paula. Me too."

After my conversation with Paula Pendergast ended, I didn't write any more notes, not right away. Instead, I sat staring out the window some more and thinking. It was starting to feel like The Tumbling Mustard was something of a game changer in our search for Ellie Foster. A few people had commented on the personality transformation that seemed to have occurred, and that roughly coincided with Ellie's time at the club.

That thought continued to be my focus as I spent an hour at the upstairs camera watching the house across the street. Eventually my thinking morphed into wondering again if the people who lived there now knew that a little girl's body had been found in their backyard. I wondered, too, if something like that would impact my own decision to buy a property or not.

I went downstairs, made coffee, and called Cobb.

"You're not paying me enough," I said, when he answered the call.

"You're assuming that I'm paying you at all," he replied.

"Good point," I said. "I had an interesting chat with a woman named Paula Pendergast this morning. Paula performed at The Tumbling Mustard around the same time as Ellie Foster did. Had some interesting insights into the place and the two people who owned it."

I recounted in detail my conversation with Paula and threw in my opinion that the place was of significance, certainly measured against the change that people had indicated came over Ellie at about that time. I added in that the place might even be related somehow to her disappearance.

When I'd finished, Cobb said only, "Hnh," which I took to mean he was thinking about what I'd just told him. Half a minute or so later, he shared his thinking.

"Let's not get ahead of ourselves on this thing. We need more about the place, or at least about Laird and Fayed. Let me think about how we should go about getting that information. How's everything over there?"

"Nothing new here. Kennedy gets back tomorrow. I'm glad I could help the guy, but I haven't achieved anything."

"Which is exactly the same as what he's achieved over, what did he say, nine thousand days?"

"Yeah, well, I'm looking forward to getting back to my own place and spending time with the people I love."

"Yeah, I love you too, man."

I laughed. "Aw, shut up."

"I'll call you later after I've had time to consider some things."

"Right."

We ended the call, and I made four slices of toast to go with the coffee. Another hour, maybe a little more,

at me in two languages — one was English, the other something European, maybe. Oh, and two more calls from Bernie.

When my own cellphone rang, I was so relieved I actually fist-pumped before I answered. Pathetic.

"Mr. Cullen?"

My enthusiasm waned. The caller sounded at least two years away from puberty. *But hey, look at the good stuff,* I told myself. *It isn't Bernie.*

"My name's Darby O'Callaghan."

The words that popped into my head were, *You gotta be shitting me,* something I hadn't actually said since maybe college. But I stifled that urge and said instead, "Mr. O'Callaghan, I appreciate your calling me back."

"I wasn't going to."

"Why is that?"

"You said in your message you wanted to talk to me about Ellie. And whenever I talk about her, even after all this time, I feel like crap, you know?"

"I understand. But I'm sure you'd want to help us find her if there was any chance at all, right?"

"You won't find her."

That got my attention. Not only the words, but also the change in his voice. Suddenly assertive. Definite.

"You drink coffee, Darby? Or beer? I'd be happy to buy you either one if you could spare a few minutes to chat."

A long pause. "I guess I could do that."

"Great. I know you live out of town, but I wonder if you get into Calgary from time to time."

"Sure, I grew up in the city. Got lots of family and friends in there."

"What high school did you go to?"

"Crescent Heights."

"No kidding? Me too, Darby."

"Seriously?"

"Seriously. Want to hear me sing the school fight song?"

He laughed. Instant connection.

"I was going to run in there tomorrow, but I could push it up a day. Could probably be in the city in an hour or so."

"There's a Starbucks on 16th Avenue, right at 10th Street, near the Earl's restaurant. Should be fairly handy for where you're coming from."

"It's not bad at all. And I know the place."

"Perfect. But please, don't rush. Let's make it a couple of hours from now. In case there's traffic and stuff."

"Fair enough. Two hours it is."

After the call ended, I fielded two more calls on the second cellphone and was beginning to hate that I'd put the story in the *Herald*. And that was only one paper. What would happen when it appeared across the country? I tried telling myself again that even one call that yielded useful information would make the thing worthwhile, but I was having trouble believing me.

I took a long, hot shower, got dressed, and gathered my notes on the Foster case, stuffing them in a tired leather briefcase that I'd had for almost a decade. It was a birthday gift from Donna — couldn't remember which birthday.

I called Cobb and got his message. I told him I was meeting O'Callaghan and to feel free to join us if he had time and was in the area.

The drive to 16th Avenue was uneventful; the traffic was relatively manageable at that time of day. I stepped outside my comfort zone, abandoning my CDs in favour of sports talk radio. I lasted ten minutes; the American broadcaster, who was clearly very fond of himself, drove me back to the refuge of Prism, then the Sam Roberts Band. I was four cuts into Roberts's *Collider* when I pulled into the parking lot of the Starbucks on 16th.

I looked around the place, didn't see anyone who I thought could be Darby O'Callaghan, and decided to stick with my determination to think outside the box. I ordered a green tea — about as outside the box as a coffee lover like me can get.

There was a trio of easy chairs available, so I threw my jacket on one and sat in another. I waited for O'Callaghan, checked messages on my phone ... and drank tea.

Five minutes into my ordeal, a short sixty-something guy came in the front door. He was wearing a faded ball cap with a capital *C* that had been red once, but was now the pink of medium-rare meat. Could have been a Cubs cap, but I couldn't rule out Cleveland or Cincinnati, either. Decided not to ask and spoil the mystery.

He was also wearing thick glasses, and he squinted through them as he walked tentatively into the Starbucks and looked around. If I wanted a single word to describe Darby O'Callaghan — if this was, in fact, him — that word would be *moist*.

He spotted me, nodded, and made his way to the table and chairs I was guarding.

"Mr. Cullen?"

I stood up. We shook hands, and I pointed to the vacant chair. "What can I get you to drink?"

He looked down at my cup. "What are you having?" The adolescent-sounding voice that had fooled me earlier.

"Green tea," I said, as quietly as possible.

"Pretty much anything but that," he said.

I headed for the counter, unsettled in the knowledge that even moist guys drank coffee. I ordered him a Pike, almost made it two, but decided reluctantly to stay the course. When I got back to where we were sitting, O'Callaghan had removed the ball cap to reveal the unsurprising news that he was mostly bald.

Moist *and* bald.

I sat, and we sipped in silence for a minute, maybe more.

"I appreciate your taking the time to meet me," I said. "You were quite definite on the phone that we wouldn't find Ellie. Mind telling me what makes you so certain of that?"

Everyone I'd talked to had an opinion, it seemed, as to the likelihood of our finding Ellie, dead or alive. I suppose I had an opinion of my own, but so far I'd kept myself from admitting it … at least out loud.

O'Callaghan ran a finger around the rim of his cup and nodded. "I mean, I wish you could. I wish it was possible, you know? But I don't believe it is."

"And why is that, Darby? Is it all right if I call you Darby?"

He nodded again. "Two guys kill two people in cold blood and grab the only person who saw them do it. You think they took her for a spin in the countryside and then dropped her off? Or maybe she was the reason they drove down that alley in the first place. And the two guys they shot were just unlucky witnesses. Either way, it wasn't going to end well for her. It just makes no sense that she'd be alive after all this time."

"Well, you've pretty well summarized the two possibilities as to what happened that night. But her granddaughter is hoping that your conclusion about what happened to her after that night is wrong. I suspect most people who've thought about it at all share your conclusion, but until we have absolute proof of that fact, we'll keep on believing and we'll keep on looking."

O'Callaghan shrugged. "And I wish you very good luck."

He had a face that looked like it wasn't used to smiling. And it wasn't smiling now.

"I'm told you were around The Depression quite a lot."

"Yeah, I was. I loved the music, and I loved the feel of the place. Interesting people, terrific acts. The conversation was sometimes funny, sometimes energetic. It was a great place to be."

"Energetic?"

"Yeah, you know — humour, rumour, people arguing, debating, laughing, yelling. It was a big-energy place, and I couldn't get enough of it."

"Sounds more like Studio 54."

He shook his head vigorously. "Don't get me wrong. When Ellie or Joni was singing a ballad, there wasn't a sound except what came from that stage. The energy I was talking about didn't always manifest itself in noise. But even the quietest moments … they were special, too."

"The discussion you mentioned — much of it focused on politics?"

"Sure, some."

"You remember any of the other topics?'

He shook his head. "That was a long time ago. I just remember politics — global, local, all of it, I guess. I'm pretty sure there was a fair amount of establishment bashing — both in the conversation and in the music.

But to be more specific than that after what? Fifty-some years? Yeah, I'm afraid I can't make that happen."

"Fair enough," I said. "So how did things unfold that night?"

"What do you mean?"

"How do you remember it all happening?"

"It happened in the alley, and I was inside. I don't know how it came down except from what other people told me and what I read in the papers, heard on the news."

"What were you doing about the time Ellie was taken?"

He thought about that.

"Well, Ellie was on a break, and when the acts were taking a break, that's when things tended to get noisy. A lot of fairly loud talking. I was up at the counter helping to serve coffee and snacks to people. Then that guy, the one who hid behind the garbage cans, he came running in, yelling. And he — oh shit, I made a mistake."

"What do you mean, Darby?"

"I got it wrong. I said before there was only one person, Ellie, who saw those guys shoot the two people in the alley, but there was also the guy who was hiding. I forgot about him."

"Right. Go on."

"Well, with all the noise, we didn't hear him, at least not right away. I guess that's why we didn't hear the shots either — the noise, I mean. The guy ran over to where we were, and three or four of us went out into the alley to take a look. I hadn't heard him say that Ellie had been kidnapped — I'd only heard him say some guys got shot. It wasn't until we were outside that he pointed and said, 'Right over there, that's where she was when they grabbed her.' That's when I found out … that … she was …"

O'Callaghan didn't finish the sentence, and when he stopped talking he was looking down.

"Everybody went back inside to phone the cops and shit, but I ran down the alley, thinking maybe I'd see the car. Of course, I didn't."

"Who were the people who ran into the alley with you?'

"Hell, I have no idea. Couple of customers, maybe. I wasn't looking at them. I was looking for Ellie. I remember — it was like if I just looked hard enough and ran fast enough, she'd be there. Dumb, huh?"

His voice had grown fainter and fainter, fading to almost a whisper. I felt sorry for the guy and was working on what to say to him when Cobb stepped through the entrance to the place. He got a drink of something from a barista and strode over to where we were. I moved my jacket and he sat down, looking at O'Callaghan, who hadn't lifted his head.

"Darby O'Callaghan, this is Mike Cobb."

At that O'Callaghan looked up, then slowly leaned forward and shook the hand Cobb had offered.

"Mr. O'Callaghan was just taking me through his recollection of what happened the night Ellie Foster disappeared."

Mike nodded but didn't say anything, clearly not wanting to interrupt O'Callaghan's narrative.

"You were just at the point where you ran down the alley, hoping to catch a glimpse of the car Ellie had been forced into."

O'Callaghan nodded. "I didn't see anything," he said again, "so I went back to the club, and we waited for the cops to get there, spent most of the night there. They wanted to talk to everyone … it took a long time."

"Did Ellie take her break at about the same time every night?" I asked him.

O'Callaghan looked at Cobb, then at me. "I'm not sure I can remember that, but my guess would be no. She might have taken a break at roughly the same place in the set, but that could be at different times, because she would have started at different times. Things were a little casual that way, not just with Ellie, but with all the performers. If they were supposed to start at eight, they might not actually start their set until ten or fifteen minutes after eight."

I looked at Cobb to see if he wanted to take over, but he shook his head slightly, leaving it to me.

"What we're wondering, Darby, is how the kidnappers knew she'd be out there at exactly that time. We're thinking there had to be someone in the club that night, maybe even one or both of the guys who took her, or maybe someone to let them know that Ellie had gone into the alley."

O'Callaghan nodded his head slowly. "I guess you could be right about that."

"Do you remember anyone leaving the club about the same time as Ellie went out to the alley for a smoke?"

He shook his head. "I mean, people came and went, especially during the set breaks. So it's more than likely that some people might have gone outside or left altogether. I wouldn't have paid much attention to it."

He closed his eyes as if trying to visualize the scene inside the club that night, then shook his head. "I have no idea," he said.

"You were in love with Ellie, weren't you?" I said.

He looked at me for a long time before shaking his head. "No, but only because being in love implies a mutual thing. I loved her. Will always love her. But I was ... I was going to say I was *nothing* to her, but that's not true. We were friends. She was always decent, even kind to me, but that was all she felt. And I knew that."

"Some people have said she was different in terms of her personality during that last gig."

"Different how?"

"Different from the person she'd been when she'd played The Depression the previous time. What would you say to that?"

No hesitation this time.

"She was different, yes. I guess if I can use a cliché, I'd say she went from glass half-full to glass half-empty."

"Negative," I said.

"Yeah, and that wasn't Ellie."

"You ever ask her what was bothering her?"

He nodded. "I asked, but she didn't answer. At least, not with real answers. It was more like, 'I don't know what you're talking about,' or 'I guess I'm just tired.' Stuff like that."

"You ever hear of a place called The Tumbling Mustard?"

"Yeah. Yeah, I think so. Coffee house, maybe. I'm not sure where or how I heard about it, but I'm pretty sure I've heard that name before."

"Ellie ever mention it?"

O'Callaghan sipped his coffee, then scratched his chin as he thought. "I don't think it was Ellie I heard about it from. But don't hold me to that.… I'm just not sure."

"Ever hear anything *about* the place, what kind of place it was?"

"Nothing that stands out in my mind. Why? What about it?"

"You're right. It was a coffee house in Ottawa. Ellie played there. We're just trying to find out more about the place."

I looked again at Cobb. I'd exhausted my list of questions for O'Callaghan. At least for the moment.

Cobb set his cup down. "Mr. O'Callaghan, you said Ellie wasn't in love with you. Were there other men she was interested in?"

O'Callaghan didn't like the question. He wriggled around in the easy chair and looked unhappy. Finally, he shrugged. "I guess so. We didn't talk about that."

"But you would have seen other guys in The Depression who seemed interested in her."

"Sure, lots of them." O'Callaghan answered, still grumpy. "But I don't know how interested she was in them."

"That ever bother you, all those guys buzzing around someone you cared about?"

O'Callaghan shrugged. "Not really. It wasn't like I had any claim on her."

He suddenly sat up straight, made leaving motions. "I hope I've been able to help, but I've got some things to do, so if that's everything …" He stood up.

Cobb and I stood up as well. "Thanks for your time, Darby," I said. "It is appreciated."

"Good to meet you," Cobb said, extending a hand again.

When O'Callaghan was gone, Cobb and I sat back down. "You sure know how to make new friends." I grinned at him.

"It's a gift," he answered. "Definitely struck a nerve though, didn't I?"

"Jealous, maybe?"

"Maybe." Cobb nodded. "And there have been a hell of a lot of nasty crimes motivated by that particular emotion."

I drank more tea, then set my cup down.

"What *is* that?" Cobb pointed accusingly.

"Green tea."

"They out of coffee when you went up there?"

"I'm trying something new. You should give it a whirl sometime."

"I don't know if we can continue to work together. Coffee has been our bond. I'm shaken."

I laughed, then turned serious. "O'Callaghan just about wraps up the people I had to talk to. I'm not sure where we go from here ... or at least where *I* go."

"I saw the story in the *Herald*. How's that going for you?"

"Just kill me now."

Cobb smiled. "We knew it was a long shot ... and I did warn you."

"I know, I know. But I had no idea how many crackpots there are in the world. Point is, I have no one else to talk to except maybe the guy who conducted Ellie's business and arranged her bookings. And I have no idea where to start looking for him."

"Okay, let's see what we've got."

"Hold it," I said, holding up my hands. "I can't stand it." I stood up, crossed to the counter, and ordered a grande Pike. When I got back to where Cobb was sitting, he was grinning at me.

"Attaboy," he said.

"Yeah." I sat down, pushed what was left of the tea out of the way. "You were saying?"

"I think it's too soon to throw in the towel," Cobb said. "I get that it doesn't look all that promising, but there are at least a couple of things we have to take a closer look at."

"And they are?"

"First, The Tumbling Mustard. We've heard from a few sources now that Ellie was a changed person in the last weeks leading up to her disappearance. And at least one person has connected the attitude change to The Tumbling Mustard. I still think we need to find out more about that place."

"Easier said than done," I reminded him. "The place was around for only a year and a half or so, and it was never a big player in the coffee house scene. I'm not sure it's going to be easy to find people who can give us much."

"Agreed, but I still think it's our best lead, and we have to do all we can to follow it up. Secondly, there are the lyrics. I'm still convinced that song doesn't just show up in Monica Brill's car, a car that somebody had to break in to, fifty years after the song was written, without it being significant. We have to take another look at those lyrics."

"Okay, here's an idea: Kennedy gets back tomorrow. Let's all of us — your family and mine — put our heads together, see if we can't come up with something."

"A lyrics bee. I like it." Cobb smiled. "How's the coffee?"

"Shut up."

Third time's a charm.

I was sitting in a booth near the back of the Kane's Harley Diner. It was the third nocturnal visit I had paid to the place. I'd just finished a chili burger and salad and was starting to think I'd be 0 for 3 in terms of what I'd gone there for.

While I loved the food and the atmosphere — diner plus Harley-Davidson kitsch, what could be better? — neither was the reason I was there watching the front door. I'd brought along the most recent Ian Rankin, perhaps hoping that reading about Rebus would give me the courage I wasn't sure I had to do what I'd intended.

I had just begun to plan other strategies for meeting the man I wanted to meet when the door opened and he strode in, accompanied by two people, both of whom I'd met before. Seeing them in person reminded me that what I was planning was both foolish and possibly suicidal. I picked up my book and the bill and started to slide out of the booth.

"Well, I'll be go to hell, it's the scribe." The speaker was Rock Scubberd, the leader of the MFs, a motorcycle gang slash organized crime syndicate that I had written about during my time at the *Herald*. More recently, Cobb and I had crossed paths with them while we were trying to find a drug-addicted teenage runaway. It had been … interesting.

Scubberd was wearing a T-shirt — the better to show off the buff body he had sculpted during what I guessed was hundreds of hours in a gym. Cobb had told me that much about him before our first meeting with the man a couple of years before. I was fairly certain some credit for the physique needed to be given to Scubberd's dedication to performance-enhancing drugs. He had a new tattoo as well — a dragon-looking thing that emerged from the top of his T-shirt to cover his upper chest and the front of his neck. Same almost-shaved head, same narrow, vivid blue eyes that felt like they were reading your soul as he looked at you.

I glanced around the diner and noted that, as had been the case the last time we'd met here, the place had magically emptied when Scubberd and company entered.

Standing next to Scubberd was his bodyguard, a behemoth whose name, I recalled, was Minnis. We weren't on a first-name basis. There had previously been a second goon, a slimy, knife-wielding psychopath who had died on the front step of my apartment, a couple of bullet holes expertly placed in his upper torso.

But it was the third member of the threesome who exerted an almost mesmerizing presence, just as she had the first time I'd seen her. She was Mrs. Scubberd — I didn't know her first name either. She was beautiful, intelligent, and, as both Cobb and I had concluded, a whole lot more than a pretty face when it came to the decision-making process for the MFs.

She slid into the booth they would occupy. Minnis and Scubberd remained on their feet, both of them facing me, neither of them looking welcoming.

I willed my legs to move and took a couple of steps toward them.

"Hello," I said, "nice to see you again."

"No need for pleasantries, scribe. Especially when there isn't any goddamn truth in what you're saying. The real truth is either you are just leaving and this was a chance encounter, or you want to talk to me about something. Either way, there's nothing *nice* about it."

"You're right, I was hoping you might have a minute. I apologize if I'm interrupting your evening." I nodded in the direction of Mrs. Scubberd, whose chin moved downward maybe a millimetre.

"Where's your private-eye pal?"

"I'm flying solo this time around," I told him.

"Well, good for you. Now fuck off, because as a matter of fact, you *are* interrupting our evening." Scubberd moved a half step to the side to allow me to get by on my way to the door.

I nodded and walked past him a few steps, then stopped. I'd invested three nights of my time in this, and I figured I owed it to myself to try a little harder. I turned back to face him.

"It can't hurt to hear what I have to say, and I promise I'll be quick about it."

Scubberd grinned at me and turned first to the mammoth Minnis and then to his wife. Minnis was unmoving and silent, like a Downton Abbey servant gone rogue. Mrs. Scubberd studied me for a full minute while I tried to keep my face as emotionless as possible. I'm not sure how successful I was.

"Maybe we can give him a moment or two, Rock," Mrs. Scubberd said, in a voice and tone that belied her role as a biker's woman and wife of a big-time criminal. Cobb had thought she was a lot closer to the top of the gang's hierarchy than the bottom, and I remembered thinking at the time he might be right. Now I *hoped* he was right.

Scubberd pointed at the seat across from his wife. As I moved into the booth, Scubberd slid in next to her, while Minnis stood alongside the booth, his eyes never leaving my face and his presence always ominous.

"Let's hear it, scribe," Scubberd said.

I took a breath and was about to speak when a server I knew from my previous time at the diner arrived with a tray full of beer. Four beers in total.

"We'll only be needing three, Davy," Scubberd said.

"Rock, I think we should be hospitable," his wife said, in a voice as gentle as Minnis was violent.

I held up a hand. "I'm fine, really. It's not necess—"

Mrs. Scubbard smiled and stopped me midsentence. "I'd like very much for you to have a beer with us, Mr. ... it's Cullen, isn't it?"

"It is, yes. And I'd be honoured."

Davy set the fourth beer in front of me and left. The Scubberds and I poured our beer into large glasses. Minnis didn't move, and his eyes hadn't moved either. They were still on me. His beer sat on the table untouched.

Scubberd raised his glass. "To prosperity ... and a good story."

Mrs. Scubberd and I drank, and I set my glass down.

"Because that's what we're going to get, am I right?" Scubberd said. "You're a writer, and I'm guessing you've brought us a story."

I looked at Scubberd. "I'd like you to think about making a donation. To a homeless shelter."

Scubberd set his glass down and leaned forward just slightly. "You came in here soliciting a donation from me? Not even a loan, a donation. Are you fucking crazy?"

I figured I better keep talking if I wanted to walk out of there on my own. "There's a shelter not far from here that's going to have to close its doors if it doesn't get some money, and soon. It's a place where addicts are able to go for a bed, a shower, and a hot meal. Things are tough economically in Alberta right now. A lot of businesses — maybe not yours — but other ... uh ... kinds of businesses are struggling and can't support the charities and causes that they have previously. And government budgets are stretched to snapping point. This shelter has lost its funding. I figured you might want to help."

Scubberd was shaking his head in disbelief. "First of all, either you are the dumbest son of a douchebag alive, or you're crazy, flat-out fucking nuts. Now, which is it?" He didn't wait for the answer. "Wrap your head around this: The MFs are not corporate Calgary. We don't donate to charities, and we don't get tax breaks. We have our own formula for economic success. I'm going to assume you bumped your head earlier today and that's why you're here. And if you don't want it bumped again" — his eyes flicked briefly in the direction of Minnis — "then you need to get your sorry ass out of here."

I knew I would be pushing it to continue. But I hated the way he felt he could blow me off like some teenager asking for an increased allowance. "One of the things about your formula for economic success, Mr. Scubberd, is that there's a fair amount of what could be called *collateral damage*. You remember Clay Blevins, the kid we were all looking for after his father shot a couple of dealers? Clay ended up at that shelter. He was collateral damage who was able to get his life back in order. And so I was thinking it might be kind of appropriate if you were to offer to donate the amount of the shortfall the shelter is facing."

"Have you ever thought of trying to get work in comedy clubs? You could do stand-up and have people in freaking tears."

I didn't have an answer to that, so I took a long drink of the beer.

"Okay, keep me laughing, scribe. How much are we talking about?"

"Twenty-five thousand."

Scubberd's eyes bulged. "Twenty-five large. Is there a camera in here?" He looked around as if he were trying to spot it. Performing. "There's got to be a hidden camera in here. Nobody is crazy enough to walk in here, look me in the eye, and ask for a donation of twenty-five grand. Nobody."

"I'm not saying it's a small amount. In fact, I realize that's a sizable figure, but I'm guessing you can afford it. I'm also guessing that the money wouldn't mean nearly as much to you as it would to the people who run that shelter and the people who use it when it's minus twenty outside."

Scubberd had jabbed a finger in my direction throughout his speech. His face was red, and he was no longer thinking that my craziness was something to laugh at. He was pissed off, and I didn't think a pissed-off Rock Scubberd was likely to get me a solid rating on my next life insurance application.

There was nothing more I could say. He was right; I'd been stupid to think this could work. I reached in my pocket and pulled out two twenties and tossed them on the table. As I started to slide out of the booth, Mrs. Scubberd put her hand on her husband's arm.

"Rock, Mr. Cullen is a journalist. There have been times when having a journalist we could talk to might have been useful. There may be other times when having a member of the fourth estate, someone we can … work with, might be helpful."

I'm not sure what my face was conveying, but I know what I was thinking: *It isn't every damn day you hear a biker's lady, someone who is arguably a gangster's wife, reference the fourth estate.*

She looked at me. "Do you know how it works in our business, Mr. Cullen?"

I shrugged and waited for her to continue. She was dressed in much the same way she had been the only other time I'd met her: like a downtown executive. Her makeup was perfectly applied, and she was a striking woman. When she smiled — and that happened rarely — she became breathtakingly beautiful. She was smiling — slightly — now.

"Let me explain it to you," she continued. "Nothing is free. If my husband gives that shelter the money you're asking for, it means we're partners. Not us and the shelter. Us and *you.*"

"If I had the money, I wouldn't be talking to you." I wasn't sure why I said that or that it was relevant. But I said it anyway.

"Not money, Mr. Cullen. This isn't a loan. We won't be asking you to pay back the money. But we will require repayment. Do you understand what I'm saying?"

I thought hard about her words. "I understand."

"I don't know if my husband will decide to donate that money or not. But if he does, I want you to understand exactly how it works. Good night, Mr. Cullen. And thank you for the beer."

I pulled myself out of the booth. Minnis moved over just enough to let me by. Like boss, like underling. I didn't look back at them as I headed for the door and out into the rain, which felt a lot less pleasant than it had earlier.

EIGHT

It was just after two in the afternoon, and I was at the downstairs location, having just fielded two more responses to my *Herald* story: one from a woman who was certain that Ellie Foster had paid the price for her sinful ways and was "burning in hell as we speak," and the other from a guy named Max who claimed to be Ellie's husband. He'd married her when she was twenty-three, and they'd been together for four years before his heart was broken by her being kidnapped. He'd received a ransom note and had paid seventy-five thousand dollars, but Ellie had not been returned to him by "them thievin' bastards" and he was merely wanting to recover the seventy-five grand, because the last thing he'd want to do is profit from poor Ellie's misfortune.

"Ellie was twenty when she was taken, Max."

"Well, damn, my girl lied to me when we got married."

"Have a nice day, Max."

I heard the key in the front door and climbed off my stool. Kennedy had set down his suitcase and was hanging up his coat in the front closet when I got to the hall.

"Welcome back," I said.

"Thanks."

"I've got some coffee going in the kitchen. Want some?"

He hesitated, and I wondered if what he wanted most was for me to be out of his house. But finally he shrugged. "Yeah, sure. Thanks."

I poured a couple of cups, and we sat at the kitchen table. I'd already packed up my computer, CDs, and sports bag, and had them in one corner of the kitchen. Kennedy noticed.

"Eager to get out of here?"

I shook my head. "Eager to get back to my family," I said.

"I get that." He nodded, added milk to his coffee, and passed the carton to me.

"How did it go out there? I mean, under the circumstances." I wasn't sure how much he'd want to talk about his ex-wife's death.

"Under the circumstances? Okay, I guess."

Conversation flagged after that, and we drank coffee in silence.

"How about here?" he asked. "Any problems? Anything interesting?"

I shook my head again. "No problems. Not much interesting."

"Not much?"

I'd thought about whether to tell him about my nocturnal visit to the alley behind the murder house, decided I would. "You ever see anything over there late at night? Something that looks like a shadow, maybe?"

"What did *you* see?"

"Just that. The second night I was here, there was something, a movement, a shadow — hard to say — probably an animal, but I wasn't sure. I went over there, but I didn't see anything."

Kennedy stood up. "Let's take a look at the tape."

I led the way upstairs, found the tape from that night, and fast-forwarded it to when I'd seen whatever it was I'd seen. We watched it through three times.

"And you went over there," Kennedy said at last.

"Yeah."

He nodded, clearly thinking about what I'd shown him. "And?"

"Nothing. Not a sign of anyone or anything."

He watched me, thinking.

"You ever see anything like that?"

He took his time answering. "Yeah," he said finally. "A few times over the years. Just the last three years or so. Maybe half a dozen times total over that period. I've gone over there every goddamned time. Nothing."

"What did you conclude?"

"About the same as you … nothing. Maybe it was an animal, like you said. I just don't know. I've even gone over there a few nights and hidden out there, waiting for whatever it was to show up. Nothing happened on any of those nights."

I looked out the window over at the house and garage, the alley behind it. "Probably nothing."

"Yeah, probably." I wasn't sure if he sounded convinced or not.

"Guess I'll be on my way."

"Sorry you didn't get to finish your coffee. I guess I wanted to see —"

I held up a hand and smiled. "I drink too much of the stuff anyway."

We went back downstairs and I gathered my gear, headed for the front door, set my computer down.

He pulled out his wallet. I shook my head. "You don't need to do that."

"Yeah, I do."

I shook my head again.

"You mentioned family. You got a new lady? You know, since …" He looked at me, somehow more kindly than I'd seen before.

"Yeah, I do."

"I want you to take her for dinner. On me. At least let me do that." He offered a hundred-dollar bill. "I mean it."

I hesitated, then took it, realizing this was as much for him as for me. "I'll make sure she knows."

"Sure." The corners of his mouth turned up slightly — it was as close as I'd ever seen him come to smiling. "Thanks. I appreciate what you did here."

"You ever see that shadow again and figure out what it is, I'd like to hear about it."

"Sure," Kennedy said again. I wasn't sure he meant it. "By the way, I know your car now."

I wondered for a few seconds what he meant. Then I got it. If I drove down the alley again, as I had a number of times in the past, he'd know it was me. And wouldn't feel the need to hunt me down, thinking I might be Faith Unruh's killer.

For a few seconds I considered telling him about my adventure of the previous night. But only a few seconds. I knew his reaction would be fairly similar to my own: *What were you thinking?*

I shrugged into my jacket, nodded, and left Kennedy's house feeling a little weird. I'd spent most of the last couple of weeks in this house and wasn't sure whether I'd ever set foot in it again. No reason to, really. Yes, we were both interested in the same cold case, but it wasn't like I'd be dropping by for a beer and a chat about it. I got to the end of the walk and looked back at the house. A house that was a surveillance site for an obsessed ex-cop who hadn't let go. And never would.

There was part of me that was relieved to be out of there. But for another part of me, yeah, it felt weird.

I didn't go directly home. I needed to think. And ever since I got my first car at sixteen, driving through the streets of Calgary had allowed me to do that. I chose Joni Mitchell to background the thinking I wanted to do. First, because it seemed appropriate. And second, because I'd loved her music for pretty well ever.

I had no destination in mind. I started toward downtown, then changed my mind and rolled back south on Elbow Drive, past the old mansions I loved to look at and dream about. As I often did when I drove this route, I thought about the people who occupied those splendid homes with their often more splendid grounds.

What secrets did those magnificent walls shield? Because there *were* secrets. That thought brought me back to the reality of Faith Unruh and that strange, sad street. Every day motorists and pedestrians meandered past Kennedy's house, their casual glances yielding nothing of the story that unfolded every day between those walls. The former Unruh house was just a few doors down.

And, of course, there was the house across the street. *Stigmatized*, I had learned, was the real estate agent term for places where violent tragedies have taken place. Yet, almost none of the people passing would know about that tragedy. Too long ago. Long ago and long forgotten. By most, but not by all.

I forced my focus back to Ellie Foster — to her life, to her disappearance — and wondered where those secrets were buried. I wondered, too, whether Cobb and I would find them. *Could* find them.

I mentally noted some of the questions that were percolating in my mind, questions that, could we answer them, might lead us to her. I reviewed what I had learned so far, recapped the conversations in my mind. There were the questions that had to do with the minute or ninety seconds — it could hardly have taken longer — in back of The Depression. Did Ellie Foster say "Bastard" or "*You* bastard" as she was being forced into the car? And if it was "You bastard," did that mean she knew at least one of the men who had just shot her band members to death? And if she did know them, was it possible that she wasn't forced into the car at all, but actually went of her own volition? Which would make her a participant in the shootings. Then why, if she were part of what had happened that night, if she was actually in league with the killers, did she call him (or them) bastards?

Then there were the questions swirling around The Tumbling Mustard. What were the topics of those conversations that had taken place at the coffee bar? Who were the participants? And how did Ellie figure in to whatever was going on there — if, in fact, it was anything of consequence?

And then there was the CD. Why leave a CD of a song if its lyrics weren't significant? Were they left by Ellie as a kind of come-and-find-me plea? If so, why lyrics? Why not just a note saying "I'm alive and living in Wichita, Kansas. Please come and get me"?

But there *was* a CD. And there was also the thorny little matter of who had left it in the car.

I had continued south, eventually curving east on Canyon Meadows Drive, then north on Macleod Trail, heading back toward Stampede Park and downtown. I was still a few blocks from what older Calgarians still called "the Stampede Grounds" when I decided I'd worked myself into a foul mood and needed to do something about it.

I stopped at a bar, the Blind Beggar Pub, not because I was especially craving a beer, but mostly just to chill, maybe hear some music … or even snippets of conversation. I'd been to the place before and figured it would work for what I wanted. Some people around, but not a ton of noise.

Once settled at a back corner table, I tried to force thoughts of my meeting with the Scubberds into the back of my mind. Not easy, as the magnitude of what I'd done and what I may have opened myself up to became clearer.

I spent a half hour scribbling in my day planner and nursing a Big Rock Traditional. I read over what I'd written and realized I hadn't progressed much beyond my earlier doubts. I very much wanted to be able to tell Monica Brill what had happened to her grandmother, but I was less and less optimistic that we'd be able to do it. *Fifty years is just too damn long.* I looked up from my notes and realized I'd vented my frustration out loud. Two women with big hair and stern mouths were staring unhappily at me.

A check of my watch told me it was time to head home, get showered and changed for our dinner date and lyrics bee. I toasted the disgruntled ladies with the last of my ale and headed for the door.

We had congregated at the Chianti Café at the south end of Macleod Trail. It had become a favourite of Jill's and mine, and Cobb admitted he'd wanted to try the place for a long time. The pre-dinner conversation was light: Cobb's son Peter's school anecdotes, Kyla's laughter at what high school apparently held in store for her.

Cobb shook his head after his son's account of sneaking a Big Mac meal into math class and consuming the whole thing without once attracting the attention of the teacher.

"My son has not set the bar all that high in the area of academic performance."

"I'm passing everything, Dad."

"Remind me. Your last math mark was?"

"Fifty-eight percent," Peter replied, with only a trace of guilt.

"But I bet he's amazing in foods class," Kyla said, which dissolved all of us into laughter and earned her a high-five from Peter.

Dinner was a potpourri of fettuccine, lasagna, veal, spaghetti, and gnocchi, and all of it disappeared quickly amongst appreciative — and hungry — diners. The adults, without anyone actually suggesting it, limited ourselves to one glass of wine, all of us apparently aware that the lyrics puzzle would require full and clear-headed attention.

As we were waiting for the dessert — tiramisu all around — Cobb chuckled and cleared his throat. "Before we get down to the serious business of unlocking the secrets of the mystery lyrics, I should update you on another fascinating element in our investigation. Well, actually, Adam would be the best person to tell you about it. Adam, why don't you share with the group some of the more memorable moments from the tip line?"

If there had still been a knife on the table, I'd have plunged it into Cobb's heart, then pleaded temporary insanity. His suggestion was greeted by several voices. "Oh, yeah, tell us about it, Adam."

So I did. Bernie's calls were a big hit, especially with the younger diners, and I have to admit I did a pretty fair job of recreating Bernie's spectacularly annoying voice.

The dinner over and the table cleared, it was time to get down to what had brought us there. I had made copies of the lyrics and passed them around the table, even though some had already seen them and brought their copies with them.

"Okay," I said. "There's only one ground rule. And that is that there are no ground rules. No one needs to worry about saying or asking something stupid. The truth is, Mike and I have studied the hell out of the words on this page and have no idea what any of it means. So any and all suggestions will be welcome. I'll take notes so that we can keep track of people's ideas.

"And just so you know how it actually sounds, I recorded the song on my phone so you can all hear it." I played it for them twice. A few heads nodded, but no one spoke.

There was general nodding around the table, and everyone buried their heads for a few minutes, either seeing the words for the first time or refreshing their memories of what they'd seen before. Though I could damn near recite the thing by heart, I refreshed my memory.

Dream of a Dying

Summer sun. Summer fun. Some were done
They walked the gentle path
At first asking only that the wind and rain wash
their shaking hands
Stopping peace to fame
That person's name
Man at the mike ... so, so bad
But good at play
And always the sadness, the love over and over
The long man points and tells
An owl sits and stares, sound around and through
his feathered force
So much like the other place. And so different ...
Midnight. Not yesterday, not tomorrow. A time
with no day of its own
The last of sun. The last of fun. The last time won
They circle the windswept block
At first telling the youngest ones it's only a dream
See the balloons, hear them popping
Are they balloons?
No more the sadness, the hate over and over
The long man points and tells
An owl sits and stares, sound around and through
his feathered force
Midnight. Not yesterday, not tomorrow. A time
with no day of its own

For a while it looked like no one was going to say anything, perhaps nervous despite my pep talk about saying
something that made them look dumb.

Jill was the first to speak. "Okay, the first thing I looked at was the shaking hands in the third line. I asked myself what might cause shaking hands, and I came up with cold, fear, or anxiety, someone elderly, maybe with Parkinson's or something like it … or maybe they're shaking from working really hard, maybe lifting something. I ruled out cold, because the first line talks about summer sun."

"That's good," I said, and jotted down Jill's thoughts in the margin next to the third line. Then I looked up. "I'm still puzzling over that first line: *Summer sun. Summer fun. Some were done.* Other than the rhyme, what's the writer saying there?"

Lindsay Cobb frowned and tapped the paper with a pencil she'd dug out of her purse. "Sounds to me like something's going on — you know, like the Stampede — summer sun, summer fun.… Maybe the *some were done* is talking about people who are tired at the end of a long day of walking around looking at things or doing stuff at a fair, or something like it."

"That's good," I said. "Or maybe not a fair … something less, something with a *gentle path*?"

"Like the lake, a gentle path near the water?" Jill wondered.

"I don't know," Mike said. "I mean, that sounds like a possibility, but later there's a mention of balloons — sounds more celebratory than a day or weekend at the lake."

Jill nodded. "Good point. And it's raining, so maybe whatever it is, it's just a one- or two-day event, not like the Stampede, ten days long."

"Back in '65, the Stampede was just six days," I said, "but I see what you mean."

"*Stopping peace to fame. That person's name.*" Lindsay pointed at her page. "I wonder if whoever that person is might be important."

"I'll bet they are," Peter chimed in, the first of the kids to venture an idea. "I was reading a thing the other day about this really old song, 'You're So Vain.' You should know that one, Dad, it's from your era."

"Carly Simon," I said. "Which I guess makes me really old too." I grinned at Cobb, who was shaking his head.

"Anyway," Peter went on, "the song is about this really rich dude who is kind of a jerk to the chick and is totally in love with himself. She never says the guy's name, but the story I was reading said it was … oh, damn, I can't remember …"

"Warren Beatty," Jill said.

"Really?" I said. "I didn't know that."

"Guess that puts me in the really old club too," Jill chuckled. "Anyway, that's one theory."

"Sorry about the *old* remark — I was mostly talking about Dad," Peter said.

"I'll have to kill 'im." Cobb glared at his son, although I was pretty sure there was some smile in the voice.

"Peter may have something, though." I stared again at the words. "There is an implied person in here who could have some significance."

"*Stopping peace to fame.*" Cobb looked back at the lyrics. "Any ideas there?"

No one said anything for a while. Jill shook her head. "I've got nothing."

There was general shaking of heads around the table, as apparently everyone was experiencing the same difficulty with that section.

"*The man at the mike*? Thoughts there?"

"I wonder if the person whose name we don't have is the same person who's really bad at the microphone." Mike rubbed his chin and looked at me. I shrugged a noncommittal response.

Around the table there was pretty much the same universal lack of ideas.

I stared at the line on the page. "All we know is that he was really bad. Singer? Emcee? Or bad as in a total jerk? Hard to say."

The truth was, I was beginning to think that our family get-together might have been equally productive if we had been playing Scrabble. I knew people were trying, but it felt like one more nail in the coffin called the Ellie Foster case.

"That brings me to something else," Jill said. "I have two copies of the lyrics: the first one you gave me, and the one you handed out today. They're not identical."

"Yeah, I saw that, too," I said.

"There's one word that's different — maybe it's just a typo, or maybe it's not."

Everyone leaned a little closer to the table to see the two versions Jill had in front of her.

"Line six," she said, pointing to the page. "In this one it says, *That person's name*, but in the first one you gave me, it says, *That pearson's name*."

"Yeah, I saw that, too. Probably a typo," I said.

Cobb shook his head. "Maybe. Maybe not." He looked at Jill. "So you're thinking that Peter's unnamed person is actually named and the name is Pearson."

"That should make it easy," I said. "There can't have been more than a couple jillion Pearsons in Canada."

The group was suddenly stone-faced, and I knew my attitude was the cause.

"Sorry," I said. "Don't pay any attention to me. I'm just frustrated."

"One of those jillion Pearsons was a prime minister." The speaker was Cobb's daughter, Layne, who was only nine and until now had been concentrating on her phone. Peter looked at his little sister in something akin to amazement, apparently having concluded she would have nothing useful to contribute to the evening.

"You learned that in school? And *remembered* it?"

"We studied Canada in social studies. And yeah, I remembered it." She threw in a roll of the eyes to indicate her feeling for her brother at that moment.

"Lester B. Pearson," Kyla added. "I can't remember exactly when, though."

"On it," Pete said and bent over his tablet.

Cobb leaned forward, his brow furrowed. "I've got nothing on the love and sadness or the tall man pointing, but I'm wondering … *owl* in French is *hibou*."

"Le Hibou was the coffee house Ellie played shortly before the gig at The Depression," I explained to the group.

"Wow," Jill said. "That feels like it could be significant."

"Just a sec, I'm getting behind here," I said as I furiously scribbled notes.

After a couple of minutes, Lindsay Cobb mused, "And the thing about sound…. *Music* is sound."

"Damn, look at that," I said.

"What?" At least three of them said it at the same time.

"That next line." I pointed, actually excited about what we were doing for the first time. *"So much like the other place. And so different …* That could be The Tumbling Mustard."

"What's a Tumbling Mustard?" Kyla asked.

I gave them the Coles Notes version of what I'd learned about The Tumbling Mustard, including the comments from Paula Pendergast.

"*So much like the other place* — they were both places where music was played, but according to at least a couple of people, there were big differences, too."

Jill was nodding. "If that singer, Paula, is right, and it wasn't about the music like the other clubs were, could it have been about something else, maybe even something criminal? Maybe drugs? Or something else altogether?"

"Got it." Peter looked up from his device. "Lester B. Pearson, prime minister of Canada, 1963 to 1968."

"That one feels a little flimsy to me." I tapped the line on the paper and shot an apologetic look at Layne, who had gone back to her phone but was clearly listening. She shrugged in reaction to my doubts.

"It could just as easily be a typo and nothing more," I continued. "Or some songwriter or bartender or anybody named Pearson."

"Could be." Cobb nodded slowly.

"Or not," his wife added.

Cobb continued to nod. "Or not," he repeated. There was silence for a while as everyone bent to the task again.

"I saw a show on TV once," Kyla said. "It was about a school shooting somewhere in the United States. And I remember the reporter was talking to some of the kids after, and a couple of them said that at first they thought it was a bunch of balloons popping."

"I'm pretty sure I saw something like that once, too," Peter added.

"And asking *Are they balloons?* could be something like that" — Lindsay looked at her husband — "couldn't it?"

"*Telling the youngest ones it's only a dream.*" Jill spoke slowly, thinking as she formed the words. "Maybe there was something they saw that scared small children, and parents told them it was a dream? I don't know … I feel like I'm floundering, just trying to attach meaning to stuff I don't understand."

"Okay, let's look at what we've got." I looked down at my notes. "A summer event of some kind, maybe like a fair. It talks about summer sun and rain, so hard to figure that part.… We're told it's at a place with a gentle path. The two folk clubs in Ottawa — Le Hibou and The Tumbling Mustard — might play a role. And there are balloons, so that reinforces the idea of a festival or something like that, whether it's a one-day thing or longer. And the then prime minister may be mentioned, or he may not be. What am I missing?"

"So maybe Ottawa is a part of this," Cobb said. "Ellie played there not long before she came to Calgary, and we know she'd played there at least a couple of other times previously as well. And there might be a reference to Le Hibou in here, and maybe even The Tumbling Mustard. Feels like Ottawa could be important."

"And the prime minister lives and works in Ottawa," Lindsay Cobb noted. "So if it is Pearson who's talked about, yeah, Ottawa seems to be a theme in the lyrics."

"Just a sec," Peter said suddenly. "There was some-thing I saw in the thing about Pearson online. Let me check again."

"Okay, while he's checking, what else have we got? Balloons popping that could sound like gunshots. We've got a bad guy at the mike.… I wish we could piece some of it together so that it actually made sense."

"Whoa," Peter said.

"What?" Cobb looked at his son.

"So Lester B. Pearson was his name, right?"

There was a nodding of heads.

"Anyone want to guess what his nickname was?"

"Nobody wants to guess, Peter," Cobb said. "So forget the drama and give it to us."

"It was Mike." It wasn't Peter who said it, but Jill. "I don't know where that came from, but I remember that. Mike Pearson."

Peter looked crestfallen.

"The *man at the mike*?" Maybe a play on words?" Lindsay Cobb wondered.

"This whole thing feels like a play on words," I said.

"Maybe," Jill said. "Sorry, Peter. I didn't mean to steal your thunder."

Peter smiled. "It's okay, because I've got something else that might fit too."

"What is it, Peter?"

"That line, where is it — something about peace and fame?"

"It's right here," Kyla said. "*Stopping peace to fame*, right before *That person's* — or Pearson's — *name*, and then *Man at the mike … so, so bad*."

Peter nodded. "Pearson was famous before he became prime minister. Guess what for."

This time nobody spoke, letting Peter make his announcement.

"He won the Nobel Prize for Peace."

No one said anything for a while. Lindsay Cobb patted

her son's shoulder and nodded. Cobb finally said, "*Peace to fame* ... good job, Pete."

"So maybe it *is* Pearson," Jill said.

"Could be, but what *about* him?" Cobb sat back and stared at the ceiling.

"*Summer sun* and *summer fun* could be the Parliament Buildings," Lindsay said.

"Where I'm betting there are gentle paths," Jill added.

"You put it together, it sounds like an indictment of the prime minister that maybe ended with a shooting. An assassination attempt? Only trouble is, to my knowledge, nobody ever shot at Pearson," I pointed out.

"It would explain the *shaking hands* reference, though," Lindsay said. "Nerves."

"Except it didn't happen," I repeated. "Which means we could be totally off base."

"Let's set that aside for now," Cobb said. "There's something else here that's interesting. We know one of the shooters at The Depression was tall, and there's a mention of a tall man in the lyrics. And didn't Paula Pendergast tell you one of the guys who ran The Tumbling Mustard was tall?"

"Yeah." I nodded. "Laird. She said he was tall and skinny ... but, yikes, there are millions of tall guys. That really feels like a stretch."

Another period of silence followed. I looked around the table, and it looked to me like the kids and maybe a couple of the adults were fading.

"I say we wrap this up," I suggested. "We've made some progress here. Why don't we call it a night, sleep on it, and if anyone comes up with anything else, we all stay in touch."

Cobb looked from face to face. "You guys are amazing. I may have to hire all of you."

"Thanks, but this is as close to the action as I want to get," Jill said, laughing.

"Besides," I said, "you can't afford all of them and me too."

Cobb looked at me. "You're right, Adam." He reached out his hand. "I want to thank you for all your effort. See you around."

That had the whole table laughing, as I shook my head and finally laughed too.

The party, if that's what it was, broke up.

"Seeing as this is my last day as part of the Cullen and Cobb team, I've got the bill," I said.

"No, you don't." Cobb held out his hand, wanting the bill I'd already laid claim to.

"I insist. Besides, I came into some money today, so I'm good with this."

Cobb shook his head, continued to gesture for the bill.

"I'm serious," I said. "I'll tell you about it later."

He finally withdrew his hand. "Hell, if I'd known I'd get a free dinner out of it, I'd have fired you a long time ago."

I was the last one out to the parking lot, and when I got there everyone was in the two cars except Cobb.

"Thanks for the dinner," he said. "You didn't have to do that."

"Actually, I did," I said. "Kennedy insisted on it."

"Ah," he said, nodding. "This was useful. Hard to say *how* useful, but there are some things that came out of this that we need to talk about."

"Sure. When do you want to do that?"

"How about in the morning? My office. Say, ten?"

"See you then."

We shook hands, and I climbed into the Accord. Kyla looked like she was already asleep in the back seat.

I looked over at Jill. "Thanks for your help in there. You were amazing, which doesn't surprise me."

"Do you really think it was helpful?"

"Cobb does. We're going to talk about it in the morning. And yes, I think we're further along in attaching meaning to the lyrics than we were before."

"Good." She smiled at me with a glance over her shoulder at Kyla, who was definitely in dreamland. "I hope that means I've earned the right to have my way with you tonight."

"I believe that is a distinct possibility."

She pointed at the ignition.

"Home, James, and don't spare the horses."

When I got to Cobb's office, he was at his desk, staring again at the lyrics to the Ellie Foster song. He had a coffee on his desk, so I crossed to the coffee maker and Keuriged myself a cup.

I sat, took a couple of sips, and said, "What do you think?"

He looked up at me, and his eyes were narrow and red. I knew he hadn't slept much.

"What do you know about Lester B. Pearson?"

I shrugged. "Beyond what we learned in school and what was said last night? Not much. Although I seem to remember he was the big push behind Canada getting its own flag."

Cobb nodded. "I spent a lot of last night and this morning learning as much as I could about him."

"I thought research was my job."

"It is, and you're a lot better at it than I am, but I couldn't sleep and decided if anything could possibly make me drowsy, it would be delving into Canadian political history."

"Did it work?"

He laughed. "Yes, but regrettably not until about five-thirty this a.m."

"Thus, the coffee." I pointed.

"Thus, the coffee."

"Find anything interesting in your studies?"

"A few things. First of all, you were right — there was never any record of an attempt on Pearson's life."

"Pretty bland stuff back then?"

"Yes and no. Peter mentioned the Nobel Peace Prize that Pearson won."

"Before he became prime minister."

Cobb nodded, sipped coffee. "Feel like a history lesson?"

"Professor Cobb." I grinned. "It has a nice ring to it." I leaned back, coffee cup in hand. "Hit me."

"Pay attention; there's a test." He smiled, then turned serious. "First of all, the Suez Canal links the Mediterranean Sea to the Red Sea. It was built by Egyptian workers, but it was owned by the Suez Canal Company, which was itself jointly owned by the British and the French. The canal opened in 1869, and it was a big deal as a main transportation artery for … guess what."

"Oil," I said.

"You just might ace this course. The canal was a vital route for oil travelling to Britain. So now let's fast-forward to the mid-twentieth century. By the 1950s, things were a little complicated in the world. You had the Cold War going on between the United States and Russia; there was growing Egyptian dissatisfaction with the two Imperialist powers — Britain and France — and, of course, there was the ever-present Arab-Israeli strife going on. Nasser was the president of Egypt, and he was worried that Britain was trying to increase its influence in the region by establishing closer ties with Iraq and Jordan and would use that as a way of controlling Egypt. So Nasser did a couple of things. First, he bought a huge quantity of arms from Russia in the fall of 1955, and then in 1956, he seized the Suez Canal. Obviously, this was a major headache for Britain."

He paused and looked at me for some kind of validation.

I nodded and said, "With you so far."

Cobb glanced down at his notes, but it was clear he didn't need them. "I'm not going to go into all the reasons for Nasser doing this — it's not important for our purposes — but clearly the political problems in the area were instantly amplified. So Great Britain, France, and Israel launched an attack on Egypt, wanting to take back control of the canal and oust Nasser from power. A couple of little problems. They neglected to inform the United States of the plan, and the Soviet Union, wanting to back up their guy, Nasser, threatened to use nuclear weapons."

I sipped some of my coffee, nodded. "I remember some of this, but not well and not in detail."

"I'm going to keep this as short as I can," Cobb said.

"You're doing fine," I told him. "I'll let you knew when I get bored."

"Okay, so the invasion was a big success militarily but a nightmare diplomatically. Instantly there was a big-time rift between the U.S. and Great Britain, and there was a worry that the action would drive the rest of the Arab world into the welcoming arms of the Soviet Union. Enter Lester B. Pearson, who was at the time the Canadian secretary of state for external affairs. He'd already served as president of the United Nations General Assembly in 1952, so he was a player on the international stage. He managed to get the United Nations to agree to form a United Nations Emergency Force and send it to the region to settle things down and separate the warring parties. This allowed Britain, France, and Israel to ease their way out of the conflict — and the area — without losing face. Essentially peace and stability were restored, and Pearson was awarded the Nobel Peace Prize for 1957."

"Let me guess," I said. "Even though things cooled down somewhat, there were leftover hurt feelings and pissed-off folks all over the place."

"Of course. The British prime minister had to resign, the French and Americans didn't trust each other for decades after that, and Arab-Israeli tensions were ratcheted up several notches. Even in Canada, there were people who weren't happy with their own Nobel winner because they felt he and the government had abandoned Mother England in her time of need. So, yes, there were lots of grudges that carried on for a long time."

I scratched my chin and thought about what Cobb had said.

"And you think there might have been motivation in this long-simmering anger that could have led some individuals or groups to want to do something — if not assassinate the PM, at least do something to make a statement?"

Cobb shrugged. "It's possible. And one more thing. Pearson's crowning glory, the new Canadian flag, was unveiled in February 1965."

I whistled. "And Ellie Foster disappeared in February 1965."

Cobb said, "It's entirely possible that the two are totally unrelated and all my overnight reading was a pleasant exercise in learning some Canadian history and nothing more."

"Why is it I have a feeling you don't believe a word of what you just said?"

Cobb shrugged, drank some coffee, and made a face.

"Cold?"

"Ice cold." He set the mug down, glared at it like it was at fault, then looked up at me. "It would damn sure help give this whole thing some meaning if there was a connection between Ellie's disappearance and that section in the song."

"Can't argue that." I sat and watched Cobb as he gathered up the pages of notes he'd written throughout the night. When the stack of paper was relatively neat, I said, "So what's next?"

"Next?" He stood up. "Next, we walk over to Red's for breakfast. And we think and we talk … and maybe we plan."

Red's Diner was about four blocks from Cobb's office, and the walk seemed to revive Cobb at least a little. We studied the menu for a couple of minutes. I went with eggs Benny, and Cobb opted for chorizo hash and eggs. We were only a couple of bites in when Cobb set his knife and fork down and looked hard at me.

"Am I crazy on this thing?"

"Depends on which thing you're asking about."

"I keep asking myself the same damn questions. I'm sick of the questions, and I'm even sicker of my non-answers."

"The key question being the importance of the lyrics?"

He nodded. "They *have* to matter. Don't they? And another question. I'll throw this one to you. Did last night's family gathering amount to nothing more than a fun parlour game to pass the time while our dinner digested, or did we learn something? Did we actually figure out some stuff?"

"Valid questions, and pretty much the same ones that have been rolling around in my head as well. Unfortunately, the questions — that's the easy part. Answers are a little tougher."

"Humour me," Cobb said. "Throw some answers out there."

"Well," I said slowly, "I agree that there has to be some significance to the song. I might be less convinced than you are that it's a key element in our investigation. But let's assume it is — because you're right in asking why someone would have placed the CD in Monica Brill's car if it didn't matter.

"But whether we broke new ground last night — who the hell knows? There was a good discussion and some really creative ideas being thrown around. And obviously it led to some interesting historical research. But I don't know if we're any closer to knowing what happened to Ellie Foster. I just don't know that."

Cobb looked at me for a while, then picked up his knife and fork and went back at the food. But it didn't look to me like his heart was in it. And sure enough, half a dozen bites later, he pushed the plate aside and pulled out a notebook and a pen.

"You keep eating," he told me. "I just want to jot down a couple of things."

"Okay," I mumbled between bites. "Feel free to verbalize."

"Let me throw out a theory … actually, a bunch of theories I've woven together to suggest a direction we might want to pursue."

"Okay, go ahead."

"Here's the thing. I'm making a lot of assumptions, and I know some of them are shaky. But I'm just trying to construct even one possible scenario for us to kick around."

I shrugged, mostly because I wasn't sure what I was supposed to say.

"So, first of all, let's assume that Ellie knew her abductors, that the 'You bastard' was directed at a person or persons known to her. And let's assume that the two band guys who were shot that night were collateral damage. Wrong place, wrong time. We know that one of the shooters was tall. So now we've got two guys, and Ellie being forced into a car that is leaving the back alley behind The Depression. We have to ask ourselves why. I see this as a well-orchestrated abduction required having someone in the club — either one of the kidnappers or an accomplice — let the bad guys know when Ellie went outside for a smoke."

He stopped and raised an eyebrow to invite a response.

"Go on," I said.

"So let's go back to why. I find any suggestions that involve jealous or desperate lovers, no matter how enchanting Ellie Foster may have been, to require more of a leap of faith than I'm prepared to make. And we know it wasn't a robbery. There was never a ransom demand, so that rules out the most common reason for kidnapping — financial gain. That takes us down some less-travelled roads."

He paused as the server came by with a coffee pot in hand. She eyed Cobb's abandoned food. "Was there anything wrong with your breakfast, sir? I can get you something else, or —"

Cobb held up a hand. "The food was great. I'm sorry, I'm just not hungry, but please tell whoever prepared this that there was absolutely nothing amiss with the food."

The server smiled. "Thank you. I'll be sure to do that," she said. "More coffee for you, gentlemen?"

"Please," Cobb said, and I nodded.

After she'd gone, I said, "I'm guessing one of the less-travelled roads you see us travelling down has a political overtone to it."

Cobb nodded, a little more animated now. "It was a time of political upheaval. I came across another note last night. February 11, 1965, Malcolm X was killed. I'm not suggesting there's any connection with this case, but I am saying it indicates the kind of political ... I don't know if *turmoil* is the right word, maybe *turbulence* ... anyway, there was a lot going on."

"And you think there might have been some political element behind what happened to Ellie Foster?"

He shrugged. "I don't know for sure, but there are two strands of this I keep coming back to that I can't help but feel *are* interconnected: the song lyrics and The Tumbling Mustard."

I thought about that. *The same two things I keep coming back to.* I finally nodded. "Seems like a pretty good bet."

"And I think we took a pretty good run at the lyrics last night," he continued. "And it felt like they were maybe pointing to a political thread in there somewhere. Which brings us back to …?" He stopped talking and looked at me.

"The Tumbling Mustard."

"Bingo."

"That might be a bit of a challenge," I said.

"Understood," Cobb agreed. "But you've already made some progress there, in your conversations with the guy from Le Hibou and the singer from Saskatoon."

I didn't answer but thought back to my conversations with the two of them. As far back as my first chat with Paula Pendergast, I remember thinking that The Tumbling Mustard might be worth concentrating on.

"How would you feel about taking another run at them?"

"Sure." I shrugged. "Anything in particular I should be concentrating on?"

"I'm not sure. We know a little more now than we did when you first talked to them. How about you just see what else you can find out? And see if you can get us a few more names — staff, performers, regular customers — anybody else we can talk to."

"Got it." I pulled out my own notebook and dashed off a few notes.

"Meantime, I'm going to see if I can find out anything from any of the law enforcement folks down there. I realize all the cops will be retired or deceased, but maybe I can find someone in Ottawa who might recall something. If there was anything that had a political feel to it — especially something that smelled a little bad — there ought to be some records somewhere."

"So you're saying The Tumbling Mustard is our focus for now."

Cobb nodded. "And I'm saying that for two reasons: First, I have a feeling there's something there. And second, we've got bugger-all else."

"Both excellent reasons," I said.

The Saskatoon Princess picked up on the third ring. After we exchanged hellos and she brought me up to speed on the weather situation in Wanham, I decided to get right to it.

"Paula, I was wondering if you'd thought any more about The Tumbling Mustard since our first conversation."

"Actually, I haven't thought about much else. See what you did?"

"Sorry about that." I chuckled. "Come up with anything that might help us with our investigation?"

"I don't know for sure if it's helpful, but there was one more thought I had, something I remembered."

"Go on."

"I recall that there was a rather nasty argument one night. I was there as an audience member, and I've tried to remember who was playing, but I'm just not sure. But the discussion was loud and quite unpleasant, as I recall."

"Do you remember who was arguing?"

"It was Fayed and Laird — I'm sure it was both of them — and they were yelling at some guy. I thought at first they just wanted him out of there, that maybe he was drunk and bothering people or something, but it wasn't anything like that, as I remember."

"What was it, then?"

"I'm not sure. The only thing I really remember was the guy yelling 'This is bullshit! It's all bullshit!' And the only reason I remember that much is that there was an emcee guy there that night, and after the argument was over he stepped up to the mike and said, 'And now let's get back to the music. Here's (whoever it was) with a special rendition of that old favourite, "Bullshit."' It was pretty good — brilliant, actually — because it got people's minds back on the music and off the unpleasantness."

"And you don't know who it was they were arguing with?"

"No, I didn't know him."

"You ever see him in there before that?"

"I don't think so, but I can't say for sure. I wouldn't have taken notice of everybody who came and went from there — even when I was performing."

"Of course not," I said. I thought about what else I could ask her.

"I guess it's not much," she said. "I mean, it could have been a bad cup of coffee, or the guy not liking where he'd been seated. It could have been a lot of things that didn't matter at all."

"Or it could be something significant, and I thank you for sharing it with me. One more thing, Paula. Can you remember any other names besides Fayed and Laird? Anybody at all — staff, performers, people in the audience, anybody we might be able to talk to?"

"Are you thinking the place might be important?"

"I don't know that, Paula, I really don't. But we'd like to find out all we can about it."

"Names," she said. "I should be able to come up with

one or two at least. Can you let me work on it for a couple of hours?"

"Of course I can. How about I call you back?"

"I'll look forward to it. And I hope I can do some good."

"We'll be happy with whatever you're able to put together. Goodbye, Paula."

I had some time, so I pulled a Rolling Rock from the fridge and sat for a while enjoying the view outside my living room window. It wasn't an amazing view, but I was especially appreciative after spending over a week in Kennedy's house, where the only views were of two houses forever linked to a violent tragedy.

I went over everything I knew about The Tumbling Mustard, and after twenty minutes realized it wasn't a hell of a lot. Two guys: one tall, one maybe Middle Eastern and muscular. Discussions at the bar during and around the performances onstage in a place that, according to Paula Pendergast, was not all about the music like most other coffee houses. And Ellie Foster seemed changed in a negative way after her time there. That was it.

It wasn't much. I opened a second beer and pushed Rose Cousins's *We Have Made a Spark* into the CD player. I flipped open my Day-timer and found the number for Armand Beauclair, the guy who had been an assistant manager at Le Hibou for a time.

I was on a roll. He picked up even faster than Paula Pendergast had. I thought this was a bit of a long shot, that he'd be unlikely to tell me much more than he already had. But, of course, the truth was we didn't have a lot of hot leads on a club that had sprung up, lingered, then fizzled out all in about eighteen months, as near I could figure.

"Armand? Adam Cullen. We talked a while back about Le Hibou."

"Of course. How can I help you?" A bit formal, maybe unhappy at my calling again.

"During our previous conversation, you mentioned The Tumbling Mustard."

"Yes, I did."

"We're just trying to get a better handle on the place, and I wonder if you can remember anything else, anything you didn't think of until after my earlier call. Or even any names, people I could call and chat with."

"Christ, that was a half century ago."

"I know I'm asking a lot," I agreed, "but if there's anything at all that comes to mind, it just might help."

He didn't say anything, and I wasn't sure whether he was thinking or waiting for a prompt from me.

"How about the owners?" I prompted. "Anything more on them? Fayed and another guy, real tall, skinny. Name of Laird, Cameron Laird."

Still Beauclair said nothing, at least for another minute or so.

Finally, he cleared his throat and spoke: "You know how it is. You hear stuff. You're in the same business, and naturally, I guess, people think you're interested, so, yeah, I'd hear rumours from time to time."

"What kind of rumours?"

"Oh, just that the two guys who ran the place weren't real solid citizens, that maybe there was some shady stuff going down in the place."

"Shady stuff," I repeated. "Anything specific?"

"God, I can't remember now. Back then you'd think it might have been drugs, but I can't say for sure if that was it."

"You ever hear of anything subversive going on at the TM?"

"The TM," he repeated. "Wow, I'd forgotten that's how people used to refer to it. Subversive … subversive how?"

"I don't know," I admitted. "I mean, it was a time of protest. Any of that protest get to be more than just songs and talk?"

A pause. "I can't say one way or the other. Like I said, I was busy helping run our own place. I didn't have the time or, frankly, the interest in what was happening in Little Italy."

"Where exactly in Little Italy was it?"

"On Preston — not far from Dow's Lake. There's something else there now. Actually, I think there's been a few different businesses in that spot since the TM. Maybe it jinxed that location." He chuckled.

"Yeah, maybe."

"Sorry I couldn't be more helpful, but I'm glad you guys are still working on finding Ellie. It must be tough."

"Damn tough," I admitted, "but I appreciate your help once again."

After ending the call with Beauclair, I still had a little over an hour before I was to call Paula Pendergast. I didn't want to rush her and have her miss a possible contact. I decided that, rather than sit and wait for the minutes to tick by, I'd have another go at the Ottawa newspaper. After all, my last search had yielded the *Saskatoon Princess*.

I grabbed my jacket and cellphone, jotted Paula's number on a piece of paper, stuffed it in my pocket, and headed for the Accord. Twenty minutes later I was once again settled at a table at the downtown library, scrolling through automated pages of fifty-year-old *Ottawa Citizens*.

I looked at countless stories, checked Entertainment pages, and flipped through ads — all to no avail until about five minutes before I was to call Paula. I stumbled across something by sheer accident.

I'd confined much of my search to the Entertainment section and had found no mention of The Tumbling Mustard. But as I was scrolling through papers pre-dating the place's existence, I happened to see a small story not in Entertainment, but in the Lifestyle section of the June 19 edition. The three-paragraph piece talked of a new coffee house opening soon in Little Italy. The place was to be called The Tumbling Mustard, and the owners planned to compete for the best folk and blues acts in the business.

But what was of particular interest to me was that there were *three* owners mentioned — Laird, Fayed, and a third man, Daniel Gervais, who at the time was a successful movie theatre operator in Ottawa and nearby Hull.

Silent partner? Folk music lover? And why hadn't his name shown up previously? I had no idea. I did an online search, got nothing, and called Paula Pendergast.

"I did come up with one name," she told me, after we had exchanged greetings. "Real nice guy — Ben Tomlinson," she offered, with more than a trace of pride in her voice. "He was the doorman."

"Doorman? At a folk club?"

"I know, right?" Paula said. "It was weird, the only place I ever played that was like that. There was this little portable box office thingy outside the front door. People bought tickets and then they'd go inside. The doorman, Ben, would tear their tickets. It was more like going to a movie."

Going to a movie.

"Any idea where I might find Ben?"

"That's what's so cool. I did a search and found a mention of him on an obscure little website called Seniors: The Circle of Life. It contains information on taking care of elderly family members. The site looks like it's been inactive for a really long time, but there was a list of board members for 2008 to 2009. And there was Ben's name — if it's the same Ben Tomlinson. I think it might be, because he was still living in Ottawa at that time in what sounds like Gloucester. And I even found a phone number for him."

"Did you call him, Paula?" I hoped the answer was no. I didn't really want my call to be announced.

"No, I wasn't sure the number would still be valid. And I thought I'd better leave that to you."

Good girl. She recited the number, and I jotted it down in my notebook.

"One more thing, Paula. You ever hear of somebody named Daniel Gervais?"

A pause while she thought about it. "No, I don't think so. I don't recall that name. Should I have heard of him?"

"I read a report that he might have been a third owner of The Tumbling Mustard — along with Laird and Fayed."

Another pause. "If he was, I don't remember him. And I'm sure I'd remember one of the owners if I'd ever met him — they're kind of important to performers."

"I understand," I said.

"But maybe Ben can help you with that."

"Maybe he can," I agreed. "And thanks for this, Paula. You've been tremendously helpful again. This is much more than I'd asked you to do, and I won't forget it."

"I just hope it helps, Adam. Do you feel you're getting any closer?"

"Depends on what time of day you ask me."

"I'm sure there must be frustrations."

"A few," I admitted. "But you've been great," I said again.

We ended the call, and then I phoned Armand Beauclair, who informed me he'd never heard of Daniel Gervais. This time I was sure Beauclair was getting tired of hearing from me.

Next, I called Cobb.

"I've got a new name, but beyond the name I haven't got much else." I told him about Gervais's name being mentioned prior to the opening of The Tumbling Mustard.

"Maybe he dropped out of the deal before the place opened," Cobb suggested, "and was never a player."

"That's absolutely possible, but I'm not sure we should blow the thing off without checking, if we can."

"I agree," Cobb said. "Leave it with me. I'll make some calls."

"Okay, and while you're doing that, Paula gave me the name of the doorman: Ben Tomlinson, possibly still living in Ottawa. She also dug up an old phone number for the guy. Or at least for a guy with that name."

"Maybe we should hire the Saskatoon Princess full-time."

"So far, she's at least as effective as the journalist guy you've got working for you."

"Feeling sorry for yourself doesn't look good on you, my friend."

"Point taken. Let me see if I can reach Tomlinson."

We rang off, and I stared at my computer screen for a while, willing it to start flashing clues. Cobb was right.

I had been feeling sorry for myself and was becoming a pain in the ass — even to myself.

Except, of course, what I was feeling was more self-blame than self-pity, my ill-conceived Faustian arrangement with the MFs never out of my mind. More and more, I was hoping they'd just let it drop and not follow up on my requested donation to the Let the Sunshine Inn. And, more and more, I was convinced that was not going to happen. I repeatedly had to force myself to concentrate on what I should be doing and not what I almost certainly should *not* have done.

I called the number Paula had given me, struck out, tried 411, and was given another number for a Ben Tomlinson. I tried that number, got a man's voice mail, and left a brief message saying I was freelancing a story about Ellie Foster and would like to talk to Ben Tomlinson, if this was his number, about his time at The Tumbling Mustard. It was the old fallback lie, but I wasn't comfortable talking about our investigation on the voice mail of a man I didn't know.

I decided to call Jill next.

"Hey," I said. "Miss me?"

"More every day. And just so you know, there are two of us over here who feel that way."

"Actually, that's what I was calling about."

"Oh?"

"Listen, I feel like I haven't been there for either of you guys lately. I spend ten days or whatever it was at Kennedy's house, then I swing back into this case full bore. I wouldn't be a bit surprised if the pair of you have started to wonder about your choice of male companion."

"You're not serious."

"Actually, I am. The last time we did anything that could be categorized as fun was … hell, I can't even remember. I mean, Kyla has Crohn's disease, for God's sake, and I bet it's been days since I even asked how she's doing, and —"

"Hold it right there, mister." The laughing lilt that was almost always in Jill's voice was gone for the moment. "First of all, I think it should be up to Kyla and me to decide if we're feeling neglected. And we're not. You've been wonderful to both of us, and Kyla adores you. So get all the really dumb thoughts out of your head. We both know you've been busy, and we're making a list of all the things you're going to have to do to make it up to us right after you find Ellie Foster."

"Yeah," I said.

"What's going on, Adam? This doesn't sound at all like you."

I wanted so badly to tell her about what I'd done, my ill-thought-out approach to the MFs. But, of course, I couldn't do that. Instead, I said, "It's been fifty years, Jill. I'd give anything to find her, or at least be able to say what happened to her, but it just seems so …"

"Wasn't last night helpful? I thought we —"

"Last night was totally helpful," I said, cutting her off. "You guys were all amazing. It's not that. It's just … I don't know what it is."

"Sounds like a good old-fashioned case of the blues to me. Is there anything I can do?"

I sat up. "Yeah, actually there is. You can let me come over and barbecue up some burgers and tell me how great they are after we've eaten them."

"Deal."

"And then you and your daughter will be crushed by yours truly in the game of your choice."

"Hey, we're good, but we can't do the impossible here."

"Ha ha."

I hadn't even set my phone down when it rang again.

"What, you've already decided which game will establish my male superiority?"

"It's Kennedy."

"Sorry," I mumbled. "Thought you were somebody else."

"No shit. That's why they have caller ID."

"For the record, that's not why they have caller ID. How can I help you, Marlon?"

"You got any time today? I have a couple of things I'd like you to see."

I thought about whether I wanted to spend any time with Marlon Kennedy today. If Jill was right and I had the blues, Kennedy was very capable of turning blue to black. But if he had something to share on the Faith Unruh case, I didn't want him running off and doing something impulsive, then saying, *I called, but you didn't have time for me.*

"I can be there in an hour."

"Good. Except not here. I'll buy you a beer at the Rose and Crown. You know it?"

"I know it. I'll see you there."

NINE

I had some time and was still feeling the invariable lift I got from talking to Jill. I decided I could face what Cobb called the *tip line* and what I called the *phone messages from hell*. This time there were twenty-one messages, three deserving of callbacks. The good news was that Bernie had apparently taken the day off.

The first two callbacks netted me nothing I didn't already know. The third call was to someone named Alfie Keller. He picked up after two rings.

"Adam Cullen, Mr. Keller. You left a message that indicated you might have some information concerning the disappearance of Ellie Foster."

"Yes, I did."

"I appreciate the call, sir. Why don't you tell me what you know?"

"I was at The Depression that night."

I sat up. Interested but cautious. I'd had big first lines from callers before — *I saw the getaway car*; *I saw Ellie arguing with two guys the afternoon of her kidnapping*; *Ellie and I were lovers* — but in every case, the statement proved to be false.

So this could go nowhere. But better to be ready.

"What night was that, Mr. Keller?"

"February 28, 1965. I was a big fan of Ellie Foster's. Sat through her shows maybe ten or twelve times between that last string of gigs and the one before it."

Promising.

"What can you tell me about that night, Mr. Keller?"

"I don't know if I can tell you anything useful, but I thought I should at least call to see if I could help somehow. It was terrible that she disappeared like that, but to still be missing … or … after all this time, it's horrible beyond belief."

"I agree, Mr. Keller. Were you there by yourself, sir?"

"I *was* by myself that night, actually. Most of the time there were three of us — a couple of my buddies usually came along — but that night I guess they were busy or something, I can't honestly remember, but I do remember being by myself that night."

"Go on."

"Well, *by myself* is probably not totally accurate. It was a friendly place, so after a few minutes you were usually in conversation with someone — between sets, I mean. You know, it was just a really social atmosphere in there."

"You remember any of the conversations that night?"

"I don't know. There were probably lots of them. I remember trying to chat up this girl, but she was three or four years older than me. I was eighteen, and when she found out how old I was she couldn't get rid of me fast enough. I remember that because back then I was kind of a strikeout artist, not much luck with girls, so I remember her as sort of another brick in the wall." He followed the admission with what sounded like a laugh of embarrassment.

"I've been there, believe me," I said, knowing self-deprecation was never a bad thing when wanting to win the confidence of an interviewee. "You remember any other conversations from that night?"

"Conversations, no. But I remember that was the night I almost got in a fight with a couple of guys. Well, one guy, anyway."

"What was that about?"

"I'd just got a coffee, and this guy kind of ran into me, which was no big deal. It was pretty crowded in there that night because both Ellie and Joni Mitchell were performing."

"Except she wasn't Joni Mitchell back then, was she?"

"Nope … Joni Anderson. I think it was a year or two later she got married."

You just passed the test with flying colours, Mr. Keller.

"Okay, so this guy jostles you. I imagine he caused you to spill your coffee."

"Knocked it right out of my hand. The reason I remember that was because this cup smashes to smithereens on the floor, and I look up, and who's standing there looking at me like I've got dog shit on my shoes but the girl I'd been trying to move on earlier.

"Anyway, the guy was pretty big, which, by the way, I'm not, and if he'd said 'Excuse me' or 'Sorry about that' — anything — I would have left it alone. But first he looked at me about the same way the girl had been, and then he told me to watch the fuck where I was going, or words to that effect. I think I'm pretty close."

"When you say he was a big guy, Mr. Keller, what do you mean? Football player big, lots of muscles, what?"

"No, that was the other guy. This guy was tall but not much for physical presence. But just an ignorant prick, you know what I mean?"

"I do, yes. So what happened after that?"

"Nothing. Some people got between us, and his friend, the dark guy, pulled him away, and that was it."

"Dark guy?"

"Yeah, I don't know — sort of foreign — Arab or something."

"And he was the football-body guy?"

"I don't know about football, but he was pretty big — tough-looking. I was glad it wasn't him who had knocked my coffee on the floor."

"And you remember all this fifty years later."

"I guess it's kind of like you remember where you were on 9/11, or when Kennedy was assassinated — stuff like that. If Ellie Foster hadn't been kidnapped and those guys shot out behind The Depression that same night, I might have forgotten about it by now. And, of course, I had to go through it with the cops a few times, so that kind of set it in my mind a little firmer, maybe."

"So tell me about that, Mr. Keller."

"The cops part?"

"Yeah, that part."

"Well, after we found out what had happened outside, there was a lot of milling around in there. I wouldn't call it panic, but pretty close. Then the cops showed up — they got there pretty fast, really — and nobody could leave after that. They questioned all of us. We were there for a really long time."

"Did you see the two guys you had the altercation with? Were they still there when the questioning was happening?"

"I don't remember seeing them, but that doesn't mean they weren't there. Although I did hear that quite a few people hauled ass out of there when they heard about the shooting and stuff."

"Mr. Keller, would you have time to meet me? I'd like to chat further, and maybe it would be better if we could talk face to face."

"Yeah, I guess that would be okay."

"Any chance you could meet my partner, too? He's the detective; I just do research, and I'd really like for him to chat with you."

"Sure, if you think it would help at all. You think there's anything I've told you that might be useful?"

"I can't say, Mr. Keller. But I think it would be helpful if you talked with Mike Cobb."

We set up a time for the next morning at the Good Earth at Glenmore Landing in the south part of the city. After the call ended, I gathered keys, phone, and wallet and headed for my Accord, which was parked behind my apartment at a neighbour's, who had kindly rented me space in his backyard.

I didn't often use the space — even less so since Kennedy had taken me down and threatened to kill me some months earlier. Most of the time, I just parked on the street. Now as I got to the car I looked over my shoulder, a habit that had developed after the unpleasantness with Kennedy.

The remastered two-CD edition of Glass Tiger's *The Thin Red Line* did two things: it made the time pass more quickly as I made my way downtown to the Rose and Crown and it improved my mood even more. I was already feeling somewhat buoyed by my conversation with Alfie Keller. I hoped my impending meeting with Kennedy wouldn't undo Glass Tiger's good work.

He was at a back table on the second level of the pub, laptop already on the table and fired up.

I'm not sure why that surprised me — maybe I somehow thought his technological expertise applied to surveillance equipment only. In any event, he looked up at me and moved the chair on the opposite side of the table to a spot on the side, I assumed so I could see whatever it was he had ready.

But before I could say anything, he waved to a young server who looked like she was a regular at a gym somewhere.

"Bud Light for me. What are you having?" Kennedy asked.

"Same," I said, and she disappeared down the steps to the main floor.

"What have you got?" I looked at the computer.

"Wait till she brings the beer." Kennedy held up a hand. "No sense starting and having to stop right away."

The buff server was back quickly, and I had my wallet out when she arrived.

"No, no, no," Kennedy objected. "My invitation. My bill."

"Wrong," I said. "You were far too generous with my staying at your place, so this is on me."

He looked like he wanted to argue further but also wanted to get on with whatever it was he wanted me to see. So he nodded to the server. I paid, and she headed off to see to the needs of three young guys a couple of tables away who looked and sounded like they were getting ready for a large night.

Kennedy held up his beer. "Cheers."

"*Skol*," I said.

We drank, set our glasses down, and Kennedy swung the computer around to face me. He clicked the mouse once, and I was back looking at the garage and alley behind the house where Faith Unruh's body had been found. Same scene I had looked at for ten days and nights at Kennedy's house. I leaned forward and concentrated hard on what I was seeing, which for about forty-five seconds was nothing.

Then it changed. Something fleeting. A shadow? It was as if a portion of the screen had grown darker, then the dark patch moved across the screen from right to left, starting from up the alley a bit and then moving toward the yard and garage. I strained hard, almost hurting my eyes, willing them to see something more. But the shadow was gone, and there was nothing else.

"That's it? I showed you this the night you got back."

Kennedy shook his head. "Uh-uh. This is from last night." He clicked the mouse a couple more times. "*This* is what you showed me."

Another piece of tape played, and it was virtually identical to what I'd just seen. Then he played both pieces again, back to back.

"What do you think?" I said.

"I want to know what *you* think."

"I don't know. They're so similar, it's hard to imagine an animal doing exactly the same thing, almost taking the same steps."

"But not impossible. I told you I'd seen that same thing a few times before. I went back and looked at those tapes, too. And it's like watching a replay over and over — almost no variation."

"Did you go over there last night?"

"Yeah. Nothing. Just like the other times."

"Hard to figure," I said. "I wish I had some idea what it is that's making that shadow, or whatever the thing is. But I just don't."

"Yeah, well, that makes it unanimous."

"I mean, all these years later — you said it's happened only in the last two, three years — it's hard to believe that it could have anything to do with the murder of Faith Unruh."

"But again, not impossible."

"No, not impossible."

"There's one more thing." He tapped away at the computer and after a few seconds angled it again for me to see. "Recognize that?"

I didn't at first and shook my head.

He enlarged the image, and I looked again. This time I nodded. Garbage cans on a stand. With all the focus on the garbage cans behind The Depression where Guy Kramer had hidden during the abduction of Ellie Foster, that's where my mind went. But only for a few seconds.

"Is that the alley behind the mur—" I checked myself, not wanting to sound callous. "The house where Faith's body was found?"

Kennedy's eyes moved from the screen to me. His chin moved up, then down, the movement slight but definite.

"Okay, I remember seeing them the night I went over there," I said. "I'm not sure the signifi—"

He held up a hand to cut me off, then manipulated the zoom on the screen. Finally, he pointed again. I guessed that what I was looking at was a two-by-six board painted white. It looked to be one of the pieces along the bottom of the stand that housed the two garbage cans.

He zoomed again, and what appeared in the wood looked like scratches — no, not scratches. Tally marks. Two groups of five, and one more. Eleven marks in all:

卌 卌 |

"What do they mean to you?" Kennedy asked, his voice flat and low.

"Looks like the marks someone makes when they're keeping track of a number — one, two, three, four, five, then one, two, three, and so on over again."

"Right. So what does it mean *there*?"

"When did you notice these?" I asked him.

"Last night. I never saw them all the other times I was there."

"I missed them, too," I admitted, "if they were there when I checked the alley that night."

"I'm betting they were there … or at least some of them were," Kennedy said.

I stared at the screen for a while longer and then finally looked up at him. "Jesus, you don't think it's some tally of times the guy came into that alley …? No, that can't be possible."

"Somebody made those marks. Those aren't the work of an animal."

I didn't answer. I had no answer.

"I think there are two possibilities," he said slowly. "One is that someone somehow knows about my setup and that I'm watching that spot and is fuckin' with me."

I nodded. I could see that as a possibility. Hard to believe that someone would get some kind of kick out of messing with a person's head in that way, but not impossible.

"There aren't many people who know about this," he said.

"You said nobody — except Cobb and me and your wife."

"That's right," he said, and sat back in the chair looking at me. Hard.

It suddenly dawned on me. "Wait a minute. You think one of us put those marks there to screw with your head?"

"I'm saying there aren't a lot of possible explanations."

I couldn't believe what I was hearing. "That makes absolutely no sense."

"You still pissed at me for what happened behind your place that night?" He leaned forward, his face now close to mine. "Is that it?"

"I'm only going to say this once, Kennedy" — I didn't care at that moment that this man could take me apart in seconds — "I've never seen those marks before now. I didn't put them there, and I'll guarantee you Cobb didn't put them there either. Now you can believe that or not, I don't really give a shit." I stood up.

"Hold on," he said, holding up a hand. "I didn't really believe it, but I had to ask."

I stayed standing, still angry.

"I'm sorry," Kennedy said. "I'd appreciate it if you sat back down. I have something else to show you … please."

I sat down, pushed my beer to one side.

"I said there was another possibility."

"And that is?" I wasn't sure I wanted to hear the answer.

Neither of us had spoken loudly even during the confrontation, but he lowered his voice still more. "The killer's been back there eleven times and has logged every one of those times."

"Jesus," I said.

"Yeah."

"But why? Why would he do that?"

"Like I said … fucking with my head."

"But for that to be true, he'd have to know about your house and what's in it and what you do with it."

"That's how I see it."

I shook my head. "That doesn't seem possible. There's another possibility," I said.

He lifted his eyebrows to invite my suggestion.

"The marks mean nothing," I said. "Maybe the guy who lives there made them to indicate how often he took out the trash, to show his wife how overworked he is — who the hell knows? — but I'd bet my backside those weren't made by the killer."

"Be careful what you bet. You could lose your ass." Kennedy sat back and thought about what I'd said, then leaned forward again. "Okay, what's your email address?"

I gave it to him.

"I'm not going back through years of tapes to look at every time Dennis Bevans — that's the name of the guy who lives there — took out the goddamn garbage. Which, by the way, was a hell of a lot more than eleven times. But I'm going to watch from now on — and if he so much as bends his knees, I'll be over there to see if there's another mark."

"Fair enough," I said. "Just make sure you don't jump the guy because you think he might be up to something."

"Don't worry. I'll be cool. And if another mark shows up that I know he didn't make, I'll email it to you."

I looked at him, seeing a bit more of the guy who'd dropped me in the alley behind my apartment. I nodded. "Just remember your promise."

"I'll keep my promise." He gave me a mirthless grin. "You and Cobb will be the first to know. Oh, and one more thing. I did go back through the tapes to count up how many times I'd seen that movement, that shadow over there, the same one you saw."

"And?"

"Counting the one you saw and the one last night: ten times."

"Ten times," I repeated. "Eleven marks."

"Yeah," Kennedy said, his voice as cold as Arctic ice. "Maybe he was there one other time … a long time ago."

I had no answer for that. We drank beer for a couple of minutes, neither of us saying anything. Finally, he reached into the inside breast pocket of his blazer.

"One last thing I've got for you."

I set my glass down. "What is it?"

"You remember I told you and Cobb I figured maybe there was a cop factored into the thing somewhere, either as the perp or maybe doing some shit inside to make it harder to investigate?"

"I remember."

"I told you I'd make a few notes about some of the things that I see as a little irregular."

"I remember that, too."

He unfolded a piece of paper and spread it on the table in front of him. Then he once again turned it so I could see.

It was brief, containing just four points.

1. Lack of forensic evidence. Only prints on plywood belonged to the owner of the house where Faith's body was found. No DNA

match. This is not impossible or even unusual, but it makes you wonder, especially when you think about the other stuff.

2. One piece of Faith's clothing was recovered but later disappeared from evidence room.

3. No tip line — senior police administrators (or someone else) argued successfully against it.

4. The case was taken away from Hansel and Gretel after only seventeen days; they were then reinstated as the primary investigators three weeks later. Why were they removed, and why were they reinstated?

I wasn't sure what Cobb would say, but I had to agree that there were a couple of points on Kennedy's list that, first of all, I hadn't been aware of, and second, that bothered me. I didn't know, for example, that Hansel and Gretel had been pulled from the case and then put back on it. *Who were the investigators in the interim? And where was their report?* I was quite sure I hadn't seen a secondary report in the homicide file.

And which piece of clothing had been found and then gone missing?

Definitely points to consider.

"You can keep that," Kennedy said.

"I'll make sure Cobb sees it."

"Good, thanks."

I drained the last of my beer. "There's something I want to ask *you* about."

Kennedy's eyes narrowed, but he didn't say anything.

"Cobb and I have been working another cold case, one from a really long time ago — 1965, to be exact."

"That's damn cold," Kennedy said. "Maybe when you've wrapped that one up you should take a run at solving Jack the Ripper."

"Yeah, right. Anyway, a folksinger, a girl named Ellie Foster, disappeared from a coffee house that used to be in the basement of a building on 1st Street West, right near 12th Avenue."

"That's the one you were talking about."

"What?"

"That morning I met you guys at the Belmont Diner. You mentioned a case you were working on."

I nodded. "I remember that now. Yeah, this is that case."

"Anyway, it was well before my time," Kennedy said. "Don't think I know the case."

For the next half hour, and over another beer, I told him everything I could remember without my notes in front of me, right up to the present and including my chat with Alfie Keller. The one thing I did have with me was a copy of the lyrics of Ellie's song. I showed those to Kennedy as well. For a long time, he didn't say or do anything. I was about ready to leave when he looked up at me.

"I bet you're wondering if Fayed and Laird were the two dudes Keller got into it with that night."

"The thought had crossed my mind."

"I have two thoughts."

I relaxed, watched him. "Okay. What are they?"

"First ... I think it's Pearson. The guy in the lyrics ... I think it's Pearson, the prime minister."

"Why do you think that?"

"A lot of the same reasons you boys and girls talked about during your dinner. But I've got one more. You any kind of an athlete?"

"Played some baseball," I answered. "College ball at Oklahoma State."

"Full ride?"

"Yeah, but I tore my rotator cuff in my junior year, and that was the end of my career. Not that there would have *been* a career after college, but I would have liked to have finished that year and played my senior year. We had a pretty good club."

Kennedy nodded. "I was a student athlete as well. Football."

"What's that got to do with —"

"Just this. I'm interested in athletes. I don't read novels and stuff, but when I can I do read non-fiction. I've read a lot about the psychology of athletes. Always did. Still do. What makes them, what drives them ... shit like that."

"I saw your book collection at the house."

He nodded. "A few years ago, I read a book about Lester Pearson, sort of a biography, I guess, except I wasn't interested in the political stuff. In fact, I doubt if I even knew he was once our prime minister before I read that biography. What *did* interest me was that he was quite an athlete. Played on a hockey team that won the Spengler Cup, and like you, he was a pretty fair ball player. Played semi-pro, I think."

He tapped the paper containing the lyrics. "*Good at play*. I don't know a hell of a lot about songwriting, but if those other lines are about Pearson, not some anonymous *person*, then *good at play* fits."

I sat for a while, thinking about what he'd said. For me, the line could have applied to a lot of people. And it could have been about a lot of things, sports among them.

"You said you had two things. What's the second one?"

Kennedy's mouth came close to forming a smile. "I think if the answers are out there at all, they're a long way east of here. If it was me, I'd be getting my ass to Ottawa."

I thought about that, too. I nodded my head and started to thank him, but I didn't get the chance. Kennedy suddenly rose from his chair. The look on his face was the one I'd seen that night in the laneway behind my house. And seen again moments earlier, when he'd suggested I might have left the marks on the trash can stand behind the murder house. I thought for a second he was going to hit me.

I was wrong. He went by me and in three strides was standing in front of the three guys who'd come in just after us. His body language told me he hadn't gone over there to invite them to our table for a beer.

I barely had time to turn and track his movement over my shoulder.

I knew I couldn't just sit there enjoying my beer while Kennedy squared off with three guys, all of whom looked to be both willing and in pretty good shape. So I eased my way over, hoping I was lining up opposite the smallest of the three.

"I heard your friends call you Todd," Kennedy said to the guy in the middle just as I got there.

"Yeah?"

"Well, Todd, you and your boys here got bad mouths," Kennedy growled. "And I'd say you got bad minds, too, but for that to be true, you'd have to have minds, period. And there's no guarantee of that, is there?"

When Kennedy asked the question at the end, I was hoping he wasn't directing it at me. I stared straight ahead, just over the head of the guy in front of me. Old hockey adage: you want to fight, you make eye contact. I don't think of myself as a coward, exactly, but bar fights often go badly — for everybody. And I didn't have any beef with the three guys. I'd heard them talking, but as hard as I was concentrating on the various subjects Kennedy and I had covered, the conversation from the nearby table had been white noise.

So far, none of the three have stood up, which is a positive si—

Todd stood up with enough force that his chair went crashing over backward behind him.

"What are you talking about, fuck?"

"I heard you asswipes talking about nailing young girls," Kennedy shot back. "*Young* girls. Bragging about it. Guess I don't think that's anything to brag about."

"Well, get over it, fuck, because it really isn't any of —"

Things happened rather quickly, like a movie on fast-forward.

Kennedy's hand shot out and grabbed the guy called Todd by the hair, then he brought his arm — and Todd's face — down at a very high rate of speed, the face making heavy contact with the surface of the table. The crunch of the man's nose as it came to a sudden stop on the thick wood surface of the tabletop was unpleasant, to say the least.

Kennedy then shoved hard, and Todd stumbled back, falling over the chair that lay on its side behind him. Blood was streaming from his nose. I'd seen the face-slam move before — in a movie, maybe a western — but it was much more impressive in person.

Two bartenders from another part of the pub and the female server arrived, all at the same time. None of them looked like bouncers, which was maybe a good thing. Kennedy didn't look like he'd be easily bounced. He stepped around one of the other guys at the table and helped Todd to his feet, picked up the chair and sat him back down. Then he looked at the pub staffers.

"Poor guy," he said, "he got up to go for a whiz and he stumbled, and his face must have hit the table as he fell. Can we get a couple of towels, Miss?"

When the server didn't move, he said it again. "Towels, Miss? He's bleeding on the furniture."

Another guy now arrived. He looked like a manager and had his cellphone in hand. I figured he had the cops on speed dial. One of the bartenders shook his head. "Says he fell, hit his face on something. Nicki, grab those towels, okay?"

Nicki hustled off.

Kennedy looked at each of Todd's friends. "Maybe you guys should take Todd down to the washroom, help clean him up a bit."

The two guys, who had been statues since the action began (as, by the way, had I), each took an arm and led Todd in the direction of a nearby washroom. As they went by me, I could see that Todd was going to need more than towels and a sink full of water. I'd seen broken noses before. This wasn't a broken nose. This was a nose that had been crushed and was now red pulp. To his credit, Todd hadn't said anything or even whimpered since it had happened. He may have been in shock. But the fight had clearly gone out of him.

When the three of them disappeared into the washroom, the manager looked at Kennedy and me. "I know those guys. I'm guessing Todd had it coming, but I need you guys out of here. Now."

Kennedy nodded, stepped back to our table, and drained the last of his beer. He stuck out his hand, and we shook.

"Good luck with your cold case," he said.

"Good luck with yours."

I followed him to the door of the pub, and once in the parking lot we went in separate directions without saying another word.

TEN

I drove south for a while, eventually connecting with Elbow Drive. Still shaking from the excitement at the Rose and Crown, I pulled into a Safeway parking lot, called Cobb, and told him first about my meeting with Kennedy and the dust-up that was its conclusion. "I haven't been thrown out of a bar since my sophomore year of university," I said, hoping I didn't sound proud of the incident.

"Kennedy had a reputation for having a short fuse when he was a cop. Busted up the occasional suspect, but for the most part was a little careful about whose faces he punched."

"Yeah, maybe he had a good reason. I didn't hear what these guys said, but I guess if you've been investigating the murder of a child for over a quarter of a century, maybe you don't take kindly to guys talking about sexually abusing young girls."

"Maybe not," Cobb agreed. "You okay?"

"Fine. I was just a bystander. Anyway, that's not the reason I called. I think maybe I finally got a response to the article — the *tip line*, as you call it — that might be useful."

He agreed to meet Keller and me the next morning. I heard him cough on the other end of the line. Then he said, "So what are you thinking — that maybe Fayed and Laird were in The Depression that night?"

"I don't know. It's worth considering."

"Be nice if somebody remembered them being away from The Tumbling Mustard around that time."

"That would be good," I concurred. "Oh, and one more thing."

"What's that?"

"I told Kennedy about the case."

"Yeah?"

"Yeah. Not quite everything, but I gave him a pretty comprehensive overview."

"And?"

"And he thinks the answers are in Ottawa."

"He might be right," Cobb said.

It was strange, and I hoped that the violence of the afternoon wasn't the reason why, but I was feeling optimistic that at last a lot of little things felt connected — maybe out of those connections we'd finally arrive at a point where we actually knew something.

I was still haunted by the thought that I'd made a mistake in approaching the MFs for help with saving the shelter. But I succeeded in pushing even that black cloud a little further away, at least for the moment.

I carried the positive vibe into the barbecue, played catch with Kyla while the burgers cooked, then lost (again) at Clue. This time it was Jill's turn in the winner's circle — Colonel Mustard in the study with the lead pipe. *Yeah, like the ex-military guy would off somebody with a pipe. Stupid game.*

"This isn't a team sport, you know," I told Jill and Kyla. "I'm pretty sure you two were working together somehow. And, just so you know, high-fiving isn't appropriate." I glared at Kyla. "You *lost*."

"But so did you!" She beamed at me.

"I rest my case. Next time, we play Monopoly."

Kyla kissed her mother, hugged me, and headed off to bed, chortling all the way down the hall.

"Think hugs are great," I told Jill, "but the real deal is so much better."

"Can't argue that." She smiled. "So what happened to my man between this afternoon and now to bring him out of his funk?"

"I'm not sure," I admitted. I told her about my day, including the incident at the Rose and Crown.

"Great. One of my favourite pubs in the city, and you're probably banned from there for life."

"I'll work up a disguise. Maybe I'll go as Colonel Mustard.… But to answer your question, I don't know. I just feel that there are actually answers out there and that maybe we're getting closer."

"I'm glad one of us had a great day," she said.

"Uh-oh, what's up?"

Jill was one of the most positive people I'd ever known, so for her to say anything like that meant something was decidedly wrong.

"We got word that our grant is definitely gone. And with the economic climate the way it is right now, it doesn't look like the business community is going to be able to res-cue us. If something dramatic doesn't happen, and pretty darn soon, we'll have to close the shelter."

"Damn," I said. I was having trouble looking at her,

fearful that she might see something that would give me away. I didn't want to tell her about my approaching the MFs, but I also didn't want to lie.

"Yeah," she said.

"How much time have you got?" I asked, trying to think of the questions I would ask if I hadn't talked to Calgary's underworld about bailout money.

"If we aren't able to find some serious cash in the next couple of months, we'll be shutting down — just as the weather starts to turn cold. Couldn't be a worse time."

I pulled her closer to me, put an arm around her. I marvelled at the fact that, as we had gone through dinner and the game with Kyla, Jill never let on even a little the disappointment she had to be feeling over something as important to her as the Let the Sunshine Inn having to close its doors.

"I know things look pretty black right now, but let's not give up just yet," I said, trying to comfort her. "We have to let the sunshine in."

I regretted it almost the second the words were out of my mouth. Jill's body tightened as I realized that not only had my attempt at humour missed the mark, but also I had unintentionally trivialized something that was anything but trivial.

"Jill, I'm so sorry, that was a stupid thing —"

Bryan Adams mercifully interrupted my awkward attempt at an apology. It was Cobb.

"I'd better take this," I said. "Sorry."

"Sure." Jill stood and moved off toward the kitchen.

"What's up?" I said.

"Not a lot, and I know this is a long shot, but when you talk to the doorman, ask him if he can remember Fayed and Laird being away from the place for any extended periods of time."

"I tried him once, didn't get him, left a message on his machine. He didn't get back to me. I'll try him again tomorrow, see if I have better luck."

"Anything the matter? You sound a little off."

"No, nothing's the matter. I guess I just …" I didn't have any idea how to finish the sentence, so I just quit talking.

"Listen, I'm sorry if I called at a bad time. I'll talk to you tomorrow."

"No, really, you're fine. Any luck talking to the Ottawa cops?"

"I kind of thought we might want to hold off on that," he said. "Sometimes these things are better done in person."

"I've been leaning that way myself." I turned just as Jill came back into the room, slid her arms around my waist, and kissed my neck.

I could still hear Cobb's voice on the phone. "I'm not sure yet, but give it some thought and let's talk about it tomorrow."

"Can do."

"Tell Jill and Kyla hi."

Jill was close enough to hear Mike's voice. She lifted her head and said, "Love you, Mike."

"Love you, too, Jill," Mike said.

"By the way," I said, "being a former policeman, you should know this — are there fairly severe penalties for cheating at Clue?"

"There should be," he answered with a laugh. "I don't think I've ever actually won a game. I recommend Monopoly."

"Exactly."

"Whiners," Jill said, as I ended the call.

I held on to her and kissed the top of her head. "Jill, I know how you feel about the Inn, and I'm really sorry I was an insensitive ass, and —"

"Shut up and kiss me," she said.

After the kiss — there may have been more than one — I poured two glasses of wine and we sat together on the couch, quiet for a few minutes, enjoying the red, the fire I'd lit earlier … and each other.

"I know this sounds almost foolish, but maybe it's too early to panic about the Inn's funding just yet."

"That might be true if I had even one idea, short of banging on corporate doors and demanding money. And I'm pretty sure that won't work."

I nodded. "Probably not. But try to keep your chin up. I hate to see you get down. There has to be a way through this."

She kissed me on the chin. "Thanks, babe. I really appreciate that you care. Have I mentioned I think you're quite a nice guy?"

Have I mentioned I may have made a huge mistake? Have I mentioned I'm keeping something from you? Have I mentioned I'm not the nice guy you think I am?

It was time to change the subject. "There's a chance we may have to go to Ottawa. Things are starting to point in that direction."

"I was wondering about that."

She moved in closer to me, and again we let the silence surround us. Several minutes passed before either of us spoke.

"Jill, I wasn't sure I'd ever love again like I loved Donna. I know I've said that before, but I have to add something to that now. I do love you that much … I really do. And the best part is that I'm glad I love you."

"You mean, the feeling of betrayal you felt before — that you were being disloyal to her memory, all of that — you're okay now?"

"I am."

She set her wineglass down and leaned forward to kiss me again. After a long moment, she pulled away.

"Are you going to come into the bedroom with me, or will I have to get the lead pipe to convince you?"

The lead pipe wasn't necessary.

I arrived back home just after nine the next morning. I went for a long, slow run through the streets of Bridgeland, then showered and made coffee.

I called The Tumbling Mustard doorman, Ben Tomlinson, again, and this time he picked up on the fourth ring.

"Mr. Tomlinson? Adam Cullen. I called yesterday."

"Yeah, sorry about that. I didn't check my messages until this morning. Was going to call you in the next few minutes."

It was hard to tell if he was feeding me a line. I hoped the rest of the conversation would go well.

"Whereabouts do you live, Mr. Tomlinson?"

"Aylmer. On the Quebec side. Moved out here a few years ago from Gloucester. And prior to that, I lived in the Glebe."

"Finally got tired of the big city?"

"Something like that. I can be in Ottawa in a half hour, if I need to be. The rest of the time, we can look at it from across the river. Best of both worlds."

"You said 'we.' You have a family, Mr. Tomlinson?"

"Just me and my father. He's confined to a wheelchair."

"I don't know Ottawa that well, but if I remember correctly, the Glebe isn't all that far from Little Italy, is it?"

"No, not very far at all."

"Which brings us to the reason for my call."

"You mentioned The Tumbling Mustard in your message. A story you're writing."

"That's right. I'm a freelance journalist, and I've been looking at the disappearance of Ellie Foster. I'm sure you're familiar with the incident."

There was a long silence.

"An absolute tragedy. I met her when she performed at the TM. Then, just a few months later, she was gone. Hard to believe."

"I was given your name by another of the performers, Paula Pendergast."

"Paula … Paula. Yeah, yeah, now I remember. Terrific kid. Not Ellie Foster or Joni Mitchell in terms of talent, but pretty good … and just a really nice person. Kind, you know? How's she doin'?"

"Quite well, I think. She lives in Alberta now. She mentioned you were the doorman at the TM. I wasn't aware coffee houses had doormen."

"I can't speak for the others. I wasn't in that many. But we had one, yeah."

"So why did The Tumbling Mustard have one, do you suppose?"

"I can't say," Tomlinson said slowly. "Just the way management wanted it, I suppose."

"And management was who, exactly?"

"That was Mr. Fayed and Mr. Laird."

"There wasn't a third owner?"

"Sorry?"

"I came across a third name — Daniel Gervais. Apparently he was a part owner. I wondered if you knew the guy."

"Hmm …" There was another long pause. "Sorry, that name doesn't ring any bells, and I'm pretty sure if he was an owner, even a silent partner, he would have been around the place. I saw pretty well everybody who came and went. Don't remember a Daniel whatever, and I never heard anything about a third owner."

I didn't want to give up on the idea just yet. "Let's go back to that doorman thing. Whose idea was it to have a doorman at the TM?"

"What?"

"We just agreed most coffee houses didn't have doormen. The Tumbling Mustard did. I was just curious as to how that came about."

"Actually, we didn't agree on that," he said. "You said most coffee houses didn't have doormen, and I said I hadn't been in that many."

"Fair enough," I said. "I didn't mean to put words in your mouth."

"Anyway, I have no idea why the TM had one, or whose idea it was." A little snark had crept into his voice. "Like I said, maybe Fayed, maybe Laird, who the hell can remember that long ago, right?"

"Yes, it was a long time ago."

"And I'm curious," he said. "What exactly has the fact that there was a doorman at the TM got to do with Ellie Foster being kidnapped?"

"You're right," I said. "Probably nothing at all. Just trying to get a feel for the place."

I thought for a moment before making my next foray, trying to decide how hard I wanted to go at him. Decided to go for it.

"Thing is," I said, "this rumoured third owner was apparently in the movie theatre business. Lots of movie theatres had doormen, especially back in those days. Seems a strange coincidence, doesn't it?"

"I'm afraid I'm not following you."

"Theatres had doormen. Coffee houses didn't. Except for the one that may or may not have had a theatre guy as a part owner. Just seems weird."

"Jesus Christ," he said, his voice decidedly less friendly than it had been at the beginning of our conversation. "First of all, it's beginning to sound like you're calling me a liar. And second, I told you I didn't know that Gervais guy or any other owners who weren't named Laird or Fayed. So, if that's all your questions —"

"I have just a couple more," I said quickly. "And I'm sorry if I gave the impression I didn't believe you. That wasn't my intention. I was wondering if I could ask you to think back and tell me if you recall a time when Mr. Fayed and Mr. Laird were away from the TM for a while ... a few days? A week? Anything like that come to mind?"

He paused. "I really can't recall anything like that. A day or two, maybe, and even then it was one or the other of them, not both at once. Again, that's as near as I can remember."

"How well did you know Ellie Foster?"

Another pause. Longer this time. "I guess I knew her about as well as I knew most of the performers."

"And how well was that?"

"Again, I'm not sure I know what you're getting at."

"Was it 'Hey, how's it going?' Or was it sitting around the dressing room shooting the breeze? Maybe a drink after the place had emptied out?"

"I guess somewhere in the middle. Mostly it was just 'Hey, how's it going?' but once in a while we'd have a coffee between sets and talk a little bit. That's about it, I guess."

"How would you describe Ellie Foster?"

"As a performer or as a person?"

"How about both?"

"Amazing performer, and as far as I knew a very good person — friendly, easy to work with. Not all of them were, you know. Other than that, I guess I can't say much more about her."

"I understand there were frequent conversations between Fayed, Laird, and other people around the coffee bar — sort of intimate, maybe secretive conversations. You recall seeing much of that sort of thing?"

"Can't say I did."

"From where you were located as the doorman, could you see the coffee bar?"

"Sure, if I looked in that direction, I could see it."

"But you didn't notice the kinds of conversations I've described happening?"

"Didn't notice, so it couldn't have been all that big a deal."

I thought about that. Had to decide whether to keep pushing hard or to go in another direction. Seeing as being aggressive hadn't worked that well earlier, I decided on the latter course of action.

"You ever run into anyone from The Tumbling Mustard days — former staff, performers? Like you said, everyone who came and went from the place had to pass right by you. I just wondered if you still keep up with anyone."

"Nope, nobody. Kind of sad, really, but that seems to be the way it goes. You think you're going to be friends with this person or that person forever, and then life gets in the way and you drift apart."

"So you didn't really keep up with anybody from those days?"

"I think I just answered that question. Listen, I have to run here. I'm meeting some people right away, and —"

"Just one last question, Mr. Tomlinson. What did you do after The Tumbling Mustard?"

"What do you mean?"

"For a living. I just wondered what you did after the TM shut down." I wasn't sure why I'd asked that — maybe just curiosity.

"I went back to school. Had a few different careers after that — you know the deal, right? A guy moves around some. Maybe that's why I lost contact with the people. Anyway, like I was saying, I'm gonna have to end this."

"Thanks, Mr. Tomlinson. If you think of anything you feel might help me in my research, I'd appreciate a call."

"Sure. Will do."

And he was gone. There was more I would have liked to ask him, but I knew that wasn't going to happen. At least not right then.

The meeting with Keller was brief, a one-coffee chat. He didn't give us much more than what we'd discussed the day before, but I was nevertheless glad Cobb heard it as well to corroborate my opinion that Keller was legit and had given us real information. And that there was at least a chance that Fayed and Laird had been in The Depression the night Ellie was abducted.

When Keller had gone I said, "I'm assuming you will never again scoff at the efficacy of the tip line."

Cobb smiled. "It's like call-in shows on sports radio. You listen to fifty calls that are total shit, and then — bang! — somebody who has actually thought about things and is coherent and sober calls in. Makes the whole godawful night worthwhile."

I shook my head. "Where did you come up with that analogy?"

"Am I right or wrong?"

I thought about the Bernie calls and had to laugh. "You might be right."

I stood up and got us more coffee. When I was back and we'd each sipped a couple of times, Cobb said, "By the way, I got less than nothing on Gervais. The guy hasn't existed for a few decades. I'm guessing either he's long dead or he moved to a Third World country and is living in a hut on a beach."

"Okay, so what's next?"

He didn't answer right away. We'd finished most of the coffee before he set his mug down and looked at me.

"You ever seen the Parliament Buildings?"

"I have, yeah."

"Maybe it's time to see them again."

ELEVEN

Cobb, earbuds in, was watching Sportsnet highlights of games from the previous night. I was reading Louise Penny's latest. We were maybe an hour into the WestJet flight from Calgary to Ottawa, and so far there'd been little in the way of conversation.

I noticed that Cobb was now watching the same set of highlights for the second, maybe third time, so I closed my book and tapped him on the shoulder. He looked at me, pulled the earbuds out, and dropped them in the seat pocket in front of him.

He looked at me again, clearly waiting for me to say something.

"We haven't talked strategy, and I'm curious," I said. "Is the idea for us to split up, or to talk to people together? Are we going to call people, or just randomly stop folks on the street and ask if they happened to know anything about a singer who disappeared a half century ago?"

"Well, that's certainly one approach, but I think we'll leave that for later. For now, we have an appointment with a retired RCMP man." Cobb worked at unwrapping the cookie things the flight attendant had brought earlier. I hadn't had the courage. "Pretty high up in the force by the time he retired. He spent quite a few years working on national security cases. He wasn't in that department in the sixties, but he knew what was going on. Or at least that's what he told me. We start there."

"What are you hoping to hear from him?"

"I'm not sure," he admitted. "I don't really know what he'll tell us. But the lyrics of the song, if we've interpreted them even somewhat accurately, point to something going on at some political level. Maybe he can enlighten us a little."

"Enlightenment would be helpful."

He looked over at me. "Everything okay with you?"

"Sure, why do you ask?"

"It's just that some of your quips seem to have more of an edge than usual. Feels like there's some bitterness there. Everything okay with you and Jill?"

"Never better."

"And Kyla's all right?"

"Kyla's fine." I realized that my waspish answers were probably reinforcing his belief that there was something bothering me. And I wasn't about to tell him what that was.

"Sorry," I said. "I guess I'm just frustrated with the case … wishing we could move ahead a little faster."

"I remember going to my uncle's farm in the summers." Cobb leaned his head back on the seat, closed his eyes like he was seeing the place. "He had some cattle, a few horses. And he used to say 'The only way to move cows fast is to move them slow.' Grammar issues notwithstanding, he was right. This case feels like that. The more we try to rush things, the less progress we make. A lot of cases are like that. Our job is to stay focused and not overlook anything that might be important."

I nodded, trying to look less stressed than I was, wondering if my face was a better liar than my voice was. "So first stop, retired RCMP guy."

"Then we see about tracking the doorman, Tomlinson, and with any luck at all he'll be a little more forthcoming in person than he was with you on the phone. And the movie theatre guy, the maybe-or-maybe-not third owner — I'd like to find him, have a visit with him, too. That's a start. Anybody you'd like to add to the list?"

"The one guy I haven't been able to get any sort of track on is her manager-agent. All I have is a last name, Bush. No last known whereabouts. I've got nothing on the guy. And maybe he doesn't matter, but if we could find him maybe he'd be able to tell us something about Ellie's mental state in those weeks leading up to and including her time at The Depression."

"What have you done on him?"

"The usual stuff. Google, phone directories ... I mean, I don't even know how old he was at the time. He may have been dead for thirty years or so by now."

Cobb nodded. "Bit of a long shot, but let's keep him in mind."

I turned and looked out the window at the prairie landscape thirty-eight thousand feet below. I looked back at Cobb.

"Something I've been thinking about."

"And that is?"

"Somebody put that disc in Monica Brill's car."

"Uh-huh."

"But without a note or anything, how would they know that she'd turn it into a search for her missing grandmother?"

Cobb frowned, considered, finally nodded again. "You raise a good point. She could just as easily have played the thing a few times and then set it aside, and that would've been the end of it. Except for one thing."

"What's that?"

"The very fact that someone actually broke into the car and left the disc there. I mean, if it was just a gift from someone who thought it would be nice for her to have this remembrance of her grandmother, then why not walk up to her on the street and hand it to her, or put it in the mail with a note that said, 'Thought you might like to have this'?"

I thought about that, didn't really have the answer, so I responded with a shrug.

"The thing *was* done surreptitiously, by an unidentified individual with no note, no clue, nothing — I'm guessing the whole point was to pique her curiosity and get her thinking about seeing what she could do to solve a fifty-year-old mystery."

"But again, why not just tell her or write to her and say 'Hey, your grandma's out there somewhere, and you should look for her'?"

Cobb nodded. "I've thought about that, too, and the only thing I can come up with is that the person responsible for getting the disc to Monica feared for his or her own safety if it became known that he ... or she ... had been in contact with Ellie Foster's granddaughter. That, and the lyrics themselves — I know I'm beating the thing to death, but they have to matter."

I turned back to the window and closed my eyes. I slept for a while, but I've never been a good airplane sleeper. I had a weird dream in which I was looking at a

giant screen with strange, off-kilter pictures in the foreground — pictures of Ellie Foster, The Depression, the
alley behind the Unruh murder scene, even Jill and Kyla
— and in the background a video was playing. The video
showed a bunch of MFs lined up on their Harleys, with
Mrs. Scubberd front and centre. She was speaking to me,
explaining how the arrangement that I had just agreed
to — in fact, *asked for* — worked. Then she laughed and
said, "What's the expression — the devil is in the details?
Well, if you leave off the *d*, that makes it the *evil* is in
the details. Thanks for the beer, Mr. Cullen." And she
laughed again. Her husband was standing next to her,
and he wasn't laughing.

I woke up with a headache. I felt cold. I looked over
at Cobb. He was sleeping and looked like he was a whole
lot more relaxed than I was and enjoying his high-altitude
nap more than I had. *Probably hasn't sold his soul to the
devil,* I thought.

Jack Beacham had retired from the RCMP in 2013. He
was an inspector at the time of his retirement.

He was a big man with greying brown hair that
hadn't seemed to co-operate with whatever plan Beacham
had had for it that morning. He was wearing an Ottawa
Redblacks hoodie, jeans, and sneakers. He looked like
a guy who got some exercise and could still be a pretty
effective cop. The smile creases around his eyes were
those of a man who appeared to be enjoying retirement,
and the enthusiastic grin with which he greeted us said
he was also a man who was happy with where life had
taken him.

We had agreed to meet at the Pasticceria Gelateria Italiana, a bakery and restaurant on Preston Street. After five minutes in the place, I decided that if they rented rooms, I'd move in later that day. The mix of baking and cooking smells, as well as the ambiance of the veranda on the front of the building where two older Italian guys were having an enthusiastic conversation, made it a place where I could spend some serious time.

I liked Jack Beacham right off, and I think Cobb did, too. He was already set up at a table in the main part of the place when we arrived. Beside his chair was a briefcase, open. In it we could see file folders, notepads, and computer discs. He was carrying an iPad and had it sitting on his lap. Ready. We probably liked him even more at that point.

But first came the job of sampling three or four of the baked items that graced display cases along two sides of the place. That, and coffee. Small talk that morphed into Cobb and Beacham trading cop stories: some hair-raising, others pretty funny.

The food dispensed with — quite industriously — it was time to see if the inspector could tell us anything that might be helpful.

Cobb had already spoken to him on the phone, but went over again what we were looking for some help with.

"I have to be vague, Inspector, because the truth is, we don't know what exactly we're after or even if we're in the right area code when it comes to finding out what happened to Ellie Foster."

Cobb went over first what we knew and second what we theorized. Beacham listened carefully, nodding a couple of times and asking only one question — he wanted

Cobb to repeat the name of the third possible owner of The Tumbling Mustard.

When Cobb was finished and I'd arranged refills of coffee, Beacham leaned forward. "Okay, first of all, a little background. You're right, those were turbulent times. President Kennedy had been assassinated, and that seemed to be the trigger — and I realize that's a terrible pun — for so much of what followed. Vietnam had taken centre stage; Cuba wasn't all that far in the rear-view mirror, and groups like the Black Panthers were pissed off and wanting to do something. People tend to think that it was all happening in the States, and that's true to some extent, but we had our pockets of dissidents up here, too. Most of them were relatively benign, but don't forget, we were only a few years away from the FLQ Crisis.

"After you called me, I did some digging." He held up a hand. "And don't say I shouldn't have gone to the trouble, because this is the stuff I've lived for all my life. It wasn't trouble; it was interesting, and it was fun to be back in the game even in a limited way. By the way, I studied the lyrics of the song you sent me, and I found them interesting, too. I'll get to that later. The bad news is, I don't know how much good I've been able to do for you."

"Anything you've got, Inspector, is likely more than we've got now, and it's much appreciated," Cobb told him, as I nodded my agreement.

"Okay. For starters, you don't have to call me Inspector. Jack will do nicely. So what I did was try to focus on stuff we were looking at during late 1964 and into 1965. And you'll be interested to know that The Tumbling Mustard was on our radar, although not in what I'd say was a big way. And that's not as much of a rarity as you might think. We also looked at Le Hibou, not because it was some kind of radical hotbed but because we were interested in any places that brought poets, musicians, playwrights — the artistic types — together." He looked at me with a slight smile. "Everybody knows what a breeding ground of dissent you damn writers are."

I held up my hands in surrender. "Guilty as charged, sir."

He laughed, then reached down into the briefcase to pull out a file folder. I glanced at Cobb, and he put a finger to his lips — the message being that it might be best not to ask Jack Beacham how he had come to possess the stuff that was in that briefcase.

We were quiet for a few minutes as Beacham rifled through papers, sorted, organized, finally narrowing his search down to just a few pieces of paper that he looked at long and critically through half-frame reading glasses. Finally, he looked up at us again, removed the glasses, and used them to tap one of the pages he'd laid out in front of us.

"By the way, I was in the force at that time, but it was early in my career and I wasn't immersed in this stuff until a couple of decades later. But it appears my colleagues were interested in three different groups around that time. TFR, which stood for Time for Revolution — you can tell from the name alone this wasn't a group that had a lot of deep thinkers in it. Their chief claim to fame was having Ken Kesey and Timothy Leary up here to speak. Their 'revolution' was all about LSD and not much more.

"They drew big crowds for those two, and it looked like this was an organization with some traction, but it fizzled and disappeared within a few months of that event.

That was in '64. The second group was interesting. But it was really in its infancy in '65; became more of a force in '67 and '68, when the protests against the Vietnam War became bigger and better organized. The group was first called Part of the People, acronym POP, but they changed their name to Doggers in '67. I think they wanted to align themselves with Diggers, which was a pretty prominent radical action force in the U.S. The American group was led by Peter Coyote. I don't know how closely aligned the two groups became, but several members of the Doggers were arrested, some repeatedly, as they protested the war and the 'fascist campus leadership' — a lot of the same stuff that was going down all over North America and elsewhere.

"As near as we can tell, the Doggers just kind of faded away; we didn't hear much from them after '68 or '69."

"Either of those groups have any real connection to The Tumbling Mustard?" I asked.

"Didn't find any references to it or Le Hibou, which isn't to say they never went there, but I don't think we can look to The Tumbling Mustard as any kind of headquarters."

I nodded.

"Which brings us to the third group, a little more colourful … and maybe a little more relevant."

Cobb glanced at me, noncommittal but interested. I leaned forward, took a drink of the now-cool coffee.

"They were called Five Minutes to Midnight. I don't know the significance of the name other than as a kind of countdown, maybe — midnight being the time they were going to do something dramatic?" He shrugged. "They staged a teach-in at the University of Ottawa during the first week of classes in September 1964. That's really the first we heard of them. Then, not much but a couple of meetings and a protest against a prof, guy with a Polish name, at Carleton, some student boycott deal — got the prof suspended for a term. Don't know the reason the group disliked him. That was it until the last week in December that same year. There was an attempted armoured car holdup in Little Italy; it was late at night, not far from The Tumbling Mustard, now that I think about it. Not that we saw any link to the place at the time, and there's no particular reason to lean that way even now. We're not sure how many people were in the gang; it was dark, but the guards thought five or six. There were shots fired on both sides, first by the robbers, then by the armoured car guards. One of the guards received a minor wound, but two of the gang members were hit. One was dragged off by fellow gang members, and they tried to take the other one as well. The two guards were veteran guys and, by all accounts, pretty damn fearless. They were able to drive off the bandits, leaving the one guy lying on the ground. He died in hospital two days later without regaining consciousness."

Beacham tapped a finger on the paper in front of him. "The guy's name was Calvin Bush. Born in Ottawa, but the family moved to upstate New York, came back in 1959. Bush finished high school here and was kind of an on-and-off student at Carleton. Was one of the organizers of the teach-in at the University of Ottawa a few months before. By the way, the guard who wasn't injured — his name was Payne — insisted that one of the people involved in the attempted holdup was a woman. It was dark, so he couldn't be 100 percent certain, but it was a claim he stuck to right up to his dying day."

"Shades of Patty Hearst," Cobb murmured.

Beacham nodded. "Except Hearst was ten years later."

"Any idea as to whether the woman in Five Minutes to Midnight was forced to participate, like Hearst alleged she was, or if she was a willing participant?" I asked.

Beacham shook his head slowly. "I've read a fair amount of stuff on the attempted holdup, and it doesn't look like that was ever determined."

Cobb and Beacham started to look through some of the documents Beacham had brought. I said, "Ellie Foster's manager's last name was Bush. I don't have a first name."

Cobb looked up. "That's right — the guy you've had trouble tracking. Maybe now we know why."

Beacham looked up and whistled. "Interesting. I wonder if it's the same guy."

Cobb thought about that, then said, "Okay, let's say for the sake of argument that the Bush in the holdup was Ellie Foster's agent and manager. She obviously had a number of bookings, including Le Hibou and The Depression, after the guy was killed in the attempted armoured car heist. I wonder how she got those bookings."

I said, "Most performers' bookings — I think even back then — were made a few months ahead of the actual gigs. So it's possible that they were made by Bush before he died — if this guy is the same Bush. Let me make a call." I stepped away from the table and walked outside, where I dialed Armand Beauclair's number. I hoped he was close to his phone.

He was, and clearly he recognized my number. "I don't talk this often to my kids," he greeted me.

"Yeah, and I'm sorry to bother you again. Just one quick thing."

"Sure … shoot."

"You mentioned that you booked Ellie with a guy named Bush but couldn't remember his first name."

"That's right."

"How about I throw a name out there? You think if you heard it, it might ring some bells?"

"We can try it. I'm not sure the bells are ringing as clearly as they were a few decades ago, but go ahead."

"Calvin Bush."

A pause. "Calvin," he said slowly. "Calvin … I won't say yes for sure, but I won't say no either. It sounds like it might be right, but that's about as definite as I can be — which I realize isn't very definite at all. Sorry."

"You remember a shootout involving an attempted armoured car holdup? Tail end of '64?"

"Yeah, maybe. That *does* ring a bell. What about it?"

"A guy named Calvin Bush was shot and killed by the armoured car guards. We don't know if there's any connection, but we're just trying to make some pieces fit the puzzle."

"Guess that makes me look like a putz — here's this guy that I might know, gets killed trying to rob an armoured car, and I don't put it together. I can't remember, but either I didn't read the reports all that closely or I didn't tie the name to Ellie Foster's manager. Or it's just possible I was stoned at the time and it didn't really register. There was some of that happening back then. Sorry again."

"No need to apologize," I said. "One more for you — ever hear of a group called Five Minutes to Midnight?"

"*Group* as in musicians?"

"*Group* as in sixties radicals."

"Sorry, that's not registering at all. Calvin Bush part of that group?"

"Yes."

"So it would really help if I could confirm that Calvin Bush was also the guy I booked Ellie through."

"That would make my day."

"Wish I could."

"Hey, you've helped us a lot, and I appreciate it."

"I don't know about that, but I'm still hoping you find her. And I don't mind you calling, I really don't."

"That's also appreciated, Armand. Have a great night."

I went back inside and joined Cobb and Beacham at the table.

"I phoned a guy who used to help run Le Hibou — he's not sure, but says it might have been Calvin Bush who did the booking for Ellie. I'll keep chasing that."

"*Might* have been," Cobb repeated.

"He couldn't say for certain."

Cobb nodded. "Fair enough." He then turned to Beacham. "You have any other names of people that were part of the Five Minutes to Midnight group?"

Beacham nodded, pulled another sheet of paper out of the manila folder. "Three of them: Andujar Nuno, deceased July 6, 1977; Jonathan Kempner, deceased November 9, 1990; and Hazen Tribe, name suspected to be an alias, whereabouts unknown. Clearly there were others, but those are all the names on record. Or at least that I could access."

He passed the list to Cobb, who stared at the names for a time, then shook his head. "Mind if I keep this?"

"That's a photocopy," Beacham replied. "I made it for you."

Cobb nodded. "We appreciate what you've done. One last thing — the deceased former members of Five Minutes to Midnight — Nuno and Kempner — any details as to cause of death?"

"Not in the file, but let me ask around, see if I come up with anything."

Cobb shook his head. "You've already gone way above and beyond. I can't ask you to do any more."

"You didn't ask. I offered. Let me see if I can find anything."

Cobb, as he usually did, looked at me to see if I had anything I wanted to ask.

"Just the three events?" I said to Beecham. "The teach-in, the attempted armoured car holdup, and the boycott of the professor. Doesn't seem like they were very active."

"At least in terms of things we knew about, but yeah, I agree." He nodded and leaned back in his chair. "This is just me talking now, but I'm betting they had some more plans. Having a couple of people get shot tends to be a bit of a deterrent."

"Any rumours around that time about somebody wanting to mount something against the prime minister?"

"I never heard any, but I wouldn't have. I was pretty junior. Again, let me talk to a couple of people." He held his hands up before Cobb could object. "Listen, I'm at a point in my life where having a reason to get up in the morning is a blessing. So don't take away the blessing." He smiled.

Cobb returned the smile. "Just so you know, we appreciate it, and we don't expect it."

"Understood."

"There's something else," I said. "Five Minutes to Midnight — there's a midnight reference in the song lyrics. Nobody said much about that during our lyrics-deciphering bee, probably because no one was able to make any sense of it. But this might be a connection. I don't know."

"Yeah, I'd mentioned I had a thought or two about the lyrics — especially that line about midnight." Beacham pulled out the copy of the lyrics, and the three of us grouped around the lone copy. Beacham read aloud, "*Midnight. Not yesterday, not tomorrow. A time with no day of its own.*"

"It's repeated twice, once in the middle and once at the end," I said.

"But does it mean anything?" This time it was Cobb who was casting doubt.

"You told me on the phone some of the thoughts your group came up with on the lyrics," Beacham said.

Cobb nodded. "What I don't know is how accurate our deductions were."

"I've always been a where-there's-smoke-there's-fire kind of guy. To me, a line like that and a group like Five Minutes to Midnight that was active at the time you're looking at — that looks and smells like smoke to me. Like I said, if midnight is a kind of D-Day-now-we-go reference, and you're thinking Pearson could have been a target, that song starts to become pretty damn significant."

I tapped the paper. "If there were only one or two things that sounded meaningful in something like this, it might be hard to give it much credibility. But the truth is, there are a lot of references that might be linked. And now here's another that seems to be pointing in one direction."

"And what direction is that?" Cobb asked.

I looked at Beacham. "Which way to The Tumbling Mustard?"

The former RCMP inspector told us it wasn't far, and recommended walking if we wanted to get the feel of Preston Street, the central artery of Ottawa's Little Italy. We took his advice, and the three of us headed south. Preston was a busy, bustling thoroughfare with noisy energy. I liked it.

The potpourri of smells, most of them to do with food, some less pleasant than others; the rise and fall of shop and street noise; and always the hurried motion of people, some from the neighbourhood and others, like us, clearly not — all of it provided a vitality that made me like Ottawa much more than I'd thought I would.

After fifteen minutes or so, Beacham pointed to a building up ahead on our side of the road. "That's where The Tumbling Mustard stood. The building was torn down in the mid-1990s. I think it was offices — low-end real estate types, maybe — at the time of its demise. It was pretty decrepit by the end."

"And where was the shootout?"

Beecham pointed. "Again, not all that far — corner of Booth and Somerset. Not sure what business the armoured car was picking up at, but it's likely long gone too. There's been a fair amount of renewal in this area."

The opening bars of "The Boys in the Bright White Sports Car" emanated from the inside breast pocket of my jacket, so I wandered off a few feet to take the call. It was Jill.

"Hey, cowboy, how are things in our nation's capital?"

"Slow going so far, but we remain ever optimistic."

"You are not going to believe what's happened."

"Kyla's been admitted to Harvard," I said.

"How did you know that?" Jill laughed. "No, not that, but almost as good. Celia just called, and an anonymous donor has stepped up with twenty-five thousand dollars for the shelter. We're back in business."

For a second, I stopped cold. I was hoping Cobb wasn't watching me. I'm sure that at the very least I turned somewhat white at Jill's news. Until that call, a part of me had hoped Scubberd and the MFs would forget about our conversation and just go away. That clearly hadn't happened. I wasn't dumb enough to believe that out of the blue, some other anonymous benefactor had stepped up just days after I had made what I was now convinced was one of the biggest mistakes of my life. And the worst part was I'd have to continue to deceive a woman I had promised myself I'd never lie to.

"That's great, babe." I made my voice sound excited, hoping she wouldn't sense it was fake. "See, I told you there was no reason to worry."

"You can't even imagine the relief all of us at the shelter are feeling right now. The weight of the world and all that."

"I *can* imagine. We'll have to celebrate when I get home."

"Affirmative on that. Hey, are you okay? You don't sound 100 percent. You don't sound like you."

"Sorry, just a lot going on with the Ellie Foster thing. But I'm totally jacked to hear your news. That is amazing, and I'm really happy for you and Celia. I know how worried you both were."

"Listen, I'd better not keep you. I know you guys have work to do. I hope it's going well."

"Hard to say. We might be making a little progress."

"Just keep slugging, okay?"

"Okay, Coach, we will."

"I love you, Adam Cullen."

"And I love you. I'll call you later."

We ended the call, but I didn't walk back to where Cobb and Beacham stood talking. I needed a few seconds to gather myself. I kept thinking of the words of the lovely Mrs. Scubberd as she had looked at me across the table at the Harley Diner. *Nothing is free. If my husband gives that shelter the money you're asking for, it means we're partners. Not us and the shelter. Us and* you.

And now the "partnership" had been confirmed.

I glanced over to where Beacham and Cobb looked like they were wrapping up their chat. Cobb gestured at me, so I made my way back over. Beacham reached out a hand. "This is where I leave you, gentlemen. We're having people for dinner, and if I don't get home in time to help … well, you guys know how that is."

I nodded and smiled as I shook his hand. "Thanks for the help," I said. "You've been terrific."

"What he said." Cobb, too, shook the offered hand.

"Glad to try." Beacham grinned. "Hope I *was* some help. And if I find out anything more on the causes of death for the Five Minutes to Midnight group members, or any of the other things we talked about, I'll let you know."

"Thanks again," Cobb said.

We watched as Beacham crossed the street and disappeared into the growing crowd of people who were beginning to populate Preston Street.

"Bad news?"

"What?" I said.

"The phone call. Everything okay?"

"Better than okay." I forced a big smile. "A donor has come forward to rescue Let the Sunshine Inn. It was looking more and more like they might have to close the doors, but this anonymous donor came through, so there's jubilation all around."

Cobb regarded me for a few seconds before nodding. "That is good news. Tell Jill I'm happy for her next time you talk to her. Okay, we'd better get to work. We need to find your doorman buddy."

"I've got an address in Aylmer for the guy," I said, as we started the walk back to where we'd parked the rental car.

"I'm thinking we might be able to take the time for one more pastry before we hit the road. Celebrate the good news from home."

"You won't get an argument from me," I said, although I knew I wouldn't enjoy it. Jill's phone call and the sure knowledge that I would be hearing from the MFs one day had killed any potential appetite I might have been able to muster.

I liked Aylmer right off. Of course, it wasn't Aylmer anymore, having been amalgamated with Hull, Gatineau, and some others to form the city of Gatineau, Quebec.

Cobb had decided against calling ahead, preferring an unexpected visit that would lessen the possibility of the interviewee prepping for our questions. The GPS directed us through the urban parts of Gatineau and eventually to the gorgeous fall colours of the Gatineau Hills. I had Tomlinson's house projected in my mind, and I expected something you might see in the Blue Ridge

Mountains — a hillbilly shack with Tomlinson and his toothless father resting on a rickety wooden porch, chewing on straw and knocking back moonshine.

I was glaringly wrong.

The house was a two-storey brick affair that sat gleaming in the late fall sun. I wouldn't have guessed that brick could gleam, but this did, or at least gave that very pleasant impression. The yard that surrounded the house was well-kept — not manicured, but a long way from neglected. The porch was where my projection had come closest. It was a wood construction, protruding out and over white double doors — definitely not rickety. The driveway leading up to the house was flanked by tall, thin, perfectly shaped cedars. In that driveway was a newer-looking blue Ford Explorer, spotlessly clean, its chrome glistening in the afternoon sun. I'm guessing my mouth was open as I looked at the place. I checked the GPS and the address I had, convinced that one or both was incorrect.

"I'm thinking a doorman's wages didn't pay for this place," Cobb said, as we climbed out of the car.

"A Canadian senator could be very happy here."

"Five bucks says a butler answers the door," Cobb said, as we advanced on the house.

"Uh-uh," I said. "Not touching that one."

"When we get in there, I think you should take the lead," Mike said. "You've already talked to the guy. And we stay with our cover story that we're writing something on Ellie — let's hang on to that as long as we can."

I shrugged. "I'm not sure you want me to lead the charge on the interview. When we talked on the phone, I got the feeling I might have pissed the guy off."

"That's okay," he said. "You piss everybody off."

"Ha ha."

We were wrong about the butler.

When the door opened, the man looking at us appeared to be in his mid to late sixties, maybe a little older. He was tall, on the thin side, and casually dressed in sweater, slacks, and loafers, with an Ottawa Senators ball cap resting atop grey fringes around his head. His face was a road map of lines and creases. If this was Ben Tomlinson, this was not how I had expected him to look. What I had done, of course, was see in my mind's eye the doorman at The Tumbling Mustard — a wide-eyed twenty-year-old learning about the world around him.

But that man was fifty years older now, and as I looked at the unsmiling, silent figure who stood in the doorway, I realized this could very well be him.

"Mr. Tomlinson?"

When he didn't answer, I took a step forward. "I'm Adam Cullen. I spoke to Mr. Tomlinson on the phone a couple of days ago. About Ellie Foster. We were out here to follow up on a few things and thought we'd stop by." I offered a hand.

He ignored it and didn't indicate we should come in.

"Yeah," he said.

"Are you Ben Tomlinson?" I asked again.

"I told you everything I remembered when we talked on the phone the other day."

"Yes, sir, I'm sure you did. We just had a couple more things we'd like to ask you about."

"What kind of things?"

There was no doubt the former doorman at The Tumbling Mustard was not happy that we were there.

There had been a decided change in his attitude near the end of our first conversation, and clearly there had not been a thaw since.

"This is Mike Cobb." I gestured to Mike. "He's working on the story with me."

Cobb smiled, stayed silent. Tomlinson eyed him for a minute, then turned his attention back to me.

"What kind of things?" he repeated.

"I wonder if we could come in just for a few minutes," I said.

"How about some ID?"

I looked at Cobb, who gave the slightest shrug — my call. I knew I didn't have long, and made my decision. "Mr. Tomlinson, I'm afraid we haven't been totally truthful. While it is true that I'm working on a story on Ellie Foster's disappearance, Mr. Cobb here is a private investigator I've engaged to assist me. As you know, there are elements of the story that have a criminal connotation, and I thought it best to involve someone with that kind of expertise as an adviser."

Tomlinson thought about that. Finally, he said, "I'll still need to look at that ID."

Cobb and I pulled out our wallets and presented our credentials to him — mine as a journalist (out of date, but impressive if given only a cursory glance, and happily Tomlinson's glance was cursory), and Cobb's as a private investigator. While Tomlinson looked them over, Cobb gave me an approving wink that said *Nice cover*.

Tomlinson returned our IDs, then, as if he'd turned a switch, offered a broad smile and shook both our hands. "Sorry, guys, I haven't been very hospitable, and that's not like me. I guess I was just a little suspicious, and I let it get the better of me. Come on inside and let me get you something to drink."

I wasn't sure what had precipitated the attitude change but didn't really care. Tomlinson stepped back, and Cobb and I followed him into the house. The front hallway was spacious and opened up into the main living room, with the dining area straight ahead.

Tomlinson gestured at a long L-shaped couch, and Cobb and I sat.

"What can I get you gentlemen? Beer? Wine? Apple juice?"

"Just water's fine for me," Cobb said.

"I'll have an apple juice," I said.

"I'll be right back." Tomlinson smiled and headed off toward the kitchen.

I watched him go. He still moved fluidly, not at all like a man taken hold of by arthritis or other afflictions of the aging. I glanced at Cobb, looking for his take on the man, but he was checking out the house, his attention, it seemed, on a series of photographs on one wall of the living room. I followed his gaze to a small table that sat directly in front of the photos on the wall, and it, too, was festooned with framed pictures, some in black and white, others in colour, but all weathered and faded. Old photos.

Tomlinson returned with a tray bearing the drinks. He passed the water to Cobb and the apple juice to me, then took the last glass from the tray — another apple juice.

"Thank you." Cobb pointed his chin in the direction of the photos. "Family?" he asked.

"Some," Tomlinson replied. "Actually, not many are family. Most are friends, people we've known. Some from a long time ago, as you can see."

"Any Tumbling Mustard memories?"

Tomlinson crossed to the photos. "Just one," he said, "but it might interest you. It's Ellie Foster."

He crossed the room and returned with one of the framed colour photos from the table. He handed it to Cobb, who held it so that both of us could look at it. I recognized Ellie Foster from the photos Monica Brill had brought us the morning of our first meeting at Cobb's office. In this photo, Ellie was standing next to a dark-complexioned, unsmiling man. Ellie was smiling, but the smile lacked warmth or any sense of joy.

"Is that Fayed?" I asked Tomlinson.

"That is Mister Fayed, yes."

"Mister" Fayed, even after all this time.

"Do you remember when this was taken?" Cobb asked.

Tomlinson shook his head. "Uh-uh. I'm guessing it was from when she played The Tumbling Mustard, but I don't know that for sure. The picture is right outside the TM, so that's certainly possible — and if that's when it was, that would make it the fall of '64."

I leaned closer to get another look at the photo, this time concentrating on what looked like the front of the coffee house. Not much to see, really. Large double doors were set into a yellowish (mustard?) concrete and brick wall; protruding from the entrance was a kind of box office like you see outside movie theatres, exactly as Paula Pendergast had described. Above the entrance, a sign, also inexpensive, maybe hand-painted in what looked like tie-dyed lettering — The Tumbling Mustard Coffee House. Frankly, it looked like a place I'd walk by, looking for something a little more user-friendly. But maybe it was all the rage in the mid sixties, and maybe I wouldn't have felt that way if I'd been part of that time and that scene.

"Pretty lady," said Cobb. He'd been looking at Ellie while I was checking out the building.

"Yeah, I guess she was," Tomlinson agreed, "but not beautiful. *Pretty* is the right word. But when she smiled, man, that was a little bit of magic right there."

He set the picture back on the table, then sat down opposite us, took a sip of his juice.

"Mr. Tomlinson," I began, "we'd like to know more about The Tumbling Mustard."

Tomlinson shrugged. "Fire away. I can't say I'll be much help a half century after the fact, but I'll do all I can."

Before I could ask my first question, there was a noise behind us. We turned to see a man in a wheelchair rolling slowly into the room. If I'd had to hazard a guess, I would have put him at least twenty years older than Tomlinson, making him in his late eighties or early nineties.

Tomlinson jumped up and hurried to the old man, turning to us as he reached the wheelchair. "Gentlemen," he said, "I'd like you to meet my father, Arnold. He likes people to call him Arnie. Dad" — he bent slightly toward the old man — "this is the gentleman I was telling you about. Mr. Cullen. It was Mr. Cullen I spoke to on the phone. Mr. Cobb is his … associate. They're working on the story about Ellie Foster."

"Adam and Mike," I corrected, as both Mike and I stood, unsure of whether we should offer to shake the old man's hand, whether he'd be able to respond.

He wasn't just old. Unlike his son, this was a person who did not look well. I couldn't tell how tall he'd be when standing, but I guessed that he weighed less than a hundred pounds. Maybe considerably less.

"Welcome to our home." The old man smiled as he spoke in a soft, croaking, slightly halting voice, another indication to my untrained eye and ear that he was not well. "I'm pleased to meet you both." He pulled a wizened hand from beneath the blanket that covered his lap and legs and shakily extended it. I took it first, found it to be bony and cold, though the room was, if anything, a little too warm. Cobb moved alongside me, and he, too, shook the old man's hand.

"Good to meet you, sir," I said, as Mike nodded and smiled.

The old man looked up at us somewhat questioningly, as if wondering why we were there. I wondered if he had understood his son's explanation, or even remembered the earlier conversation.

As if to confirm my doubt, Tomlinson went through the explanation a second time. "These are the newspaper guys, Dad," Tomlinson said, as he moved behind the wheelchair and moved the old man farther into the room. "I told you about Mr. Cullen ... Adam. He called a few days ago. They're doing a story on Ellie Foster — she's the singer who performed at The Tumbling Mustard and then was abducted out in Calgary. We've talked about it a few times over the years."

Tomlinson had elected not to note Cobb's actual profession, I guessed to keep things simple for the older man, whose eyes hadn't left Cobb and me.

"Yes, I remember," he said.

I wasn't sure if he was referring to my phone call to his son or to Ellie Foster's disappearance.

"Would you like a juice, Dad?"

The old man shook his head, and Tomlinson came around the wheelchair, sat back down, and regarded Cobb and me. Ready. I pulled a notebook and pen out, partly for show and partly to note anything I thought might be useful.

"How long were you at The Tumbling Mustard, Mr. Tomlinson?"

"I think we're all on first names here, so let's make it Ben. And as for the TM, I was there the day they opened the doors and I was there when they shut the place down."

"How were you hired?"

Tomlinson smiled and scratched his jaw. "Well, now, *hired* is maybe the wrong word. Initially, I volunteered to help out. I liked the music, and I wanted the place to be another Le Hibou or maybe better. It never was, but ..." He stopped talking, and I wasn't sure whether he'd lost his train of thought or just didn't want to finish the sentence with some negative comment about the establishment.

I thought back to my conversations with Paula Pendergast and her statement that The Tumbling Mustard had never been about the music. I wondered what Tomlinson would say to that, but decided to leave that question for the moment.

"So you weren't paid to be there?" Cobb asked.

"Not at first, but then I wasn't doing a whole lot. I'd help performers set up on stage, pour the odd coffee, take out the trash — odd jobs guy, that was me. Didn't have to pay for coffee — I guess that was my payment. But maybe a month after the place opened, they decided they wanted a doorman and I got the job. Turned out to be a long-running gig."

I wanted to go back over the doorman thing and whose idea it was, but that was when things had turned testy when we'd spoken on the phone, so I decided to let it go.

"Tell us about Fayed," I said.

"As in …?"

"As in what kind of guy he was. What was he like to work for?"

"He was fine, same as Laird. Thing is, at the TM there wasn't a lot of employer-employee dynamic going on. You came in, you did your job; at the end of the night after the customers were gone, you maybe hung around for a while, visited with the performers, had a coffee, or sometimes there'd be beer or wine and we'd have a glass or two. Then you went home, and the next day you came back and did the same thing."

Cobb looked over at me, and I sensed he wanted to jump into the conversation. I gave a little nod. It's not like I was enjoying some kind of rapport with Tomlinson. He was answering the questions but not really giving me much.

Cobb must have been thinking the same thing. He leaned forward on the couch. "You really didn't say much about Fayed. Can we try that again?"

A cloud came over Tomlinson's face, and I thought we might have lost him, but he recovered and pulled the half smile back into place. "You're right," he said pleasantly. "The problem was, I really didn't know him very well. He tended to hang out with certain people, and I wasn't really one of them. I didn't know much about him. I knew he was born in Egypt, moved to California as a teenager, then to Ottawa a year or two before The Tumbling Mustard opened its doors."

"He have a family?"

"Not then."

"Later?"

"No idea."

"What did he do with his time away from The Tumbling Mustard?"

"No clue." Tomlinson shook his head. "Like I said, I didn't hang with the guy. I know he worked out a bunch, and somebody said he was a big soccer guy. I don't know if that was as a player or a fan, but I remember hearing that. And that's about the extent of how well I knew him."

"How about Laird?"

"Same answer."

"What answer was that, Ben?"

Again a hint of a frown, then, "Didn't know him beyond seeing him at work. Except he was the guy who paid us. We handed in time sheets, and at the end of the month he came around with the cheques, handed them out."

"When the news hit that Ellie Foster had disappeared, what was the reaction of Fayed and Laird?"

Tomlinson shrugged. "Shock, I think, like everybody else. I mean, it was a terrible thing, and when you actually know the person this has happened to ... I guess it hit all of us pretty hard."

Cobb glanced at me, an invitation to jump back in.

"Ben, I know I asked you about this when we talked on the phone, but we were given to understand that there were a lot of conversations between Fayed and Laird and a number of other people ... conversations that seemed almost secretive, maybe conspiratorial. Often these conversations were around the coffee bar area and were long and somewhat intense. Can you tell us anything about that?"

"Conversations?"

I nodded but didn't say anything.

"I mean, sure, there were conversations. Hell, coffee houses were all *about* conversation. People singing about and talking about fixing the world. But what you're suggesting … conspiratorial … I didn't see any of that."

"I know you said you didn't get to know the performers that well, but can you tell me your impression of Ellie Foster?

"Impression?"

"Truth is, Ben, several people said she seemed somehow different after her gig at the TM. Did you notice that at all?"

"Different?"

Tomlinson was a master of the delayed response. Repeat a word from the question to buy time while you thought about your answer. I'd seen it in lots of interviews I'd conducted over the years — often when the person being interviewed was feeling uncomfortable.

"Changed," I said. "Maybe more serious, not as happy."

He thought for a while before answering, finally shaking his head as he spoke. "No, I didn't see that. But then I wouldn't have, would I? I didn't know her before she played there, and I never saw her after. So I can't comment on whether she was … changed. I can't recall her being unhappy, though. Seemed to me that the way she was on stage was all about happy. She gave off this vibe. It was the love generation, after all. And Ellie was definitely a part of that generation."

"But not everybody who was part of the love generation was happy," Cobb said. "I mean, I wasn't there, but it was also a time of unrest, of wanting change and being willing to do things that didn't feel much like love to effect that change. Did you see any of that around the TM, Ben?"

A pause, then a shrug. "Hell, I'm sure there were radicals came into the place. I mean, they were everywhere, so they'd have to be in the TM occasionally, wouldn't they? But if you're asking me if suddenly Ellie went all radical, I really didn't see that. Sorry."

Cobb sat back again.

I said, "Something else I think I asked you earlier — Ellie Foster disappeared on the twenty-fifth of February. Can you recall if Laird and Fayed were around the TM at that time?"

"You mean were they in Ottawa and not out in Calgary shooting guys and kidnapping Ellie? Yeah, I think I can say they were around the club at that time. Like I told you, they were never away for more than a day or two at a time. So no, they didn't kidnap Ellie, which is what I think you're asking. Sorry to ruin your story."

Tomlinson had switched again — the voice was once again cold, and his body language was leaning toward *Get the fuck out of here.*

Cobb stepped back in, undeterred by our host's suddenly unpleasant demeanour. He spoke to Tomlinson's father.

"Did you ever get to The Tumbling Mustard, sir?"

I was looking at Tomlinson when Cobb asked his question, and it was obvious he was uncomfortable with his father having to answer. "Just a min—" he began, but the elder Tomlinson held up a hand to stop him.

He looked at Cobb, and the halting voice spoke: "I was there from time to time, yes. Liked the place, at least the music. Loved the music."

Cobb smiled and nodded. "Did you ever see Ellie Foster perform, Mr. Tomlinson?"

The old man swallowed a couple of times before answering. I continued to watch the younger Tomlinson, who seemed to be worried that the effort to answer questions was taking a toll on his father.

The old man nodded. "Yes, I did. She was wonderful. Quite wonderful." He swallowed a couple more times. It seemed to require an effort.

"Dad, I think we'd better get you back to your room for now. You're looking pretty tuckered. And we've got a big day tomorrow — doctor's appointment in the morning and lunch at your favourite place."

The old man looked like he wanted to argue the point, but he finally responded with a slight nod. I was disappointed to see him go. Other than the swallowing, he didn't appear to be in a great deal of discomfort. At least, not any *more* discomfort.

Tomlinson rose, turned his father's wheelchair, and started in the direction of the bedroom. "I'll just be a minute," he said, without turning to look at us.

I looked over at Cobb, my eyebrows raised. The bedroom was too close for us to say anything that wouldn't be heard. Cobb got up and crossed to the part of the living room where the old photos were displayed. I also stood up, more to stretch my legs, and wandered around the room.

It was a pleasant space. There were older paintings on the wall; at least, I assumed they were old. Certainly the frames were. Antique tools and kitchen implements hung on nails here and there. It was an attempt at rustic, and I thought it worked.

I stepped closer to examine the paintings and artists' names. Not all were signed, and those that were tended to be by artists I didn't know — maybe locals, though clearly some were very good. Lots of landscapes — I wondered if they were of nearby places.

Among those that were signed, several were French Canadian names. Some were only initials. One of the paintings stood out, at least for me. It was a vibrant splash of greens and golds, with a young boy in the foreground sitting on the bank of a pleasant stream. The boy was leaning against a tree but not facing the stream, at least not face on. Instead, he was to one side of the tree, facing what looked to be downstream. A forest canopy stretched out behind the boy and the stream. His knees were pulled up, and he rested his arms on his knees, his chin on his arms. And he looked unhappy, or at least deeply contemplative. It was an image that drew you in, almost forcing you to wonder what the boy was thinking so hard about.

I looked for the artist's name, hoping I'd see more of his or her work. No name — only the initials *D.G.*

I was about to wander the place to see if D.G. had anything else on display when Tomlinson returned from the bedroom. "Sorry about that." He rubbed his hands together. "Well, if that's everything, I do have some work to do. I don't know if I was much help with your story. But I look forward to reading it when it comes out." His voice conveyed something, I wasn't sure what — maybe it was my imagination. I got the feeling he doubted there would be a story. But I couldn't tell if it was because he thought we weren't capable of writing it or he sensed our cover was bogus.

Cobb wasn't in a hurry to leave. He finally turned to face Tomlinson without moving from the photo gallery corner.

"Ben, let me ask you something," he said. "Do you have any idea who might have kidnapped Ellie Foster?"

"I really don't." Tomlinson shook his head sadly. "I won't say I haven't thought about it, especially in the months and even the first few years after it happened. And that's what makes it so tough — she truly was as wonderful as my father said she was."

Cobb nodded and looked at me. I gave a small head shake to tell him I had nothing more. He started for the door, then stopped and turned to Tomlinson, who was behind us.

"One last thing. I'm wondering if you might be able to give us a list of other people who worked at The Tumbling Mustard."

Tomlinson shook his head. "After Adam called" — he gestured in my direction — "I did some thinking about that. I actually wondered if there was someone at the TM who might have been involved in the incident out in Calgary. And I came up with nothing at all. Truth is, a lot of the people who worked there were there for only a short time — students making a little money to help with their schooling, hippie types who just wanted to work a few hours. I came up with maybe two or three names in all, and those people have been dead for some time. So I'm afraid I can't help you on that score. Sorry."

Cobb looked like he wanted to pursue the point but changed his mind. He continued to the door. I followed as Tomlinson moved past us to open the door. "I hope you enjoy the rest of your stay in our part of the world," he said, smiling. "And I wish you every success with the story."

Again, the slightest hint of sarcasm. I was pretty sure our cover had been blown.

"Thank you," I said.

Cobb merely nodded. And then we were out of the house, the door closed behind us. *Firmly*, I thought. Not exactly rudely, but definitely firmly.

Once we were in the car and out of the driveway, I said, "Well, what did you think?"

"He kind of blew hot and cold," Cobb observed, "depending on where the conversation was going."

"Does that tell you anything?"

Cobb shook his head slowly. "Other than the fact there were things he liked talking about more than some other things, not much."

"Did you believe the thing about the names, that there wasn't anybody he could give us?"

Cobb shrugged. "Hard to say. It *was* a hell of a long time ago. So maybe he was telling the truth. I can't say I have a warm spot in my heart for Mr. Tomlinson the younger, but that isn't a good reason to suspect he was lying."

"The guy felt a little oily to me," I said.

"Has that about him, all right." Cobb nodded. "I would have liked to spend a little more time with his father. Got the impression Ben didn't want that. But in fairness, that might have been because of the old man's health. He may simply have thought a lot of questions would tax his father's strength, and looking at the older Mr. Tomlinson, that might have been the case."

We drove in silence for a while. I wanted to enjoy the scenery, but the realization that we were pretty much at the end of our leads spoiled the view at least somewhat.

"You think Ben believed we just wanted to write a story?" I asked.

"I can't say for sure." Cobb shrugged. "But I don't know that it matters. I don't think he would have given us any more either way."

"Any thoughts as to what we should do next?"

"Not really," Cobb replied. "But while we ponder our next move, I think we should sample some Ottawa cuisine."

TWELVE

We were upstairs in the Vittoria Trattoria, an Italian restaurant in the ByWard Market. We had already worked our way through some excellent bruschetta and were wrapping up the pasta dishes. Mine was a *funghi e pancetta*, a penne with ham and sautéed mushrooms in a brandy rosé sauce, and it was damn good. Cobb, ever the conservative gourmand, went with the meatballs and spaghetti, which he pronounced "just as damn good."

We had not discussed the case, neither of us wanting to spoil a terrific dinner with a depressing recap of our lack of progress. The waiter had just delivered two more glasses of wine when Stompin' Tom's "The Hockey Song" announced an incoming call on my cell and brought smiles to neighbouring diners' faces. I looked at the call display — no name, but an Alberta number with a 780 prefix, meaning that the call was from the northern part of the province. I told Cobb I'd better take the call, relieved that it wasn't the MFs with the dreaded payback demand.

I answered the call as I was making my way down the stairs and out onto the street. A female voice said, "I hope I'm not taking you away from anything."

"Not at all," I answered, noncommittal until I knew who the caller, whose voice was familiar, actually was.

"It's Paula, Adam. Paula Pendergast."

"Hi, Paula. What's up? You come up with any more names?"

"I wish I had," she said. "No, I just haven't been able to think about anything else but Ellie Foster and what happened to her. I guess I was just hoping for an update. I hope that isn't too presumptuous of me."

"Not at all, Paula. I understand, but unfortunately I'm afraid we haven't really gotten any closer to determining what happened to her."

"I'm sorry to hear that."

"Funny coincidence, though, that you should call today. Cobb and I spent the afternoon with Ben Tomlinson. He has a place out in the Gatineaus. Pretty cool place. Unfortunately, he wasn't able to give us anything we didn't already have."

"Ben. My goodness. How is he, anyway?"

"Well, I'd say he looked pretty good. I wish I could say the same for his father. But I think the old man isn't going to be around much longer. He looked pretty emaciated and sickly. I'm no expert, but I'd say it might be cancer."

She was quiet for a long while. I guessed she was upset at the news about Tomlinson's father. When the silence continued, I said, "Did you know Ben's dad, Paula?"

"Are you sure it was Ben Tomlinson you were speaking to?" she asked me.

I wasn't sure how to react to a question so odd. "I'm not sure I know what you mean."

"Ben Tomlinson's dad is dead."

I didn't understand. "But he seemed —"

"No, I mean he died *a long time ago*."

It was my turn to fall silent. After a few seconds, I said, "How do you know that?"

"It was really sad." Her voice was so soft I had to press the phone harder to my ear to hear her. "It was when I was performing at The Tumbling Mustard. One night Ben wasn't at his usual spot at the door, and I asked Laird if anything was wrong. He told me that Ben's dad had died that morning of an aneurysm. It was terrible; I think he was only in his forties. When Ben came back to work a couple of days later, he was so terribly down. I think they must have been really close. I guess I kind of became the person he could talk to, and we spent a couple of long nights with him telling me about his dad. That's why when you said you met his father ... well ... that's just not possible."

I took a couple of deep breaths while I processed what she'd said. "Paula," I said, "do you happen to know if Ben ever married?"

"I don't know for sure. I thought we'd stay in touch after my time at The Tumbling Mustard, especially with him losing his dad and all, but you know how it is — it just didn't happen."

"Listen, Paula, I have to run, but thanks for the call, and believe me, you weren't bothering me one bit. And if we find out anything definitive about Ellie Foster, you'll be my first call."

"Thank you, Adam, that's very kind of you."

I disconnected and took the stairs two at a time back up to the second floor, almost laying out our waiter as I reached the top of the staircase. I apologized and made my way quickly, and a little more carefully, back to our table. Cobb had finished his dinner and was looking impatient.

I sat down. "Sorry, but that was a call I'm glad I took. It was Paula Pendergast, the Saskatoon Princess, with some very interesting information."

"Good. I ordered tiramisu, so why don't you finish your pasta while you talk?"

I nodded. I took one bite of the pasta, a sip of wine, and leaned forward, lowering my voice. "There's something strange going on. The old guy we met today wasn't Ben Tomlinson's father. Paula told me that Tomlinson's dad died during the time she was performing at The Tumbling Mustard."

Cobb was about to take a drink of wine. The glass stopped halfway to his lips, and he set it back down.

"Is she sure?"

"One hundred percent positive."

Cobb was looking at me, but I could tell he wasn't seeing me or anything else. He was in an almost trance-like state as he digested the news.

After a couple of beats, he said, "So who was the old man?"

"Good question. Father-in-law?

"We can check that. But why lie about it? If he's the father-in-law, then just say that — it's hardly incriminating."

I shrugged. "I guess he could argue that he didn't lie, that we just assumed when he said 'Dad,' he meant his own father."

"That seems a bit of a stretch. My turn to make a call. I'll be right back. If you touch my tiramisu, I'll have to kill you."

He was a lot quicker than I had been, and was back after just a couple of minutes. Before we could go any further with the conversation, the tiramisu arrived, and even Paula Pendergast's revelation didn't keep us from falling onto the dessert with purpose. But after the first few bites and the obligatory visit from the server to see how it was, we slowed down and looked up from the food.

It was Cobb who finally spoke: "I called Beacham — he's going to have one of his former colleagues check with Stats Can — find out if Tomlinson ever married, and if so, the name of his father-in-law and whether that person is still alive. In the meantime, I think we need to go back there. Tomlinson said the old man had a doctor's appointment in the morning and then they would be going somewhere for lunch. I want to look around the place, see if we can turn up a few things — the real identity of the old man, for starters, and who knows what else."

"So we break into the place and do a little snooping. Is that what you're proposing?"

"Pretty much."

"Why does this worry the hell out of me?"

Cobb shrugged, then grinned. "I've kept you out of trouble so far, haven't I?"

"Actually, no, you haven't. What you've done is get me into a fair amount of trouble, and then get me out of it again. That's not the same as not getting into the mess in the first place."

"Eat your tiramisu."

By just after seven the next morning, Cobb had found us a spot sheltered by a canopy of trees from which we could observe the driveway to the Tomlinson house. The plan was to wait until Ben Tomlinson and the old man (whoever he was) left for their appointment, then get into the house and see what we could learn about the identity of the man Tomlinson had masqueraded as his father. And we'd see what else we could find that might be interesting. It all sounded so innocent when Cobb described it — like a visit to a realtor's open house on a Sunday afternoon.

We drank Tim Hortons coffee and ate old-fashioned plain doughnuts while we waited for the men to leave.

We had been there only about twenty minutes when Cobb's phone rang; it was an actual ring — Cobb, the old-school guy. He answered, mostly listened for a couple of minutes, said a couple of things in French, thanked the caller, and ended the call.

"Staff Sergeant Lapointe, RCMP. Beacham's connection. No record of Tomlinson ever having been married. He also checked if Tomlinson has a stepfather, and he doesn't — so the dad thing is a charade. I'd really like to find out why."

"What if the doctor's appointment was as big a fiction as the father thing?" I said between bites of my second doughnut.

"I thought about that," Cobb said, "but he didn't say it to us. He was talking to the old man at the time. Of course it might have been for our benefit, but to what end? And looking at the old man, I'd say he's probably a fairly frequent visitor to one or more doctor's offices."

I chose not to debate the point. Instead, I finished my coffee and doughnut and tilted my seat back. I closed my eyes. "How about you take the morning shift, and I'll handle the afternoon?"

"Whatever I'm paying you, it's too much."

"Actually, that whole pay issue is one we should discuss sometime soon."

"How about we discuss it right after your surveillance shift?"

"The world hates a whiner," I said, and slid into a sleep that ended twenty minutes later (it felt like five) when Cobb shook me awake.

"Contact," he said. "Ford Explorer just went by, heading south, two male occupants. Time to move."

I sat up, pulled the seat upright, and shook my head to dislodge at least some of the cobwebs. Cobb started the car, put it in gear, and we moved out from our hiding place. We made the three- or four-hundred-metre run to Tomlinson's house and parked behind the garage. I hoped Tomlinson was the person driving the Explorer and wasn't sitting in the living room reading the paper as we prepared to break into his home. I took some comfort from Cobb's having done this sort of thing before and his being completely calm. Or oblivious. I opted for calm.

In case we were spotted and aroused the interest of neighbours, Cobb had brought along two white jackets that read *Eastern Electric*. I suspected the jackets had already made a few trips here and there.

I liked the fact that Eastern Electric could mean a lot of things and might fool at least some people some of the time. I'd have been much more confident in the ruse had we been driving a van that had Eastern Electric emblazoned on its sides instead of a nondescript Toyota Corolla that looked exactly like what it was — a rental car.

Before we exited the car, Cobb said, "In case anyone happens to be watching, act like you belong here. Walk like you have someplace to go, and don't look around. We go straight around the back and see if we can get in the back door. I checked yesterday, and it doesn't look like the place is alarmed." Then he said, "Here," and handed me a clipboard. I wondered if Eastern Electric employees would be expected to carry clipboards but decided this was a question for another time.

We climbed out of the Corolla in unison and strode purposefully to the back gate. I hoped there wasn't a dog back there waiting to devour us and wondered if the clipboard could be pressed into service as a weapon, if need be.

There was no dog, so we opened the gate and headed for the back door. Cobb knocked, then again, harder. No one came to the door. First hurdle cleared.

Cobb pulled two pairs of latex gloves out of an inside jacket pocket and handed one pair to me. "These won't protect you from being cut or punctured, so be careful where you stick your hands. Don't reach into areas you can't see into. If you're in doubt, call me, and we'll figure out another way."

I nodded as he tried the door's handle. As both of us expected, it was locked.

Cobb shrugged. "Worth a try." He pulled a small tack hammer from a pocket and, without hesitation, broke the glass window that sat two-thirds of the way toward the top of the back door. He carefully cleared the remaining glass shards from around the frame, then reached in and down. It took a few tries, but finally he was able to locate and undo the lock, and seconds later we were inside the house.

He had told me on the way there that we would split up in our search — he'd take the main floor, while I searched the upstairs for anything at all that might provide answers. Cobb was especially interested in learning the identity of the man Tomlinson had passed off as his father. And, of course, anything that related to The Tumbling Mustard.

Wordlessly, we separated and I headed upstairs. There were four rooms on the second level of the house. Two of them were bedrooms, one was an office, and the fourth was a full bathroom. There was an ensuite off one of the bedrooms. I decided to check the bathroom first, my reasoning being that there might be a prescription or two that may have been filled in the old man's name.

I was disappointed that the only two pill bottles up there bore the name B. Tomlinson. Not surprising — yesterday we'd seen that the old man's bedroom was downstairs, and his prescriptions were more likely to be found down there as well. There was nothing else of interest in the bathroom.

I decided to tackle the office next. I opened every drawer, sifted through every piece of paper, and carefully examined each card in a fairly substantial stack of business cards, some in English, most in French, a few in both languages. I was hoping to see a name or a business that might have some significance, but there was nothing that set off any alarm bells.

I returned each pile of papers to what it had looked like before I handled it — again, an instruction from Cobb. Next, I tackled the two bedrooms. The first was almost barren; I took it to be a guest room. There was some linen in one closet, but all other drawers and spaces in the room were completely empty.

An easy but disappointing search.

That left only the final bedroom. It was clearly occupied, and I guessed it was Ben's room. I opened drawers and rummaged through the closet, checking pockets of jackets and shirts. I looked under the bed, in the night table, and even flipped through the paperback books Tomlinson had stacked there — his reading taste leaned toward fantasy — but found nothing remotely incriminating or even interesting.

I started back downstairs and almost overlooked a small table that sat inconspicuously on the landing halfway up the stairs. It had a sewing machine sitting on it, which might explain why I hadn't noticed it or given it a thought on my way upstairs. I thought about it now. It wasn't a sewing table. This was a sewing machine sitting on an ordinary end table.

I began checking it out. More meaningless stuff in the drawer, but when I went to the two doors that opened in the middle, just below the drawer, I saw only one item: a scrapbook. I pulled it out, and realized the second I opened it I'd finally found something significant.

The first third of the scrapbook was filled with yellowed newspaper clippings, all of them held in place by aged and weakened Scotch tape. Some of the tape had given way, leaving several of the clippings hanging precariously aslant.

I leafed through them quickly, my excitement building as I did. The clippings were all from the period just before and just after Ellie Foster's disappearance. There was a section that focused on the teach-in that had been staged by Five Minutes to Midnight, followed by pages of coverage of the failed attempt to rob the armoured car. Next came a series of clippings that focused on the coverage of Prime Minister Pearson's various meetings, pronouncements, and public appearances.

Only one of the clippings had any kind of notation on the scrapbook page. That was above a comprehensive *Globe and Mail* story on the impending unveiling of the new Canadian flag, scheduled for February 15, 1965. The story, dated three weeks before, talked about the celebration that was planned on Parliament Hill for that day and focused on Pearson's involvement in the ceremony.

Above the clipping was written the word "Midnight," and a bull's eye had been painted on the prime minister's chest in the accompanying photo. To me, that was just another indication of the adolescent way this group of activists, if that's what they were, had conducted themselves. But there was more to what I was seeing than juvenile silliness. These had been dangerous people, and I paused at the thought of how different so many things might have been had they carried out was at least a preliminary plan to assassinate the prime minister.

The clippings took up about a third of the scrapbook. Several blank pages followed before I came to another significant section — this one a series of photographs. Though I hadn't been to the Parliament Buildings in several years, I recognized the Peace Tower. On the next page was a sequence of photos with a handwritten note underneath identifying an RCMP constable who was in each of the photos. The note identified him as Constable Joseph Secours, whose job it would be to lower the Red Ensign for the last time and raise the new Canadian Maple Leaf flag above the Peace Tower.

There were crowd shots taken at Parliament Hill — I guessed maybe from a previous July 1 celebration. In two of the photos, the prime minister, Lester B. Pearson, was at a podium. The thousands of onlookers gathered in front of him looked to be taking in whatever it was he was saying.

There was one photo that gave me pause. It was of the policeman and the prime minister together, both smiling and looking at the camera. Behind them, the new Canadian flag flew above the Peace Tower. The photo clearly had been taken in the minutes just after the first raising of the flag. This time, a large *X* had been drawn through the photo. *Frustration at not being able to carry out the plan?*

The last few pages were like a catalogue — lists and pictures of high-powered rifles and the ammunition they fired, details about several kinds of explosives, and instructions on how to use them. I didn't take the time to read any more, but picked up the scrapbook and took it downstairs to show Cobb, who was just emerging from the old man's bedroom.

He looked up at me and shook his head, an indication that he hadn't found anything useful.

I held up the scrapbook.

"This looks like pay dirt," I said, and headed for the kitchen table, where I set it down. I let him open it and look at it. I looked over his shoulder but didn't comment — I wanted to let him make his own assessment of what we were looking at.

Twenty minutes later, he finally straightened and turned to look at me.

"What do you think?" he asked.

"It looks to me like Five Minutes to Midnight had planned or at least thought about assassinating Pearson and maybe the RCMP guy who raised the flag that day."

"I get going after the PM, but why the cop?"

"Symbolism?" I shrugged. "It would have been pretty powerful if, as Constable Secours was raising the new flag for the first time, both he and the PM were gunned down or killed in some other way. You can imagine the chaos and confusion that would have followed, not just here but across Canada. I mean, it's so outrageous it doesn't even seem possible, and clearly if that's what they had planned, they didn't pull it off. We know there was no attempt. I wonder what happened."

Cobb tapped the scrapbook and nodded. "That's what I take from this, too," he said. "And I'm betting that whoever put this together was a member of Five Minutes to Midnight. Tomlinson, or the old man … or both?"

I shrugged. "Or someone else who then gave the scrapbook to one of them."

"We need to know what happened," Cobb said. "And that isn't in here." He tapped the scrapbook again.

"The other big question remains. Who is the old man?"

"Roger that," he said. "Come on, I want to check out the garage."

We'd taken only a couple of steps toward the back door when the front doorbell rang. I stopped moving and stopped breathing for a few seconds, trying to take comfort in knowing it was unlikely that Tomlinson would ring the doorbell of his own house. Cobb moved to a front window, pulled a curtain back, and peeked out.

"I think it's one of the neighbours," he whispered. "Grab your clipboard and look like you're inspecting stuff. I'll get the door."

I grabbed the clipboard off the kitchen table and bent down over an electrical outlet. Cobb opened the door. I forced myself not to look up, thinking a real electrical inspector wouldn't give a damn who was at the door. I glanced from the clipboard to the outlet and back to the clipboard, hoping whoever was at the door knew as little about electricity as I did.

"Hi," I heard Cobb say. Very cheery.

"I live across the way," I heard a male voice say. "Thought I saw somebody over here, and I knew Ben and his dad weren't home. Thought I'd better check it out."

"Good idea, Mr. …"

"Burkowsky. Who are you guys?"

"Private contractors," Cobb answered, still the soul of congeniality. "The power company hires us to inspect the older homes. They haven't got enough manpower. Burkowsky, did you say? You got a Burkowsky on your list?" he called.

I knew the last bit was directed at me so I made a show of checking the clipboard. "Burkowsky … Burkowsky. Yeah, we got him down for next week."

I went back to intently examining the electrical outlet.

"I don't blame you for checking, Mr. Burkowsky," Cobb said. "Mr. Tomlinson's lucky to have a neighbour like you. We'll see you next week. Marge in the office will call to make an appointment. And, by the way, there's no charge for the service call."

"Never had an inspection before."

"I know. New government regulations. Pain in the butt for everybody, believe me."

I still hadn't looked back, so I couldn't tell if Burkowsky was going to be difficult or not. I heard the door close and glanced back for the first time. Cobb was back at the window, I assumed to make sure the neighbour was actually leaving. He stayed there for a few more seconds, then turned back into the room.

"Okay, he's heading back toward his place. We'd better pick up the pace. We don't know that he won't call Tomlinson to ask him about the electrical inspection that's happening in his home."

"You ever think of switching teams, you know, maybe becoming one of the bad guys? You're a natural with the bullshit," I said.

Cobb snorted and pointed to the back of the house. "Let's get out to that garage."

The next three quarters of an hour we spent rooting under benches, opening boxes that were stored on shelves, moving equipment and tools to peer into grease-stained corners. And we found nothing. We were halfway through the morning, and all we had was the scrapbook. And though I knew it was important, there was nothing there to incriminate Tomlinson, the old man, or anyone else. I hadn't seen names or photos of anyone associated with Five Minutes to Midnight. Tomlinson could say he'd found the scrapbook, or it had been given to him, or he'd bought it at a garage sale, and there was nothing in it to disprove that.

I looked at my watch — just after ten. I was beginning to get nervous. I'd heard Tomlinson talk about the doctor's appointment and the lunch after, but I was beginning to feel a little uncomfortable hanging around the place. If Tomlinson and the old man did show up and found us prowling around, things could become a lot more uncomfortable.

I looked at Cobb, but he didn't seem to share my concern.

"Back to the house — this time, you take the main floor and I take the second level."

I'd read enough cop procedurals to know that this was often the way searches were conducted in order to give every part of the search area two complete looks. That knowledge did nothing to alleviate my growing nervousness.

I also knew that there was no point arguing. The quicker we got started, the quicker we'd be out of there. Again I started with the bathroom, and again came away empty-handed. I moved to the living room and was meticulous, even checking under and between couch cushions and looking at each of the boards on the hardwood floor to see if any of them looked like a hiding place. I could hear Cobb upstairs as I turned my attention to the living room and dining area. I was still a little spooked after the Burkowsky visit but tried to stay focused and thorough as I examined bookshelves and the entertainment centre. I paid special attention to the photo area.

I studied every photo in the hopes of seeing a face I could recognize, but it wasn't until I turned one of the photos over that I found something of interest.

On the back of a photo of three people — two men and a woman — I noticed that the cardboard backing looked worn at one corner, an indicator perhaps that the backing had been removed on a somewhat regular basis, or at least more than once or twice. I eased the little metal pieces holding the cardboard in place and eased the cardboard off. Inside was a folded piece of paper.

It was old and felt like it could crumble if I handled it at all roughly, so I slowly and carefully unfolded it and spread it out on the kitchen table. It was a note with the words *Five Minutes to Midnight* scrawled across the top of the page alongside an almost comical logo or symbol. It was the face of a clock with the hands at — no surprise — 11:55.

The note read:

February 11, 1965

The time of our proud moment draws near. Each of us must maintain our silence, our courage, and above all, our belief in the inevitability and rightness of our cause. In just days we will re-write the history of our nation and avenge the atrocity of the Suez at the same time as we destroy the hated flag that Pearson wishes to inflict on a proud people.

With victory in our sights, I rely on each of you to do what must be done to ensure our victory.

Abdel Fayed

It was childish in its fervour and desperate appeal to whomever the intended readers were and would have been almost funny if it weren't for the seriousness of the subject matter, which I was sure included the attempted assassination of the prime minister of Canada.

I reread the brief note, then turned my attention once again to the photo. I wished there was a way to enlarge it to get a better look at the three people. I was fairly confident that I could rule out Fayed being one of the people in the photo based simply on the description I'd been given of him as a well-built man who looked as if he could be

Middle Eastern. Neither of the men in the photo fit that description.

The two men flanked the woman in the photo, and I concentrated first on her. I thought it might be Ellie Foster, but I wasn't certain. Her hair was different, and she was somewhat in the shadow of the bigger man standing next to her. I checked against the photo Tomlinson had showed us the day before and was fairly certain it was Ellie. I wished we'd thought to bring the photos Monica Brill had left with us, but they were at our hotel. I recalled that Tomlinson had said there was only one photo on the table that pertained to The Tumbling Mustard. He might have lied.

I looked again to the two men, concentrating first on the man on the left, the tallest of the three people, thin, with hair that was longer, though not *long*, and an unkempt beard. I tried to see any resemblance between this man, whom I would have guessed was twentyish, and either Tomlinson or the old man. I couldn't say, but lose the facial hair and long locks and add fifty years, and who the hell knew?

The man on the right looked a little older and was clean shaven, with shorter hair. He was wearing a sweater that looked like it cost more than the other man's entire ensemble. I was wishing I could get a look at Tomlinson and the old man again to try to compare the facial structures, see if I could get a read on whether one or both of them were in the photo.

I got my wish.

THIRTEEN

"Research for the article?" The voice dragged out the word *article*, making all three syllables into words of their own.

The voice was maybe ten feet behind me, and I knew without looking that it wasn't Cobb. I set the photo back on the table, straightened up, and turned slowly, just in case the speaker was as hostile as the flat, monotone voice indicated.

Turned out it wasn't a bad idea to exercise caution.

Ben Tomlinson was standing there with a pissed-off look on his face and a shotgun in his hands. He had to have arrived while we were searching the garage and wouldn't have heard a vehicle or someone entering the house. The shotgun, a double barrel, was aimed at me. I moved my hands out to the sides, away from my body, to indicate I wasn't a threat. I wasn't at all sure that right at that moment it made a difference.

"Hey, asshole!" Tomlinson yelled. "I've got your friend right here, and if you aren't out here in less than five seconds I will blow this son of a bitch into the great beyond."

I didn't turn my head toward the stairs, just in case Cobb had some plan to come in, gun blazing, and catch

Tomlinson off guard before he could send me into the great beyond.

Cobb did not have that particular plan in mind, and he appeared at the top of the stairs, moving with the same caution I had exercised earlier.

He didn't say anything, and Tomlinson was silent as well, choosing to gesture with the barrel of the gun to indicate he wanted Cobb standing next to me. Cobb, hands raised slightly, reached the bottom of the stairs, crossed the floor to where I was, and turned to face Tomlinson.

"Burkowsky?" he asked, the hint of a wry smile at the corners of his mouth.

"Pays to get along with the neighbours," Tomlinson answered, his thin lips stretched into a decidedly unpleasant horizontal line.

"So what now?" Cobb said. "Seems to me you've got a decision or two to make. Right now what we've got is our suspicion that you were a member of Five Minutes to Midnight and that you may have had something to do with the disappearance of Ellie Foster. That, and maybe a charge of illegal use of a firearm. You take this any further, and you end up in some serious shit."

Tomlinson laughed, without a trace of mirth. "I believe what we call that is trying to make a silk purse out of a sow's ear. The only people in shit here are you two, and all of us know that. I shoot both your asses, tell the police that here's me, a helpless senior citizen finding you in my home, and I panicked a little and shot to protect myself, my father, and my home. Might get a reprimand — more likely a hero's reception." He looked at me. "You're a newspaperman — be a great story, wouldn't it? Too bad you won't be the one writing it."

"Yeah, about that father thing," Cobb said. "Speaking of not being 100 percent honest — you feel like telling us who the old man really is?"

I wasn't sure Cobb's strategy of challenging Tomlinson, even verbally, was the one I would have employed. But I decided to keep my mouth shut and concentrate on having my legs continue to keep me in the upright position.

"I don't feel like telling you shit." The look on Tomlinson's face reminded me of the one I'd seen on Marlon Kennedy's a couple of times.

"Which brings us to the only other question we have," Cobb went on. "What did you do with Ellie Foster?"

"No, that isn't the question at all." Tomlinson shook his head. "The one question is, what do I do with *you*? Which, by the way, I already have an answer for, but then we've been through that, haven't we?"

I was convinced the verbal sparring was about to come to an end, and if Tomlinson actually planned to shoot us, that he would do it sooner rather than later. There was a movement behind him, and I saw the front door open and the old man in the wheelchair enter the house, his eyes moving from us to Tomlinson and back to us as he rolled farther into the room. He took up a position a little to Tomlinson's right.

"I told you to wait in the car," Tomlinson barked, his eyes never leaving Cobb and me.

The old man nodded. "Yes, you did."

It had to have taken a tremendous effort for him to get himself and the wheelchair out of the car, transfer himself into the chair, and roll it in here without help.

I looked at him and realized that if I was looking for a saviour, this frail little man, who looked like what he'd done had taken a tremendous toll on the little strength he had, was not that person.

"Get into the bedroom." Tomlinson growled the command with a quick glance at the old man before returning his attention to us.

"Shortly," the old man managed in his husky wheeze.

"Now!" Tomlinson's voice carried the threat of what would happen if he was disobeyed.

The old man shook his head and placed his withered hands on the wheels of the chair, as if he could somehow keep it from moving. Like a child making a fist. Determined.

"There are things I want to know. Things I want to say."

"There's nothing you need to know. And you'd be wasting your breath saying anything to these two. They're not leaving here alive."

Cobb was looking at the old man. "I don't know who you are, but I'm wondering if you're okay with a few more killings … to go along with the ones at The Depression, for starters. Were there others? Ellie Foster?"

The tug-of-war between Tomlinson and the old man wasn't about to settle. I watched the old man. Whoever he was, he wasn't intimidated by the shotgun or by Tomlinson's menace.

Tomlinson was alternating between watching us to make sure we weren't trying anything and glaring at the man in the wheelchair. And still the frail old man made no move to leave the room.

I was willing him to stay. I thought as long as he was there, Tomlinson might not pull the trigger. But I realized that even that thought wasn't rooted in reality as Tomlinson's fury continued to mount. He was clearly not accustomed to being disobeyed. And now I feared that the old man's stubborn refusal to leave might actually prove the snapping point in the man holding the shotgun. I wasn't sure that he wouldn't turn and shoot the old man first. Except that he would be left with only one shell for Cobb and me.

Cobb must have been thinking the same thing, because I noticed he was inching away from me — very slowly.

"It doesn't really matter now, sir, but I would like to know your name." I spoke to the old man, partly to keep Tomlinson's focus on me and partly because I really did want to know who this man was.

The old man looked at me, and there was a small smile playing at his eyes and mouth.

"You shut the fuck up," Tomlinson snarled in the old man's direction. He was waving the shotgun around now, and I knew there was a danger that we could push him too far.

"Daniel Gervais," he said softly. "Not words I have said in a very long time."

"The third owner of The Tumbling Mustard," I said, watching Tomlinson as I spoke.

He turned again on Gervais, spittle flying from his mouth as he yelled, "I told you to shut your goddamned mouth!" He spun back to me, and I knew then that he was close to the breaking point. I held my hands up in a gesture of surrender and to show I wouldn't ask any more questions. I hoped he received the message.

But Gervais wasn't finished. "The Tumbling Mustard was nothing but a front for a bunch of amateur anarchists. And I was one of them. I actually believed —"

Tomlinson raised the gun, aimed it at Cobb. He was savvy enough to realize that of the three people in that room, Cobb posed the greatest danger to him. Take him out, then me, and he'd have all the time he needed to reload and shoot the old man, too, if that was what he decided to do.

I know I winced and maybe even closed my eyes for a second, almost missing Daniel Gervais as he used the only weapon he had. In what for him had to be a superhuman effort, he rolled the wheelchair into Tomlinson, hard enough to almost take him down. The old man's spindly arms flailed uselessly as he pummelled Tomlinson with blows that had the force of a small child's. They were no more than an irritant. And a distraction.

Tomlinson didn't go down. He was knocked back a step by the wheelchair but recovered his balance, reaching down instinctively to his lower legs, which had been hit by the chair's footrests. He swore at the pain as he stepped forward again and raised the shotgun over his head, clearly intending to bring the butt end down on Gervais's head.

"Hold it right there!" Cobb yelled, and I turned to see that he had his own weapon — the Smith & Wesson .38 Special he often carried — out and aimed at Tomlinson. Cobb had assumed the attack stance, the two-handed grip of his police training.

"Put the gun down, Ben," Cobb said, quietly at first, then louder a second time. "Put the gun down!"

Tomlinson hesitated, and I watched as reason duelled with fury, the internal conflict playing out on a face contorted with rage and surprise. But I thought I saw something else on that face. Hard to know, but maybe he was resigned, knowing it was over and it wasn't ending as he'd wanted.

He'd made his decision.

He swung the shotgun around, bringing the barrel back toward Cobb and me. The move was fast, so fast that when I heard the two loud bursts that echoed through the room, I wasn't sure at first which gun had fired.

Tomlinson hadn't been fast enough.

The force of Cobb's shots jerked him back, and the shotgun fell to the floor behind the wheelchair. Tomlinson crashed down, one horrible final curse, if that's what it was, escaping his lips.

For several seconds, no one moved. No one spoke. I looked to my left and saw Cobb, still in the position, his weapon still aimed at the fallen Tomlinson.

When it was clear Tomlinson was not moving, Cobb stepped forward. I followed him, Cobb kneeling next to Tomlinson, me moving to Gervais to see if he was okay.

Cobb straightened. "Are you all right, sir?" he addressed Gervais.

The old man, shaken by all that had happened, nodded to both of us. Then he turned his gaze to the man on the floor and, in a voice filled with hate and rage, said, "Amateur son of a bitch. Didn't check for weapons."

"Call 911, Adam," Cobb said, as he looked back to Tomlinson. "He's alive, but I'm not sure for how long."

I made the call, my fumbling fingers struggling to hit the right buttons, watching Gervais as I spoke to the operator. I knew the old man was ill, perhaps even terminally so, and I wasn't sure his body could withstand the shock of what had just taken place.

I gave the operator the information she demanded, her voice all business after I told her the reason for the call. I wasn't on the phone long. The woman I was talking to — she told me her name was Susan — was both efficient and fast. She told me an ambulance and the police would be dispatched immediately and I could expect both very soon.

She wanted me to stay on the line until they arrived.

"I have to go," I told her. "I'm needed here."

I could see that Tomlinson hadn't regained consciousness and Cobb had holstered his weapon. I realized that Tomlinson and Gervais weren't the only ones feeling the effects of what had just happened. I was shaking violently and couldn't make myself stop.

Watching someone who was quite possibly in the final throes of a violent death was a horror I hadn't expected and had never wanted. Yet here it was. The shaking continued.

"You okay?" I heard Cobb's voice off in the distance somewhere.

"Adam!" The voice was near now. In fact Cobb's face was inches from mine, and I could feel myself coming back from wherever I'd been.

"I need you to focus," Cobb told me, his voice sharp, staccato. "I know this is tough, but I don't want you folding up on me now. Are you okay?"

I blinked a couple of times and nodded.

"Get yourself a glass of water, and bring one for Mr. Gervais."

I forced myself to do as I was instructed. I had to act, believing that if I didn't do something, keep moving, I'd slump down in a corner and end up staring at the floor, useless to Cobb and not a hell of a lot of good to myself, come to that.

I walked to the kitchen, poured two glasses of water, and gulped one down before returning to the living room with the other gripped in two hands to keep it from spilling.

I made my mind concentrate on something other than what had happened moments before. As I handed Gervais the glass, I said, "Daniel Gervais. D.G. You are a fine artist, sir."

Gervais was able to take the glass, and after a long drink he handed it back to me, then looked at Tomlinson, the pool of blood beneath him spreading across the hardwood floor. "You got what you deserved," he said, and spat in the direction of the fallen man.

I knew Cobb would have questions for him, but I had one, and it wouldn't wait.

"Mr. Gervais, can you tell us if Ellie Foster is still alive and where we might find her?"

I watched him turn slowly in my direction; then, after a few seconds, he shook his head, a look of great sadness creasing the gaunt features.

"Ellie died four years to the day after she was kidnapped."

The room was very still, even Tomlinson's gasps now near-silent in his attempt to breathe.

"Did he kill her?" I asked.

The old man looked at me for a long time before he said, "I suppose he did. I think she died of a broken heart ... but yes, he was the one."

FOURTEEN

There was little Cobb could do for Tomlinson, other than try to stop the bleeding as best he could.

As he did that, the wounded man spoke only one word: "Cold." Cobb and I covered him with blankets and bedcovers. While Cobb and I worked over Tomlinson, Gervais, unprompted, began the telling.

And while the old man's body may have been in its final stages of life, his mind and memory were remarkably intact and his ability to recall details of long-ago conversations was singular.

"I was older than the rest, and I'd already been successful in business, though mostly by accident," he began. "I got into the movie theatre business as a high school student, working as an usher and doorman at the Capitol, one of the great old Famous Players houses. It was at the corner of Bank Street and Queen Street. I loved the movie business, and I especially loved the theatres themselves — all of them are gone now, but it was a grand age. My family had money, and I guess maybe to keep me from indulging my other passion of the time — radical dissidence — they bought three smaller independent theatres in the city. I ran them, but it wasn't the same. The romance of the great old movie palaces was gone. I decided to move in the other direction. Abbie Hoffman and Jerry Rubin were starting to make noise in the U.S. I wanted to be that guy in Canada."

He stopped talking then and took several deep breaths.

"More water, Mr. Gervais?" I was worried that it was too taxing for him and that he might not say anything more. But after a minute or two, he shook his head and began again.

"I knew a guy named Calvin Bush. He was at Carleton for a while studying political science, but after a year or so he dropped out. Still went to some classes even though he was no longer registered, dropped a fair amount of acid, and sometimes spent entire days listening to Dylan and Guthrie and Pete Seeger. I remember spending one afternoon at his place smokin' dope and listening to *Like a Rolling Stone* over and over for hours.

"I made the mistake of introducing him to a young woman I knew. It was something I would forever regret. I'd met Ellie when she was performing at Le Hibou, and I wanted to help move her career along. I knew I couldn't do that. Bush swore he could ... had all these amazing contacts in the business. That was bullshit, but Ellie and I, we didn't know that. He became her agent. Bush had a friend named Cameron Laird, and the three of us hatched an idea for a folk club. Laird was going to run the place. Bush saw himself as this music genius who could recognize talent that nobody else noticed. He told us he knew about Dylan when the guy was still a student at the University of Minnesota and nobody'd heard of him. That was likely more BS, but that was Bush. He was going to be out there finding all this talent and introducing it onstage at the

TM. Of course, neither Bush nor Laird had any money, which is why I must have looked attractive to them. It was my money that set up The Tumbling Mustard. I leased the building, paid for all the renos, and bought a damn good sound system. Then Laird brought in another guy, a guy from Egypt."

"Fayed," I said, wanting to speed up the story. It was all interesting background, but I wanted him to get to Ellie Foster and what had happened to her. And I wanted to get there before the cops arrived. I wasn't sure he'd keep talking or that the cops would allow it once they were on the scene — at least not with Cobb and me present.

I knew that showing my impatience would be rude and might even stop the story altogether. I glanced at Cobb, who was alternating between watching Tomlinson and paying attention to what Gervais was saying. He seemed fine with the pace of the telling.

"Yes, Fayed." The old man nodded. "He actually had some money — not a lot, but he was willing to put what he had into the coffee house. So we brought him into the partnership. I didn't like him much. He was an intense, pompous bully, and he had almost no interest in the music. He said he was a businessman and he saw The Tumbling Mustard as a business opportunity. More bullshit."

Gervais's speech had slowed and his eyes were half closed. I thought he was ready to stop, didn't have the strength to go on. But he gathered himself with a couple of deep breaths and continued.

"I stayed in the background. I still had the theatres, and I wasn't sure I wanted to mix the two. Or maybe I wasn't quite ready to turn my back completely on the real world. We opened the TM in the late summer of

1964, and it was clear pretty fast that we weren't all on the same page. I was excited about the music, but Laird and Fayed were about anything but. The only good thing that happened was that one of the first acts we booked was Ellie. Bush conveniently forgot that it was me who had introduced him to Ellie. It was like *he* had discovered her. He kept saying she'd be the next Baez. Or maybe he said she'd be bigger than Baez, I forget. Thing is, for once he was right. She was our first … maybe our only sold-out house." He smiled at the memory.

"She was that good?" Cobb asked.

"She was that good," Gervais stated, his voice the strongest it had been since he'd started talking. "And then everything changed. Ben Tomlinson had read about the coffee house opening in the paper, and he came to us, said he'd volunteer until we determined if the place could be profitable. Then we could talk about wages. That seemed fair, and we were glad to have him. I wanted a doorman because I thought having one gave theatres class and would do the same thing for a folk club. Ben was that person, and at first he did a wonderful job. But slowly he became less interested in the place as a folk club. He and Fayed started scheming … the TM became a home for the counterculture element. I was part of it, too — a bunch of us standing around plotting the overthrow of the capitalist world. But slowly the three — Tomlinson, Fayed, and Laird — took over the running of the coffee house, and then they took over everything else. I went along — willingly, by the way. I don't want to give the impression I was coerced or forced to do something I didn't want to do. I was right there. But the part I have regretted every day since is that I brought Ellie with me."

"What about Bush?" Cobb asked.

"He was there, too, but he was on the fringes. He wasn't smart enough to be a player."

"Bush represent any other musicians?" Cobb asked.

"None that I knew of."

He paused. A beat, then another. "It wasn't long until the TM was nothing more than a clubhouse for a group of dissidents. But we weren't Hoffman or Rubin or anybody that mattered. We were just some fucked-up punks. The three of them — Fayed, Laird, and ... *him*" — his eyes flicked in the direction of Ben Tomlinson — "they didn't merely want to protest or march or write angry poetry. They wanted to pursue violent means to achieve their goals, whatever they were."

He paused again, shook his head. "No, that's wrong. They *had* goals. Fayed, as I said, was Egyptian and pissed off at the role Canada, specifically Pearson, had played in the Suez Crisis." He looked up at me. "You know about the Suez?"

I nodded and pointed my chin at Cobb. "We do, sir, yes."

Gervais turned his head in the direction of Tomlinson's body splayed out on the floor, the pool of blood beneath him still spreading, despite Cobb's efforts to at least slow the bleeding. "It was him," Gervais said, voice filled with contempt, "who came up with the plan to assassinate the prime minister on one of the biggest days of this country's political history — the unveiling of Canada's new flag."

"February 15, 1965," I said.

"That's right. He said it would be Canada's Kennedy moment." The voice was growing weaker, the cadence slower.

"Let me help, sir," I said. "Ellie Foster did something to undermine the plan."

Gervais shook his head, his eyes now filled with tears. "They thought she did. But it was me." He raised a hand, I think to tap himself on the chest to emphasize the point he was making. But the hand slumped back down before he completed the gesture.

He stopped talking and looked like he was struggling again, swallowed a couple of times. Cobb looked back at Tomlinson, and I looked at my watch. Eleven minutes since my call to 911. I thought I could hear the first hint of sirens in the distance.

"Would you like more water, Mr. Gervais?" I asked again.

He licked his lips, shook his head one more time, and spoke again.

"I overheard Fayed talking to someone on the phone. I remember him saying that the red in the new flag would be very appropriate on that day. I thought at first it was a joke, but one night after we'd closed up and I was there by myself, I stumbled across five high-powered rifles, a bunch of ammunition, and some explosives. They'd kept all that stuff hidden away right there at The Tumbling Mustard. That pissed me off. And I was worried about Ellie. It was like Tomlinson controlled her, and I was afraid she might be mixed up in whatever it was they were planning. And she was."

The sirens told us the first responders, cops or the ambulance or both, were getting closer. The old man was barely able to talk anymore. Cobb told him to rest, that we'd find out what happened to Ellie later. But Gervais shook his head stubbornly.

"Just a little more," he insisted. "Most of it I'm guessing, you know. The fuck-up with the armoured car was another one of *his* schemes." It was like the old man couldn't bring himself to say Tomlinson's name anymore. No longer a man determined merely to stand up to his oppressor, his eyes, his voice radiated loathing.

"Ellie was part of that thing. She told me later she even fired the gun they'd given her, just shot in the air, but I could see the whole thing had been exciting to her, at least at first. Bush was killed that night, and another punk they recruited for that deal got shot. He wasn't hurt all that badly, but he got scared — or maybe he got smart — and took off. I don't even remember his name. Probably has a nice life somewhere in New Brunswick. You'd think that night would have told them that this man couldn't plan a three-car parade, let alone devise a plot to kill the prime minister. But he was like Manson; they all followed along.

"After I found the weapons, I tipped off the RCMP about what they were planning. Anonymous phone call. I didn't give the cops any names, but I told them as much as I knew about the plot. I wasn't part of the actual plan, but I went to Parliament Hill that day anyway. You never saw so many cops and military. Only an idiot would have thought they could pull it off. You see, this wasn't going to be some suicide bombing or shooting. They wanted to get away with it and believed they would — well, until they saw all the RCMP, the cops, the soldiers. They finally realized it wasn't going to work. There was nowhere within a couple of miles of Parliament Hill that they'd be able to set up rifles. They'd have been arrested in seconds."

"You did that, sir. You did the right thing." I knew it sounded patronizing, but I felt bad that he blamed himself for so much of what had happened.

He shook his head, more vigorously this time. "Bullshit! The right thing would have been to tell them it was me who gave away their scheme." He hesitated, had a coughing spasm before he resumed. "But I didn't. I'm a coward. I've let him run my life out of fear ... a coward."

This time it was Cobb who spoke. "You weren't a coward today, sir."

The sirens announced that the police and ambulances had arrived. I knew the cops wouldn't rush the house, not right away, not until they knew the situation.

"I better get them in here ... for him," I said.

"No need to hurry," Cobb said. "He's dead."

"Are you sure?"

"I'm sure."

I realized my shaking had slowed some, but now as I looked at Tomlinson, I began shaking harder again. The phone rang. I guessed it was the cops.

"Don't answer it," Gervais said. "Not yet."

He coughed again, wiped spittle from his mouth. "Ellie finally realized this thing was all so goddamn wrong. For a while she was just depressed, but then she came out of it, at least enough to leave, wanted to get back to her career. That pig on the floor wasn't about to allow that. He wanted to do something dramatic, something spectacular, after the failed Parliament Hill plan. To show the others that the next time he planned something as big and as crazy as the Pearson thing, he could pull it off. And, most of all, he wanted revenge because he still thought it was Ellie who gave it up to the cops. They could have just taken her, but instead they killed those innocent men. Fayed and Tomlinson were in the car. Laird in the club. When Ellie and the other two went out into the alley, Laird went out the front door, stood on the street, and lit a smoke. That was the sign. Like a goddamned B movie. You know what happened after that."

"Do you know who the shooter was, Mr. Gervais?"

"Oh, yeah" — his eyes glanced again at the figure on the floor — "he shot both of them."

He looked back at me as I nodded. I started to ask him about the most important part — what had happened to Ellie after that. He looked at me, and his eyes, still moist with tears, wrinkled a little. He knew this was the part that mattered most to Cobb and to me.

"Fayed panicked, maybe realized he had thrown in with a crazy person, and soon after he fled back to the U.S., I heard California. I never heard from him or about him again. Laird disappeared, too, not long after."

It was Cobb who spoke next. Like me, he wanted to hear the end of the story. "You and Ellie stayed with him. Why?"

"At first she was literally a prisoner. Tied up all the time … she was in one room of this little house Tomlinson rented on Bayswater. It was like when someone is taken hostage in the Middle East…. Laird hadn't left yet and him and Tomlinson, they brought her food and water — they didn't starve her, and they took her to the bathroom. They never left me alone with her — maybe they didn't trust me, I don't know. The only time they ever talked to her was to try to get her to admit she'd ratted them out. Of course, she never did. Finally Tomlinson decided to change things … decided he wanted her. Maybe he always had.

"He swore he'd turn her in for her part in the armoured car fiasco, then kill her child if she didn't go along with what he wanted. Ellie became a slave to that man. Sexually, psychologically — I guess in every way possible, really. She couldn't leave, at least not at first, because she believed — we both did — that he meant what he said. And even if we murdered the bastard — and believe me, we talked about it — he told us he had people in place who would kill Ellie's daughter if anything happened to him. I guess we thought we really couldn't take the chance. Ellie stayed to save her daughter.

"She was writing songs during that time; I gues it was the one thing that felt normal ... that felt right to her. Tomlinson even encouraged it. He had this insane scheme: one day he'd bring her back, make up this story that he's rescued her, and then she's start perming again, and recording, and he'd make all this money. It was crazy. But *he* was crazy. And that was our lives — Ellie writing and the two of us planning, scheming, and working on our exit strategy." His mouth formed a small smile.

"But then," he gestured at his wheelchair. "This happened."

I looked at Cobb, who was sitting next to Tomlinson, still pressing down on the wound, now using his Eastern Electric windbreaker and a blanket from the couch to try to stanch the flow of blood.

"What happened?"

"Car accident. Right in front of the old Capitol Theatre. Ironic, eh? Broken back. Paraplegic." His voice was flat as he said the words.

"I'm sorry ... I — we didn't know. We thought you were in the wheelchair because of an illness."

"Oh, I have that too. But I've been in a wheelchair a long time. Long before my more recent ... challenge. The bad part of the accident was it kind of made our escape a whole lot tougher. But Ellie wasn't a quitter and I guess I wasn't either, so we kept planning, figuring how we could get away *and* protect Ellie's daughter. We were just waiting for the right time. But there never was a right time. Finally we had pretty much decided to make our move. I don't know if Tomlinson suspected something or what, but one day he called us into the kitchen and showed us a photo of Ellie's little girl. It was clearly taken in the yard of the people who were raising her. He didn't say anything other than, 'isn't she a lovely girl' and stuff like that. But if it was meant to scare the hell out of us, it worked. We didn't know what to do.

"One day we'd both be ready to call his bluff and take off. But the next day we'd be thinking *what if he wasn't bluffing?* Eventually Ellie stopped writing, and it was like she began to fade away. It wasn't long after that she became ill. Tomlinson refused to let her see a doctor. Instead we moved out here to this place, and he concocted the story about his invalid father, and Ellie, his sister. I guess there was no real reason for people not to believe it. Ellie died a few months after we moved here. She's buried not far from the back of the house."

It was quiet again for a long minute.

"And you still stayed," Cobb said. "You didn't even try to escape with ..." Cobb looked at the wheelchair as his voice trailed off.

"Escape to what? My family was gone. My parents had both died quite young; I had no brothers or sisters. So what was left ... some institution? Besides, Ellie's out there," he pointed his chin toward the back of the house. "I know it sounds strange, but I wanted to be here."

I thought about Kennedy and his compulsion, his fixation with a dead girl. While his was for a different reason — he was trying to find a killer — the two obsessions were similar ... and equally sad. A man wanting to be near where the woman he loved was buried.

"And he let you stay," I said.

"He let my money stay. My parents were gone, and they left me pretty well off. My money bought this place and paid for the life we lived. My money and a few ... enterprises he had going, criminal stuff, I don't know the details. Besides, I was harmless," Gervais said bitterly. "Gutless. He knew that, and kept me around for the money and to do the things he didn't want to, the bookkeeping and and all that. I knew his books were as phony as he was, but I didn't care." There were tears now, flowing unchecked. He didn't raise a hand to wipe them away.

"And now I'll finally be with her." He pointed to his abdomen. "Pancreatic. We'll finally be together without him, and it took this to make it happen."

I waited for him to regain control. It didn't take long. In his own way, Daniel Gervais was tough. "What about the CD?" I asked. "Was that you?"

He nodded. "I didn't know Ellie ... had a granddaughter until a few months ago. Tomlinson let it slip. I figured Ellie would want her granddaughter to have something. Afrer she died, Tomlinson burned all the songs Ellie had written — pissed off that her dream of a big comeback died with her. But I'd had that one tape for a long time. Made sure he never found out about it. It took some doing, but I knew a guy out in Calgary, thought he might be able to get it to her. It was a song Ellie had written just before the day of the flag raising — like an anthem. I got some money and the tape, and one day while he was getting a haircut, I rolled over to the post office and sent the CD and the money. I told the guy I wanted him to break into the car. I had this crazy thought that if there was a little intrigue involved, and especially with *that* song, maybe she'd go to the cops or somebody … somebody like you. I wanted her … or someone to know about her grandmother."

"Something I don't understand," I said. "Tomlinson seemed almost dedicated to you yesterday when we were here. Concerned — taking you to the doctor … I heard earlier that he was reading seniors' magazines, presumably to be able to help you, and even served on the board of a senior's organization."

Gervais weakly waved a hand. "All part of the charade. Every day of his life, everything he did was play-acting. If he read a seniors' magazine it was to learn strategies that would help him exercise control. Not that he needed help with that." He laughed a bitter, gurgling laugh. "The neighbours thought he was a devoted family guy … a great guy."

I thought about Burkowsky coming by to check up on his neighbour's place.

The phone rang again. I looked at Cobb, and he nodded. But as I crossed the room to the phone, I heard him ask Gervais one more question: "Mr. Gervais, would you like us to arrange a meeting with your granddaughter?"

FIFTEEN

I hadn't seen it, hadn't sensed it. I asked Cobb about it after.

"I wasn't sure," he admitted. "But there were clues, not so much in what Gervais said, but in how he spoke of Ellie. He said he'd known her before The Tumbling Mustard, so the timing was right for them to have had a relationship. And his staying with her through all those years of what had to be hell with Tomlinson when he could have left, that got me to thinking. I knew he felt guilty, but I got a sense there was something more there. He loved her, of course, but I started to wonder if he felt a greater bond than even love or guilt. And his being the father of Ellie's child just made sense."

We'd gone through several hours of questioning by the cops, not knowing for sure if Daniel Gervais would live long enough to corroborate our story. He and Tomlinson were both taken away in ambulances. Tomlinson's death was confirmed not long after his arrival at the hospital.

I was still shaken by all that had happened there that day, and knew it would take some time for me to recover. A doctor in Ottawa who worked with soldiers with PTSD spent time with me and recommended a colleague he thought I should see when we got back to Calgary.

It was the third time I had been face to face with someone threatening to kill me. And it was the second time since I'd begun working with Cobb that I'd seen someone gunned down right in front of me. The second time wasn't any easier than the first time had been. Both of the victims had been extremely bad men, but that didn't lessen the horror.

We remained in Ottawa for a few days while the police completed their investigation and introduced Monica Brill to her grandfather. She virtually lived at the hospital and was at his side when he died three days later.

Cobb and I visited Gervais a couple of times at the hospital, too, but though we both had questions, we asked none of them. The old man had given us all he had, and it would have to be enough. He did manage a smile when I told him I admired his art.

When Monica learned we had been staying at a Super 8, she booked us rooms at the Lord Elgin, despite our objections. When we checked in, we were told our bill had already been taken care of.

It was our last day in Ottawa, and we were having lunch with Monica at the hotel's Grill 41. She and I had opted for salads, hers a Caesar, mine roasted beet, while Cobb went with the butternut squash ravioli.

Cobb eyed my selection suspiciously, and after what looked like a particularly satisfying bite of his ravioli, said, "You should have gone with this instead of the purple stuff."

I told him the "purple stuff" was penance for having run only once since I'd arrived in Ottawa. He said he could see that. "Looks like something that would do the job as penance."

Monica laughed. "If you two can quit bickering, I want to ask you something."

"Geez, I don't know." Cobb chuckled. "We're all about bickering."

I wasn't feeling quite as buoyed by our success as he was. There was still the matter of the MFs and the inevitable call that would be coming one day — that thought left a black cloud in even the bluest skies.

I nodded at Monica. "Ignore him. What's your question?"

"I remember our first meeting," she said, "and your reluctance to take the case — especially you, Mike. I know it had to be frustrating trying to track people and leads that had disappeared a long time ago. I guess I'm wondering why you stayed with it. I mean, I'm so glad you did, but I wouldn't have blamed you for a second if you'd put this one aside and got on with more ... user-friendly investigations."

Cobb smiled and nodded at me, offering me first kick at offering an answer to a question I'd asked myself several times along the way.

"I guess for me it was such an intriguing case," I told her. "This wonderfully talented singer who simply disappeared; it became personal. Ellie Foster mattered to me, and I wanted — actually I *needed* — to know what happened to her. For you, but for me, too."

Cobb set his fork down. "This is how I make my living, but it's more than that. I'm a stubborn bastard. I don't want to let go — ever. I won't lie. There were times when I thought this thing wasn't doable. We were out of people to talk to, we had nowhere else to look, but it seemed that every time we got to that point, there was some little ray of light, one last thing to check on that led to one more thing, then finally … here we are."

I wasn't all that happy with my answer to a question I had never been asked before. *Why* do *we do the things we do? Why did I become a journalist in the first place? And why do I still write today?* Maybe the answers to those questions changed with the times we lived in. I knew that in a world that seemed to value truth less and less, I cared about writing it more and more. Despite my stumbling answer, I liked that Monica had asked. And I liked what she did next even more.

She signalled our waiter, who disappeared for a moment, then came to our table carrying two wrapped parcels, one for Cobb, one for me. We opened them, and inside each was a painting by Daniel Gervais. I was delighted that the one I received was the one of the boy by the stream that I'd seen on the wall of the house in Aylmer.

We expressed our appreciation, and both of us meant it. It was a nice end to a case that had had more than its share of unpleasantness about it, the most unpleasant part being that we hadn't found Ellie Foster alive. I would have loved to meet the woman whose voice and personality had captured so many hearts.

Maybe if our plane hadn't been delayed, I wouldn't have told him, at least not then. But, sitting around an airport for over an hour with nothing to do but talk and drink coffee, I guessed the time seemed right.

"You did *what*?"

"I was desperate — I had to do something."

"You didn't have to do *that*." Cobb's voice was low, controlled, but there was no denying the disbelief and the anger that were simmering below the surface.

"The shelter was going to close if I didn't do something. They'd exhausted the more conventional fundraising methods, and it was either start making random calls and talking as fast as I could before people hung up on me or see if I could get Scubberd to do a good deed."

"That's how you see this? The MFs doing a good deed?"

"I don't know, I was just —"

"This isn't a joke, Adam! Take me through it. Tell me exactly what they said."

"I just did."

"Do it again. I want every word they said, especially the lovely Mrs. Scubberd. Don't leave anything out."

I'd seen Cobb boil over before, and I knew his anger was a force it was better not to unleash. And I'd never seen that anger directed at me before.

"Can we just be rational about this?"

"Rational? I'll tell you what's not rational. Making a deal with gangsters. Tell me again."

I took a sip of coffee, then went back over the evening at Kane's Harley Diner in painstaking detail. When I finished, Cobb said nothing for quite a long time, which I discovered was considerably less pleasant than when he was speaking, even when he was angry.

When he finally did say something, his voice was flat and cold. "You really don't know how it works, do you?"

"Listen, I realize I was a little naive about the whole thing," I said. "But if I had it to do again —"

Cobb held up a hand. "If you finish that sentence the way I think you're going to finish it, then you are even stupider than I thought. Let me explain how this works."

"Scubberd's wife already did that."

"She told you nothing. Here's what you've done. One day, they will come to you wanting you to do something. I guarantee you it will be something you will not want to do, but you'll do it because you have no choice … and believe me, *you have no choice*. And when it's done you'll think to yourself, 'that was bloody awful, but at least it's over.' And that's where you'll be wrong. They'll be back, wanting something else. And then again … and again."

"Mike, I know all this …"

He rumbled on, unstoppable: "Let's say a couple of years from now you're assigned a feature, or maybe a series of features, on Calgary's underworld. And you labour over this thing and you're about ready to see it published, and you are paid a visit. It might be Scubberd, or it might not be. It damn sure won't be Mrs. Scubberd. The message will be simple and painfully clear. And it won't be, 'Leave out the part about the MFs.' It will be, 'Here's what we want you to write, and we want to see it after you've written it.' And you will do exactly as they say because you owe them and, more important, because they know where you and Jill and Kyla live, and if you fuck with them they will not hesitate to hurt those you love in ways you can't even imagine. And there will be other things they will want you to do, and you will do them because there are no options. No options at all."

I opened my mouth to argue but shut it again, the words unsaid. Because I knew that what Mike Cobb had just said was exactly the way it was. I'd known it since the night I'd walked out of the diner. I'd hoped I was wrong — told myself I was wrong. But I knew better. I knew what I'd done. And Mike Cobb, who'd spent much of his life pitted against forces like the MFs, had just confirmed it.

"What do I do, Mike?"

He rubbed a hand over his face and shook his head. "I don't know, Adam. I do not know."

"Jill doesn't know. She thinks the money came from some anonymous philanthropist. I figured … Jesus, Mike, I've put the people I love in danger. I've …" I stopped talking then and held my head in my hands, my body shaking with fear and, most of all, self-loathing.

Mike sat for a long time, staring into the distance. He was silent but for the sound of his hand rubbing his chin, which sported two days of growth.

Finally he turned to me. "I want you to listen very carefully to what I'm about to say."

I nodded.

"If you are contacted by any of them — phone, email, or in person, I don't care if it's just 'Let's have a cup of coffee' — you agree to nothing, you *do* nothing, except get ahold of me."

"Mike, I don't want you taking this on for me. This is on me, and I'm the one who has to see it through."

"I repeat" — he leaned a little closer to me, and I'm pretty sure if we hadn't been in a public place he might have hit me — "you listen to what they are saying, and then you call me. I need you to understand me on this, Adam, and I need to know you're going to do exactly what I just told you to do."

I looked up at him and nodded. "I understand. I'll call."

"And now we say no more about it. Because if we talk about this anymore I might forget we're friends and kick your ass around the terminal." As he said it, there was no hint of a smile on a face that loved to smile.

We didn't talk about it anymore.

The launch of my new book, the sequel to *The Spoofaloof Rally*, this one called *The Spoofaloof Goof,* took place on a cold November night. There was a pretty good crowd on hand.

Despite Cobb and me agreeing that the inevitable publicity and associated interviews arising from the solving of one of Calgary's longest unsolved cases would be left to Monica Brill, I knew that at least some in the audience were curiosity seekers, wanting to catch a glimpse of and maybe chat with someone who'd been in the news lately.

The launch was at Owl's Nest Books, and I'd been looking forward to it. During the two or three weeks before, I had begun to feel more like my old self, recovering at least a little from the trauma of what had taken place in the house in Aylmer.

The evening went well. Kyla and I did the reading together. She was awesome; I managed not to screw up. The question-and-answer session afterward was actually fun, with lots of thoughtful questions — none of them about Ellie Foster or The Depression. The presentation completed, there was a healthy lineup of book buyers waiting to have me sign their copies, reminding me again that the improbable had happened — I was an author of children's books. And loving it.

The lineup had thinned, and I looked up at the last couple of people wanting to have their books signed. One of them was Cobb. He wasn't holding a book. We hadn't seen one another since we'd returned from Ottawa, and I hoped his being there was maybe a sign that all, or at least some, was forgiven after my MFs blunder. I had yet to receive the dreaded call from the bikers. With every day that went by without a call, my hope built that there wouldn't be one, but I knew that was completely unrealistic.

"Congratulations," he said. "Looks like it went well."

"Thanks, and yes, it was a pretty cool evening. I didn't see you in the audience. Sorry I missed you."

"You didn't miss me. Lindsay and I had planned to be here, but something came up. I'm sorry to do this, but I wanted you to get it from me and not hear it on the news or see it on Facebook or something." He looked serious, and I had a feeling that what I was about to hear wasn't likely to add to the amiable atmosphere of the event that was just wrapping up.

"What's up?"

He stepped closer to the table, bent toward me, his palms down on the tabletop. "Kendall Mark … Marlon Kennedy … is dead. They found his body in the alley behind the house where Faith Unruh's body was discovered. I just came from the scene."

For a long moment I said nothing. Trying to make sense of the senseless. "It wasn't accidental." I didn't phrase it as a question because I already knew the answer.

"No, it was a hit and run. The driver hit him, then drove back and forth over him three or four times. Making sure."

"Jesus."

"Yeah, sorry to put a damper on the celebration."

I waved him off. "Anyone see it happen?"

He shook his head. "A couple people heard the squealing tires and roaring engine. But by the time anyone got out there, the car was gone."

I shook my head sadly, remembering the man who had dedicated his life to trying to right a wrong, to finding the person who had committed an act so horrific that even a cop's tough mind had not been capable of coping with it. Now he would never know the answer he so desperately wanted to find. And he himself was a victim of an equally brutal crime.

"Mike, the tapes!" I blurted out, loud enough to turn the heads of the people still remaining in the store. I brought my voice down to a whisper. "It'll all be on tape in Kennedy's place — the upstairs camera was pointed at that spot all the time."

Cobb shook his head. "There is no tape."

"What are you talking about?"

"I told the cops exactly what you just told me. They checked it out. Somebody — likely the killer — had been in the house. Both of the surveillance locations were ransacked — there was stuff strewn everywhere, and I know that's not how Kennedy operated. There was no tape in the upstairs camera."

I stared at Cobb, the reality of what he had just said hitting me like a hammer. "Then the killer had to know about the surveillance."

"That would seem extremely likely. I'm heading back there now to see what else I can find out."

"Do you think this is Faith Unruh's killer at work again?"

"I don't know," Cobb said slowly. "You know how I feel about coincidence, but I can't say for sure. Again, I'm sorry to interrupt the party — you'd better get over there and have a glass of wine with your fans. I'll let you know what I find out."

Mike gave Jill a quick hug on the way out, then was gone. I did as he'd suggested and went over to where store owners Michael and Susan Hare were pouring wine. I had two glasses.

On the way home, with Kyla asleep in the back seat, I told Jill about Cobb's reason for stopping by the bookstore.

She laid a hand on my leg. "I knew, when I saw him there without Lindsay, and just in and out like that — I knew it wasn't going to be good."

We drove in silence for a few minutes until, at a red light, Jill put into words the question we were both thinking: "What happens now?"

"I don't know," I said. "I just don't know."

Once we were in the house and Kyla was tucked away for the night, I sat down at the laptop I kept at Jill's, figuring I'd look for more news about what had happened earlier that night.

I went to my inbox first. There was an email from Marlon Kennedy. It had been sent at 7:12 p.m. I shivered as I considered the reality that Kennedy had sent the email in the minutes before he crossed the street and returned to the alley for the last time.

The email was cryptic. It read, "I promised, and I know you'll want to see this."

Below that line of text was a photo of tally marks: two groups of five … and two more lines.

And below that, Kennedy had typed: "Twelve marks."

ACKNOWLEDGEMENTS

I am indebted again to Dr. Adam Vyse for his wisdom; to Mike O'Connor for his knowledge and encouragement; and to the editorial team at Dundurn under the steady, guiding hand of Jenny McWha. I found Ken Rockburn's book *We Are as the Times Are: The Story of Le Hibou* both helpful and a delightful read, and the online notes for *A History of Folk Music in English Canada* by Gary Cristall were also useful. Special thanks to the owners of the Amantea Restaurant that, when I began this project, sat above what was once the basement home of The Depression; and to Chad Ares from Parm, which is the newest (and very cool) incarnation of that location.

ACKNOWLEDGEMENTS

Mystery and Crime Fiction from Dundurn Press

Birder Murder Mysteries
by Steve Burrows
(BIRDING, BRITISH COASTAL TOWN MYSTERIES)
A Siege of Bitterns
A Pitying of Doves
A Cast of Falcons
A Shimmer of Hummingbirds
A Tiding of Magpies

Amanda Doucette Mysteries
by Barbara Fradkin
(PTSD, CROSS-CANADA TOUR)
Fire in the Stars
The Trickster's Lullaby
Coming soon: *Prisoners of Hope*

B.C. Blues Crime Novels
by R.M. Greenaway
(BRITISH COLUMBIA, POLICE PROCEDURAL)
Cold Girl
Undertow
Creep

Stonechild & Rouleau Mysteries
by Brenda Chapman
(FIRST NATIONS, KINGSTON, POLICE PROCEDURAL)
Cold Mourning
Butterfly Kills
Tumbled Graves
Shallow End
Bleeding Darkness

Jack Palace Series
by A.G. Pasquella
(NOIR, TORONTO, MOB)
Coming soon: *Yard Dog*

Jenny Willson Mysteries
by Dave Butler
(NATIONAL PARKS, ANIMAL PROTECTTION)
Full Curl
Coming soon: *No Place for Wolverines*

Falls Mysteries
by Jayne Barnard
(RURAL ALBERTA, FEMALE SLEUTH)
When the Flood Falls

Foreign Affairs Mysteries
by Nick Wilkshire
(GLOBAL CRIME FICTION, HUMOUR)
Escape to Havana
The Moscow Code
Coming soon: *Remember Tokyo*

Dan Sharp Mysteries
by Jeffrey Round
(LGBTQ, TORONTO)
Lake on the Mountain
Pumpkin Eater
The Jade Butterfly
After the Horses
The God Game

Max O'Brien Mysteries
by Mario Bolduc
(TRANSLATION, POLITICAL THRILLER, CON MAN)
The Kashmir Trap
The Roma Plot

Cullen and Cobb Mysteries
by David A. Poulsen
(CALGARY, PRIVATE INVESTIGATORS, ORGANIZED CRIME)
Serpents Rising
Dead Air
Last Song Sung

Strange Things Done
by Elle Wild
(YUKON, DARK THRILLER)

Salvage
by Stephen Maher
(NOVA SCOTIA, FAST-PACED THRILLER)